The Breaking Point

A Body Farm Novel

Jefferson Bass

HARPER LUXE

An Imprint of HarperCollinsPublishers

LP
Bass

This is a work of fiction. Names, characters, places, and incidents are products of the author's imagination or are used fictitiously and are not to be construed as real. Any resemblance to actual events, locales, organizations, or persons, living or dead, is entirely coincidental.

HarperCollins books may be purchased for educational, business, or sales promotional use. For information please e-mail the Special Markets Department at SPsales@harpercollins.com.

FIRST HARPERLUXE EDITION

HarperLuxe™ is a trademark of HarperCollins Publishers

Library of Congress Cataloging-in-Publication Data is available upon request.

ISBN: 978-0-06-234410-6

15 ID/RRD 10 9 8 7 6 5 4 3 2 1

The Breaking Point

ALSO BY JEFFERSON BASS

Fiction

Cut to the Bone

Jordan's Stormy Banks

The Inquisitor's Key

Madonna and Corpse

The Bone Yard

The Bone Thief

Bones of Betrayal

The Devil's Bones

Flesh and Bone

Carved in Bone

Nonfiction

Beyond the Body Farm

Death's Acre

In memory of Clyde Snow, Walter Birkby, and Ted Rathbun: good friends, valued colleagues, superb teachers, and crusaders for justice.

The Breaking Point

Part One

The Two Faces of Richard Janus

And thus does Fortune's wheel turn treacherously
And out of happiness bring men to sorrow.

> —Geoffrey Chaucer, *The Canterbury Tales*

One of ancient Rome's most powerful and mysterious deities, Janus—the god of two faces—was guardian of gateways and transitions. The two faces signified not hypocrisy, as people often assume, but dual vision: One face turned toward the past, the other toward the future, Janus stood sentinel on the threshold of birth, as well as the threshold between death and the afterlife. In one hand he held a key; in the other, a cudgel.

—Sofia Paxton, *Ancient Teachings, Modern Wisdom*

Prologue

McCready stopped and knelt beside a rut in the dirt road, raising a hand to halt the six men and two women fanned out behind him. The road, if a pair of faint tracks through grass, weeds, and leaves could indeed be called a road, meandered down a hillside of oaks and maples, their trunks girdled with vines. The mid-June morning was sweet with honeysuckle blossoms; the exuberant lushness of June had not yet given way to the duller green of July and the browning scorch of August, but underneath the perfume lurked something darker, something malodorous and malevolent hanging in the air.

McCready—Special Supervisory Agent Clint "Mac" McCready—studied the rut, which was damp and also deeply imprinted with multiple layers of sharply defined tire tracks. He pulled two evidence flags from a back pocket and marked the ends of the tracks, then, with the camera slung around his neck, took a series of digital photographs. The photos were wide-angle views at first, followed by tighter and tighter shots. As he snapped the final, frame-filling close-ups, he said, to no one in particular, "It rained, what, couple days ago?"

"Night before last." The answer came from behind him, from Kimbo—Kirby Kimball, the youngest, newest, and therefore most eager member of SSA McCready's Evidence Response Team. "The front passed through about thirty-six hours ago. Rain stopped shortly after midnight."

McCready nodded, smiling slightly at the young agent's zeal, and lowered the camera, focusing now solely with his eyes. "These tracks look like they've been *machined*. What does that tell us?"

"New tires," said Kimball. "Deep tread blocks. Almost no wear. But there's a nick—a cut—here. At the outer edge."

"What else?"

"Big, off-road tires," Kimball added, squatting for a closer look. "SUV or four-by-four. Just one, looks like. One set of impressions heading in, another—on top—heading back out."

"Right." McCready glanced over his shoulder at the other agents. "Mighty quiet back there. I thought maybe the rest of you guys had gone for coffee." The agents exchanged sheepish glances. "Okay, what else can we tell from these tracks? Somebody besides Kimbo jump in. Anybody?"

"The vehicle passed through after the rain stopped." This from Boatman, an earnest, thirtysomething agent who looked and listened a lot more than he talked.

"Right, far as it goes. But can you pin it down any tighter than that?"

Boatman stepped forward and bent down, his brow furrowing, his gaze shifting from the tracks to the surrounding vegetation—crabgrass and spindly poison ivy. "Quite a while after the rain stopped. Hours later, I'd say; maybe yesterday afternoon or even last night."

"Because?"

"The impressions wouldn't be so crisp—so perfect— if there'd been a puddle there when the vehicle went through," Boatman said. He surveyed the margins of the rut, then inspected the undersides of some of the blades of grass there. "Plus, if there'd been standing water, there'd be mud spatter on the vegetation. There's no spatter."

"Good." McCready focused on Kimball, who stood motionless yet somehow seemed cocked and ready to fire: his T-shirt stretched by the tension in his shoulders and biceps; the heels of his boots hovering a half inch off the ground, as if he were ready to spring into action. "Kimbo, you're an eager beaver this morning; you wanna cast these?" It wasn't actually a question.

"Yessir. On it." Kimball jogged back to the truck, a Ford Econoline chassis with a big cargo box grafted behind the cab; the vehicle might have passed for an ambulance on steroids if not for the prominent FBI logo on the side and the foot-high letters reading EVIDENCE RESPONSE TEAM. Opening a hatch on the side of the vehicle, Kimball hauled out a large tackle box and lugged it to the tracks. He unlatched the lid and took out a gallon-sized Ziploc bag, half filled with powdered gypsum crystals—dental stone—and a graduated squeeze bottle. Squirting ten ounces of water into the bag, he resealed it and began kneading, creating a slurry the color and consistency of thin pancake batter: runny enough to flow into every block and groove of the tire tracks, thick enough not to seep into the soil itself.

McCready had already moved on, following the tracks in a hunched-over crouch: half bloodhound, half Quasimodo. "Looks like they parked here," he said, stopping to study the ground again. The soil was covered with leaves, and McCready frowned at the lack of castable shoe impressions. A trail of scuffed leaves led toward the trees at the edge of the clearing, but the undergrowth beyond the tree line appeared to be undisturbed; indeed, the scuff marks led only as far as a large, convex oval of mussed leaves situated just short of the trees. McCready began circling the oval, pausing occasionally to take photos. "This matches the C.I.'s description of where it went down," he said. Heads nodded in agreement; earlier, McCready had passed out transcripts of his interview with the confidential informant. "Boatman, you and Kimbo . . ." He paused to glance over his shoulder at Kimball, who had already finished pouring the slurry of dental stone into the rut. "You and Kimbo set up the total station and start mapping. Rest of you, suit up and get ready to dig in." The other six team members returned to the truck and wriggled into white biohazard suits and purple gloves. They came back laden with rakes, shovels, trowels, plastic bins, and a wood-framed screen of quarter-inch wire mesh.

As they laid their tools neatly beside the oval mound, Boatman latched the 3-D mapping unit onto a tripod. Kimball returned to the tire tracks again, this time holding a long, reflector-topped rod, its length marked in alternating, twelve-inch bands of red and white. Boatman swiveled the instrument toward Kimball and sighted on the reflector. "Lights, camera, *action*," he deadpanned, and he began pressing buttons to capture the position of the track. Checking the small display screen, he nodded. "Got it," he said, rotating the unit toward the oval mound, to which Kimball jogged with the reflector.

The mound, uncovered by careful raking, was red-brown clay, roughly four feet by six feet. The clay was broken and infused with pale, shredded roots, freshly shorn and torn from the soil—a raw, ragged wound in the earth's smooth, dark skin. McCready's gaze ranged over the lumpy surface, then zoomed in on something no one else had seen, tucked beneath a clod of clay. Kneeling just outside the margin of the oval mound, he leaned down, his nose practically in the dirt. "Cartridge case," he said. "That was careless of somebody." Then, without looking around: "Kimbo." By the time he'd finished saying the name, Kimball was already placing the end of the rod beside the piece of brass.

"Got it," Boatman called a moment later.

Still kneeling, McCready took a twig from the ground and used it to lift the shell from the clay. Angling it to catch the light, he peered closely at the marks in the base. "Remington. Nine millimeter." A paper evidence bag materialized beside his knee, held open by one of the agents; McCready dropped the case into it, and the agent sealed and labeled it, then set it in one of the plastic bins.

He sat back on his heels. "All right. We're burning daylight, so let's get to it. Boatman, you and Kimball keep mapping. The rest of you, dig in: shovel till you see something, then switch to trowels. Screen everything—dirt, leaves, twigs, everything but the air. Hell, screen the air, too." He waved a hand in a sweeping gesture that encompassed not just the mound of clay but the surrounding area as well. "Might be more brass, buried or scattered around the periphery. Maybe cigarette butts, too, if we're lucky or the shooters are stupid. Maybe they left us some DNA."

"Maybe a signed confession, too," joked one of the agents. McCready did not laugh, so no one else did, either.

"All right," he said. "Dig in. Easy does it, though. If our C.I.'s playing straight with us, we've got three bodies here—the two buyers and our undercover guy. Way the C.I. tells it, the traffickers never intended to sell; their plan all along was to kill the buyers, keep the coke, and move their own distributors into the dead guys' turf."

"Nice folks," muttered someone.

"Aren't they all?" someone else responded.

They began by defining the margins of the grave with probes—thin, four-foot rods of stainless steel, each topped by a one-foot horizontal handle. Pressed into the soft earth of a fresh grave, the slender shafts sank easily; encountering hard, undisturbed soil, though, they balked and bowed, resisting. The probes weren't actually necessary; the perimeter of the grave was clearly visible, once the leaves and the slight mound of excess fill dirt had been removed. Still, the Bureau prided itself on thoroughness, and McCready was a Bureau man all the way. There would be no shortcuts today, for himself or his team.

Once the grave's outline was flagged and mapped and photographed, three of the agents—already sweating inside their biohazard suits—began digging. They started with shovels, working at the margins, digging down a foot all the way around before nibbling their way toward the carnage they expected to unearth at the center. After a grim twenty minutes, marked mainly by labored breathing and the rasping and ringing of shovel blades against soil and rocks, one of the agents—Starnes, a young woman whose blond hair spilled from the hood of her moonsuit like a saint's nimbus—paused and leaned in for a closer look. "Sir? I see fabric. Looks like maybe a shirtsleeve."

McCready knelt beside her. With the triangular tip of a thin trowel, he flicked away crumbs of clay. "Yeah. It's an arm. Lose the shovels. Switch to trowels. Let's pedestal the remains."

Two sweaty hours later, digging downward and inward from all sides, they'd uncovered a tangle of limbs, torsos, and heads. The pedestaled assemblage resembled a macabre sculpture—a postmortem wrestling match, or a pile of tacklers on a football field. It also reminded McCready, for some odd reason, of an ancient Roman statue he'd seen years before, in the Vatican Museums: a powerful sculpture of a muscular man and his two terrified sons caught in the crushing coils of sea serpents. Maybe the reason wasn't so odd after all, he realized: like the chilling figures frozen in stone, these three men had died in the coils of something sinister, something that had slithered up behind them as surely and fatally as any mythological monster.

McCready photographed the entwined bodies from every angle, seemingly oblivious to the stench that grew steadily stronger as the day—and the corpses— got hotter. "All right," he said finally. "Give me three body bags over on this patch of grass. Let's lift them out one at a time. I'll want pictures after each one."

It took another half hour to lay out the corpses, faceup, on the open body bags. By then, several of the techs were looking green around the gills, though no one had vomited. The last of the bodies to be lifted from the grave—the eyes gone to mush, the cheeks puffed out—was recognizable, just barely, as the man whose photograph McCready had passed around in the morning's briefing. "This one's Haskell, our undercover guy," he said grimly.

"So the C.I. was telling us true," said Kimball. "The drug buy goes bad, turns into a shoot-out."

"Looks like it," said McCready. "But just to be sure, let's ask him." He turned, looking over one shoulder toward the trees on the far side of the clearing. "*Hey*," he called out. "You—Brockton. Step out from behind that tree. And keep your hands where I can see them."

The team turned as a man emerged. He did not appear to be a seedy specimen from the sewers of the drug-trafficking world. The man looked more bookish than dangerous, and as he raised his hands, a broad smile creased his face.

Chapter 1

"You—*Brockton*," I heard McCready calling. "Step out from behind that tree. And keep your hands where I can see them."

"I'm unarmed," I yelled, stepping from my observation post behind an oak tree. "But I've got a Ph.D., and I'm not afraid to use it. One wrong move, and I'll lecture you to death!" The joke—*mostly* a joke—drew laughs from the weary FBI agents, as I'd hoped it would. "I'm Dr. Bill Brockton," I added as I approached. "Welcome to the Body Farm." I approached the rim of the empty grave, which was ringed with evidence flags and sweat-drenched FBI forensic techs. Peering into the hole, I saw that they had excavated all the way down to undisturbed soil, four feet down. The clay there was deeply grooved, as if it had been clawed by an immense monster. I, in fact, was that monster, and I'd left those marks the day before, when I'd dug the grave with a backhoe.

I'd missed most of today's excavation, having spent the morning entombed deep inside Neyland Stadium, the colossal cathedral to college football that the University of Tennessee had erected beside the emerald waters of the Tennessee River. Wedged beneath the stadium's grandstands, caught in a spiderwork of steel girders, was Stadium Hall: a dingy string of offices, classrooms, and laboratories, most of them assigned to the Anthropology Department, which I chaired. The rooms were strung along one side of a curving, quarter-mile corridor, one that underscored the *hall* in Stadium Hall. At midafternoon, when McCready had texted to say that the training exercise was nearly finished, I'd hopped into my truck, crossed the bridge, and slipped through a high wooden gate and down through the woods, stepping carefully to avoid treading on the bodies and bones scattered throughout the three-acre site: donated corpses whose postmortem careers were meticulously scrutinized, itemized, and immortalized, in photos, journal articles, scholarly dissertations, and law-enforcement anecdotes.

Officially, my macabre laboratory was named the Anthropology Research Facility, but a few years before, one of McCready's waggish FBI colleagues had dubbed it "the Body Farm," and the moniker—popularized by crime novelist Patricia Cornwell—had caught on so thoroughly that even I, the facility's creator, tended to call it by the catchy nickname. For several years now, the FBI had been sending Evidence Response Team members to the Body Farm for training exercises like this one. With a ready supply of actual human corpses, plus plenty of privacy, the facility was the only place in the nation—possibly in the entire world—where forensic teams could hone their skills in such realistic scenarios.

The three corpses just unearthed by McCready's team had gradually attracted a cloud of blowflies, some of which strayed—either at random, or in an excess of eagerness—from the faces of the dead to the eyes and nostrils of the quick, causing the agents to squint and swat at the unwelcome intruders. Off to one side was a large mound of sifted dirt, plus piles of clay clods and rocks too big and too hard to pass through the quarter-inch wire mesh. On the ground beside the dirt lay the screen and—atop the mesh—three cartridge cases, two cigarette butts, and one wad of chewing gum, plus a gum wrapper.

I scrutinized the screen, then the bodies, then the hole in the ground, taking my time before turning to face the assembled agents. "That's it? That's all you got?" Their expressions, which had been confident and proud a moment before, turned nervous when I added, "So y'all just ran out of steam before you got to the fourth body?" Exchanging worried glances, they returned to the edge of the grave, their eyes scanning its floor and walls. I chuckled. "Kidding," I said, and a chorus of good-natured groans ensued. "Okay, so tell me what you've learned from the scene."

I pointed at Kimball, the eager young agent who'd cast the tire tracks. "Agent Kimball," I said. "You like to make a good . . . *impression*." More groans, as the dreadful pun sank in. "What else does that rut tell us, besides the fact that the puddle had dried up by the time the tracks were made?" McCready had texted me a few notes on the team's findings, starting with their observations about the tire impressions. Kimball frowned, so I gave him a hint. "How many sets of tracks did you cast?"

"Just the one," he said. "That's all . . ." He hesitated, his eyes darting back and forth, then the light dawned. "Ah—they all rode in together."

"Bingo," I said. "But they didn't all ride out together. And what about the grave? What does the evidence there tell us?"

"The cartridge cases are from two different weapons," said one of the dirt sifters. "They're all nine-millimeter Remington, but there's two differ-ent firing-pin impressions. One's round, the other's rectangular." I nodded approvingly; when I'd asked a friend on the campus police force for spent shells, I'd specifically requested shells from two different hand-guns, so I was pleased that the difference had been noticed. "Also," he went on, "the cigarette butts are two different brands. So we might get two different DNA profiles from those."

"Good," I said. "Maybe there's DNA in the gum, too—and maybe the gum chewer's not one of the smokers. So there could be *three* DNA profiles, right?" Heads nodded. "Okay, let's talk taphonomy—the arrangement of the items you excavated. What did you learn as you unearthed the bodies?"

"All three were killed with a single shot to the back of the head," said a guy whose nerdy, Coke-bottle glasses were offset by immense, chiseled jaw muscles, gleaming with sweat and smears of clay. "Execution style." I nodded, slightly self-conscious about this part. The shots to the head were the least realistic part of the exercise, because the shots—unlike the corpses themselves—were fakes. It had struck me as unnec-essary and disrespectful to fire bullets into donated bodies, so I'd settled instead for daubing a small circle of red dye onto the back of each head, and a larger circle on each forehead, to simulate entry and exit wounds.

"What else?" A long silence ensued. "Did you find blood in the grave?" Heads shook slowly. "Did you find blood *anywhere* besides on the wounds themselves?" More head shaking; several of the agents now cast nervous sidelong glances at one another. "So what does that suggest to you?"

The blond woman raised a hand. "It suggests they were killed somewhere else," she said. "And then brought here."

I gave her a thumbs-up. "Which explains why there was only one vehicle. Tell me—how often do drug traffickers and drug buyers carpool to the place where the deal's going down?" A few of the agents laughed, but Kimball, the tread caster, winced, as he should have: Kimball, of all people, should have given more thought to the absence of a second vehicle. "Also," I went on, "how likely is it that only three bullets would be fired during a drug-deal shoot-out? All of them to the back of the victims' heads?" I could see them rethinking the scenario. "Anything else?" The agents looked from the grave to the bodies and back to the grave, then at me once more. My questions made it clear that they were still missing something—still failing to connect important dots—but apparently they needed a hint. "Look closely at the three faces," I said. "See any differences?"

"Ah," said the nimbus-haired blonde. "The two 'buyers' look a lot better than our guy. A lot . . . *fresher.*"

"Bingo," I said. "They show no signs of decomposition, and no insect activity. Look at your 'undercover agent.' He's a mess—he's starting to bloat, and he's got maggots in his mouth and nostrils. Anybody look in there?" Several of the agents grimaced; most shook their heads sheepishly. "So if you compare the condition of the bodies, what does the difference in decay tell you?"

"He was killed before the other two," said Boatman, the agent who'd noticed the absence of mud spatter beside the tire tracks.

"Exactly," I said, pulling on a pair of purple nitrile gloves. "Also, your undercover guy was probably outdoors, or maybe stashed outdoors for a while— someplace where the blowflies could get to him." I pointed a purple finger at the puffed-up face again. "Blowflies like to lay their eggs in the moist orifices of the body," I went on. "The mouth, the nose, the eyes, the ears, even the genitals, if those are accessible. But especially, *especially*, any bloody wound." I stooped beside the dead "agent" and lifted his head. I had gone to the trouble of mixing a bit of actual blood— pig blood—with the red food coloring on his head, and I'd brought him out to the Body Farm two days before I'd brought the other bodies. During that time, his "gunshot wound" had attracted legions of flies, and by the time I'd placed the bodies in the ground, maggots had begun colonizing his hair, forehead, and orifices. "Next time, check for maggots. And collect the biggest ones." I bent down and plucked a quarter-inch specimen from an eye socket, holding it in my palm for them to inspect. "A forensic entomologist could tell you that this maggot hatched three or four days ago," I said. "Which—if I remember right—is just about the time your undercover agent dropped off the radar screen. Is that correct, Agent McCready?"

"That's correct, Dr. Brockton."

I flicked the maggot into the woods. It was time to reveal the final plot twist in the scenario. When I'd first phoned to suggest the idea, McCready had sounded dubious. As we talked, though, he warmed to the idea, and by the end of the call, he'd embraced the scenario enthusiastically: "A good lesson in investigative skepticism," he'd called it.

"So," I said to the team of trainees, "knowing that these other two guys were killed a couple days after your agent—and knowing that all of them were brought out here and buried together . . ."—I paused, giving them time to think and rethink before offering the final hint—"what does that tell you about your confidential informant?"

"It tells us he's a lying sack of shit," Kimball blurted. His face was flushed and his tone was angry, as if the corpse really *was* a murdered FBI agent, rather than a married insurance agent who'd had a heart attack during a tryst with his mistress. "It tells us the C.I.'s whole story is bullshit," Kimball fumed, smacking a fist into an open palm. "Hell, maybe he even set *up* our guy—ratted him out to the traffickers."

I nodded. "Maybe so. So be careful who you trust. Bad guys lie through their teeth. But bugs?" I pointed to the bloated face and the telltale maggots. "You can always believe them. Whatever they tell you, it's the truth."

Chapter 2

The familiar arc of a rib cage filled my field of vision as I leaned down and peered through the smoke. On the rack of my charcoal grill, two slabs of baby back ribs sizzled, the meat crusting a lovely reddish brown. Ribs were a rare treat these days—Kathleen, invoking her Ph.D. in nutrition, had drastically cut our meat consumption when my cholesterol hit 220—but she was willing to bend the dietary rules on special occasions. And surely this, our thirtieth wedding anniversary, counted as a special occasion.

As soon as the FBI training at the Body Farm had ended, I'd headed for home, stopping by the Fresh Market, an upscale grocery, to procure the makings of a feast, southern style: ribs, potato salad, baked beans, and coleslaw.

As I fitted the lid back onto the smoker, I heard a car pull into the driveway, followed by the opening and slamming of four doors and the clamor of four voices. A moment later the backyard gate opened, and Jeff, my son, came in. Leaning into the column of smoke roiling upward, he drew a deep, happy breath. "Smells great. Almost done?"

"Hope so. The guest of honor should be home any minute. She's been dropping hints all week about celebrating at the Orangery." The Orangery was Knoxville's fanciest restaurant. "Way I see it, only way to dodge that bullet is to have dinner on the table when she gets here."

"You know," he said, "it wouldn't kill you to take Mom someplace with cloth napkins and real silverware once every thirty years."

I raised my eyebrows in mock surprise. "You got something against the plastic spork? Anyhow, I thought it'd be nicer to celebrate here."

The wooden gate swung open again—burst open, whapping against the fence—and Tyler came tearing into the backyard, with all the exuberance of a five-year-old who'd just been liberated from a car seat. "Grandpa *Bill*, Grandpa *Bill*, I could eat a *horse*," he announced, wrapping himself around my left leg.

A few steps behind came his younger brother, Walker, age three, grabbing my right leg and crowing, "I can eat a elephant!"

Jeff's wife, Jenny—a pretty, willowy blonde, who carried herself with the easy grace of an athlete—came up the steps after them, closing the gate. "Stay away from the grill, boys," she called. "It's hot. Very, very hot." She leaned over the boys to give me a peck on the cheek. "I don't know about the ribs, but you smell thoroughly smoked," she said. "Are you *sure* you want us horning in on your anniversary dinner?"

"Absolutely. What better way to celebrate thirty years of marriage?"

"Hmm," Jeff grunted. "Hey, how 'bout you and Mom celebrate with the boys while Jenny and I eat at the Orangery?"

"Listen to Casanova," scoffed Jenny. "For *our* anniversary, he took me to the UT-Vanderbilt game. *Super*romantic." She shook her head good-naturedly. Then, with characteristic helpfulness, she asked, "What needs doing?"

"If you could set the table, that'd be great. Oh, and maybe put the slaw and potato salad and beans in something better looking than those plastic tubs?"

She nodded. "Hey, kiddos, who wants to be Mommy's helper?"

"*I* do, *I* do," they both shouted, abandoning me to follow her through the sliding glass door and into the kitchen.

"What on earth did you do to deserve her?" I asked Jeff as the door slid shut.

"I think she likes me for the foil effect," he said. "I make her look so good by comparison. Same reason Mom keeps you around."

At that moment I heard the quick toot of a car horn in the driveway, followed by the clatter of the garage door opening. Kathleen was home.

Soon after, delighted squeals—"Grandmommy! Grandmommy!"—announced her arrival in the kitchen.

The slider rasped open and she emerged, the strap of her leather briefcase still slung over her shoulder. "Bill Brockton, you *sneak*. You didn't tell me you were cooking."

"I wanted to surprise you."

"I wanted to surprise you, too," she said. "I made us a seven o'clock reservation at the Orangery."

"Oh, darn—I wish I'd known," I said. She shot me a dubious look, which I countered with an innocent smile. "That would've been nice, honey. But I guess you'd better call and cancel."

"I'll call," she said, "but I won't cancel; I'll reschedule, for Saturday night. You don't get off the hook *that* easily. If I can survive thirty years of Cracker Barrel vittles, one fancy French dinner won't kill you."

She turned and headed inside. The instant the sliding-glass door closed, Jeff and I looked at each other and burst into laughter.

Dinner was loud, rowdy, and wonderful, with three terrible puns (all of them mine), two brotherly squabbles, and one spilled drink (also mine). The ribs were a hit—smoky, succulent, and tender.

Sitting at the head of the kitchen table, I surveyed my assembled family, then, with my sauce-smeared knife, I tapped the side of my iced-tea glass. "A toast," I said. The three adults looked at me expectantly; the two boys gaped as if I were addled.

"Toast?" said Walker. "Toast is breakfast, silly."

"A toast," Jenny explained, "is also a kind of blessing. Or a thank-you. Or a wish."

Walker's face furrowed, then broke into a smile. "I toast we get a dog!" His toast drew laughs from Kathleen and me, and nervous, noncommittal smiles from his parents.

"A toast," I repeated. "To my lovely wife. To thirty wonderful years together."

We clinked glasses all around. Kathleen looked into my eyes and smiled but then, to my surprise, she teared up. "To this lovely moment," she said, her voice quavering, "and this lovely family. The family that almost wasn't."

Now I felt my own eyes brimming. We almost never spoke of it, but none of us—Kathleen, Jeff, Jenny, or I—would ever forget the near miss to which she was alluding. The grown-ups clinked glasses again—somberly this time—and Kathleen reached out to me with her right hand. Instead of clasping hands, though, she bent her pinky finger, hooked it around mine, and squeezed. It was our secret handshake, of sorts: our reminder of what a sweet life we had, and how close—how terribly close—we'd come to losing it, right in this very room, right at this very table, a dozen years before. I lifted her hand to my face and uncrooked her finger, tracing the scar around the base and then giving it a kiss. By now the scar was a faint, thin line—barely visible and mostly forgotten, except when something triggered memories of that nightmarish night, and that evil man: Satterfield, sadistic killer of women. Satterfield, emerging from our basement, gun in hand, to bind us—Kathleen, Jeff, me, and even Jenny, Jeff's girlfriend at the time—to the kitchen chairs. Satterfield, putting Kathleen's finger into the fishlike jaws of a pair of gardening shears, and closing the jaws in a swift, bloody bite.

Odd, how memories can open underfoot, in the blink of an eye, taking you down a rabbit hole of the mind to some subterranean, subconscious universe where different rules of time and space and logic hold sway. Part of me remained sitting at the table, my fingers smeared with barbecue sauce, but part of me had gone down that bloody rabbit hole.

Kathleen's finger, which had sent me spinning there, now beckoned me back. She stroked my damp cheek and smiled again. "Will you marry me, Bill Brockton?" she asked.

"Yes, please," I answered. "Again and again. Every day." Half rising from my chair, I leaned over and kissed her—a grown-up kiss, on the mouth, taking my time.

"*Gross*," said Tyler.

"Gross gross *gross*," agreed Walker.

It was ten-thirty by the time Jeff's family was gone, the kitchen was clean, and Kathleen and I were showered and in bed. I rolled toward her on the mattress and cupped her face in one hand. "Not as romantic as the fancy French dinner you wanted," I said, "but tasty."

"Says the man who thinks turkey jerky is a delicacy," she said. "But yes, delicious. And it's always so sweet to see Jeff and Jenny with the boys. They're such good parents, Bill."

"They should be. You're a great role model."

"You, too," she said, then—from nowhere—"You still sad we couldn't have more?"

"No," I said, though that wasn't entirely true; deep down, I would always wish I'd had a daughter as well as a son. "I'm the luckiest man alive. I couldn't be happier." I felt the stirrings of desire, and I slid my hand down to her hip. "Well, maybe I could be a *tiny* bit happier."

She smiled, but she also shook her head. Taking my hand from her hip, she brought it to her lips and gave it a consolation-prize kiss. "I need a rain check, honey. Bad time of the month."

"Still?" She nodded glumly. "That doesn't bother me," I assured her. "You know I'm not squeamish."

"I do know, and I appreciate that," she said. "But I'm just not up to it. I'm sorry, sweetie; I'll be off the sick list soon, and I *will* make it up to you. I promise."

She crooked her little finger at me again, to make sure I knew she meant it.

"I'm sorry it's giving you trouble," I told her, my disappointment giving way to sympathy. "Seems like that's gotten worse again. You need to go back to the doctor?" She'd had outpatient surgery a year or so ago, to remove a uterine fibroid—a knot of benign tissue— and her cramps and bleeding had lessened afterward. For a while.

"I think it's just menopause, letting me know it's headed my way," she said. "Now turn out the light and spoon me." She rolled over and snuggled against me. Switching off the light, I wrapped an arm tightly across her chest. Her breathing slowed and deepened, her body twitching as she sank into sleep. As my own breathing found the same cadence as hers, I made a silent wish for her—one last anniversary toast, Walker style: *I toast you sleep well and feel better tomorrow.*

Chapter 3

Brown Field Municipal Airport
San Diego, California

Twin shafts of light—one green, the other white—sliced the hazy night in opposite directions, like luminous blades, as the airport beacon turned with blind, unblinking constancy.

Poised at the western end of the runway was a small twin-engine jet, its airframe quivering like a living creature: like a racehorse trembling in a starting gate, its entire existence—bloodline and breeding and birth and indeed every moment prior to this one—mere preamble and prelude to the impending instant of release and freedom, of exultant headlong hurtling.

Within the indigo glow of the cockpit, the pilot, his face ghostly in the glow of gauges and screens, worked his way down the takeoff checklist, item by item: engine instruments, check; fuel, full; altimeter, set; radio frequency, 128.25; flaps, ten degrees; flight controls—rudder, ailerons, elevator—free, clear, and correct. Satisfied, he throttled back the engines. He did not hurry; he could take all the time he needed or wanted—hell, he could take a three-hour nap right here on the active runway, if he pleased, with no risk of being disturbed. The control tower had closed for the night at seven, and at the moment—a moment shortly after midnight—the dawn's early light, and the first stirrings of human and aircraft activity, were still hours away. And by then he would be long gone.

Finished with the checklist, he tucked it into a slot in the center console and sighted down the runway, an eight-thousand-foot ribbon of black, outlined by jewel-like orange lights, which seemed to converge and merge at the far end. It was pure coincidence, but it was none-theless an interesting and apt coincidence, that Mexico, too—specifically, the quarter of Tijuana known as *Libertad*, "Liberty"—lay almost exactly eight thou-sand feet away as well: a mile and a half due south of him; less than thirty seconds away, if he banked hard right immediately after takeoff. Not that he would, though; a half mile off, he'd be banking left: toward the northeast, and Vegas.

He folded the paper copy of the flight plan he'd phoned in an hour before—"visual flight direct to Las Vegas"—then took one last look at the sectional chart, the detailed aviation map for Southern California. The map's green and tan landforms were splashed with yellow splotches, which denoted cities; in addition, the area above and around the yellow splotch of San Diego was overlaid with a crazed cross-hatching of blue lines—a tangle of arcs and angles, rhomboids and trapezoids and skewed chevrons, like the web-work of some deranged spider, one of those given LSD during a Cold War CIA experiment. The lines represented a 3-D maze in the sky—borders and boundaries and NO TRESPASSING zones in the air above San Diego. Surrounded by U.S. Navy and Marine Corps airfields nearby—Miramar, North Island, Imperial Beach—the city's airspace was the most complex in the nation, exponentially more intricate than L.A.'s or New York's. Blessedly, though, Brown Field—a sleepy municipal airport whose traffic was mostly single-engine private planes, plus a few bizjets and charter aircraft—lay just beyond the navigational nightmare; just outside the edges of the tangled web. Consequently a pilot could get in and out of Brown Field with little hassle and no red tape: no queue, no clearances, and no control-tower bureaucrats, at least not at night or on weekends.

It was time. With his right thumb he pressed a red button on the jet's U-shaped control yoke. "Brown traffic," he radioed to the empty night sky, "Citation Alpha Romeo One is rolling on runway eight. Departing the pattern to the northeast." Grasping the twin throttle levers with his left hand, he pushed them all the way forward. The engines spooled up again and the plane's racehorse tremble resumed, intensifying as the turbines reached full power, the brakes barely able to keep the craft in check. Then, easing the pressure on the brake pedals, he unleashed the shuddering beast. Forward it sprang, with gathering speed and single-minded purpose and a double-throated roar of joy.

Southern California Air Traffic Control Center
San Diego, California

Amos Wilson rubbed his eyes and reached for his coffee mug. The night was quiet—*too damn quiet,* he thought blearily; the flurry of inactivity made it hard to stay awake, let alone alert. The radar screen showed only two aircraft: a Navy F-18 inbound for Miramar, and a civilian plane twenty miles southeast, just off Brown Field and climbing fast, turning northeast. *Vegas,* he guessed. *Some fat cat—banker? no; real estate developer—dashing up for a weekend of blackjack and hookers.* It was a game Wilson played when he worked the graveyard shift alone: making up stories about who was transiting his sector; where they were headed, and why.

His mug was empty. "Dad-*gum*-it," he muttered. Spinning in his chair, he snagged the handle of the coffeepot and poured himself a refill, then took a swig. Grimacing, he spat it back into the mug. The coffee had been cooking for upwards of three hours, thickening to a bitter sludge, now more suitable for fossilizing fence posts—rendering them rot resistant and bugproof—than for reinvigorating humans. Wilson took another glance at the screen, assured himself that the two aircraft posed no possible risk to each other, and hurried to the sink. It took him just thirty seconds to dump the sludge, rinse and refill the pot, pour the water into the machine, and jam a fresh filter pack into the brew basket.

When he returned to his seat, the F-18 was already on the ground at Miramar; the civilian aircraft had leveled off at twenty-seven hundred feet; oddly, though, it had changed course by ninety degrees, a right bank so steep the turn was almost square cornered. "What the *hell?*" said Wilson. The plane was heading southeast now, streaking toward the border like a scalded cat; in less than a minute—*hell, not even,* he realized—it would enter Mexican airspace, due south of Otay Mountain. Then, as Wilson stared, mesmerized and paralyzed, the icon on the radar screen began to blink, and three words appeared beside it, flashing in sync with a harsh electronic rasp: LOW ALTITUDE ALERT.

Otay Mountain Wilderness
Southeast of San Diego

A shape as tan as the rocks, as fluid as quicksilver, flowed down the stony slope, the very embodiment of stealth and predatory focus. Below, something moved, and the creature—an adult male mountain lion, 150 pounds of cunning, sinew, and hunger—froze, its belly pressed to the rock. After a long pause, punctuated only by the sound of labored, painful breathing twenty feet away, the big cat flowed forward again, its tail twitching as it closed on its prey.

Its prey was Jesús Antonio Gonzales, a new, illegal, injured, and unsuspecting immigrant. Fleeing what he'd feared to be a Border Patrol truck jolting along the ridge in the darkness, Jesús had darted off the road and scrambled down the slope. Suddenly he'd taken a step into nothingness—one moment the mountain was solidly beneath his feet, the next moment it was gone. Tumbling off a ledge, he'd landed on his left side, hard, atop a boulder. He'd tried to regain his feet but quickly sank back against the rock, the pain in his ribs causing him to gasp and groan. He now lay twenty feet below the rim of the outcrop, and even if he hadn't been injured, he felt sure he wouldn't be able to climb back up the way he'd come down. He dared not risk another fall in the steep terrain—he'd barely missed cracking his head on the boulder, and if he fell again, he might not be as lucky—so he resolved to stay where he was, to wait until dawn before limping out of the mountains and into the outskirts of San Diego. There would be other, different risks in daylight—for one, he'd heard that *La Migra,* the immigration police, had cameras and motion detectors and dogs everywhere—but Jesús would just have to take his chances. He closed his eyes and shifted against the rock. The movement caused the ends of his splintered ribs to grate against one another, like shards of glass grinding inside him, and he grunted in pain.

Jesús could have paid a coyote, an immigrant smuggler, to bring him across—he probably should have, he realized now—but the coyote had demanded an outrageous sum: five thousand U.S. dollars, which Jesús didn't possess, and for what? A bone-jarring ride across the desert inside the hot cylinder of an empty water truck, followed by a two-day hike to the nearest city.

Cheaper and safer to find his own way, he had decided; after all, coyotes weren't infallible, either; some, he'd heard, had been known to leave people dying in the desert—abandoned hundreds of miles from the nearest town, or even locked inside a cargo container. Besides, he consoled himself, maybe everything would still work out just fine, despite his fall and his broken ribs: maybe, by daylight, the stabbing pain in his side would ease, and Jesús would find a good path down, and San Diego would spread itself before him like a glittering kingdom—a kingdom so rich that even his namesake, Jesús Cristo, would have yielded to temptation and bowed for the sake of such glory and wealth. *Sí*, Jesús Antonio Gonzales told himself, *San Diego será mío.* He practiced it in English: *Yes. San Diego will be mine.*

Somewhere in the darkness, he heard the throaty hum of an aircraft engine—or was it two?—and he prayed it was not Border Patrol helicopters scouring the hills. As he listened, trying to place the source of the sound, a pebble clattered down the rocky face above him. Bouncing off a nearby boulder, the stone tapped Jesús Antonio on the arm, as if to get his attention. Puzzled, he looked up, and in the darkness above him, he saw the gleam of jewels: a pair of green-gold eyes. They glittered, brighter and brighter in the light—the light that had inexplicably appeared in midair and was now rushing toward him, its glare accompanied by a deafening roar. A cone of incandescence encircled Jesús Antonio—Jesús and the mountain lion, too, spotlighting them as neatly as if man and beast were actors on a rocky stage. And as the single-minded beast made its instinctual leap, closing the gap between its fangs and Jesús Antonio's neck, the cone of light narrowed, narrowed, narrowed, so that at the precise instant Jesús Antonio reached up to cross himself, his trembling finger touched the very tip of the hurtling jet.

It was the briefest of touches—less than a millisecond—yet in that fleeting touch, Jesús's fingertip wrought a miracle: Night became day; darkness was transformed into light, a burst of red and orange and yellow, with pyrotechnic sparks and spokes of purple and green and magenta shooting off in all directions; Jesús himself was transubstantiated—the injured immigrant, the indigenous mountain lion, the hurtling airplane, and the high-octane fuel, all of them—transformed from mundane matter into dazzling energy, a radiant bloom upon the blackness that engulfed the wider world beyond.

Chapter 4

I was humming, halfway through my morning shower, when Kathleen flung open the bathroom door. "Bill, come quick!" she shouted, then turned and ran, adding, "Hurry. *Hurry!*" She sounded not just urgent but upset.

I flipped off the water and grabbed my towel, calling after her, "What's wrong? Kathleen? *Kathleen!* Are you hurt?"

"No, I'm fine," she yelled from the other end of the house. "There's something on the news you need to see."

I mopped the suds from my head and chest and wrapped the towel around my waist. Still dripping, I hurried to the kitchen, where I knew Kathleen would be watching *The Today Show,* as she did every weekday morning over coffee and granola. On the countertop TV screen, a tanned, silver-haired guy—a tennis pro or investment banker, judging by the well-kept, self-satisfied look of him—was slow dancing with a gorgeous younger woman. "Viagra," intoned a deep voice, smooth and confident. "Make it happen."

"So . . . honey," I began, turning toward her, "is there something you're trying to tell me?" I turned toward her, expecting to see amusement in her eyes—she was a good prankster, when she wanted to be—but her coffee cup was trembling in her hand, and her expression looked distraught.

"What? No, not *that. This.*" She tapped the television, where *The Today Show*'s news anchor, an attractive woman whose name I could never remember, had just appeared on-screen for her 7 A.M. rundown of the headlines. Superimposed across the lower part of the screen were the words "BREAKING NEWS—FIERY CALIFORNIA JET CRASH."

The newscaster's sculpted face was solemn, her impeccably manicured eyebrows furrowed with concern. "Authorities are investigating a fiery plane crash that occurred outside San Diego in the early morning hours today," she began. "The crash is believed to have claimed the life of pilot and humanitarian Richard Janus, founder and president of the nonprofit organization Airlift Relief International." The image cut to aerial footage of a steep, rocky hillside at night, lit by a fire blazing high into the sky. "According to the FAA," the anchor's voice-over continued, "Janus was on a solo night flight from San Diego to Las Vegas in his agency's twin-engine jet. Minutes after takeoff, the aircraft slammed into a dark mountainside and exploded." The camera cut to another aerial, this one showing emergency vehicles and firefighters gathered on a ridge above the blaze. "Darkness and rough terrain are hindering search-and-rescue efforts," continued the woman. She reappeared on camera, her face brimming with compassion. "And with high winds, wooded terrain, and hundreds of gallons of jet fuel feeding the fire, authorities say the blaze could continue to burn for hours."

The newscast moved on—another psychotic meltdown by some pop-culture princess—and I turned down the sound. "That's awful," I said. "Poor Richard."

"Poor Richard," Kathleen agreed. "And poor Carmelita. She must be devastated." I nodded. We didn't actually know Richard Janus or his wife, Carmelita, but we felt almost as if we did. Kathleen and I deeply admired Richard's work, and we were regular contributors to his nonprofit, Airlift Relief, which delivered food and medical aid to areas ravaged by natural disasters or human violence. "Funny how the mind works," Kathleen mused. "I've always half expected him to die in a crash someday, but I figured it'd be in some jungle somewhere. To crash on his way to Las Vegas? Seems extra sad, somehow."

She was right; it *did* seem cruelly ironic. "Well, one silver lining," I said, "if you can call it that. He must've died instantly. Probably didn't even see it coming." I had worked a few plane crashes, including an air force crash in the Great Smoky Mountains, and I was familiar with the swiftness and force with which airplanes—and the people inside them—could disintegrate.

Kathleen laid a hand on my arm. "Let's send a donation."

"We sent a big check six months ago," I reminded her. "At the end of the year."

"I know, I know. But this is a huge blow to Airlift Relief. He was the heart and soul of that organization. They'll be struggling without him—and they'll lose donors, you know they will. Please?" There were many things I loved about Kathleen, but her instinctive compassion and reflexive generosity—qualities I myself had benefited from, time and again—ranked high on the list.

I smiled and kissed her forehead. "You're a good-hearted woman, Kathleen Brockton."

She responded by wrapping her arms around me and giving me a full-body hug. "You're an observant man, Bill Brockton." After a moment, she reached down and untied her bathrobe, opening the front to press against me, skin to skin.

"Oh my," I said. "A lucky man, too." After three decades of marriage, Kathleen and I had settled into a companionable relationship, one in which fiery passion had given way to steady warmth. Still, she retained the capacity to surprise me and even, when something enkindled her desire, to take my breath away. "Not that I'm complaining," I managed to say, "but didn't you tell me last night you were on the sick list?"

"I feel *much* better this morning," she murmured. "And I was thinking how bereft I'd be if I lost *you* suddenly. So *carpe diem*, I guess."

"*Carpe me-um*," I murmured back.

She gave me a squeeze, one hard enough to make me yelp. "One more bad pun," she breathed in my ear, "and I might just change my mind."

"My lips are sealed," I breathed back. I began kissing and nibbling the side of her neck, seeking what I liked to think of as the magic spot. When she groaned, I thought for sure I'd found it, but gradually I realized that the telephone was ringing, and I echoed her groan.

"Don't," I said. "Don't answer it." But it was too late; she was already pulling away and picking up the handset. "Damn," I muttered. "So close and yet so far."

"Hello?" Kathleen sounded breathless, as if she'd run to catch the phone; her eyes were shining, the pupils still dilated wide. "Yes, it is. . . . May I tell him who's calling?" Her gaze grew focused and serious— her brows knitting together the way the newscaster's had—and she held the receiver toward me, mouthing something I couldn't quite make out.

Moments later, I felt my own forehead furrowing, as images from the television news—images of flames and smoke and emergency vehicles—flashed through my mind. "Of course," I said after a moment. "I'll see you there."

An hour after the phone call, I was standing on the tarmac, my "go" bag slung over one shoulder, as a white Gulfstream V—its only markings an aircraft registration number stenciled on the two engines— touched down at McGhee Tyson Airport and taxied toward Cherokee Aviation, the small terminal for private planes and charter aircraft.

The jet stopped, but its engines continued spooling as the cabin door flipped down and Special Agent Clint McCready appeared in the opening, beckoning me up the stairs that were notched into the door's inner surface. McCready gave me a hand up—a gesture that merged into a quick handshake—then he pulled the door closed and latched it. "Thanks again," he said. "We figure this I.D. will be quite a challenge. Glad you can help us out on such short notice."

"Anytime," I said. "I sure didn't expect to see you again so soon. Where'd you just come from, anyhow? We were out at the Body Farm till four yesterday. Did you even have time to get back to Quantico last night?"

He gave a rueful smile. "I had just enough time to take a shower and unpack." He turned and pointed to two closely cropped young men in the second row of seats. I recognized them both from the prior day's training at the Body Farm. "Doc, you remember Kimbo—Kirby Kimball—and Tim Boatman from yesterday?"

"Of course," I said. Kimball stretched out a bronzed paw and gave me a crushing handshake. Mercifully, Boatman, thin and sallow, had a grip that was as limp as Kimball's was fierce.

McCready added, "You saw how good they are with the Total Station. Best in the Bureau, actually."

I nodded, projecting more knowledge than I felt. I understood what a Total Station was—a high-tech mapping system, one that could record and document, in three dimensions, the exact position of bodies, bones, bullets, and other pieces of evidence at a large, complex crime scene—but I'd never witnessed one in action until the prior day's training exercise. "A crash site," I said to Kimball and Boatman. "I'm guessing you guys'll have your work cut out for you." They grinned, and I understood the sentiment behind their happy expressions. It wasn't that they were pleased someone had died; it was, rather, that they loved the challenge of helping solve the puzzle that awaited them at the scene. The truth was, I felt exactly the same way, and I also felt honored by the FBI's confidence in my identification skills.

The engines spooled up and the plane began rolling, so McCready motioned me to my seat. In less than a minute we turned from the taxiway to the runway, and without even stopping, the Gulfstream hurtled forward, the acceleration pressing me deep into the glove-soft leather, as if I were on some luxurious theme-park ride. "This thing has some good giddyup," I remarked as the plane leapt off the runway, still accelerating.

"Sure beats a Crown Vic," McCready replied. "Took me eight hours to get home last night. Took me forty-five minutes to get back here this morning. This thing climbs four thousand feet a minute. Has a five-thousand-mile range. Top speed of nearly six hundred miles an hour."

"No offense," I said, "but since when does the FBI have such a need for speed?"

"Since 9/11. Gives us quick-response capability to terrorist threats anywhere in the world."

I nodded reflexively, then—when his words sank in—I narrowed my eyes and stared at him. "Wait. Are you saying Richard Janus's plane was brought down by terrorists?"

"God, no," he replied, then hedged, "I'm not saying it *wasn't*, either. All I'm saying is, when the G5 isn't needed for a national security mission, we can deploy it for other high-priority investigations."

"And an accident involving a private plane is a high-priority investigation because . . . ?" He didn't answer, so after a moment's thought, I answered my own question: " . . . because the accident wasn't actually an accident?"

He shrugged. "Too soon to know."

"But you have reason to think Richard Janus was murdered?"

He shrugged again.

I'd worked on enough FBI cases over the years to know that the Bureau liked to hold its investigative cards close to the vest. So I wasn't surprised that McCready didn't seem inclined to show his hand. Nor was I surprised, a moment later, when he pulled a laptop from the briefcase beneath his seat, mumbled something about catching up on paperwork, and busied himself with the computer.

I opened the outer compartment of my bag and took out a fat three-ring binder, which Kathleen had handed me on my way out the door. It was a collection of monthly newsletters and annual fund-raising appeals from Airlift Relief International, Richard Janus's non-profit organization. Kathleen had first learned about Airlift Relief three years before, when she'd decided to create a nonprofit organization of her own. At the time, she was teaching a course on nutrition in develop-ing countries, and she'd been astonished and appalled to learn that five hundred thousand children a year go blind simply from vitamin A deficiency—a defi-ciency that can be remedied for less than a dollar per child. Never one to sit idly by, Kathleen had created the Food for Sight Foundation—and she had modeled her newsletters and fund-raising appeals on materials from Janus's agency, Airlift Relief International. Janus had built an organization that was lean and agile; vir-tually every dollar he raised went toward direct ser-vices; his mission was clear and compelling; and his agency's communications were informative and inspir-ing. Kathleen's binder on Airlift Relief was thick—four inches, at least—and contained newsletters dating back five years, all the way to the organization's founding. The inaugural issue featured a large photo of Janus and Jimmy Carter and a slew of other dignitaries lined up on the tarmac of an airport in Georgia. Above them loomed a battered DC-3 cargo plane, given by an anonymous donor. The caption proclaimed, "Airlift Relief is ready for takeoff!"

As I began leafing through the binder, I found myself captivated anew by the newsletters, which recounted dreadful disasters and daring relief missions. When a pair of powerful earthquakes killed more than twelve hundred people in El Salvador in 2001, for instance, Janus made a dozen flights to devastated villages, delivering food, antibiotics, water purifiers, volunteer doctors and nurses, even portable field hospitals. By the time the bigger relief agencies got into gear, Janus had already delivered tons of supplies—and had also survived two minor crashes: one when his landing gear collapsed, another when a child had darted onto the airstrip, forcing Janus to veer into the bush. Luckily, neither mishap was serious, and he and a mechanic had managed to make temporary repairs in the field. The series of photographs documenting the landing-gear collapse and repair was remarkable: First, the crippled plane sat lopsided and askew on the ground, beside a deep furrow plowed by the broken gear leg. Next, dozens of villagers pitched in to hoist one of the DC-3's wings up onto a makeshift scaffold of crisscrossed tree trunks. Then Janus and his mechanic wrestled and welded the mangled gear leg, their labors lit by a pyrotechnic shower of sparks. In the final photo, the villagers all sat perched atop the airplane's wing, their faces grimy, greasy, and grinning with pride. No one grinned more broadly than the pilot at the center of the crowd.

I was only halfway through the newsletters when I felt my ears popping from the Gulfstream's swift descent. As I tucked the binder back in my bag, I felt the plane bank sharply. Looking out my window, I saw a rocky peak below the right wingtip, and for one brief, disorienting moment—perhaps because of my immersion in accounts of cataclysms—I had the startling impression that we were circling an active volcano, one that had just erupted and sent a plume of smoke roiling skyward. Not until I saw the emergency vehicles clustered along the ridgeline of the peak did my brain register the fact that I was looking down on a plane crash—the crash I had just flown across the country to work. From the television footage I'd seen, I'd expected the entire mountainside to be ablaze, but luckily—or thanks to the trucks spraying water around the margins of the site—the fire had been confined to a narrow section of slope, at the blackened center of which now smoldered a tangle of wreckage. A line from a James Taylor song popped into my head: *Sweet dreams and flying machines in pieces on the ground.*

Soon I would sift through those smoldering pieces, seeking the shattered remains of a man whose dreams I had long supported—and whose actions I had deeply admired.

Chapter 5

The Gulfstream straightened and leveled off, leaving the crash scene behind. A minute later we streaked low over the coastline, then made a U-turn back toward the east, back toward Brown Field, the airport from which Janus had taken off just nine hours before. A thousand feet below us, the Pacific glittered in the morning sun like polished pewter. When the waves reached shore—a pristine stretch of sand and grass—they curled into a white line of surf, broken only, at a single point, by a high, blank wall, dividing one featureless stretch of sand from another, splitting wave after wave of the ceaseless surf. I was puzzled for a moment, then I realized that the wall must be the border fence separating the United States from Mexico.

A few hundred yards inland, on the Tijuana side of the fence, I noticed a large, circular structure, like a high-sided bowl—it appeared to be a stadium of some sort, but it was proportioned more like Rome's Colosseum than Knoxville's Neyland Stadium. Encircled by the steep grandstands was a small patch of bare, brown dirt, barely a hundred feet across. "Hey, Mac," I called across the aisle to McCready, "what's this stadium-looking thing? Looks way too small for soccer, and I *know* that's not a football field."

"That would be the Plaza de Toros," he said, without even looking. "The 'Bullring by the Sea.' Holds twenty thousand people. If it's a big festival, every seat will be filled, and more people hanging over the railings. We should go, once we finish working this crash scene."

I shook my head. "I don't think I'd have the stomach for it. I'm no animal-rights crusader, but a bullfight seems just plain cruel."

"Nothing plain about it," he said. "Very elaborate. But cruel? Define 'cruel.' You eat beef?" I nodded, knowing he was leading me into a trap. "Beef cattle get castrated," he said, "force-fed growth hormones, crammed into feedlots and trucks, and then carried by conveyor belts into the slaughterhouse to have their brains knocked out. Me, I'd rather hang on to my *cojones*, service some heifers, and go out with a splash—maybe even take a matador down with me, just to even the scales. Sure, it's a raw deal. But bulls make lousy house pets, Doc. And none of us gets out alive, remember."

Just then I heard a click in the overhead speaker, followed by the pilot's drawl. "Guys, we're on final. Touchdown in about thirty seconds."

I checked my watch. I had kissed Kathleen good-bye in my kitchen in Knoxville, two thousand miles to the east, at 7:30 A.M.. It was now 8:55. The Gulfstream wasn't quite as swift as the transporter beam on *Star Trek*, but it would do in a pinch. It would definitely do.

We were on the ground at Brown Field for less than ten minutes—just long enough for the group to make a pit stop and then cross the tarmac to our next vehicle, a helicopter labeled SAN DIEGO COUNTY SHERIFF. It was parked near a twin-engined cargo plane—a battered DC-3 that had seen not just better days, but better decades, and a fair number of better decades, at that. Faded paint along the side of the fuselage read AIRLIFT RELIEF INTERNATIONAL, and I recognized it as the same plane I'd seen in many of the newsletters I'd read on the flight from Knoxville. Crime-scene tape was stretched between stanchions placed around the plane's perimeter, creating the odd impression that the aircraft was an exhibit in some bizarre history museum devoted to aviation outlaws. The same tape was stretched across the front of a large metal hangar, which was considerably newer and less battered than the DC-3. The hangar, too, bore the organization's name.

The helicopter that awaited us, its turbine whining and its rotor spinning, was painted white, with blue lettering, but the paint did little to camouflage the craft's military lineage: It was clearly a plainclothes version of the Huey, the U.S. Army's helicopter work-horse during the Vietnam War. Nearing the whirling rotor, I ducked into a crouch—probably unnecessary; as far as I knew, no one had ever been decapitated because of good posture—but why take chances? Kimball and Boatman stashed their equipment and our bags in the back of the cabin, then clambered into the middle seats, leaving the seats directly behind the pilot to McCready and me. As we settled in, the pilot—a leathery deputy in aviator sunglasses—tapped his ear, then pointed to a pair of headsets hanging beside us. We nodded and tugged them on, their rubber seals shushing the urgent whine of the turbine and the jackhammer thud of the rotor. "Welcome, gentlemen," he said. "Strap in and we'll hop on up there."

The FBI's jet had been equipped with simple lap belts, like a commercial jetliner—as if a lap belt would have done any good if we'd hit the ground at almost the speed of sound. The sheriff's helicopter, on the other hand, was equipped with five-point, military-style harnesses. As I struggled with the fittings, McCready leaned over to help, tugging the straps so tight I could scarcely move. The instant I was clipped in we took off—an upward leap and a forward tilt so swift that I decided the pilot, like the aircraft, probably had some links to Vietnam service. Two minutes later we reached Otay Mountain, which lay only a few miles beyond the end of the runway. "There it is, gents," said the pilot. "Want to look it over before we land?"

"If it doesn't cost extra," McCready answered.

Without another word, the pilot put the helicopter into a bank so steep the rotor blades were almost vertical; if not for the centrifugal force, and the harnesses holding us in our seats, we might have tumbled down against the cabin door. For the second time in a quarter hour, I found myself circling the column of black smoke. This time, though, I was much lower and closer, and the helicopter bucked in the vortex of turbulence generated by the fire, the wind, and the rocky terrain.

Just as I was getting used to the steep bank, the helicopter plunged downward, dropping into a hover below the ridgeline, crabbing sideways, closer and closer to the mountainside. Looking out the right-side windows, I found myself at eye level with the wreckage of Richard Janus's jet—a mess of mangled metal that appeared to have been run through a junkyard shredder, doused with gasoline, and then set ablaze. "Damn," came McCready's voice through the headset. "That's what I call a crash."

"Nobody walked away from that one," agreed the pilot. "I don't get it. Richard was a damn good pilot."

"Friend of yours?"

"I knew him. Flew with him a few times. He was too good a pilot to just auger in like that. Unless something went bad wrong. Or unless he did it on purpose."

"Why would he do it on purpose?" asked McCready, his voice neutral.

"No clue. Beautiful wife, high-minded work, plenty of adventure. The perfect life, seems like. I guess you just never know."

I didn't join the conversation; I was too busy wondering how the hell I'd recover a victim—or even identifiable parts—from the devastation that lay just beyond my window. Almost as if he'd read my mind, the pilot added, "I don't reckon you guys'll be needing a body bag. Couple sandwich bags, more like it."

Years before, I'd helped recover and identify remains from the wreckage of an air force transport that had hit a cloud-shrouded ridge in the Great Smoky Mountains at high speed. The debris from that crash had been strewn for half a mile, and—on the basis of that experience—I'd expected a similar debris field here. Instead, everything seemed to be contained within a narrow wedge of valley, which sloped away to the north. The valley stretched for miles, but the debris seemed confined to its final, highest hundred yards or so. Judging by the tightness of the wreckage, the center of impact appeared to be the base of the bluff that formed the valley's upper terminus—a bluff that rose all the way to the mountain's ridgeline, where a long line of emergency vehicles was perched. Fire trucks at either end of the line sprayed feathery plumes of water onto the evergreen trees at the margins of the smoldering debris field.

As I studied the destruction, I heard and felt a boom as the mountainside erupted. Chunks of metal and rock hurtled against the shuddering helicopter, and with a crack like a rifle shot, my window shattered into thousands of shards, held together only by a thin film of plastic embedded in the glass. With a yank on the control stick, the pilot spun us away from the mountainside. "Dam-*nation*," he yelled. "Thought for a minute I was back in 'Nam. Oxygen cylinder blew, I guess. Sorry. Anybody hurt?"

"I'm all right," I said. "Nothing a quick shower and a clean pair of pants won't fix."

McCready glanced back at Kimball and Boatman, who gave him thumbs-up signals. "We're all fine," he told the pilot. His words sounded calm, but I noticed that his voice was pitched half an octave higher than normal.

The pilot lofted us above the ridge and then eased down toward a flat, rectangular surface—a concrete pad, I saw as we descended, its surface weather-beaten and cracking, a cluster of battered meteorological instruments huddled at one corner. He landed the big machine softly—tenderly, almost—as if to make up for his earlier recklessness and our near-death experience.

I heard the inner echo of Kathleen's recent words— *carpe diem*—and also heard myself adding a silent "thank you." But for what, and to whom? To the helicopter pilot, for not quite killing us just now? To Kathleen, for being a loving wife and loyal friend for thirty years? To God, for blessing me—far beyond all deserving—with a fine family, good health, and work that I loved doing?

Maybe all of them, I realized as the turbine spooled down. All of those, and more besides. *Thank you. Thank you. Thank you.*

Chapter 6

The rotor was still spinning as a man approached the helicopter with a limp in his stride, a scowl on his face, and a pair of outstretched arms that silently shouted the question "What the *hell*?!?" Tight on his head was a navy blue baseball cap, monogrammed NTSB in large letters. He made a beeline for the cockpit door, but the pilot pointed a thumb over his shoulder, indicating that McCready was the one he should talk to. A moment later the cabin door was yanked open. "Who are you," shouted the man in the cap, "and what the hell did you think you were doing, besides jeopardizing my crash scene?"

"Actually, it's my crash scene now," McCready said, flashing his badge. "Supervisory Special Agent Clint McCready. Federal Bureau of Investigation."

"FBI?" The man in the cap glowered, but he dialed back the anger a few clicks. "What brings the Bureau up here?"

"We're . . . *investigating*," McCready said drily. "We'll be working this as a crime scene. I've got an identification expert and a mapping team with me, and an eight-man Evidence Response Team is headed up the mountain now from our local field office." McCready clambered out of the cabin and extended a hand. "We appreciate your help, Mr. . . . ?" The final sentence was more than just a way of asking who the pissed-off guy in the cap was; it was also McCready's efficient way of putting the guy in his place, of showing him whose jurisdictional penis was larger. McCready's smile, as he waited for an answer, was polite but tight, underscoring the message that the Bureau was running the show now.

"Maddox," said the man in the NTSB cap. "Patrick Maddox, National Transportation Safety Board." He unfolded his arms and shook McCready's hand with understandable coolness. In less than thirty seconds, Maddox had been demoted from head honcho to hired help. Henceforth, he was a consultant who might provide useful insights, but his investigative procedures and priorities now carried far less weight than they had before our arrival.

Wriggling out of my harness, I lurched out of the cabin with my bag. Kimball and Boatman were close on my heels, nimble despite their load of gear and baggage.

As the rotor spun up again, Maddox surveyed the lot of us, then shrugged. "It's all yours," he shouted. "Knock yourself out." The helicopter lifted off and spun away, wheeling westward and dropping down toward Brown Field. Maddox watched it, then turned to McCready again. "By the way," he added, as the rotor's noise faded in the distance, "do you realize that you guys nearly made history?"

"How's that?" asked McCready.

"First crash ever witnessed—in person, in real time—by an NTSB investigator. You'd've been famous at the Safety Board. Legends, all of you."

I had to admit, he had a point—and maybe a sense of humor, too. "No offense," I chimed in, "but I'd much rather be a *living* legend."

McCready and Maddox both smiled, and I hoped I'd helped ease the tension.

McCready pointed at me. "Mr. Maddox, this—"

"Call me Pat," said Maddox.

"Okay, Pat. Call me Special Supervisory Agent McCready." Maddox stiffened again, but then McCready laughed. "I'm kidding, Pat. Call me Mac. Sorry to get in your business here." He gestured at the two young agents. "Pat, meet Agents Kimball and Boatman. They'll use a Total Station to map the site." He indicated me. "And this is Dr. Bill Brockton, a forensic anthropologist from the University of Tennessee. Doc here specializes in human identification and skeletal trauma."

Maddox shook my hand, nodding in the direction of the crash. "Plenty of trauma here, but probably not much human left to identify." He furrowed his brow at me. "Remind me? How many bones in the human body?"

"Two hundred and six, in adults."

"Uh-*huh*. Ever work one of those thousand-piece jigsaw puzzles?"

I shook my head. "Never had the patience."

"Well, better start cultivating some," he said. "Just a guess—but it's a fairly educated guess—you've got one hell of a puzzle waiting down there, and the pieces are gonna be damned tiny."

"You mean 'we,' don't you? *We've* got a puzzle. You'll be down there with us, right?"

He shook his head. "I wish. Can't." He hoisted up the left leg of his pants to reveal a contraption of straps, buckles, and hinges that resembled a medieval implement of torture. "Knee surgery three weeks ago. I'm not supposed to be walking on anything rougher than wall-to-wall carpet. My orthopedist went ballistic when I asked what to do if I had to climb around on a mountainside. 'Schedule a knee replacement,' he said."

"Knee surgery's tricky stuff," I said. "Your doctor's right to be cautious."

Maddox sighed. "I hate being on the sidelines, though."

"Not to worry, Pat," said McCready, clapping me on the shoulder. "If anybody can put the pieces together, it's this man right here. The best there is." Then he frowned. "I have a question, though. That little kaboom a minute ago—what the hell was that? It rang our chimes pretty good."

"I've seen planes brought down by less," said Maddox. "A lot less."

"Hovering beside a burning aircraft." McCready looked rueful. "Kinda dumb, I guess."

"You said it."

"So what was it?" persisted McCready.

Maddox shrugged. "Won't know till we start combing through the debris. Just guessing, though, I'd say an overheated oxygen cylinder."

"That's what the helicopter pilot said, too." McCready looked puzzled. "But the fire's about out. Why would it blow now, not earlier?"

"Well . . ." The crash expert glanced away, then met McCready's gaze. "Frankly?" McCready gave a yes-please nod. "Probably the buffet from your rotor wash," Maddox said, "stirring things around. Maybe knocked the cylinder against something sharp—a metal rod, or a shard of rock—and it popped. Like a balloon."

McCready grimaced. "So it was my own damn fault?" I looked at him, surprised; it had been the pilot, not the FBI agent, who had dropped down beside the wreckage. McCready was choosing to let the buck stop with him, though, and I admired that. Maddox gave a half nod, half shrug, which I also admired: He was confirming what McCready said, but without rubbing his nose in it, as he could've. McCready shook his head. "Hate that," he said. "I put my people at risk, and I altered the scene, too. If anybody should know better, it's me, Mr. Save-the-Evidence. Sorry about that."

"Well, look on the bright side," Maddox said. "If it hadn't blown now, it might've blown later, with your guys right there beside it. Somebody's boot bumps it, the thing tips over, hits a sharp edge, and *kaboom*. Could've taken off a foot, maybe blinded somebody. So you probably did us all a big favor." He paused. "Hell, now that I think about it, maybe you oughta call that chopper back to stir things around some more; set off anything else that's about to blow." He smiled, making sure we knew it was a joke, not a jab. McCready smiled back. Olive branches had been accepted all around, it seemed.

McCready shifted gears and got down to business. "Seriously, how soon you think it's safe to get down there and start working it? We got more oxygen cylinders down there? What about other hazards?"

Maddox shrugged. "Well, the fuel's just about burned off. Hydraulic fluid—for the brake lines and the flight-control systems—that's combustible but not explosive, and it's probably burned off by now, too. I doubt that there's another oxygen cylinder—one's the standard on a Citation, but some have two. I've got somebody tracking down the maintenance guys, back at the hangar, so we'll know for sure."

"I haven't had a chance to read up on the Citation," McCready said—another surprise to me, since I'd noticed him unfolding a big cutaway diagram of the jet during our cross-country flight. "It's a twin-engine bizjet? Like a Gulfstream or a Learjet?" Was he doing more fence mending—giving Maddox a chance to demonstrate his knowledge?—or was he testing to see how much the man knew?

Maddox gave a half smile. "*Sort* of like a Learjet. The first version of the Citation was a little sluggish;

some pilots called it a 'Nearjet.' Newer ones are faster, though still not as fast as that Gulfstream horse you guys rode in on—that *was* you that circled on your way in, right?" McCready nodded, and Maddox rattled on. "But the Citation's a good design. Solid. Simple, relatively speaking—it's the only jet approved for single-pilot operation. Sensible, for a multimillion-dollar minivan. It—"

McCready broke in. "Excuse me? Did you just say 'minivan'?"

Maddox nodded. "It's the Dodge Caravan of biz-jets. Not too fast, not too fancy, but functional and roomy, and plenty good enough, you know?"

"So much for the magic of flight," said McCready.

"Hey, I'm all about the magic of flight," Maddox answered. "It *is* magic. But tell me: What's Europe's biggest aircraft maker called? Airbus, that's what. Air. *Bus.* I rest my case."

A cell phone at McCready's belt shrilled; he flipped it open, turning his back to Maddox and me. "McCready," I heard him say. "Go ahead." He listened a moment, then said, "Got it; we won't start the party without you. Thanks." Snapping the phone shut, he turned to us again. "That was Miles Prescott, from the San Diego field office. He's the lead agent on this case. He's on his way up—almost here, he says—and he's bringing the cavalry with him."

McCready pointed down at a jeep road, and sure enough, a quarter mile below, I saw a minicaravan snaking up the ridge. "Hail, hail, the gang's all here," muttered Maddox.

The lead vehicle, a black Chevrolet Suburban—its windows tinted nearly as dark as its paint—sped past the line of emergency vehicles and pulled onto the concrete pad. It was followed by the familiar, boxy shape of an evidence-recovery truck. Lumbering up behind them was a massive vehicle labeled MOBILE COMMAND CENTER. It looked like the offspring of a Winnebago that had somehow managed to mate with a fire truck.

The doors on all three vehicles opened simultaneously, almost as if the move were choreographed, and a dozen FBI agents emerged, one wearing a suit and spit-shined shoes, the others decked out in cargo pants, boots, and T-shirts. *One of these things is not like the others*, I thought. It was an absurd echo from my son's *Sesame Street* days, twenty years or more ago, and yet it fit. And maybe, I realized, what was silly was not the song, but the wearing of a three-piece suit on a rocky mountaintop in the wilderness.

A round of introductions ensued—a litany of names I promptly forgot, except for that of Prescott, the Suit—and when it was done, Prescott turned to McCready. "So we good to go?"

McCready frowned and shook his head slightly. "I don't think we can start working it quite yet," he said.

"I agree," said Maddox, taking the opportunity to step forward and reclaim a seat at the figurative table. "The fire's mostly out, but that wreckage is gonna be hot as hell for a while yet. An oxygen cylinder exploded half an hour ago. Why put your men at risk?" He didn't mention the helicopter's role in triggering the explosion, and McCready didn't either, so I kept quiet about it, too.

Prescott looked impatient, and at me. "Dr. Brockton? What's your take on this, forensically speaking?"

"Forensically speaking," I said, "this reminds me of something a Tennessee sheriff said to me at a death scene years ago, on a mountainside in the middle of the night." The other FBI agents and the crash investigator edged closer so they could hear better. "We were discussing whether to start working the scene right then, or to wait until daylight. The sheriff mulled it over and then said, 'Well, Doc, I reckon he ain't gonna get any deader by morning.'" Maddox grinned; Prescott gave a tight smile; McCready kept his expression as neutral as Switzerland. "I reckon Richard Janus won't get any deader if we let things cool down for an hour or so while we figure out the best way to work this thing."

What I didn't say, but couldn't help thinking, was that in an I.D. case with a celebrity victim, every minute we delayed would cost us, too. The throng of reporters—and therefore the authorities whom the reporters would be badgering for updates—would want us to hurry, to push, to make up for lost time. Looming even larger in my mind was another person who would surely be waiting impatiently, perhaps even desperately: Mrs. Richard Janus.

Chapter 7

The FBI agents and I shifted in our chairs in the command center—adjusting and readjusting our personal-space boundaries, like people crammed into an oversized elevator—as crash investigator Patrick Maddox began briefing us on what to expect in the wreckage. Using the command center's satellite link and computers, Maddox had, in ten minutes or so, downloaded a batch of files and created a PowerPoint presentation. I was impressed. Maddox appeared at least ten years older than I was—a leathery, rode-hard sixty, probably more—but he seemed far more Internet savvy and PowerPoint positive. My relationship with PowerPoint could best be characterized not as love-hate, but as *loathe*-hate. I despised the software, with a deep and abiding passion. Drop my 35-millimeter slides into the slots of a Kodak Carousel projector, and I'm a happy guy; import them into PowerPoint—whose default settings seem to include a permanent "blur" feature—and I'm one pissed-off professor.

"Okay, guys," Maddox commenced. "I'll give you the supercondensed version of 'Aircraft 101.' So I guess that makes it 'Aircraft 0.1.' Maybe some of you know some of this stuff already. Hell, maybe *all* of you know *all* this stuff already. Tough shit—I like talking about it. And it'll be easier to recognize the 'after'—the debris you'll be recovering—if you've taken a look at the 'before,' inside and out." He reached for the power button on the projector, but stopped before switching it on. "By the way, anybody remember anything particularly relevant about this mountain?" None of the younger guys seemed to, but Prescott, as a San Diego old-timer, nodded, and so did I, a middle-aged Tennessean. "A twin-engine Hawker jet crashed up here thirteen years ago, about a quarter mile from here. It was carrying a band. Doc, what's the name of that Nashville singer they played for?"

"Reba McEntire," I said. "She lost her whole band."

He nodded. "She and her husband were supposed to be on the plane, too, but they decided to spend the night in San Diego and catch a flight the next day. Lucky for them. Too bad for everybody else."

"What caused that one to crash?" asked Kimball.

"Bad luck and stupidity," said Maddox, shaking his head. "The night was dark and hazy. The pilots didn't know the area or the terrain. The FAA briefer they talked to on the radio gave 'em bad advice—practically steered 'em into the mountainside. Shouldn't've happened. But it did. And I can tell you, it was a mess to clean up. Anyhow." He switched on the projector, and a photo of a sleek little twin-engine jet filled the screen. "Here's a Cessna Citation." He clicked forward to another, bigger jet. "Here's another Citation." He fast-forwarded through a series of jets, each different from the others. "These are *all* Citations. Some have straight wings, some have swept wings. Some carry four passengers; some carry sixteen. But they're all Citations—Cessna calls it the 'Citation family.' Confusing as all get-out, unless you're an airplane geek like me." He flashed a photo that I recognized from an Airlift Relief newsletter: a smiling Richard Janus standing beside a jet, freshly painted with the agency's name and symbol. "This is the one we're recovering here. Donated to Janus's organization four years ago, in 2000. It's a 501—an early Citation—built in 1979. Funny thing, most of us wouldn't dream of driving a car that's twenty-five years old, but we routinely zip around the sky—six miles up; five, six hundred miles an hour—in vehicles built before some of you guys were even born. This Citation wasn't new by any stretch, but two years ago, it was upgraded—retrofitted with bigger engines and bigger fuel tanks—so it could fly faster and farther. In the end, of course, that meant it crashed harder and burned longer."

"Excuse me," McCready interrupted. "I've been wondering about that."

"About which—the crash, or the burn?"

"The burn. How come the fuel didn't all explode on impact—one giant fireball?"

"Because this wasn't a scene in a Bruce Willis movie," Maddox deadpanned, earning another round of laughs. "Actually, that's a good question. Evidently the fuel tanks didn't rupture completely. So instead of vaporizing and exploding, the fuel—some of it, at least—stayed contained within the wing structure, and it dribbled out or poured out, sustaining the fire. More on that in just a minute," he said. "First, let's back up to some basics. Structurally, an aircraft has a lot in common with a bug." He looked around, noticed puzzled looks on many of the faces, and smiled, clearly pleased by the response. He turned to me. "Dr. Brockton, how would you describe the structural framework of humans?"

"Well," I began, "we're primates—upright, bipedal vertebrates—with an axial skeleton and an appendicular skeleton. The axial skeleton—"

He held up a finger to interrupt me. "Full marks," he said. "To translate that into terms that even I can understand, you're saying our skeleton is an endoskeleton—an interior structural framework—right?"

"Right."

"Whereas bugs have . . . ?"

"An exoskeleton," I supplied, feeling a bit like a student being nose-led by a professor—and not particularly liking the feeling. "An external shell, made of chitin—a bioprotein or biopolymer, if I'm remembering my zoology."

"I'll take your word for the chemical details," he cracked. "A bug's shell is light, strong, and rigid. So is an aircraft's. Trouble is, when either one—a bug or a plane—gets squashed, the shell crumples, and the guts go everywhere."

"The plane's guts," asked Kimball, "or the pilot's?"

"At four hundred miles an hour? Both," Maddox answered. "As we dig down through it, we'll certainly recognize parts. I'm pretty good at identifying airplane pieces, and I'm told Dr. Brockton here is terrific at identifying *people* pieces. But basically? That plane and anybody in it? Squashed like a bug."

"Oh, goody," Kimball joked. "Can't wait."

It was gallows humor—a sanity-saving necessity in work this grim. But the truth was, I *couldn't* wait. And unless I missed my guess, neither could eager-beaver Kimball.

I was halfway through my part of the briefing—I had passed out diagrams of the human skeleton and had worked my way from the skull down through the spine and into the pelvis—when I noticed that my voice wasn't the only thing droning. Maddox was ignoring me by now, his head turned in the direction of the sound; a moment later, I saw McCready and Prescott turn toward it, too. In the distance but closing fast was the distinctive thudding of a helicopter rotor.

When it became clear that the helicopter was landing, McCready and Prescott headed for the door, trailed by the rest of us. Maddox and I stayed in the background, watching from the command center's steps.

The agents fanned out on the concrete, facing the helicopter—the sheriff's helicopter again, as I'd guessed from the low, military muscularity of the pitch. As the rotor slowed, the left cockpit door opened and a woman got out of the copilot's seat—a woman I recognized, even through the dark hair whipping across her face, as Carmelita Janus. She was dressed in black from head to toe, but the outfit was a far cry from widow's weeds; it looked more like a commando's uniform for night ops—but night ops with style. She wore billowy cargo pants of what appeared to be parachute nylon, topped by a long-sleeved, form-fitting pullover; the pants were tucked into tight, knee-high boots that sported tapered toes and a hint of a heel.

Maddox nudged me, muttering, "Is that who I think it is?"

"If you think it's the grieving widow," I muttered back.

"Christ, what's *she* doing here?"

"Trying to find out if her husband's dead, I guess. Or maybe trying to make sure we're not sitting around playing video games." I glanced at McCready and Prescott; to say they didn't look thrilled to see her would have been the understatement of the century.

Mrs. Janus strode toward the FBI agents, who stood shoulder to shoulder, like some posse of Wild West lawmen, minus the six-shooters and the ten-gallon hats. Her gaze swept across the group, then returned to the central figure, the one wearing the power suit. "You must be Agent Prescott," she said.

"Yes, ma'am," he said. "Special Agent in Charge Miles Prescott. So, Mrs. Janus? Why are you here?"

"To identify my husband's body, if it's been found. To help search for it, if it hasn't been."

Prescott shook his head slowly, seeming pained. "Ma'am, I'm very sorry, but I can't let you do that."

"Why not? I'm trained in search and rescue. I'm also a paramedic. Not that I think Richard could have survived this crash."

"How did you get the sheriff's office to fly you up here?"

"Our organization has a good partnership with the sheriff's office," she said. "We often work together. Quite closely." Prescott frowned. "Mr. Prescott, I'm here to help any way I can. Even if it's just to identify the body."

He held out his hands, palms up. "Mrs. Janus, we haven't even started the search. It's not safe yet. I can't put you at risk. And once we do start, we'll be collecting forensic evidence—evidence we're counting on to tell us what happened last night. You wouldn't want any of that evidence to be overlooked, or damaged, or destroyed, would you?"

"No, of course not. But—"

Their dispute was interrupted by the whine and whump of the helicopter revving. Prescott looked puzzled for a moment. Then, as it became apparent that the chopper was about to take off—without Mrs. Janus—his expression changed from confusion to fury. "What the *hell*," he snapped, then whirled and barked at the agent standing beside him. "*You.* Get on the radio with the sheriff's office. Tell them to tell that pilot—" The helicopter lifted off. "Shit. You tell them to get that helicopter on the ground—right here, right now—to pick her up. Or I will come down on them like the wrath of God."

The young agent pushed past me into the command center, and I could hear a terse exchange of voices. Sixty seconds later, the helicopter returned. It hovered directly over the cluster of federal agents, its downdraft buffeting them and yet somehow leaving Mrs. Janus—standing twenty feet from them—unruffled. Then it edged sideways and touched down. Without a word, Carmelita Janus turned, strode toward it, and climbed back into the copilot's seat.

As the machine leapt up again—buffeting the agents once more on its way out—I noticed something I hadn't noticed before: a second helicopter, hovering a hundred yards away. The cabin door was open; perched on the sill, his feet propped on a landing skid, was a man—a man with a boxy black object balanced on one shoulder. A cylinder projected from the front of the box; at its center, I saw a glint of blue: the reflection of a telephoto lens, watching and recording the scene that had just transpired. Judging by the logo emblazoned on the side of the helicopter, Fox News viewers across San Diego—or across the entire nation—would soon be seeing Mrs. Richard Janus being banished from the site of her husband's smoldering jet, her brave offer to help spurned by the heartless forces of the FBI. I felt sorry for Prescott; his Bureau bosses might well—and his media critics surely would—take him to task for being so unsympathetic . . . or for being caught on camera. At the same time, I couldn't help admiring Mrs. Janus's moxie and resourcefulness. Her maneuver could end up complicating our work, though, I realized, especially if it increased the pressure for us to work fast.

"Damn," said Prescott.

O Brother, I thought, *you can say that again.*

"Damn," he repeated. "Damn damn *damn.*"

Chapter 8

An hour had passed since Carmelita Janus flew off, but the cyclone of grit and grouchiness she'd stirred up continued to swirl long after the helicopter had vanished. Prescott spent some quality time fussing into his phone; I heard the word "grandstanding" at least three times; I also heard him say, "I want to know everything there is to know about her husband's life insurance. How much? Does it pay double for accidental death? Is there a suicide exclusion? Most important—is she the sole beneficiary?" There was more muttering I couldn't quite catch, then he snapped the phone shut and glared at the group as if we were his problem, saying, "So? *Now* what are we waiting for?" I was wondering that myself, though I wasn't in a position to ask.

McCready looked startled—or was it angry?—
for a split second, but his answer was matter of fact.
"We're waiting for a couple key pieces of gear," he
said. "Should be here any minute." He recapped the
team's assignments, concluding, "Remember, safety
first. Followed closely—really, *really* closely—by evidence preservation." He scanned the agents' faces.
"Any other questions for me? For Dr. Brockton or
Mr. Maddox? No?" He pointed toward the door.
"Okay, fellows, let's go get it."

Remembering the thirty-foot bluff we'd have
to descend to get to the wreckage, I couldn't help
wondering, *Get it? How?*

I didn't have to wonder for long. As we exited the
command center, I heard a deep, powerful roar. A
moment later a crane lurched into view and rumbled
along the rocky ridge road. McCready, Prescott, and
Maddox huddled briefly, and then Maddox limped
into the crane's path. Waving his arms to get the driver's attention, he headed toward the rim of the bluff,
motioning the crane to follow. As they traversed the
edge, silhouetted against the sky, I imagined for a
moment that Maddox was a farmer, leading some
immense, long-necked, bellowing beast out to graze.
He stopped, peering down the bluff, and then pointed
to the ground at his feet, indicating the spot where he

wanted the crane. Then he raised his arm overhead and slowly lowered it to horizontal, pointing straight out over the abyss, miming the motion of the machine's boom.

The crane had a capacity of sixteen tons—thirty-two thousand pounds—according to prominent warnings stenciled on the vehicle and on the boom. *No problem,* I thought; from where I stood, it looked as if most pieces of the wreckage weighed less than I did. Sidling over to Maddox, I joked, "Reckon we've got enough muscle?"

Maddox shrugged, looking more dubious than I'd expected. "It's not the load capacity I'm worried about, it's the boom length," he said. "The plane only weighed six tons, dripping wet, so this thing could easily hoist a whole Citation. Plus another whole Citation. The trick'll be reaching out far enough. The boom's a hundred feet long." He studied the debris field below, then looked again at the boom, now swinging out in a gargantuan imitation of Maddox's pantomime. "Might be enough. Wish we had another fifty feet." He frowned at the rough jeep road the crane had lurched up to reach us. "Might be tough to get a bigger rig up the mountain, though."

I thought, *Might be?* I was amazed that *any* rig had managed to make it up.

I felt sure the crane could get the wreckage up the bluff. But I still wasn't clear on how we could get down.

That answer, too, was quick to materialize. Two of McCready's agents emerged from the back of the ERT truck, big coils of rope slung over their shoulders. The ropes were red nylon, interwoven with diamonds of black—a pattern that made them look more like rattlesnakes than I liked. Two other agents brought out bundles of harnesses, racks of carabiners, and other climbing hardware. The agents with the ropes tied them off to cleats at opposite ends of the crane, then flung the coiled bundles off the edge of the bluff. For a moment, as the bright red loops separated and unspooled, they looked like party streamers, and the juxtaposition—the festive unfurling against the grim backdrop—gave me a surprising pang. *Poor Richard,* I thought, followed by a line of Shakespeare's: *So quick bright things come to confusion.*

"Yo, *Doc.*" I turned to find McCready staring at me.

"Sorry. Were you saying something to me?"

"Only three times. You wanna stay up top till things cool off some more? Or would you like to get a closer look? Probably too soon to start the actual recovery, but you could start getting the lay of the land down there—figure out a plan of attack—if you want to."

I hated the notion of a whole posse of agents tromping around the wreckage unsupervised—specifically, unsupervised by *me*. I imagined fragile, burned bones crushed into cinders by careless footsteps. No matter that the FBI's crime-scene techs were the best in the nation. The Bureau had brought me out here for a reason, and I meant to give them their money's worth. "Beam me down, Scotty," I said.

"You got it." He nodded toward the rope-throwing agents, who were now laying out climbing harnesses near the rim. "You ever done any rappelling?"

"A little. It's been a while, but I reckon it'll come back to me once I'm harnessed up." In fact, it came flooding back to me only a heartbeat later: a death scene I'd roped down to, in a rugged part of the Cumberland Mountains. "Here's the thing," I hedged. "Can somebody else go first?" He looked puzzled. "Ten or twelve years ago, I recovered a woman's body up near the Kentucky border. She'd been dismembered and thrown off a bridge into a ravine."

He nodded. "I think I remember reading about that case. Serial killer? What was his name?"

"Satterfield. Sick, sadistic sonofabitch. Anyhow, I roped down a bluff to this woman's body, and I landed right by a rattlesnake—a coiled-up, pissed-off timber rattler. It struck at me; missed my leg by about that much." I held up a thumb and forefinger, practically touching. I took another glance down at the rocky terrain. "I'm thinking this terrain looks kinda snaky, and I've had enough fun with snakes to last me a lifetime."

He nodded, tucking back part of a smile. "I'll send Kimball and Boatman down first, with the Total Station," he said. "They'll stomp around and scare off the varmints."

He turned toward the two agents, who were uncoiling a pair of ropes and tying them to their gear—a hard-shell tripod case, about the size of a golf bag, plus a suitcase-sized aluminum box containing the electronics. "Yo, Kimball," McCready yelled. The ever-eager agent looked up. "Got a job for you."

"Instead of the Total Station?"

"In addition. You're on snake-bait duty."

"Snakebite duty?" The young agent cocked his head. "You want me to take the antivenom kit with us?"

"Not snake *bite*. Snake *bait*. You're the designated snake bait."

"Boss. Seriously? Did you really just call me snake bait?"

"I did. Doc here is snake-phobic. Your job is to run interference. If he gets bit, you get transferred. To Fargo."

Kimball pondered this for a fraction of a second. "Hey, Doc," he said. "Do me a favor, will you?"

"If I can."

"If you get bit, chuck that snake over at me, so it'll bite me, too. I'm *Fargo*-phobic." He turned to his partner. "Hey, Boat-Man, toss me that figure eight, would you?" A piece of polished metal arced through the air toward Kimball; he caught it deftly, looped the rope through it, and then clipped it to his climbing harness. Then, easing the tripod case over the rim, he lowered it down the bluff, feeding the rope smoothly through the figure eight until the line went slack. Boatman did the same with the aluminum case.

Once the hardware was down, the two men clipped themselves to the rappelling ropes, backed off the precipice in sync, and dropped from sight. "Look out, all you rattlers and cottonmouths and king cobras," I heard Kimball call out as he descended. "I'm coming down, and I am one snake-stompin' son-of-a-mongoose badass!"

"Yeah, right," I heard Boatman taunting as he slithered down the other rope. "You proved your badassedness in Baton Rouge, didn't you? How many times did you hurl at that scene? Four? Or was it five?"

"I *told* you, man, that was food poisoning from the night before. Toxic gumbo. Tainted crawdads. A lesser man—you, for instance—woulda keeled over and died."

"Yeah," mocked Boatman. "You just keep on telling yourself that, Mr. Badass."

I was the last to rappel down. If any snakes remained nearby, they were doing a good job of hiding. As I unclipped, though, I changed my assessment: If any snakes were in the immediate vicinity, they were thoroughly cooked. The earth was scorched, and heat continued to radiate from the rocks.

Unclipping from the rope, I stepped back and studied the rock face I had just descended. Some thirty feet high by fifty feet wide, it was unremarkable, at least geologically: merely the upper terminus of a long valley; a vertical transition up to the mountain's ridgeline. In human terms, though, it was momentous: the rocky hand of death, smashing Richard Janus's hurtling aircraft as effortlessly and heedlessly as I might reflexively crush a gnat in midair.

Head high above the base of the bluff was a shallow crater, rough and raw, six or eight feet in diameter, with additional fracture lines radiating beyond the edges of the depression. Mangled debris was piled almost as high as the crater's center, and it sprawled outward to either side in approximately equal measures.

"Must've impacted right there," I said to Kimball and Boatman.

"Sure looks like it," Kimball agreed. He shook his head. "Man. A hundred feet higher, he'd've cleared it. A flick of the wrist—that's all it would've taken." He scanned the debris scattered behind and to the sides, then turned to Boatman. "So, Boat-Man. I'm thinking we ought to set the station off to one side, so we're not standing right on ground zero." He pointed to a narrow shelf of rock at one edge of the draw, just outside the zone of destruction. "How about that flat spot?"

Boatman studied the shelf. "Works for me," he said. "Gives us a clear view of the whole debris field, far as I can tell. Also a line of sight to those trees"—he pointed at a swath of broken branches a short ways down the valley. "Looks like the wings clipped 'em on the way in." He hoisted one of the gear cases and started across the slope to the shelf. I snagged the tripod case and began following him.

"Hang on, Doc," Kimball called after me.

"Might as well make myself useful," I said, trudging on. "I hate just standing around. Besides, I want to look over your partner's shoulder while he sets that thing up."

Kimball caught up just as I reached the rock shelf. He took the tripod case from me and set it down carefully. Unlatching it, he lifted out the tripod, extended and unfolded the legs, and set it on the flattest spot, then made a few adjustments to level it. Then, reaching into the case again, he removed a telescoping rod marked with twelve-inch bands of red and white, one end topped by a jewel-like prism. "You made off with my piece of the gear, Doc," he squawked good-naturedly, waving the rod like a scepter.

"Oh. Sorry. No wonder you were trying to stop me. I thought you were just afraid I would break something."

"That too." He grinned, then turned and headed across the draw, toward the broken branches that marked the beginning of the end of the Citation's flight.

Boatman, meanwhile, had opened the aluminum case that contained the system's brains: a boxy yellow instrument that looked like a cross between a fish finder, a surveyor's transit, and an overgrown camera. Bolting it to the head of the tripod, he powered it up, leveled it, and began scrolling through menus on a small digital screen. I edged closer and leaned in. "Mind if I look over your shoulder? I saw y'all using this at the Body Farm, but I didn't have a chance to pay much attention."

"Be my guest." Boatman leaned back a bit so I could see the screen. "A Total Station's like a cross between a GPS receiver and a surveyor's rig, with a laser pointer and a microcomputer thrown in. The way it works is, first you mark your reference point—this point right here, where we've set it up." He pressed a button. "Okay, so we have our reference point; ground zero. Guess I shouldn't call it that anymore—not since 9/11. Anyhow. Now we can measure the position of any other point or object out here—those broken branches; that wheel over there; whatever—in relation to the reference point. All we need to know is the distance, the heading, and the angle up or down. Kimball holds the prism beside whatever we want to map, I bounce the laser off the prism, and I hit this button to capture the data. Easy as pie."

"Don't you have to label it somehow?"

"Ah. Good question. Yeah. I've got a bunch of captions preloaded—we worked a plane crash about six months ago—so mostly I'll just scroll down the list and click on whatever caption I need. But I can add new ones, if I need to, using this." He tapped a small keyboard. "Then Kimbo moves the reflector to the next point, I hit the button again, and so on. All those coordinates get stored in memory, and when we dump everything onto the computer up there in the command center, we can spit out maps in 3-D, from any angle we want to."

"Cool," I said. "And that's accurate to within, what—a few feet? a few inches?"

"More like a millimeter—less than a *tenth* of an inch."

"Amazing."

From across the way, Kimball called to Boatman. "Yo, pard, you 'bout ready to rock and roll?"

"Ready. Gimme that broken branch right over your head, would you? The one with the big rattlesnake on it?"

"Ha ha," Kimball said drily, but all the same, I saw him sneak a glance at the branch before raising the prism.

Boatman punched the "save" button, then scrolled down and clicked on a caption. *Tree strike*, I read over his shoulder. "Got it," he called. "You want to work that whole side first? Come back up to the base of the bluff, then go across and down the far side?"

"Work the edges first, then go in? Makes sense," said Kimball. "Gonna be some backing and forthing, though, any way we do it."

"Not for me," chuckled Boatman.

"Your job does seem a bit cushier," I remarked. "All you have to do is swivel that thing around and push some buttons."

At the moment, I would have killed for a button-pushing job—for *any* job that would have helped me feel productive. As it was, I felt like a fifth wheel; the young agents treated me with politeness, respect, and possibly a bit of misplaced awe, but clearly this was the FBI's show, and I was an outsider, waiting for my cue. And I hated waiting.

"Hey, Boat-Man," came Kimball's voice from across the way, as if to confirm my glum thoughts. "Less talk, more action. There's a wingtip here."

"Got it," called Boatman, and with that, the pair settled into a smooth routine, Kimball scampering around the edges of the debris field, pausing just long enough to hold the prism and call out a description of the object he was marking. He didn't mark everything—that would've taken forever; instead, he sought out large, recognizable components ("engine cowling"; "turbine blades"; "wheel and strut") and concentrations of debris ("structural members"; "aluminum skin"; "hydraulic lines").

After an hour—an hour in which the temperature climbed from eighty degrees to an unseasonably hot ninetysomething—they'd mapped the crash scene's entire perimeter. Kimball rejoined Boatman and me on the ledge long enough to chug a bottle of water and scarf down a nut bar. "Okay," he said, looking at the central pile of wreckage. "You ready?"

Boatman nodded. "I'm always ready."

"Wasn't asking you, Mr. Button-Pusher," scoffed Kimball. "I was asking Doc, the one who's got some real work ahead." He looked at me. "You ready to get dirty?"

"That's what I'm here for," I said.

"Okay, I'll talk to the man upstairs." He tapped a shoulder-mounted radio mike. "Hey, Mac, it's Kimbo. We've got the first layer mapped. Doc says he's ready to dig in. You want to send down the other guys, so we can start moving some metal?" He listened, nodded, and gave me a thumbs-up. I took a deep breath and blew it out, relieved that the standing and waiting was over, glad to be getting into the game.

Kimball and I started back toward the blasted base of the bluff. As we neared it, a shadow flowed across the ground toward us, then enveloped us, eclipsing the sun. I looked up to see a large rectangular silhouette, rotating slowly beneath the outstretched boom of the crane. As I watched, the rectangle grew larger, and larger still, descending toward us: a wooden platform, suspended from the steel cable. It was framed of stout lumber; it was decked with heavy-duty plywood; and it was laden with six FBI evidence-recovery specialists. As it came down, I stepped to one side to avoid being crushed.

Our system for retrieving and removing wreckage was simple—primitive, even—but it made sense, given the challenging terrain. Four of the evidence techs were assigned to work directly with me, combing the central debris field for human remains and other potential evidence. Kimball and Boatman would float: using the Total Station to map significant or unusual finds, but also photographing and logging our progress. The other two would fan out across the crash site to scan for evidence of explosive devices, retrieve scattered wreckage, and load it onto the platform. The platform had a foot-high plywood rim all the way around it, to keep pieces of debris from falling off. In addition, at its center was a sort of corral or fence, sized to hold a five-gallon plastic bucket securely in place. The bucket would be the repository for whatever pieces of bone and soft tissue we could find and bag, as well as any small objects the agents considered forensically significant. As soon as either the rack or the bucket was filled, the crane would haul up the load. Topside, Maddox and two other FBI evidence techs would transfer the aircraft wreckage to a pair of shipping containers that had arrived shortly after the crane: one container for large chunks, the other—in which shelves had been hastily installed—for the countless small pieces. Whatever human material we found, on the other hand, would be taken from the bucket and stored in coolers in the command center, for transport to the San Diego County medical examiner at the end of each day. The FBI might trump the locals when it came to crime-scene investigation, but it was the M.E., not the Bureau, who had the authority to issue death certificates.

Apart from the crane and the high-tech nature of the artifacts we were collecting, our system reminded me of my early summers in field archaeology: field digs where local workers had hauled dirt in buckets, and graduate students had placed potsherds in baskets. Like most physical anthropologists, I had paid my grad-school dues in the trenches of archaeology, excavating sites that were hundreds or thousands of years old, unearthing the past year by year, century by century, burrowing deeper and deeper into the basement of time. In every dig, the topmost layer is "now"; the deeper you dig, the farther back in time you travel, inch by inch, foot by foot—and sometimes skull by skull.

Excavating the Janus crash would likewise mean traveling back, but through a far, far thinner slice of time. The surface layer of debris—"now"—was the tail, the final part of the plane to hit, and the deeper we dug, the earlier in the crash event we'd be. But the interval we would cover, from end to beginning—from the uppermost scrap of tail debris down to the lowermost layer of nose cone—would span only a single second. *Not even,* I realized. *A fraction of a second.* I did some rough, quick calculations in my head. Four hundred miles an hour was . . . upwards of five hundred feet a second, if my math was right. Maddox had told us the Citation was about fifty feet long. That meant the entire plane, nose to tail, had crumpled in less than one-tenth of a second. I blinked. *The blink of an eye,* I realized. *That's how quick it can all come crashing down.*

All these things ran through my mind as I approached the main debris field. Its center appeared to be a spot near the base of the cliff—a wide, shallow crater now—where the nose of the jet must have first hit, followed—a hundredth or a thousandth of a second later—by the nose of the pilot himself.

Shards of twisted metal and tangled wires radiated outward from the ground beneath the crater. Mixed and mingled throughout, I assumed, were cinders of flesh and bits of burnt bone. The only way to find them would be bit by bit, piece by piece—removing the metal, shaking and perhaps even scraping the scraps, scouring everything for bone shards and teeth.

McCready had assigned two of the ERT techs to work the perimeter of the debris field, gathering scattered wreckage to load onto the rack and hoist up at intervals. Four more—plus Boatman and Kimball, when they weren't mapping things with the Total Station—would help me dissect the heart of the debris, in search of human remains. Before we began, I reiterated what I'd said earlier, up top, in my minilecture on osteology. "We won't find much that's recognizable," I reminded them. "Look for bone shards and tissue, but teeth are the big prize. The soft tissue—even the bones—might be too burned for DNA testing. But teeth are tough. Our best shot at a DNA profile is inside the teeth—the molars, especially. But even if we can't get DNA out of the teeth, we can still make an identification, if we can find fillings or bridgework or something that matches our guy's dental records." They nodded and fanned out, and in near-perfect synchrony—as if we'd all been transported to a church service in the smoldering shell of a ruined cathedral—we dropped to our knees.

Four hours later, we were still on our knees, but my prayers of finding Richard Janus had gone unanswered. Over the course of the afternoon, our plywood platform had been filled, hoisted, emptied, and lowered time and again. The two wider-ranging agents had also sent up load after load of bigger pieces on their rack—turbine blades; wheels; sections of wing and tail—and my four assistants and I had contributed plenty of smaller pieces as we'd picked our way into the central pile of debris. But the five-gallon bucket designated for human material remained empty—stubbornly, frustratingly, accusingly empty—and I'd begun to feel less like an anthropologist than like a miner, or a trash picker in a scrapyard. Kathleen and I had recently watched a documentary about poverty-stricken Brazilians who lived beside an immense landfill in Rio de Janeiro, and the people—men, women, even children—spent ten hours a day, every day, picking through load after load of garbage dumped at the landfill—some seeking plastic bottles, others seeking circuit boards, still others in search of scraps of wire: lifetimes of drudgery, dredging through the detritus of modern materialism. Not long before—less than twenty-four hours before, in fact—these bits of smoldering scrap had been a multimillion-dollar jet aircraft. But in one catastrophic instant the Citation had been reduced to trash, and we had been reduced to trash pickers.

Hour by tedious hour, the shadows grew long, and the mountainside began to cool. When the freshly emptied rack descended once more, demanding to be filled again—for the fifteenth time, or the fiftieth?—McCready leaned over the rim and called down to us. "Hey, guys. Six o'clock. Quittin' time. Come on up." He didn't have to tell us twice. Hours before, I had rappelled down, but now that we had an elevator, I would ride up. The ERT techs and I clambered aboard the swaying platform. They sat around the perimeter, legs dangling into space; I stood at the center, straddling the still-empty bucket, and braced myself by holding the cables bolted to the platform's four corners.

Overhead, the crane rumbled and whined, and with a slight lurch we began rising up the rock face. After we cleared the rim, the crane's boom pivoted and began easing us down toward the concrete pad—my third landing of the day, I realized, this one a bit more primitive than the prior ones in the Gulfstream and the helicopter. As we hovered briefly, McCready threw us a mock salute, then called out, "You guys look like that painting of George Washington crossing the Delaware." Glancing around, I saw the visual resemblance—the aging general, my stance wide, surrounded by a boat-load of loyal troops. But Washington's boat had been carrying the Stars and Stripes, while all we had was a plastic bucket. As the platform settled, the cables I was holding went slack, and I staggered forward; only the quick reflexes of the closest agents kept me from falling. "More like Brockton going overboard," I said, but the joke came out sounding bitter, and it fell as flat as I had nearly done. As I disentangled myself from agents and cables, I said what was really on my mind. "So what if there was nobody in the plane?" Everyone turned, eyeing me intently. "We haven't found any remains so far. Is it possible he jumped? Maybe he was having engine trouble and bailed out?"

Maddox spoke before McCready or Prescott had a chance. "*Jump?*" he said. "From a *Citation?* At four hundred miles an hour?" He gave an amused, dismissive grunt. "First off, you can't do it," he said. "The cabin door pivots forward to open; can't be done in flight—too much air pressure. Second, even if you *could* do it, which you *can't,* it'd be guaranteed suicide to bail out—you'd hit the left engine about a millisecond after you did. Easier to stay on the ground and just blow your brains out. Third, he *didn't* do it—that cabin door was sealed tight as a drum."

"You sure about that?" asked McCready. Prescott was listening closely.

"Here, I'll show you." Maddox crooked a finger, beckoning, and led us across the cracked concrete pad to one of the shipping containers, which by now was half filled with mangled metal. Tugging at a wadded-up chunk that was leaning against one wall, he laid it flat and dragged it toward the container's opening, where the light was better. "This came up a couple hours ago," he said. "It's the cabin door. Some of it, anyhow." He pointed to a crumpled lever. "This is the latch. Banged up and burned, but you can still tell that it was in the 'closed' position. Also"—he pointed to one

edge of the door, which was fringed with torn metal—
"here's a piece of the door frame, which got ripped apart
by the impact. See these bolts?" He tapped two metal
rods, which—despite their thickness—were bent, their
ends crowned with jagged aluminum. "When the door
latches, a dozen of those bolts—spaced around the rim
of the door—slide out and lock into the frame."

"Like the door of a bank vault?"

He nodded. "Or a watertight door on a ship. The
whole hull is pressurized, so the latches and seals
have to be really robust." I could feel myself starting
to recalibrate—to get interested in the puzzle pieces
again—when he added, "Look, he's gotta be in there.
You'll find him. You just gotta keep digging."

He was right—in my heart of hearts, I knew he
was right—but I was tired, and my back hurt, and his
confidence and encouragement seemed slightly con-
descending, so my frustration returned, this time as
annoyance. Prescott didn't help my mood any when
he said, "Maybe you're looking too close, you know
what I mean?"

I turned and stared at him. "No," I said. "I have
no idea what you mean."

If he sensed my anger, he didn't let on. "You know
how, if you look at a photograph through a microscope,
you might not be able to recognize the picture?"

I stared at him. "So you think maybe we've all been stumbling over a body down there, but nobody's noticed it, because we're too close to see the shape of the arms and legs and head?"

"No, I don't mean *that*," he hedged. "I'm just wondering if you might get a better feel for the bigger picture—for how things are . . . *arranged*—if you take a step back, get into a groove, and get some momentum going."

"Three years ago—after 9/11—I spent ten days sifting through rubble from the World Trade Center," I told him. "In those ten days, I saw four intact long bones. *Four.*" I held up my right hand, fingers splayed, for digital emphasis. "I didn't see a single complete skull. Mostly what I saw were shreds and splinters. Even the teeth were in bits and pieces. I could be wrong—Pat, please correct me if I am—but I'm guessing this crash is like a scaled-down version of that rubble. Yes? No?"

Maddox hesitated, looking reluctant to choose sides. "Well, I hadn't thought about it in those terms. But a straight-on impact at that velocity?" He considered it only for a moment. "The pilot probably fragments from the initial impact. Then the rest of the plane slams into him like a pile driver. Then comes the fire." He shrugged at Prescott in what seemed a sort of apology. "This reminds me of some military crashes I've seen. Fighter jets. Sometimes all they leave is a smokin' hole." He gave us all a conciliatory smile. "But hey, tomorrow's another day, right? A juicy steak and a good night's sleep, and we'll be raring to go again."

I couldn't help wondering: *Which "we"? The "we" in the air-conditioned command center, or the "we" doubled over like field hands?* Still, I appreciated his sticking up for me, and I suspected I'd enjoy trading stories with him over dinner. "You eating with us, Pat?"

He shook his head. "Nah, I hear you guys are staying in Otay Mesa. Close to Brown Field. I'm booked somewhere in San Diego. Pain in the ass to get there, but hey, a good soldier goes where he's sent." He flashed us a peace sign and turned to go, leaving me with the FBI agents.

Chapter 9

Jouncing down from the crash site, back toward town, I was so grateful to be riding shotgun that I mostly forgave Prescott for criticizing our work pace. He was at the wheel of the vehicle, with McCready, Kimball, and Boatman in the back—a place where I'd have gotten carsick within minutes. Our Suburban, followed closely by the other one, was bucking and lurching down Otay Mountain Truck Trail—a rough-hewn route whose chief virtue, as best I could tell, was the honesty of the label TRUCK TRAIL. Between bumps, I marveled anew at the fleet of assorted vehicles that had managed to make the climb—especially the crane and the mobile command center—and I made a mental note to express my admiration to their drivers. As if to make sure I didn't forget, the Suburban tilted suddenly to the right, then abruptly to the left, whapping my head against the window. I thought longingly of the swift, smooth hop the helicopter had made from the airfield to the summit: two minutes; three, tops. *Yesterday's travel was a lot cushier than today's,* I thought. Suddenly, astonished, I realized: *No—that was today, too. I was eating breakfast in my kitchen in Knoxville this morning.*

As we descended, the kinked switchbacks relaxed, opening up into looser, looping curves, and the primitive truck trail evolved into an actual gravel road. By the time we came off the mountain's flank and into the valley floor, we had picked up enough speed to churn up a dense, dun-colored plume, and I was glad to be in the lead vehicle rather than any of the trailing ones, which had vanished inside the dust storm we were creating.

Shortly after turning onto a wide paved road, we passed a side road marked by a large sign. The sign, made of wooden boards framed by rough-hewn rock, read DONOVAN STATE PRISON. I was just about to ask Prescott about it when his cell phone rang. He frowned at the display but took the call. "No," he said tersely, "not right now." Then: "All right. . . . I *said* all *right.* . . . *Fine.* See you then." He closed the phone with an angry snap.

"Trouble?"

He made a face of minor distaste, or perhaps disdain. "Just a friendly little jurisdictional discussion. Otherwise known as a pissing contest."

"With the sheriff's office?"

He shook his head. "I wish. It's easy to outpiss the locals. Nah, this is with some of our federal brethren." He glanced at me, saw the question on my face. "Nothing serious," he said. "Case like this gets lots of media attention, so everybody wants to share the glory. 'Course, if things go south—if something goes wrong—those same glory hounds'll run for cover. Pausing only long enough to throw us under the bus." He looked into the rearview mirror and gave his backseat colleagues a slight, ironic smile. "Not that *we* would ever do that, if the tables got turned. Right, fellas?" Kimball and Boatman and McCready, jammed in the backseat, swiftly agreed that no, they would never run for cover or throw anyone under the bus.

"Bus? What bus? I see no bus," said Kimball, his tone all mock innocence. "Pay no attention to that large, fast-moving vehicle!" The agents laughed the laugh of the righteous and confident, and I assured myself that I didn't need to worry, as long as I looked both ways before crossing streets.

"**Home sweet home,**" Prescott announced, pointing through the windshield. Looking down in the direction of his point—we were on an overpass, crossing a six-lane freeway—I spotted a Quality Inn. Drab, aging, and ironically named, it huddled in the corner formed by the freeway and the overpass. Only the four out-of-towners were staying here; Prescott and the local evidence techs had the luxury of sleeping in their own beds, and Maddox, the NTSB investigator, was staying somewhere downtown. He'd made it sound like he was disappointed not to be staying with us, but now that I saw our lodgings, I suspected he wasn't all that torn up about it. *Too bad,* I thought again, wishing I'd had the chance to swap stories with him. I'd always been fascinated by planes, and flight; I'd even taken a few flying lessons years before, but I'd failed the medical exam because of my Ménière's disease, an inner-ear disorder that occasionally laid me low, sometimes for days on end, with bed-spinning vertigo and racking nausea.

"Doc?" Prescott had stopped the Suburban at the motel's entrance. He was looking at me, waiting.

"Sorry; what'd you say?"

"You ready to eat? These guys are starving. There's a Carl's Jr. on the other side of the expressway, and we're jonesing for burgers."

I was hungry, too, I realized. "Sure." Then, as an afterthought, I checked my watch. It was nearly seven, though the sun was still well above the horizon, thanks to the combined wonders of daylight saving time and the approach of the summer solstice. "On second thought, you guys go ahead. It's close to bedtime in Knoxville, and I'd like to talk to my wife before she goes to sleep."

"We can wait, if you're just touching base."

"She's pretty chatty," I said, though the truth was, I tended to be the long-winded one.

He nodded. "You want us to bring you something on the way back? Burger? Chicken sandwich? They make a mighty mean onion ring."

"A good chocolate shake, too," added Boatman.

"Sounds good," I said, "but none of that stuff travels well. Thanks anyhow." I waved a hand in cheery dismissal. "Y'all don't worry about me. I'll get checked in, call Kathleen, and scrub off some of this grime. Plenty of time to grab a bite after that."

Prescott inclined his head toward one side of the building. "There's a pool, if you want to take a dip."

"Didn't bring a suit," I said. "Didn't realize we'd be staying at a luxury resort."

He laughed. "Yeah. First class all the way." The freeway's exit ramp bordered one side of the pool, and the overpass loomed above the far end. I imagined a steady rain of dust, exhaust particulates, and rusted car parts raining down onto the pool court like volcanic ash onto Pompeii.

Opening the door, I stepped onto the parking lot's blasted asphalt. "Pop the back? So I can grab my bag?" He did, and I extricated my yellow L.L.Bean duffel and closed the hatch. McCready took my place riding shotgun. As I passed Prescott's window, it slid down a few inches. "See you in the morning. Wheels up at seven? Or is that too early for an ivory-tower guy like you?" It could have been a dig, but it didn't sound like it.

"Seven? *Early?* That's ten, Knoxville time. That's sleeping in, man."

"Hey, feel free to head on up at four. I've got a flashlight and a map I can loan you."

"Nah," I said. "You guys would be sad if you showed up and I'd already finished working the scene without you."

"Sad," he agreed. "Heartbroken, even." The tinted window slid up, hiding him from view. The black Suburban did a U-turn, and the four invisible FBI agents glided away.

Recounting my day to Kathleen helped me process it; it also helped me feel grounded, connected with her—we'd been together so long, I tended to feel unsettled and unmoored when I was away. If not for the three-hour time difference, I'd have talked her to sleep as I settled into bed myself. Instead, I'd roamed the neighborhood around the motel as we talked.

Neighborhood wasn't actually the right term for it; *industrial park* was more like it. Otay Mesa, or at least this part of it, consisted of grim blocks of warehouses, alternating with unpaved parking lots—some of them empty, others filled with semitrailers, and virtually all of them surrounded by chain-link fences topped with razor wire. Otay Mesa was a stone's throw from a border crossing, and the town appeared to revolve around it the way water revolves around the drain in a toilet bowl. Years before, attending a conference in San Diego, I'd taken a brief side trip to Tijuana; the border crossing there, a few miles to the west, had reminded me of a drive-through version of an airport terminal: a bustling crossroads traversed by throngs of tourists and business travelers. The crossing here at Otay Mesa, on the other hand, put me in mind of a freight depot or railroad switchyard: a gritty frontier outpost where produce and car parts and probably contraband came pouring in, twenty-four hours a day, seven days a week.

The nearness of Mexico was underscored every-where I looked: Brown faces, which outnumbered white faces by two or three to one. Beer trucks hauling Tecate and Negro Modelo, rather than Budweiser and Coors. Import-export brokers and warehouses with names like COMERCIALIZADORA IMPORTADORA and MARQUEZ VEJAR and INTEGRACION ADUANAL. Dual-language placards on signposts and walls and fences: STOP and also PARE; DANGER as well as PELIGRO; BEWARE OF DOG plus ¡CUIDADO CON EL PERRO!, a warning illustrated by a snarling German shepherd—a visual that made the sign trilingual, in a hieroglyphic sort of way.

From the top of the overpass that spanned the Otay Mesa Freeway, I spied the sign for the burger joint the four FBI agents had gone to—the oddly punctu-ated Carl's Jr.—as well as a closer, higher sign for McDonald's. To my left, the freeway's six lanes curved northwest toward San Diego; to my right, they ran due south for a quarter mile to the border checkpoint. As the trucks rumbled beneath me, I noticed that the southbound trucks—heading for the border—rattled and clattered, their cargo trailers empty. The north-bound trucks—fresh from Mexico—thudded and groaned beneath heavy loads.

I turned down the street toward the burger joint. I glanced inside, looking for the FBI agents, but I saw no sign of them—not surprising, given that they could have ordered and eaten and driven away a half hour or an hour before. I was reaching for the door, my stomach rumbling in earnest now, when something caught my eye and I spun in my tracks. Directly across the street was an IHOP—International House of Pancakes—and IHOP was hardwired to some of my fondest memories: Throughout my son's childhood and adolescence, he and I hit the IHOP almost every Saturday morning. Happily I headed across the deserted street and into the IHOP. By now it was nearly nine, the posted closing time, and the hostess station was vacant. Wandering into the dining room, I found a server, a sturdy young Latina. "Am I too late to eat?"

"You made it just in time," she said. "Have a seat"— she motioned me toward a high-backed booth along one wall, beside a hallway that led to the restrooms— "and I'll bring you a menu."

"Don't need one," I told her. "I know what I want." She nodded, pulling an order pad and a pen from her back pocket. "Waffle combo," I said. "The waffles with fruit and whipped cream—extra fruit and extra cream, please. Two eggs over medium. Bacon. Orange juice." I thought for a moment. "And an extra side of bacon, please." Kathleen wouldn't approve—in fact, Kathleen would be appalled—but Kathleen was fifteen hundred miles away. I knew some people who indulged in alcohol or even adultery while on road trips. Me, I indulged in bacon.

I slumped down in the booth, suddenly dog-tired; I must have nodded off, because in what seemed mere moments, I heard a thunk and opened my eyes to behold a huge helping of food. "Looks great," I said. "Smells great, too."

"Let me know if you need anything else." If we'd been in Tennessee, she'd have punctuated the sentence with a *darlin'* or a *hon,* but we weren't, so she didn't. She simply smiled and walked away.

The first bite of food—if the word "bite" can be applied to the microcosmic feast I hoisted mouthward, the fork flexing from its load—filled my mouth with layer upon layer of flavor and texture: the warm, still-crisp waffle; the sweet, juicy berries; the smooth, rich cream; the satisfying substance of the egg. My mouth was practically overflowing, but I couldn't resist cramming in half a piece of bacon for the sake of the smoky, salty crunch.

I was only beginning to comprehend the gap between how much I had bitten off and how little I could chew when I heard a familiar voice behind me: Special Agent Miles Prescott's voice. My inclination was to stand up and say hello, but my mouth was far too full to speak, so I sat, slumped and unseen in the high-backed booth.

Prescott's voice was low, but I quickly realized it had a steely edge to it; in fact, as I chewed and listened, I realized that he sounded furious, and I wondered if he was chewing out one of the other agents. Surely not Kimball or Boatman—they were too lowly to inspire such ire—but McCready might have angered him by allowing us to work too slowly. "You know the god-damn rules," he practically spat. "We had the intel first, so it was our operation."

"It was a penny-ante, pissant little operation," said another, unfamiliar voice—a voice so raspy and wheezy that the speaker was close to coughing out the words. "If you had let this thing play out just a little longer, we'd have taken it a lot higher up the food chain. Maybe—*maybe*—even gotten Goose Man. We were *this close.*"

"In your dreams."

"*This close,*" the second man wheezed again. "But no, the Bureau had to come charging in like the Seventh Fucking Cavalry—flags waving, bugles blowing—and scare everybody back into their hidey-holes. Do you realize you sabotaged a three-year investigation?"

"Do I look like I give a damn?" snapped Prescott. "It was our operation. Our call. Janus got a good agent killed two weeks ago—"

"You don't know that," interrupted the other man. "Your agent was in way over his head, playing three guys off against each other. I don't think Janus fingered him. I think your guy just fucked up."

"Janus got one of our agents killed," insisted Prescott. "And when one of ours gets killed, we don't just stand by and—how'd you put it? 'Let things play out'? We come down like the wrath of God. Maybe that's the reason we don't lose as many agents as you guys do."

My mouth was still full, but I had stopped chewing and started sweating. I didn't know who Prescott meant by *you guys,* or by *he,* and I had no earthly idea who "Goose Man" was. The one thing I understood with perfect clarity was that I'd stumbled into the pissing contest Prescott had mentioned earlier. And it sounded like a doozy.

Still slouching in the booth, I vacillated: On the one hand, I wanted them to leave immediately; on the other, I wanted them to keep arguing—*from the beginning, guys!*—so I could figure out what they were talking about. Across the room, I noticed the waitress clearing a table; she glanced in my direction, and I felt a jolt of panic. If she came over now—offering a refill of juice, or asking why I wasn't eating—she'd blow my cover. *Not now, not now,* I telegraphed her, carefully avoiding eye contact.

"You sanctimonious sonofabitch," the stranger was rasping. In my mind's eye, he was fat and sweaty, his words struggling to burrow out from within a mountain of flesh. "You wanna know why we lose more agents than the Bureau? I'll tell you why. It's because you guys are going after pussies—embezzlers and secret sellers and kiddie-porn perverts. *Pussies.* Meanwhile, we're out there waging *war.* With the worst motherfuckers on the planet."

"Are you?" Prescott's voice dripped with sarcasm. I couldn't tell if he was questioning the badness of the enemy, or the totality of the war effort.

"Damn right we are. And we're doing it with a fraction of the money and manpower you necktie-and-cufflink office boys get."

"You're breaking my heart," Prescott sneered. "Poor, pitiful you. Now if you're through whining, I've got work to do before we climb that mountain tomorrow and pick up the pieces of this operation." He walked away, his heels pummeling the tile.

"Prick," muttered the other man. I heard him turn and trail Prescott out of the IHOP. As his footsteps neared the front door, I risked raising up to take a look. I got a fleeting glimpse of a man who was short and fat, his hair a graying, greasy shade of red. From behind, at least, he looked as repulsive as he sounded.

I looked down at my plate. The now soggy waffle was surrounded by a moat of cold egg yolk, and the strips of bacon gleamed dully through a varnish of congealed grease. I pushed the plate away, my appetite killed by disgust. Or was it by fear? As I pulled out my wallet for the reckoning with IHOP, I couldn't help wondering what other reckonings awaited, and what the hell I'd gotten myself into.

I stepped out into the night—still warm, but not unpleasant. Eighty-five degrees in the sauna-dry foothills east of San Diego was a different animal from eighty-five degrees in the steam bath that was East Tennessee. It wasn't that I didn't sweat here, I'd noticed; it was that the sweat evaporated almost instantly, cooling the body a bit without drenching the clothes entirely.

"How was your dinner?" The voice came from the darkness behind me.

"*Crap,*" I exclaimed, jumping with surprise. Again I recognized the voice as Prescott's, and I turned toward it. He was leaning against the IHOP's wall, waiting for me. "You scared the bejesus out of me."

I expected him to say that he didn't mean to; instead, he repeated, "How was dinner?"

"Kinda meager," I said. "I ordered a lot, but I only ate one bite. It was a *big* bite—my mouth was too full to say anything when I heard you behind me—but I'm not sure it's gonna tide me over till breakfast." I looked at him more frankly now, embarrassed to have been caught, but relieved not to be keeping secrets. "You knew I was there the whole time?"

"Just about."

"How? I didn't think you guys could me see over the back of the booth."

"Couldn't," he said. "I noticed your reflection in the window. Hickock never did."

"Hickock's the pissed-off guy?"

"You might say that. Wild Bill. He was in the middle of his tirade when I spotted you. If I'd cut him off—if he'd known we had an audience—he'd've gone ballistic. At me and you both." He shook his head. "No point in that."

I nodded. "Well, thanks. Sorry I was sitting in the wrong place at the wrong time. Didn't mean to put you in an awkward spot."

"You didn't. From what I hear, you're one of the good guys. Besides, Hickock and I should both know better. Talking business in public? I oughta rip myself a new one for that."

I remembered old national-security posters I'd seen from the early 1940s. "Loose lips sink ships?"

"Sounds corny, but basically, yeah." He nodded across the parking lot, to the black Suburban under a streetlight, its back window thick with dust. "Come on, I'll give you a ride home."

"Thanks, but I'd kinda like to walk."

He frowned. "You carrying?"

"Carrying? You mean a gun?" He nodded, and I shook my head. "Heavens no. I've never owned one."

"Let me give you a ride, then. This ain't exactly the tourist district, Doc. You might get robbed; you might get *mistaken* for a robber. Either way, you wander around here after dark, you're liable to get shot. Or stabbed. Or worse. Not good for either of us."

"Since you put it that way," I said, "thanks."

In the privacy of the Suburban, I figured he'd tell me at least a bit about the raspy-voiced man, and about their argument, but he didn't. Instead, during the brief drive, he asked about my research at the Body Farm, then quizzed me about a couple of prior cases I'd helped the Bureau with. It was obvious that he was redirecting the conversation away from the confrontation I had stumbled into. It was also, perhaps, a reminder that he had done his research, had read the Bureau's file on me. It might even have been a subtle caution: If I wanted to keep working with the FBI, I should keep quiet about what I'd overheard tonight. As I thanked him for the lift and headed toward my room, I parsed the conversation—the things he'd said and the ones he hadn't. *Loose lips sink ships,* I reminded myself. *And maybe crash careers.*

Chapter 10

The trouble with graduate assistants, I'd noticed—well, *one* of the troubles—was their tendency to go gallivanting off every summer: for gainful employment, for adventurous travel, or for romance. My current assistant, Marty, was helping direct a student dig in Tuscany for three months, and judging by the letter and photos he'd sent in early June, he was getting both well paid and well laid. Not that I was envious.

What I *was*, though, was inconvenienced. I had a question that needed researching, but no time or tools to research it myself—and no helpful minion at my beck and call. So instead, despite the late hour, I called Kathleen.

It was only 8:45 in San Diego, but it was nearly midnight in Knoxville, and that meant Kathleen had

probably been asleep for at least an hour. To my surprise, she answered on the second ring. Her voice
sounded thick, but not sleepy.

"Hey," I said, "is something wrong? Are you
crying?"

"Oh, I am," she sniffled, "but it's just a movie I'm
watching." In the background, I heard voices and
music. "Hang on, honey, let me pause it." She laid the
phone down with a rustle, then the background noise
quieted. "You know I don't sleep worth a hoot when
you're gone," she said, "so I stopped at Blockbuster
on the way home."

"I'm jealous. What'd you get?"

"One of those chick flicks you wouldn't take me to."

"*Silence of the Lambs?*"

"Ha. Not quite. *Shakespeare in Love.*"

"I take it back," I said. "I'm not a bit jealous."

"Actually, you'd really like the scene where he's in
bed with Gwyneth Paltrow."

She knew me well. "Well then," I said, "when I get
home, we can rent it again and fast-forward to that
part."

"Hmmph." She sniffed again, and in the brief pause
that followed, I could practically hear the gears in her
mind shifting. "Why aren't *you* asleep?" Her voice was
laser sharp now, and despite the two thousand miles

between us, I could almost feel her eyes searching mine. "You called me to say good night two hours ago. What's happened?"

"I don't know." I told her about my accidental, disturbing eavesdropping at the IHOP. "I wish I understood what's going on," I said. "Not that I need to know everything, but . . ."

"But what?"

"But it feels like there's stuff here—players and politics and agendas—that I don't understand, stuff that could affect the investigation."

"Affect it how?"

Suddenly I thought, *Shit, what if my phone is tapped?* A moment later I scolded myself, *Don't be paranoid. Who the hell would want to tap your phone?* "I don't *know*, Kath. That's the frustrating thing— I don't know enough to know what else I *need* to know. What is it Donald Rumsfeld calls this kind of thing?"

"God, don't get me started on *Rumsfeld*," she said. She had a point there—she despised the man, and the mere mention of his name sometimes set her off on a Rumsfeld rant. "But I believe 'unknown unknowns' is the gobbledygook term you're thinking of."

"That's it," I said. "I'm worried that the unknown unknowns here could affect this case in ways I can't foresee or control. Distort it, undermine its objectivity or integrity. Here I am doing my thing, crawling around looking for teeth and bones. But I've got a bad feeling, like I'm wandering around in a minefield. One false step, and there goes a foot. Figuratively speaking. If I blow this case, Kathleen—the highest-profile case the Bureau has ever used me on? They'll write me off, and for good."

"Just do your best," she said. "How many times have you worked with the FBI before this?"

"Four. No, five."

"Any problems with them?"

"No. They're the best. Of course." I still felt fretful. "I wish Marty were around this summer. I'd get him to poke around a little."

"Poke around how? In what?"

"I don't *know*," I repeated in reflexive frustration. She kept quiet—her way of making me think instead of just spouting off—and after a moment I added, "I'd see if he could find out who's the FBI agent that got killed, and how, and why? Who's the fat, raspy guy that claims to be fighting supervillains? And who's this Goose Man character that the fat fellow's so hot to take down?"

"And you think Marty could dig up answers to those questions?"

"I don't . . ." I caught myself before repeating it, my mantra of mystification, once again. "I wouldn't be surprised."

"Marty's great with a trowel, Bill. And he knows his osteology forward and backward. But his skill set is—how to put this nicely?—very specific. What you need is a detective. Or an investigative journalist."

"A *journalist*? God, Kathleen, if I talked to a journalist about an open FBI case? It'd be my last case for them. Ever."

"Probably," she said. "Okay, how about a reference librarian?"

"What?"

"A reference librarian."

"Are you serious—a librarian?"

"Sure, I'm serious," she said. "Why not? They're smart, they're helpful, and they have dozens of databases at their fingertips. Remember when I was looking for stuff on child blindness and vitamin A deficiency? And nonprofits? I called the reference desk at Hodges"—the university's main library—"and maybe two hours later, a librarian handed me a stack of articles I never would have found on my own. That's how I first heard about Richard Janus and Airlift Relief."

"That's right," I said. "I'd forgotten that." I wasn't sure that confiding in a librarian was a brilliant idea, but it trumped anything else I had at the moment. "You think somebody's there now? It's nearly midnight."

"They're open another five minutes," she said. "Worth a try."

"I don't suppose you've got a UT directory there beside the remote and the Kleenex box?"

"Don't need one," she said, and I smiled as she recited the number from memory. Kathleen was smart and wise—sassy, too—and I loved her for those qualities. And more, many more.

The phone rang a dozen times—I counted the rings as I drummed my fingers. "Good *grief*," I groused as I pulled the phone away from my ear and reached for the "end" button. "Doesn't *anybody* work a full day anymore?"

As if in answer to my question, I suddenly heard a voice on the other end of the line. "Excuse me?" Then I heard a loud clatter, as if the phone had been dropped. A moment later a slightly breathless woman said, "Oops. Sorry about that. I had to vault the counter to get to the phone. Figured it must be important, as many times as it rang."

I was taken aback by the woman's breezy attitude. "Uh," I faltered, "is this the reference desk?"

"Technically, no," she said. "But I'm *standing* at the reference desk. Will that do?"

Was she mocking me? I didn't have the luxury of exploring that question. "This is Dr. Bill Brockton, head of the Anthropology Department."

"Yes?"

"I need some information. I'm afraid I can't give you much to go on. But it's important. And sensitive— it's related to a criminal investigation—so I need you to keep it confidential."

"Sounds intriguing," she said. "What do you need to know, Dr. Brockton? And what can you tell me to point me in the right direction?"

"What I need to know, Ms. . . . *What* did you say your name is?"

"I didn't," she said cheerily. "Just call me Red."

"Red? Is that a nickname?"

She laughed. "I would *hope* so!" Again I wondered if she was mocking me, though her tone sounded more amused than sarcastic.

"Look . . . Red," I said. "This seems a little . . . *strange*, not to know who I'm talking to. Would you rather hand me off to somebody else?"

"Unfortunately, at the moment, I'm all you've got," she said. "I don't mean any disrespect, Dr. Brockton; please forgive me if it sounded that way. I've been stalked a couple times—seriously stalked—so I'm skittish about giving my name to men on the phone at midnight, even if they sound legit. The guy I still have nightmares about? He sounded every bit as legit as you, at first."

"But—" I began, then stopped myself. *But what? You think if you argue, she'll feel more at ease? Not bloody likely.* "Fair enough, Red," I conceded. "Is that your hair color, or your politics?"

"Both," she said. "Also the color of my checkbook balance. Maybe short for 'Ready Reference,' too. How can I help you, Dr. Brockton? The lights in the library go out in about three minutes, so tell me quick, if you can."

I started with the thing that seemed strangest. "I need you to dig up whatever you can about someone called 'Goose Man.'" The line was silent, and I wondered if the call had been dropped—or if she'd decided I was a crank and hung up. "Hello? Red? Are you there?"

"I'm here," she said. "I was waiting for you to tell me more."

"There is no 'more.' That's it."

"That's all you've got—'Goose Man'? You're kidding, right?"

"No," I snapped, feeling defensive. "I'm *not* kidding. I *told* you I couldn't give you much to go on."

She laughed again. "So you did. I see you're a man of your word. But . . . can I ask a couple things, superquick? Just to make sure we're on the same page here—the same virtually blank page? What put 'Goose Man' on your radar? How'd you hear about him? In what context?"

"I heard a cop—at least, I *think* he was a cop—mention him to another cop."

"Was the second one also a maybe cop? Or was cop number two a for-sure cop?"

"A for-sure cop."

"Knoxville cop?"

"No. Federal cop. Both feds, I think. One's FBI. The other, I don't know—maybe Homeland Security, maybe DEA, maybe Border Patrol. Hell, maybe even CIA."

"Wowzer," she said. "You don't play in the minors, do you? Should you even be telling me this?"

"No," I said. "Almost certainly not. But something's going on that I don't understand, and it's making me nervous. I'd like to know who the other players are, and what teams they're playing for."

In the background, I heard a robotic-sounding announcement: *The library is now closed. Please exit now.* "Crap," she muttered. "Oh well—in for a penny, in for a pound. Quick, what makes you think Fed Number Two might be CIA?"

"He said they were waging war with the worst badasses on the planet. Pardon the language."

"Pardon it? I appreciate it. I hate it when people beat around the bush, all tactful and mealy-mouthed. Say what you mean, mean what you say—that's my motto. One of 'em, anyhow. So . . . presumably the Goose Man is one of these badasses?"

"Presumably," I said. "The FBI guy was getting reamed out. Apparently he scared the Goose Man away, just as Fed Number Two was about to reel him in."

"*In*-ter-esting," she said. "So the Goose Man is a pretty big fish. And he's swimming around right here in the little ol' pond of Knoxville?"

"Ah. No," I said. "Sorry. In San Diego. I mean, I don't know if San Diego's where the Goose Man is swimming, but it's where *I'm* swimming at the moment. Or treading water. And it's where these guys were arguing."

"I really have to go," she said. "How do I reach you?" I gave her my number. "Got it. Let me give you mine."

"I've already got it," I pointed out. "I just dialed it."

"I'm away from the desk most of the time," she said. "Better to call me on my cell." She rattled off the digits like machine-gun fire; I wrote hurriedly, hoping I was getting it right.

"Let me read that back to you."

"I gotta go—I'm about to get locked in."

"Last question," I said. "What are your hours—do you work weeknights?"

"Call whenever," she said. "I really, *really* gotta go."

The line went dead, and I was left staring at the scrawled phone number of a woman who didn't even trust me with her name.

Chapter 11

I slept fitfully, my dreams a patchwork of conversations, confrontations, and altercations. Some of the dreams featured a fat man with red hair, one whose shadowy, sinister face I could never quite discern. Others featured a redheaded woman, her features also veiled and vague.

I stayed in the shower a long time—hot water, then cold, then hot again—to clear the cobwebs from my brain. When I turned off the taps, I heard the warbling of my cell phone. Still dripping, I raced to answer. "Kathleen?"

"Uh, no. Sorry. Is this Dr. Brockton?"

I recognized the voice of the reference librarian. "Oh, sorry. Yes, this is Dr. Brockton." I hesitated, feeling foolish, then plunged ahead. "Red, is that you?"

"Yes. Am I calling too early?"

"No, it's fine. I was in the shower. Have you tracked down the Goose Man already?" I was speaking low and fast. "That was quick. What can you tell me about him?"

"Well, for one thing, I can tell you that there is no such guy as 'the Goose Man.'"

"It's a nickname," I said. "Like 'the Godfather' or something." I thought I heard a snort of laughter at the other end.

"Yeah, 'Goose Man'—*there's* a name calculated to strike fear into the hearts of global badasses," she said, sounding far more amused than I thought she should. "I can hear it now: 'Call off your goons, or the Goose Man is gonna come *peck* you to death.'" Now there was no question about it—she was definitely laughing.

"*Hey.*" I felt my cheeks flushing and my temper ratcheting up.

"Sorry, sorry," she said, through the remnants of a laugh. "Couldn't resist. But I swear, I've got the scoop. The guy's not 'the Goose Man'; the guy's *name* is Guzmán. Spelled G-U-Z-M-A-with-an-accent-N. Pronounced 'gooz-MAHN'—accent on the second syllable. Leastwise, that's how they say it south of the border, down Mehico way."

"He's Mexican?"

"*Sí, señor.* Joaquin Guzmán Loera. Widely known as 'Chapo,' which translates as 'Shorty'—a reference to his shape, which resembles a stout fireplug."

"But who is he?"

"A badass. One of the very baddest badasses on the planet," she said, sounding pleased with her discovery, or with the opportunity to apply the colorful label, or with both. "Also one of the very *richest* badasses on the planet."

"Do tell."

"Chapo runs the Sinaloa drug cartel, the biggest drug-smuggling operation in the world. Based in Mexico's Sinaloa Province, a rural mountainous region that's apparently perfect for growing marijuana. Also ideal for hiding big cocaine-processing labs. Giant meth labs, too."

"Giant *meth* labs? I thought people cooked that stuff in, like, pressure cookers. In trailers in the back-woods of Tennessee."

"They did," she said. "Still do, I guess. But these guys—this cartel—is all about supply and demand. Any drug there's big demand for, they supply. Marijuana, cocaine, heroin, meth: If rich gringos want it, these guys have got it. Take a guess at Shorty's net worth."

"I have no idea." From the way she put the question, I could tell it must be a lot. "Fifty million bucks?"

"Chicken feed. You're ice-cold."

"A hundred million?"

"Still frosty."

"*Five* hundred million?"

"A cool billion," she said. "That's b-b-b-billion. With a *b*."

"Get outta here. A *billion dollars*? Says who?"

"Says *Forbes* magazine. He's on their list of the world's richest people. Has been for years."

"But . . . how does he keep getting away with it?"

"Easy," she said. "Mexico's police and military are *owned* by guys like this. Bought and paid for. Case in point: Guzmán was arrested at one point, back in 1993—"

"Wait," I interrupted. "You just said he owned the police force."

"He did. Does. In Mexico. But he was arrested in Guatemala. Once he got caught, Mexico had to pretend to be glad. So they put him in prison. Maximum security, so-called. But guess what? He kept running his drug empire from inside the slammer; kept *building* it from inside the slammer; kept getting richer. Then, three years ago, in 2001? Uncle Sam started leaning on Mexico to extradite Shorty to the U.S. So what did Shorty do? He walked out of jail."

"Just like that? Walked right out the front gate?"

"Actually, he rode out the gate," she said.

"And he's a *billionaire?*"

"According to *Forbes*. And they know a lot about rich people. Apparently he's got a great business model. Plus his own fleet of boats. Planes, too: Learjets, DC-3s, even 747s. This guy's even got underground railways—secret tunnels running under the border near Tijuana."

I was stunned by the scope of Guzmán's operation. "But I thought we were winning the war on drugs."

"Define 'winning,'" she said drily.

"How is it," I asked, "that America—the richest, mightiest nation on earth—can't shut down this one guy?"

"Because we *love* this guy."

"*Love* him? He's the scum of the earth," I squawked.

"Oh, I agree," she said. "But Americans—lots of Americans—can't get enough of the stuff this guy's selling. 'The insatiable American nose,' one Mexican journalist calls it. Even our commander in chief seems to've had a taste for cocaine when he was young."

"George Bush? The *president?* I don't believe it."

"Unconfirmed fire," she conceded, "but persistent smoke. The point is, Shorty's a businessman, pure and simple. Well, not so simple, and not pure at all. There's blood on every line of coke snorted by every snotty, spoiled rich kid in America. But in the end, all Shorty cares about is the bottom line. He only supplies what we demand."

I wished I could find some fatal flaw in that piece of logic, but I couldn't. It was clear, compelling, and deeply discouraging. Suddenly the implications of her research hit me like a punch in the gut. "Well, *damn*," I said.

"What?"

"I just connected the dots, and I hate the picture." I sighed. "I should've figured this out the minute I heard those guys talking. But my brain's running in slo-mo; jet-lagged, I reckon, or maybe cooked by the sun." I hesitated, unsure how much I should reveal. "This stuff's connected to . . . a case I'm working."

"The Richard Janus crash." She didn't put it as a question.

"How the hell did you know that?"

"Well, for one thing, you're all over the local news. The *News-Sentinel;* Channel Ten. But I figured it out last night. When you said you were in San Diego."

I wasn't happy to hear this, but I was impressed. "How?"

"Easy-peasy. The crash was big news—national news—yesterday morning. Sensational story; celebrity pilot; everybody tight-lipped about whether the body's been I.D.'d. Then one of the world's experts on identifying skeletal remains turns up in San Diego. Coincidence? I don't think so."

"I like the way your mind works, Red. Ever think about getting out of the library?"

"Huh?" She sounded . . . what? confused? taken aback? No: She sounded defensive, maybe even scared. *Why?* Parsing what I'd said to her, I realized, *Hell, Bill, you dumb-ass. This woman's been stalked, and suddenly you sound like maybe you're hitting on her. Angling for a date.* "What I mean is," I hurried to clarify, "ever think about changing fields? From library science to . . . oh, for instance, forensic anthropology? We can always use smart people."

I heard a brief snort—was it laughter, or scorn? "Hey, thanks," she said. "I'll add that to my list of brilliant career moves: years of school, mountains of debt, and a one-in-a-million shot at some dead-end teaching job in Fargo—where the odds of getting tenure would be about as low as the average winter temperature."

"So you *like* the idea," I said. "Great. I'll be watching for your application." Using my shoulder to hold the phone against my ear, I began wriggling into my clothes.

"You do that. Meanwhile, *I'll* be watching for my MacArthur Genius Grant." She paused, then her tone got serious again. "Speaking of which: Your guy Janus—*he* was a Mac-Arthur Fellow, wasn't he? Didn't he get a genius grant for creating that charity?"

"Yeah," I said, saddened anew by the shame and the waste of Janus's death, or his fall, or whatever it was. "A quick-response relief force, helping people hang on till the governments and the Red Cross can get there? It *was* a brilliant idea."

"Important work," she agreed. "Bound to be frustrating, though—so much need, so little funding." She fell silent a moment. "So put yourself in his shoes. What would you say—what *could* you say—if somebody offered you a way to raise more money and help more people? A way to hire more staff, buy more planes? What if all it took to make it happen was to take a little something back with you, back across the border, on your way home?"

"Smuggling drugs? You're saying Richard Janus made a deal with the devil?"

"Not saying; just wondering," she replied. "Just thinking out loud. Playing what-if. Deadhead miles are a waste of time and fuel, right? Ask any long-haul delivery guy. Wheels or wings, same diff. Besides, *somebody's* gonna haul it; *somebody's* gonna get rich. Why not one of the good guys?"

"Because then you stop being one of the good ones,"

I pointed out. "Because running drugs makes you one of the bad guys."

"Well, yeah, there's that," she conceded. "But maybe you could rationalize it."

"Rationalize it how?"

"Same way Robin Hood did, I guess. Take from the rich, give to the poor."

"But," I started to protest, then stopped. *But what?*

"There's something else," she added.

Crack! Crack crack crack! The metal door of my room rattled, and I jumped almost as if the knocks had been gunshots. "I gotta go," I said furtively. "Somebody's at my door."

More rapping. "Hey, Doc—you in there?" It was McCready's voice. "You about ready?" I checked the bedside clock. *Crap*, I thought. I was five minutes late. "Be right there," I hollered. "One second."

BANG! "Yo, *Doc!* We're burning daylight!"

"Coming. Coming!" I muttered a quick "talk to you later" into the phone and ended the call, then hurried to the door and tugged it open. "Sorry," I said, my face flushing. "I got caught on a call to UT."

"Everything all right?"

I nodded. His question was routine—superficial small talk, without a doubt.

Almost without a doubt, I realized uneasily. Was it

just my imagination, or were his eyes boring into mine with the keen skepticism of a federal investigator?

On the rocky ride up the mountain, I mentally replayed the phone call, pondering the information and testing her Robin Hood theory: Did it fit the facts? And was it the simplest explanation that did? I had to admit, it did seem to fit with Janus's swashbuckling style, his daredevil streak. I'd seen videos of him landing a DC-3 in jungle clearings scarcely bigger than my backyard. Clearly the man didn't mind some peril—in fact, he seemed to thrive on it. Was he simply braver than most of us, more tolerant of high doses of danger? Or was it possible that Janus was an adrenaline junkie: not just accustomed to risk, but addicted to it—that danger was his drug of choice?

If so, he may have suffered a fatal overdose, I realized—an overdose supplied by Chapo Guzmán, a rich but deadly devil to dance with.

Chapter 12

"Big day today, guys," said McCready as we loaded onto the platform and prepared to descend the bluff for our second assault on the wreckage. "Summer solstice; longest day of the year. Fourteen hours of daylight."

Boatman groaned; Kimball said, "Great! We get overtime, right?"

"*Sure* you do," said McCready. "And good always triumphs over evil. And the Democrats and Republicans are about to set aside their differences and work together for the greater good."

"Hmm," Kimball muttered.

The morning wore on; the sun rose and the heat soared, the brown stone of the mountain soaking up the solstice sun. I was surprised by the heat—I'd heard that

San Diego doesn't get hot until July or even August—but somehow we had managed to catch a heat wave, which combined with the residual heat from the fire to make the crash site feel like a sauna. For much of the morning we were in shadow, sheltered by the rock wall at our backs. By eleven, though, the shadow had shrunk to a narrow band at the base of the bluff, and a hot, dry wind was funneling up the valley, swirling dust and cinders around us.

Mercifully, a few minutes later, McCready called a lunch break. Caked with dust and the salt of dried sweat, we boarded the platform and ascended the bluff. After our hours of baking on the slope, the comforts of the command center—ice water, air-conditioning, and a feast of sandwiches, fruit, chips, cookies, even ice cream bars—seemed wondrous beyond comprehension: as if we'd been released from a low, hot circle of Dante's Inferno and whisked straight to Paradise.

After lunch I staked a claim on a corner of the command center's small sofa. I must have nodded off, because I suddenly found myself waking up. The chatter in the room had ceased, and—hearing the abrupt silence—I jerked awake and said, "What?" Then, as the fog of sleep dissipated, I heard what had caused the agents to fall silent: the thrum of an approaching helicopter. My first thought was of the sheriff's chopper, but then I realized that the pitch was too high. This was no army-bred workhorse; this was a racehorse—the same Fox 5 News racehorse that had trailed Carmelita Janus up the mountain, I saw when I followed the agents outside.

McCready and Prescott—apparently the case agent had arrived sometime during my nap—frowned as the helicopter settled down, and their frowns turned to scowls as a young reporter, accompanied by a cameraman, ducked beneath the swirling blades and scurried toward us. Prescott held up a warning hand and shook his head—a clear, strong no signal—but they kept coming. The cameraman handed the reporter a microphone, and as they neared us, he held it up and began speaking. "Mike Malloy, Fox Five News. Who's in charge here?"

"I am," said Prescott.

"And who are you?" he demanded.

"I'm the federal officer who's going to arrest you both if you don't leave immediately. This is a restricted area and you know it. So get back in your helicopter and get out of here, and I mean *now*."

"Of course, of course. Just a couple quick questions before we go."

"No," said Prescott. "Now."

"Have you identified the body of Richard Janus yet?" Prescott didn't respond. "Have you found his body—or any body?"

"I won't comment on an ongoing investigation," said Prescott, his voice ringing like steel on stone. "But I will comment on this." He held up a thumb and forefinger, practically touching. "You are *this close* to being arrested for tampering with a crime scene, interfering with a federal officer in performance of his duties, and two or three other things I haven't thought of yet. When we have news, we will hold a press conference. Which you'll be welcome to attend. *If* you're not behind bars."

The reporter held up his hands and began backing away, but he wasn't giving up yet. "What's the crime? You say this is a crime scene, so what crime are you investigating?" Prescott scowled, but I wasn't sure whether his anger was triggered by the reporter's doggedness or his own revelation—I felt sure it was unintentional—that the mountaintop wasn't just a crash scene, but a crime scene.

Then I noticed Prescott's gaze lifting and shifting, refocusing on something beyond the journalists, and I saw four ERT techs edging up behind them. Prescott gave a slight nod—a gesture so subtle that I wasn't sure whether I'd actually seen it or just imagined it—and the four agents swiftly closed the gap, grabbing the TV guys by the arms and force-marching them back to the helicopter. Just before the reporter was pushed into the cabin, he shouted a final question, and the flicker in Prescott's eyes as he heard the last three words sent a shock wave coursing clear through me.

"Do you consider Richard Janus to be the victim," the reporter had yelled, "or the criminal?"

Back amid the sweltering wreckage, the air-conditioned comfort of lunchtime soon seemed a distant memory, and by midafternoon, even Kimball and Boatman had stopped bantering. We worked in steady silence, punctuated only by the thud of metal bumping metal, the rasp of metal scraping rock, the clink of rock rolling against rock. We'd still found no signs of hair or teeth or sinew, and as I stooped and straightened, stooped and straightened, I settled into a trancelike rhythm, moving like some assembly-line automaton: a metal-sorting machine, my clawlike hands gripping scraps and shards and depositing them on the rack, which—every twenty minutes or so—ascended into heaven, or into what passed for heaven out on the hellishly hot hillside. Only moments after disappearing, it seemed, the rack would return, its maw empty and mocking, sneering, *So, ready to pack it in?*

"So, ready to pack it in?" I heard the question again, this time coming from outside my head, not inside. Startled, I looked around, then looked up. McCready was peering down at me from the rim, his expression quizzical and amused.

"Sorry," I said. "What?"

"Ready to call it a day? It's after five." The insatiable rack had just come down once more, and McCready pointed toward me, then pointed toward the rack, and then mimed the act of reeling in a fish. I was exhausted, true; I'd spent most of the night fretting rather than sleeping, and I'd been keyed up all day as well.

But I was loath to end a second day without finding something: that, too, was true—truer, or at least more compelling at the moment, than my fatigue. I suspected that Prescott was still pressuring McCready, but if he was, McCready was shielding us from it. "Don't forget, it's the solstice," I called up to him. "You promised us extra fun in the sun today."

"Go for it," he said. "The rest of you guys got a little more in you?" I heard a smattering of *sures* and *why nots* from the ERT team; they sounded halfhearted, at best, but I didn't care. I wasn't going to let the sun set without finding something—even if that "something" was only clear evidence that, despite Maddox's confidence, there was nothing in the wreckage to be found.

We worked for another hour without talking, the quiet broken at intervals by sighs and grunts and occasional muttered curses; by the tin-roof clatter of scraps raining onto the platform; by the rumble and whine of the crane as it hoisted another load from the base of the bluff to the top of the ridge.

Despite my resolve not to end the day empty-handed, I realized—as the emptied platform descended for the thousandth time of the day—that I was pooped. Exhausted. Out of gas. "Okay," I groaned, "stick a fork in me, 'cause I'm done." All around me, I heard what sounded like sighs of weary relief.

"Just in time," said Kimball. "By now I wouldn't know a femur if it hit me upside the head." He radioed up to McCready. "Hey, boss, Doc's pleading for clemency. Any chance you can let us off with time served?" I didn't hear McCready's response, but a moment later, the platform eased a step closer to the ground, and Kimball offered me a hand climbing aboard.

Just as I stepped up, though, I caught a glimpse of something—or half a glimpse, or a tenth of one—in my peripheral vision. I didn't know what it was, but it triggered some subliminal sensor, set off some subconscious alarm or detector. I froze and scanned the ground, but I couldn't see anything of particular interest or importance. I stepped back, reversing course, and then retraced my steps, this time in extreme slow motion, letting my gaze brush lightly across the surface of the rubble: looking, but not too closely, for it was only when I *hadn't* been looking that I'd actually seen whatever it was I'd seen.

No luck. I repeated the maneuver twice more without success while the ERT techs watched. I had just given up, and was stepping onto the rack for good, when I saw it again, a faint glimmer of something small and smooth and lustrous. This time I got a better fix on where it was, and I bent down, maintaining the same visual angle and keeping my eye glued to the spot. "I'll be damned," I said as much to myself as to the four FBI agents. "It's a tooth—an honest-to-god tooth!" I knelt—sharp rubble dug into my knees, but I didn't care—and plucked it from the metal shards that swirled around it, like some dangerous version of a gemstone's setting. It was a bicuspid—an upper right— the roots broken and burned but the crown intact. I held it between my thumb and forefinger, studying it from all angles, as if it were a miraculous and precious object, unique in all the world. Which it *was*, of course—there was no other tooth anywhere on earth exactly like this one. Without fillings or other distinctive anomalies, it wasn't a sufficient basis for a positive identification. But it was a start, by damn. And it was proof that the plane wasn't some empty, unpiloted ghost ship after all.

"Don't tell McCready," I said to my teammates in a low voice. "I want to surprise him with it." Kimball held out a small paper evidence bag, the top open. I eased the tooth inside, then tucked the bag into my shirt pocket. Next I took an evidence flag from one of my back pockets and wiggled the thin steel shaft into the spot where I'd found the tooth, so Kimball and Boatman could map the spot when we returned in the morning. "Always park on the downhill," my granddaddy had taught me long ago, back when I was fifteen and learning to drive a stick shift. "Makes it easier to get going the next time." The advice had served me well ever since, and not just when it came to cars. Ending the day by flagging the spot where I'd found the tooth—the first of many, I hoped—was my way of parking us on the excavation's downhill slope.

Straddling the empty bucket again—*not empty for much longer*, I told myself—I caught hold of the cables, and we ascended. This time, the tide of battle seemed to be turning, and I stood taller, actually feeling a bit like George Washington this time, the Stars and Stripes fluttering beside us in the breeze.

"Hold out your hand and close your eyes," I told McCready when we disembarked topside. He looked wary, but he did it. Reaching into my pocket, I fished out the bag and opened it, then carefully laid the tooth in his palm. "Happy solstice," I said, and when he opened his eyes and saw it, a smile dawned, spreading across his face like daybreak.

Chapter 13

The solstice sun was easing toward the horizon—
a broad track of sunlight glinted off the Pacific,
though the sun was still too bright to look at—when
we adjourned to the command post to celebrate our
find, to toast the tooth with ice water and Diet Coke.
We tapped plastic bottles and aluminum cans together
as exuberantly as if they'd been crystal champagne
flutes. "To the upper right bicuspid," I toasted,
holding it aloft. "The first of many teeth awaiting us
tomorrow."

I felt the tired buzz of fatigue—or *thought* I felt
the buzz of fatigue, but as the tingling ended and then
resumed, ended and resumed, I realized that my cell
phone—tucked in my pocket and set on "vibrate"—
was receiving a call. I fished it out and saw Knoxville's

area code, 865, followed by the number that Red, the reference librarian, had given me. I noticed McCready and Maddox both looking my way, and I felt my face flush with the guilty knowledge that I was keeping secrets. "Go ahead and take that if you want to, Doc," McCready called over the din. "I'll make these guys quiet down."

I shook my head with what I hoped was nonchalance. "Naw. I recognize the number. It's just UT bureaucracy."

McCready looked up at the wall clock, which read 6:47. "Man, you ivory-tower folks work some mighty long hours."

It was nearly ten o'clock in Knoxville, I realized. *Crap, Brockton,* I chided myself, *could you have said anything dumber?* "Takes a lot of work to keep the place all clean and shiny," I said lamely. McCready returned to his conversation with Maddox, but his eyes seemed to linger on me for an extra moment.

The bone-jarring ride down the mountain seemed to take hours, although my watch suggested that only thirty minutes had elapsed. When we finally pulled into the motel's parking lot, I practically leapt from the Suburban. "I'm gonna scrub up and call home,"

I said on my way out. "If y'all are hungry, go on without me. I can fend for myself again."

"Hell, we'll wait," said McCready. "Fella works as hard as you do shouldn't have to eat alone."

"Thanks," I said, though I would rather have had the time alone. "Want me to call you when I'm ready?"

"Just meet us in the lobby whenever you get done. Maybe thirty minutes? Eight o'clock, plus or minus?"

"You sure y'all don't want to just go on without me?"

"Sure, Doc. It's not like we've got big plans."

"Hey, speak for yourself, old man," cracked Kimball. "Jack in the Box? Mickey D's? Them joints is some *happenin'*, dude—I'll be rockin' this warehouse district all *night!*" I could hear the younger agents riffing on this theme and laughing as I stepped into my room. Closing the door behind me, I immersed myself in the cool and the dark, soaking up the soothing, white-noise hum of processed air.

My phone was already in my hand by the time I'd chained the door, and I felt a surge of nervous energy when I saw that I had two voice mails waiting.

The first was a reminder about a finance committee meeting at my church the next day, one I might have skipped even if I weren't two thousand miles away. The second one, though, was as electrifying as the first one was boring. "Dr. Brockton? It's Red. I've got some follow-up info I think you'll find interesting. Call back when you can."

I checked the clock. It was 7:30 in San Diego, which made it 10:30 in Knoxville. *Too late to call,* I thought. But then again, she worked until midnight—or did on some nights, although I didn't know about tonight. *She said to call anytime,* I reminded myself. I hit the "call" button. "Hello," said the now-familiar voice. "Is that you, Dr. B?"

"It is. Sorry to call so late. Are you still working?"

"I'm always working. My work ethic knows no bounds. Well, few bounds." She paused. "Okay, truth is, my work ethic is fairly feeble. But I'm gung ho about this particular task."

I didn't have time for witty repartee. "Your voice mail said you found something interesting."

"Well, I think so, but I'll let you be the judge."

"Tell me quick, then," I said. "I don't have much time."

"Richard Janus was a pilot for Air America from 1970 to '75."

That wasn't interesting at all, I judged. "So? The man's a pilot. Was. I'd be surprised if he *didn't* fly for an airline or two."

"Air America wasn't an airline. Air America was the CIA's secret air force in Southeast Asia during the Vietnam War."

Suddenly I judged the information to be considerably more interesting. "The CIA? As in Central Intelligence Agency?"

"As in. Air America was the cover name. A shell company, it's called. Civilian pilots—get this—flying military aircraft, on black-ops missions: commando insertions, weapons drops, downed-pilot rescues. Mostly in Laos and Cambodia, where U.S. troops weren't supposed to be. There's some evidence—claims, anyhow—that Air America also trafficked in opium."

"*What?*"

"To help fund their operations. More profitable than bake sales, I guess."

"Damn," I whispered. Her news wasn't just "interesting," it was also damning, or at least potentially incriminating, on many levels. Had official U.S. agencies been complicit in the global drug trade? Had Richard Janus been part of that complicity? And had this much-admired humanitarian actually been a drug smuggler—for years, or even decades?

If so, it could explain a lot—maybe even explain everything: The investigation by the FBI. The involvement of another federal agency—the DEA, or the CIA, or whoever the redheaded fat man worked for. A desperate midnight run for the border of Mexico. It could even explain controlled flight into terrain—suicide-by-mountainside—if the demons or humans hounding Janus were sufficiently savage, if dying seemed less hellish than living.

"Gotta go," I said. "Thanks for the info. Very interesting, but damned discomforting."

"How do you mean?"

"If Janus was a serious drug runner, that could change things—change the investigation—in all sorts of ways. Maybe he was assassinated—possibly by Guzmán, possibly by the government. Maybe he was set up. Maybe this whole thing is one huge hoax."

"Maybe," she said. "Or maybe it's even more complicated than any of those. Be interesting to find out. Have a good night, Dr. B."

"Yeah," I said as I disconnected and headed out for an evening of fast food, forced camaraderie, and unshared secrets.

Chapter 14

Despite my night of fretting about Air America, the CIA, and the labyrinth of secrets that seemed to surround the life and death of Richard Janus, I resumed searching on day three with high hopes. Buoyed by the prior afternoon's discovery of a tooth, I'd assumed the rest of the remains would emerge immediately.

I'd assumed wrong. After an hour of searching and sifting, we were still empty-handed. Had the force of the impact somehow caused one of the teeth to ricochet away from the others? Or had a single tooth been planted in the wreckage, as a red-herring hoax? If so, by whom, and for what purpose?

By late morning, we'd sent up four loads of debris without having found any more teeth or bones, and my mood had gone from buoyant to discouraged to down-right mad. So when a tangle of metal tubing resisted my efforts to remove it from the wreckage, I gave a furious tug. Suddenly, unexpectedly, it came free and I toppled backward, my arms windmilling for balance. Catapulted by my flailing, a lumpy object—it looked like a charred chunk of driftwood pulled from a river-bank campfire—arched into the air, tumbling end over end. Blackened and broken though it was, I recognized it at once. I made a scrabbling lunge for it and managed to catch it just before it hit the rocks.

"Nice catch," said Boatman, on all fours, one hand working a shard of riveted aluminum free from a crev-ice. "You been practicing with the UT football team?"

"No, but I feel like I just scored a touchdown," I said. "Guys, this is the pelvis. Part of it, anyhow." The FBI techs came closer, careful not to disturb anything in the vicinity where the pelvis had been. "That tangle of tubing must be the framework of the seat." As I leaned down for a closer look, I felt my heart race even faster. "It *is*," I said. "I see vertebrae in there, too!"

"Wow," said Kimball, crouching alongside me. "Hard to tell where the seat leaves off and the skeleton begins."

"The man and the machine are pretty thoroughly mashed together," I said. "That whole aircraft—twelve thousand pounds—slamming into him like a pile driver, at four hundred miles an hour? I'm surprised it's not even more fragmented than this." I rotated the piece, studying what remained of the pelvis, then—on professorial autopilot—began pointing out structures. "This curved, triangular piece is the sacrum—the base of the spine, where it joins the pelvis. The sacrum is made of five vertebrae, and in children and adolescents, they're separate. But here, you can see, they're fused together. That tells us that this person was an adult; midthirties, at least." I pointed to the narrowest tip of the triangle. "The coccyx—that's the tailbone—attaches here, but it's been snapped off." I rotated the piece again. "Both pubic bones are broken, too. That makes it harder to tell the sex. So let's look at the sciatic notch, which is this gap where the sciatic nerve runs from the spine down the leg." I cradled the piece in one palm, so the V-shaped notch faced upward, and then pressed the side of my index finger down into the V. "I know you guys might not've noticed, but a woman's hips are broader than a male's, so the sciatic notch is wider, too. If it's a female, you can fit two fingers into the sciatic notch." I tried, and failed, to squeeze my middle finger alongside the index finger. "Here, I can't—the notch is too narrow. So we know he's a *he*."

Boatman must have been reading my mind. "Any way to tell how old he is?"

I shook my head. "It's too damaged. Normally, you can tell the age—the decade, anyhow—from the wear on the pubic symphysis."

"The what?" asked Boatman.

"The pubic symphysis. That's the joint where the left and right pubic bones meet, just above your crotch."

Kimball chuckled. "Boatman's would look like a kid's, then," he gibed. "No risk of wearing out *his* pubic bones." Grinning at his joke, he began taking photos of the pelvis and the mangled framework of the pilot's seat. Suddenly, as he hovered over the seat, he said, "Guys, look at this!" He lowered the camera, letting it hang from its strap, and bent down to extricate a charred object from the mangled metal. It was thin and small—half the size of a deck of cards—with rounded corners and a pair of thin wires, about a foot long, dangling from it.

He held it in his palm, turning it over to inspect it. "This is a circuit board. And a battery, looks like. Holy *crap*—I think this is some kind of detonator." He looked up, eyes wide. "Don't move."

He didn't have to tell us twice. A detonator implied a bomb—possibly a live bomb. I flashed back to the explosion that had nearly brought down our helicopter the day we'd arrived. Maddox had thought it was an oxygen cylinder bursting, but maybe he'd been wrong. Our eyes moved—scanning one another's faces; scanning the rocks and the ragged debris—but our bodies remained as motionless as statues.

After a long, tense silence, Boatman finally spoke. "We can't just stand here forever," he pointed out. Then, without moving his feet, he leaned forward to study the object in Kimball's hand. "So," he said, "if it's a detonator, why isn't the pelvis blown to smithereens? And why isn't the *detonator* blown to bits?" Slowly he shook his head. "I think it's just a cell phone—or maybe an iPod—with what's left of some earbuds."

"No way," Kimball insisted. "These wires aren't long enough. Besides, they're hardwired—soldered directly to the circuit board—not plugged into a jack. See?"

"Computer mouse, then," replied Boatman. "The wires are the tail."

Kimball shook his head doggedly. "Too short for that, too. And there's no USB connector on the other end. Just these weird flat tabs of copper."

"So the USB connector got sheared off," said Boatman. "Or melted." The pair of them made me think of an old, bickering married couple. He turned to look at me. "Doc? If you stare at that thing any harder, it might burst into flames. What are you thinking?"

I could feel gears turning in my mind—gears, or maybe combination-lock tumblers, their notches gradually aligning, one by one. "I think," I said, as the last tumbler clicked home, unlocking an idea, "that it's okay to move. I also think we'll know in thirty minutes whether or not this is Richard Janus."

Kimball and I went topside to the command center, taking the electronic gizmo and the camera with us. While Kimball transferred photographs from the camera to the computer, I showed the gizmo to McCready and Maddox and asked McCready to enlist some of Prescott's field-office agents for a bit of quick research. A moment later he was on the phone, calling in the cavalry.

Meanwhile, I called my friend Helen Taylor in Knoxville, hoping I'd catch her still at work. The phone rang six times, and I feared she'd left early, but finally she answered. "East Tennessee Cremation Services."

"Oh, good," I said, relieved. "Helen, it's Bill Brockton. I was afraid you'd left for the day."

"No, just processing a cremation. How are you, Dr. Brockton?"

"I'm fine, but I need a favor. Can I send you some pictures of something that's burned to a crisp and get you to tell me what it is?" If anybody could confirm my hunch about the incinerated object, I suspected Helen was the one.

"I will if I can," she said. "Do you have our mailing address?"

"I'm in a hurry, Helen. Can I fax you the pictures?"

"Well, yes." She sounded doubtful. "But they'd come through clearer if you e-mailed them—as scans, or image files, attached to a message. Can you do that?"

I turned to Kimball. "Can we send e-mail? With picture files as attachments?"

"With this computer, and the satellite data link we've got?" Kimball grinned. "We could just about send *you* as an attachment."

"Yes, we can e-mail them," I told Helen. "What's the address?" I jotted it on a notepad beside the computer. "Check your in-box in about thirty seconds. The message will come from"—I looked at Kimball as I spoke—"an FBI address?" He nodded, so I confirmed it. "Yeah, from an FBI address."

"FBI? This gets more interesting all the time. Can you tell me anything more about the pictures? Give me a little hint what I'll be looking at?"

"I have an idea," I said, "but I don't want to skew your thinking. Call me once you've had a look, and we'll see if we agree."

By the time I hung up, Agent Kimball had already hit "send."

I'd hoped we'd have the answer in thirty minutes, but I was wrong.

We had it in twenty.

Helen had called back in just five minutes—but it took another fifteen for Prescott's staff to track down the information I'd requested as a result, and to e-mail a response. Kimball opened the message, then clicked on the attachment, and a ghostly gray image filled the screen. McCready studied it closely, comparing it to the burned object Kimball had plucked from the frame of the pilot's seat. Maddox, the NTSB crash expert, peered over McCready's shoulder with keen interest, but he let the FBI agent ask the questions. "So tell me again what it is—and what the hell it does?"

"It's a spinal cord stimulator," I repeated. "It's like shock therapy for chronic back pain. The gizmo is called a pulse generator. It sends weak electrical signals out these wires, to electrical leads at the ends. The leads are surgically implanted in the epidural space of the spine, right by the spinal cord. The way I understand it, the electrical stimulation distracts the nerves—short-circuits them, sort of—so they can't send pain messages to the brain."

"Sounds scary. But it works?"

I gave a half shrug. "Sometimes. Not always. It's a last-resort kind of thing, when ordinary back surgery hasn't worked."

He peered at the computer screen, where Kimball was displaying the image we'd just received from the field office. It was an x-ray of a man's spine; of Richard Janus's spine, to be precise. Floating just above the left hip was an electronic circuit board, its metal connectors and battery showing up crisp and white against the muted grays of x-rayed flesh and bone. A pair of thin wires, attached to the circuit board, angled toward the lumbar spine and then threaded up the thoracic vertebrae, terminating in a series of flat electrical leads laid out in a geometric pattern that hopscotched from the tenth vertebra up to the eighth.

Maddox couldn't keep quiet any longer. "It looks just like somebody's connected him to a computer mouse," he said. "So you just wear that generator on your belt, like a pager?"

"Oh, no," I corrected. "It's internal. The surgeon cuts a slot in the skin—a hip pocket, literally—and sutures it inside. Looks and feels a little odd, probably—a hard, square thing just under the skin—but I don't guess anybody would've noticed it except him and his wife."

McCready appeared mesmerized by the x-ray. "And how'd you know it'd be so easy to confirm that Janus had gotten one of these things—*this* thing—put in?"

"The media loved Janus," I said, "and he loved the media. I remembered reading that he'd hurt his back in a crash, and that he'd had some kind of surgery to try to make it better. I figured there must've been a press release or a news report about that. So I suspected it wouldn't take much digging to find out if he'd gotten one of these." McCready nodded. "What I *didn't* expect," I admitted, "was that we'd get an actual post-op x-ray so fast."

McCready clapped me on the back. "Well, all I can say is, you're a wizard, Doc. And Prescott's gonna be a happy guy when I tell him we've made the I.D." He lifted his phone to make a call.

My head snapped around, and I grabbed his arm. "Wait. Don't tell him that."

"What? Why not?" He stared at me as if I'd gone mad. "You just pulled this rabbit out of the hat, and now you're saying 'never mind'? What the hell, Doc? Is it Janus, or isn't it?"

"Yes, it's him," I said, "but it's not admissible. It's a *presumptive* identification—we can presume it's him—but it's not a *positive* identification, one that would stand up in court." He still looked confused, so I went on. "The x-ray image seems to match the burned stimulator, and Janus's medical records will probably confirm that he got this brand, and this model. But unless his surgeon kept better records than any other surgeon on the planet, the records won't tell us the individual serial number—the DNA, so to speak, of this one device. And without a unique serial number, we can't prove that it's him."

He sighed. "Well, *hell*, Doc."

"I know, I know. But hey, look on the bright side. We know it's him; now all we gotta do is prove it. We just need more teeth. You've got the dental records now, right?"

He frowned: sore subject. "Working on it. The dentist is dragging his heels."

"So pull on him harder." His frown turned to a scowl, which meant I'd drilled into a nerve. I shrugged apologetically. "Hey, cheer up," I said, holding up a thumb and forefinger, separated by a hairsbreadth. "We're *this close*."

Only after I said it did I realize why the phrase—*this close*—came so easily to my lips. Prescott had used it to threaten the pushy Fox News reporter.

I had also heard another federal agent use it—the wheezy fat man who had ripped into Prescott at the

IHOP—to describe how near he'd been to nailing not just Janus but Guzmán, too.

This close. Maybe the phrase didn't exactly mean what I thought it meant.

This close. It echoed in my mind. *Presumptive, but not positive.*

During my time topside with the spinal cord stimulator, the evidence techs had begun to mine a rich vein of skeletal material: splintered ribs; incinerated vertebrae; fractured long bones. By the time I rejoined them amid the wreckage, our five-gallon bucket— what I'd taken to calling our "special bucket"—was half filled with pieces of burned bone. As I studied the bucket's contents, gently lifting and sifting my way downward, I was impressed by what they'd found— and fascinated by what they hadn't. "Hmm," I said. "So far, everything's from the postcranial skeleton."

Boatman handed me a singed scapula—the left shoulder blade. "The which?"

"Postcranial," I said. "Below the skull. If we hadn't found that tooth yesterday, I'd almost think he didn't have a head. The headless horseman, but riding a plane instead of a horse." Suddenly it hit me, and I let out a bark of startled laughter. "I'll be damned," I told the surprised agents. "Maybe he *was* headless." Their puzzled expressions prompted me to explain. "When he hits—remember, he's going four hundred miles an hour—he's strapped in, right? So his body's restrained, for a fraction of a second, by the harness. But his head *isn't* restrained, and it snaps forward really, really hard. How many g's did Maddox say the deceleration created?"

"Eighteen hundred." The answer came from Kimball, not surprisingly.

"So if his head weighed ten or twelve pounds," I mused, "then it would have jerked forward . . ." I did some mental math. "Jesus. With almost twenty thousand pounds of force."

Kimball gave a low whistle. "That's some serious traction."

"I don't know how much force it takes to pull the head clean off the spine," I added. "We've never done that particular experiment at the Body Farm. But I'm guessing twenty thousand pounds would do it." I redirected my gaze and began scanning a different area of the wreckage from where the vertebrae had been found. "I'm also guessing that we'll find the skull—the pieces of it—somewhere up here, instead of down there."

Straightening up from my crouch—I'd been stooped over the area where the vertebrae and scapula had been—I began examining the remnants of the instrument panel, the windshield, and the cockpit ceiling. The windshield itself had melted or burned away—it was plastic, not glass—but its misshapen framework remained: two rectangular openings, separated and reinforced by a stout central pillar. The pillar was bent and blackened and, down near its base, encrusted with a coating of black particles. The particles were bits of burned bone, I realized; more specifically, they were charred crumbles of skull, a few of them large enough to retain their distinctive, layered structure: hard outer and inner shells of dense bone, separated by a softer, spongy layer. My pulse racing, I leaned close and worked my way downward. A few inches below the base of the pillar—embedded in the glass-filled cavity of a shattered instrument—I spotted them: a handful of blackened pebbles. A handful of teeth. "Bingo," I said softly, mainly to myself. Then, a moment later: "Can somebody hand me the tooth jar?"

"Here you go, Doc."

Without even looking to see who'd said it, I reached back and took the container. I removed the lid and tucked it in one of my shirt pockets, then took a pair of forceps from the other pocket. One by one, I plucked teeth from their nest amid the shards of glass. They weren't all there—only ten of them; the others must have been scattered or shattered by the impact—but four of the ten were enough to send my adrenaline soaring again. "Somebody wake up McCready," I joked.

"He's standing right there," said Kimball, pointing up at the rim of the bluff.

I glanced up and saw McCready silhouetted against the sky. "Hey, Mac," I called, "can you give me another lift?"

He leaned perilously over the edge. "You okay, Doc? What's wrong?"

"I'm fine. Got something else to show you." I tucked my find into my shirt pocket, sealing six of the teeth in the small jar, folding the other four into a piece of paper.

"Climb aboard. Holler when you're set."

The ERT techs steadied the corners of the rack as I positioned myself at the center. "All set—beam me up, Scotty!" McCready spun his finger at the crane operator, and once more I ascended, swung around to the side, and settled gently onto what I had come to think of as the landing pad. "You're gonna like this," I said. "I'm . . . *positive.*"

He raised his eyebrows as my double-entendre meaning sank in. "Whatcha got? Suicide note? Signed in blood—in an asbestos envelope?"

"How'd you guess?" I fished in my pocket. "Actually, no, but probably just as good." I held out my hand, my fingers closed, then slowly opened them to reveal four teeth in my palm. "Check it out," I said. "I found a bunch of teeth. More than this, but these four are really special." With my pinky, I pointed to the first. "A canine. Dog tooth. The longest root of any tooth."

McCready leaned in, studying the tooth. "Looks kinda gnarly. *Twisted,* almost."

"Exactly—the root's got a slight corkscrew curve. Very distinctive. I've never seen one quite like this before."

He nodded. "So far, so good."

"It gets better." I pointed to a pair of teeth. "The upper central incisors—both of 'em." I tapped my own, then touched the teeth in my palm again. "Look at that."

"They're chipped—the corners broken off. By the crash?"

"No. See how the edges of the breaks are rounded off? They're worn. These teeth have been chipped for years. That picture Maddox showed us, of Janus grinning beside the jet? Look close and you'll see these chipped teeth."

McCready himself was now starting to smile. "This is good, right?"

"Good? It's *grrreeaat,*" I responded, in my best Tony the Tiger imitation. "But I saved the best for last. The most interesting, anyhow. This one's a maxillary third molar—a wisdom tooth. Upper right." I opened my mouth and put the tip of my tongue in the hollow of my tooth to show him. "*Iss* whun," I mumbled, tapping the outside of my cheek as well. "This one's interesting in a couple of ways. First, it's got a filling. That's far more common in a lower molar, because food and saliva tend to collect there." He nodded, but I could tell I was losing him, so I hurried on. "But the really cool thing about this tooth? *This.*" Plucking it carefully from my palm, I held it up, rotating it slowly to reveal the prize.

"Huh," he said. "What's that funny little knob on the side?"

"That," I said triumphantly, "is a cusp of Carabelli."

"A cusp of what?"

"Not *what*," I corrected. "*Who.* Or whom. Whichever. A cusp of Carabelli, the guy who first studied 'em, back in the 1800s."

"Oh, *him*," McCready cracked. "Sure."

"Carabelli was the royal dentist for one of the Hapsburg emperors," I explained. "Carabelli's cusp—also called Carabelli's tubercle—is a prominent bump located on the lingual surface—the 'tongue' side of a tooth—instead of the biting surface. It's found occasionally on first molars, rarely on second molars, and almost never on third molars."

"So the fact that we've got one on a third molar . . ."

"Means we've got a slam dunk on the I.D.," I finished. "If—*if*—it matches Janus's dental records." I gave him a pointed, interrogatory look.

He growled in exasperation. "Okay, okay, let me see if I can light a fire under that dentist." He unholstered his cell phone and scrolled down the display, then pushed the "call" button. When the call was answered, he spoke in an official-sounding tone I'd never heard him use before. "This is Special Agent McCready of the Federal Bureau of Investigation. I need to speak with Dr. Grant."

Through the tiny speaker, I heard a woman's tinny voice. "Sir, he's with a patient. If you'll give me your name and number—"

"Ma'am, listen closely. Are you listening? I need Dr. Grant to take his fingers out of that patient's mouth, pick up the phone, and talk to me for sixty seconds. It's a law-enforcement matter, and it's quite urgent." I saw his jaw muscles clench as she promised once more to relay a message. He cut her off. "*Ma'am,* I've spoken with you six times in the past three days, and all six times, you've told me he was with a patient, and you've assured me that he'd call me back as soon as he was free. So here's the deal. If the patient he's with right now is the president of the United States, then I'll leave a message. But otherwise, I either speak with him in the next thirty seconds, or I file charges—against Dr. Grant, and against *you*—for obstruction of justice. So I suggest you lay down the phone and go explain the options to him, because that thirty seconds? It starts . . . right . . . *now.*" He took the phone away from his ear and pressed it to his shoulder, shaking his head and muttering, "Why do some people go out of their way to make things difficult?" He put the phone back up to his ear, and a few seconds later, his eyes narrowed. "Dr. Grant, at last. Special Agent McCready, FBI. . . . Yes, you must have the world's busiest dental practice. . . . You're in the Medical Arts Building on Broadway, is that right? . . . Uh-huh. As I believe I indicated in my prior phone calls—my *six* prior phone calls—we need the dental records of one of your patients, Richard Janus, and we need 'em day before yesterday. So here's what's about to happen, Dr. Grant. In ten minutes, an FBI agent will arrive at your office. He'll have a subpoena in one hand and a pair of handcuffs in the other. If he doesn't leave with those records, he leaves with you. Your choice. Do I make myself clear, Dr. Grant?" He listened for a moment more. "Thank you, Dr. Grant. You're making a wise choice." He snapped the phone shut with a grim smile, then gave another growl.

Thirty minutes later, as I was plucking blackened shards of bone from the aircraft wreckage once more, I heard the now-familiar *whop-whop-whop* of helicopter blades approaching. "*Criminy,*" said Kimball. "Are we working a restricted crash site here, or is this now the approach to LAX?"

I looked up, expecting to see the television chopper again, the new crew waving a Freedom of the Press banner or wielding some sort of injunction giving them permission to ignore the airspace restriction. But instead of the colorful Fox 5 logo, I saw only glossy black paint.

"That must be one of ours," said Kimball. "No markings."

A moment later, his guess was confirmed when McCready radioed down, asking for me to come up. "Prescott's here with the dental records," Kimball told me.

By the time Kimball finished the sentence, I was already clambering aboard the platform for the ride up.

"Good work," said Prescott, looking up from the teeth cradled in his palm—the corkscrew canine, the chipped incisors, and the molar with the cusp of Carabelli on the side. "So now we're positive."

"Looks like it," I said.

"What do you mean, 'looks like it'? It's his plane, his battery-powered spine, and his weird teeth." He pointed at the molar. "So tell me, what are the chances that this molar, with this bump on the side, came from somebody other than Richard Janus?"

"Oh, virtually zero," I said. "One in a million, probably."

He nodded. "And what are the chances that all four of these teeth—which match his dental records perfectly—came from someone else?"

"So small, I don't even know how to say it. One in many billions."

"But you don't sound certain."

"I am," I said. "It's just . . ."

"Just *what*, Doc?" I'd heard irritation in Prescott's voice before, so I recognized when I heard it again now.

"It'd be good to confirm it with some soft-tissue DNA," I told him. "Just to be absolutely certain."

Prescott glanced at McCready, eyebrows raised. McCready gave a slight shake of his head. P rescott glared at me again. "McCready says the guy's a crispy critter. Is he telling me wrong?"

"No."

Prescott was like a dog gnawing a bone, but the bone was me. "Have you *got* some soft tissue from this guy, Dr. Brockton?"

"Not so far."

"Are you *expecting* any, Dr. Brockton?"

"Well, no."

Prescott raised his hands, as if he were Christ on the cross. "Look, no offense"—a phrase that was nearly always followed by offensive words—"but we're not living in a perfect world here, or working in some ivory-tower laboratory. We're at a crime scene that's one hell of a challenge, and we've found multiple bases for identification. Without soft tissue—or some magical video that shows Richard Janus actually steering the plane into the mountainside—this seems about as positive an I.D. as we're gonna get."

"You're probably right," I conceded.

"*Thank* you," he said. "I said it before and I'll say it again: I appreciate your contribution. And now I'm calling the boss." Prescott raised his phone, found a number, and pressed "call." "I'm up at the Janus crash site," he said. "With the dental records. We've got a solid match—it's a positive I.D. . . . Dr. Brockton, the anthropologist, just walked me through it. It's solid, sir. Very solid. We've got several teeth with very distinctive features. Any one of them would be enough, says Brockton; cumulatively, it's beyond question. There's more, too. We've also recovered an orthopedic device that Janus had implanted a few years ago." He listened, nodding. "We can be ready whenever. You want us to brief the widow first? . . . Yes, sir, I agree. But I think we should do them back to back: give her the news first, then—bam!—straight to the press conference. We don't want her to get out ahead of us and spin it. We need to be the ones shaping the story. . . . Yes, sir, we'll be ready. . . . Thank *you*, sir. Thank you very much."

He clicked the phone shut, a smile tugging at the corners of his mouth.

McCready raised his eyebrows. "Sounds like the SAC is keeping a close eye on this one," he said.

"What's the SAC?" I butted in.

"Special agent in charge," he explained. "Head of the field office. The boss."

"Yes and no," said Prescott. He no longer sounded irritated. In fact, the smile on his face was growing broader by the second.

McCready frowned. "Huh?"

"Yes and no," Prescott repeated. "It was the boss. But not the SAC." His smile widened.

"Then who?" asked McCready. He stared at Prescott, who was now grinning like a Cheshire cat. "Wait—are you kidding me?" McCready shook his head in seeming disbelief. "Whoa," he said. "That's major."

"So who *was* it?" I looked from one to the other, feeling clueless and stupid.

Finally Prescott took pity on me. "Who gave you a ride out here?"

I pointed at McCready. "*Duh.* He did."

Prescott shook his head. "Who gave you and Mac a ride? Who let you borrow his ride?"

I furrowed my brow at him, still playing catch-up. "His ride? You mean the jet—the Gulfstream?" Finally I got it. "Are you telling me that was the director—the director of the FBI—on the phone just now?" I felt myself starting to smile, too. "Whoa," I said. "That *is* major."

Chapter 15

As the afternoon wore on, we continued picking our way through the crumpled shell of the cockpit and instrument panel—a mixed-media collage of burned wires, melted knobs, shattered glass, splintered circuit boards. We found a few more shards of bone and a handful more teeth—including the other chipped incisor, which brought our total to twenty-nine of the thirty-two teeth.

Tangled amid the wiring, I came upon a pendant on a thin steel chain, the clasp still fastened around a throat that wasn't there. *A neckless necklace,* I thought ironically. At first glance, the pendant appeared to be a cross. Looking closer, I saw that the lower end had small tailfins; the pendant was an airplane, suspended from its nose in a perpetual climb. But when I rubbed it against the leg of my pants to remove the soot, I noticed that it was engraved—not with initials or an inscription, but with an etched outline of Jesus: an aeronautical crucifix; Christ on a flying cross. I held it in my palm as Kimball photographed it in detail, then I slipped it into my pocket, to give to McCready. We'd found a set of keys earlier, a charred cell phone, and the mangled remains of a stainless-steel wristwatch. The pendant, though, was the only truly personal effect we'd found, and I hoped McCready would give it to Janus's widow. What had it meant to him, I wondered: an emblem that melded elements of work and worship, worn around the neck of a man who seemed equal parts humanitarian and drug smuggler? *A man is a mass of contradictions,* I thought—a well-worn quotation, but no one had ever embodied it better than Richard Janus, I suspected—up until the split second he no longer embodied anything at all.

By now we were mining the lowest layer of wreckage—the floorpan of our excavation, down in the land of diminishing returns—and bit by bit, piece by piece, I began to smell the metaphorical barn. Finally we reached the aircraft's nose, its outer skin, which was molded to the contours of the bluff almost as closely as human flesh adheres to cheekbones, forehead, jaws. "Okay, fellas," I said, straightening up and twisting—left, right, left—to wring the kinks from my back. "Anything we haven't found by now is either decimated or incinerated. Or both. I think I smell the barn. Or maybe it's just us." My announcement was greeted by a chorus of grateful sighs and weary cheers. I stepped back and took a critical look at the nose, the last large piece of wreckage to go up. "This is gonna be tough to get onto the platform," I said. "Take some finagling to work it through those cables."

"How 'bout we just hang it underneath?" suggested Boatman.

"Be easier—more stable, anyhow—if we took the platform off altogether," said Kimball. "Fasten it right to the cable." He explained how he would do it, pointing and motioning to show places he could attach straps to the piece, and everyone agreed that the plan made sense. Kimball made a solo trip topside to unhook and park the platform. Ten minutes later he rappelled back down, followed by the crane's steel cable, the big U-shaped shackle dangling from the line like a giant fishing hook.

Kimball had brought down a half-dozen neon-hued nylon straps, which he began threading around and through the flattened nose cone. As he bent over the mangled metal, tugging and tussling to work a strap beneath the bottom edge, he paused. "Hey, Doc. Got another one for you. A stray." He reached a thumb and forefinger beneath the jagged edge of metal and plucked a small object from a recess in the rock. I held out my hand, palm upturned, and into it Kimball dropped the object: a tooth, one that had been snapped off at the gum line. I stared, blinked hard, stared again.

"Doc? What's up? You look like you've seen a ghost."

"I think maybe I have," I said. "It's an incisor. An upper central." I tapped my front teeth.

Kimball's brow furrowed. "Huh? I thought we already found both of those."

"We did." I studied the faces of Kimball and the other agents as they leaned in for a better look. "This is a third one. From a second person."

"You're kidding, right?" said McCready when I radioed him about the find. I heard him mutter to someone, "Brockton says he's found another tooth—from another person, not Janus." In the background, I heard what seemed to be a string of garbled expletives; I couldn't quite make out the words, but I recognized the voice. "Maddox says, with all due respect, that your head appears to be inserted into one of your lower orifices," McCready said. "No offense, but I'm with Maddox on this—it *can't* be from somebody else."

"Maybe it can't," I told him. "But it *is*."

"We're still short three of Janus's teeth," he persisted. "It's gotta be one of those."

"It's an *incisor*, Mac. Upper central. We've already got those, remember? Both of them chipped. Just like in the photos and the dental records."

"Then it's a lateral incisor. Or a lower. Or a canine."

"Those are all accounted for, too," I said. "All we're missing from Janus are two molars and one bicuspid. Besides, this is—*trust* me—an *incisor*."

"You're absolutely sure?"

"I'd stake my life on it. Yours, too." I turned the tooth over in my palm. "That's not all. This tooth is from a Mongoloid."

The radio went silent for a moment, then he said, "You're telling me there was a mentally retarded person on that plane with him?"

"No, no," I clarified. "Sorry, that's anthropologist lingo. Mongoloid, as in 'descended from ancient inhabitants of Mongolia.' Mongoloid, as opposed to Caucasoid or Negroid. Mongoloid, as in Asian or Native American."

"Sit tight," he said. "I'm coming down."

Five minutes later, the rappelling rope twitched and seethed as a grim-faced McCready descended from on high. Without a word, I handed him the tooth—a far less celebratory echo of the way I'd jubilantly turned over the first tooth. This time he did not smile; instead, he took it and stared at it—glared at it—as if it had done him a grievous wrong. Finally he looked up, frowning and sighing. "Well, I'm no dentist," he said, "but yeah, even I can tell it's not a molar or bicuspid. But what makes you say it's Asian or Native American?"

I plucked the tooth from his palm and turned it edgewise to show him the biting surface. "See how curved the edge is? And how the back of the tooth is scooped out?" He took it back and gave it a close look. "It's called a shovel-shaped incisor," I explained. "Unique to Mongoloid peoples. And this is a textbook example."

He nodded in acknowledgment, but the nod was followed by a baffled head shake. "I don't get it," he said. "Up to now, we've got nothing but white-guy teeth and white-guy bits—specifically, Richard Janus bits." He gestured at the last remnants of wreckage: shards of instrument-panel glass; bundles of burned wire; control levers and pedals; the empty, mangled framework of the windshield; the crushed cone of the nose. "We're all but done. How can we just now—just as the buzzer's sounding—find the very first sign of Running Bear or Miguel or whoever the hell this is?"

"Dunno," I said. Then I realized that I was a half step behind him. "You're right, it makes no sense. How could anybody be deeper in the debris than the pilot?" My mind began to race. "*Maybe . . .*" Bending down, I tugged at the piece, as Kimball had just begun to do when he'd spotted the tooth. "Maybe," I grunted, "he's not *in* the debris. Maybe he's *under* the debris."

"Come again?"

"Maybe he was already here when the plane hit."

"What are you saying, Doc? You think there's an old Indian skeleton under here?"

A flicker of movement caught my eye—an iridescent, blue-green flicker, almost like the dot of a laser pointer in midair, just above the edge of the flattened metal—and I felt a rush, as if someone had just injected pure adrenaline into an artery. "No," I said, pointing at the iridescent dot. "See that? That's a blowfly. Blowflies aren't attracted to old skeletons; they go for ripe, juicy carcasses. I'm thinking we've got a fairly fresh body under here."

"What? How?"

"Dunno," I said again, this time with considerably more excitement. "Who would be up here? A hiker? A hunter?" Suddenly it hit me. "A border jumper. We're only two miles from Mexico. Maybe it's somebody who died after sneaking across the border."

McCready considered this. "Seems like a stretch. A lot of 'em die crossing the desert in Arizona.

Dehydration—some of 'em end up walking a hundred miles or more before they keel over. But five miles from Tijuana and the outskirts of San Diego?"

I looked up at the bluff. "Not dehydration. Trauma. A fall—maybe in the dark. If he fell from up there and landed on his head, his skull would've burst like a melon."

McCready looked dubious. "So Miguel here takes a nosedive, and then—a day or a week or a month later—our guy Janus just happens to pile on? Exact same spot? Sounds unlikely to me."

It sounded unlikely to me, too. But that scenario was only a fraction as unlikely as the death scene we uncovered ten minutes later, when Kimball finished the rigging and the crane peeled the aircraft's nose from the face of the rock.

"Holy shit," McCready breathed.

I looked around. "Where's the camera?" I demanded. "We gotta have pictures. Otherwise nobody will ever believe this."

I needn't have said it. Kimball was already snapping pictures. As the camera *click click clicked*, behind me and beside me, images of the tableau began etching themselves indelibly on my mind: the hunched, crouching position of the flattened man; the arms, flung upward in a frantic, futile attempt at self-preservation;

inches above the bones of his hands, the head and fore-legs of a mountain lion, caught in midair, crushed against the rock. Shielded from the worst of the fire by a layer of aluminum, these two corpses—man and beast; prey and predator—had escaped the incineration that had consumed the fragmented remains of Richard Janus.

I had worked a few other death scenes that had pre-served, with freeze-frame precision, the drama of the deaths. I'd uncovered one of those in the rubble of a house that had burned near the Tennessee-Virginia border four years before, in the spring of 2000. Deep in the smoldering basement, seared to the concrete slab, I'd found the bones of a man's pelvis and legs—and, oddly, *only* his pelvis and legs. Thirty minutes later, and ten feet away, I found the rest of his skeleton—his skull, spine, and arms—as well as a nickel-sized disk of melted lead pooled beside the vertebrae. The man had been shot first, I realized, then blasted in half by dynamite, in an attempt to destroy the body. When that had failed—it's actually quite difficult to destroy a body—the killer had finally torched the house, hoping to make the death look accidental. He might have had a better chance of getting away with it if he'd reunited the two halves of the corpse . . . and if he'd removed the bullet from the dead man's spine. Fortunately for our side, most killers aren't geniuses.

My thoughts flashed back to ancient Pompeii, where an entire city had been entombed in volcanic ash: people lying side by side in bed, or sitting on their doorsteps; even dogs dying on their backs, pawing at the choking air. Then my mind took me back even further—nearly three thousand years back, to ancient Persia, where an invading army sacked and burned a citadel called Hasanlu. As the fire raged around the warriors, the citadel's main tower collapsed, toppling onto a stairway, flattening three soldiers in midstride as they ran for their lives. Two of them were side by side; the third man—slightly faster, and forever a few feet ahead—carried a large, ornate vase of pure gold. He clutched the vase—a death grip, in the most literal sense—for thirty centuries, as armies and empires and religions rose and fell above him, just as Hasanlu itself had arisen and flourished, then fallen and vanished. In the end, the gold vase was wrested from the soldier's grasp, not by a pursuing warrior, but by an invader of a very different sort: a scrawny, twentieth-century American archaeologist, armed only with a trowel and a camera—a man who was every bit as astonished by the transaction as the skeletal soldier himself would have been.

Motionless on the California mountainside—part of the tableau myself, though only temporarily—I stared at the dead predator, then at the intended prey. "Lucky guy," I said.

"Yeah," said Kimball. "He was *real* lucky."

I smiled. I hadn't meant the dead man. I'd meant myself, for having lived to see such a thing. So very unlikely. So very dreadful. So very beautiful.

My bubble of gratitude burst a moment later, when McCready added, "Prescott is gonna *hate* this."

Chapter 16

As I stepped through the green-glass door and into the green-glass lobby of San Diego's federal courthouse, I had the odd sensation of plunging into an aquarium, surrounded on all sides by glossy walls, through which I could see brightly lit people outside in the open air, some of them peering through the glass at the submerged specimens. After days in the windswept wilderness atop Otay Mountain, being downtown and indoors was doubly disorienting. The tie I'd cinched around my neck felt more like a noose than a fashion accessory.

The FBI had scheduled a noon press conference at the courthouse to report the positive identification of Richard Janus's body. The plan was straightforward: As the case agent, Prescott would make a brief statement, then hand the microphone to Maddox, the NTSB investigator, to summarize his preliminary crash findings; after that, I would explain the specifics of the identification. It was a no-nonsense, tightly scripted affair, one that would answer a few basic questions but leave others hanging, cloaked in the mystery of an ongoing investigation.

The media briefing would be Act Two, though. Before that, we had to get through Act One, a private briefing for Richard Janus's widow. Prescott led Maddox and me into a conference room outfitted with thick carpet, warm paneling, and heavy drapes. Inside, at a large oak table, sat Carmelita Janus, flanked by a dark-suited man who looked to be a lawyer, and a woman who Prescott had told me was an FBI victim specialist.

Even in grief, Mrs. Janus was striking. I'd noticed it from a distance the day she'd stepped out of the helicopter, hair swirling in the rotor wash; I noticed it even more now, sitting four feet across a table from her. A black-haired, brown-eyed, olive-skinned beauty, she came from an aristocratic family in Mexico. I'd seen dozens of pictures of her in Airlift Relief's newsletters— clad in cargo pants and a sweaty T-shirt, helping unload medical supplies and food for earthquake survivors in Peru; draped in a designer gown, mingling with celebrities at a Hollywood fund-raiser; wearing stained mechanic's coveralls and wielding a wrench, helping Richard change the oil in a DC-3—and none of the pictures was unflattering. For this meeting, she wore a simple black dress, with a single strand of pearls around her neck. Her eyes were red-rimmed and weary-looking, but glittering with anger as well.

I had expected Prescott to make introductions, but the lawyer-looking guy spoke first. "I'm Martin Janus, Richard's brother and attorney and executor. I'm here today in that capacity, but also, primarily, as counsel for Mrs. Janus. Just so we're clear, we won't be answering any questions today, so don't waste your time asking. This whole series of events has been unimaginably traumatic. The FBI's heavy-handed tactics and intimi-dation drove a good man—a dedicated humanitarian—to his death." I glanced at Prescott; I suspected this had something to do with the FBI's operation and with the interagency pissing contest, and I felt sure that Prescott knew exactly what the man meant. But if so, he hid his knowledge well, for his face was a chiseled mask, devoid of expression. "We appreciate the chance to hear what you'll be releasing to the press. More advance notice would have been considerate, of course. But better to hear it face-to-face than on television. So. Tell us what to expect." Having finished his curt speech, he sat back in his chair, laying a hand over one of Mrs. Janus's and giving a quick, reassuring squeeze.

Prescott ignored the attorney, focusing entirely on the widow. "Mrs. Janus," he began, his tone matter-of-fact, "these gentlemen are experts who are assisting us with the crash investigation." He gestured first toward me. "This is Dr. Bill Brockton, a forensic anthropologist from the University of Tennessee. He's an expert on skeletal trauma and human identification." I half nodded, half bowed, conveying what I hoped was both professionalism and sympathy. Her eyes searched mine, as if trying to read my findings there, but Prescott kept going. "And this is Mr. Patrick Maddox, a crash investigator from the National Transportation Safety Board. Mr. Maddox has been analyzing the accident site, the aircraft debris, radio communications, and the plane's flight path from the time it took off until the time it crashed."

Maddox also nodded; Mrs. Janus's eyes seemed to be searching his face—as if she were trying to place him from some prior meeting that she couldn't quite recall—but then Prescott barreled ahead and her attention returned to him. "As you know, Mrs. Janus, we've not yet completed our investigation—of the crash *or* of your husband's activities. But we have positively identified his remains in the aircraft wreckage, and we wanted to share that as soon as possible with you."

One of her eyebrows arched upward cynically. "With me? Or with the media?"

Prescott ignored the jab. "As you know, from the media coverage and from your own visit to the crash site, the aircraft was almost completely destroyed by the impact and the fire. That made identifying your husband's remains challenging. That's why we brought in Dr. Brockton—he's one of the country's leading identification experts."

She looked at me with what appeared to be a mixture of pain and doubt. "So Richard's body was badly burned? 'Burned beyond recognition,' is that how you people say it?"

This wasn't going to be easy, I realized. "Actually, Mrs. Janus, there was no body—not an intact one. There's no delicate way to put this, I'm afraid, and I'm sorry about that. Your husband's body was severely fragmented by the force of the impact. Fragmented and incinerated. Again, my apologies for being so blunt."

Her gaze didn't waver. "You're saying that all you found were burned bits and pieces of him?" I winced, then nodded reluctantly. "Then how can you be sure it's Richard? Have you done DNA testing?"

"No, ma'am," I said. "DNA tends to be destroyed by fire, although it's possible we could find some in the teeth." I touched the side of my jaw. "The molars can sometimes protect the DNA, if the fire's not too hot. But the best way to make an identification in a case like this—the fastest and most reliable way—is to match the teeth to dental records." I slid a manila folder across the table to her. "We've recovered almost all the teeth, and several of them had very distinctive features, which we were able to match to x-rays and photographs." She opened the chart and looked at the top image—a close-up of the chipped incisors we'd found—and then flipped to the second photo. When she saw it, she flinched, and I mentally kicked myself for not having warned her about the photo. It was an eight-by-ten enlargement of her husband's smiling face, his lips parted in a broad, boyish grin, red arrows pointing to the chips in the central incisors. *Like seeing a ghost,* I thought, flushing at my insensitivity. *An annotated ghost.* Regaining her composure, she leafed more guardedly through the remaining images: more close-ups of teeth—the corkscrew-root canine and the Carabelli-cusp molar—followed by dental charts and x-rays. She paused when she came to a photo that showed a tangle of burned wires and circuitry. "That's a spinal cord stimulator," I told her, "or what's left of it. According to your husband's medical records, he had it implanted three years ago. To help alleviate back pain."

"I am aware of why he had it implanted."

Her rebuke was subtle, but it was there. And it was probably justified. She looked up at me, so I went on. "The next page is a copy of the spinal x-ray he had taken after the surgery. You can see the electrical leads going into the spine; the impulse generator was implanted just under the skin on his left hip."

"I know where it was implanted," she said—another rebuke—still studying the x-ray. "And you found this in his body?"

"Well," I said, somewhat off balance, "as I mentioned, the body was . . . not intact. But yes, when we removed the frame of the pilot's seat, we found the device with the bones of the pelvis and the spine. The teeth are really the basis for the positive identification of your husband's remains; the spinal cord stimulator is just added corroboration." I expected her to ask more questions, but she gave a brief nod, closed the folder, and slid it aside to her brother-in-law. Prescott nudged me and nodded, so I reached into my jacket pocket and pulled out a small envelope. I had expected him to do this part, but he'd demurred, delegating it to me. "We also found this," I said, handing her the envelope. "I think I've seen it in pictures of Richard. In the newsletter."

"The newsletter?"

"Yes, ma'am. My wife and I are . . . We're on the Airlift Relief mailing list."

"I see," she said, her tone neutral and her expression unreadable. As she turned the envelope to raise the flap, the chain inside shifted and slid, rasping softly. As she opened the envelope and tipped the pendant into her palm, she gasped and seemed on the verge of a sob, but she squelched it—fought it back might be more accurate—as if she felt it important not to reveal any weakness or emotion to us.

After a few moments of awkward silence, Prescott cleared his throat to get her attention. "Mrs. Janus, there's something else we wanted to let you know before the media briefing," he said. "In addition to your husband, we found the remains of another person at the crash site."

Her eyes widened, and she clutched at her brother-in-law's hand, the tendons in her hand pulled taut as bowstrings, a spiderwork of ropy blue veins crisscrossing above them. "Who?"

"We don't know his name yet," Prescott told her. "But we believe he was an illegal immigrant from Mexico. Apparently—"

She cut in. "But who *was* he? What was he doing on the plane?"

"He wasn't on it," he said, and she looked baffled—as baffled as I had felt the day before, when we'd found the bodies of the man and the mountain lion. "Apparently he was on the ground when the plane hit," Prescott explained. "Wrong place, wrong time. We think he'd crossed the border recently—possibly even the night of the crash. If Dr. Brockton is correct, the man took a fall in the dark and was lying there, injured, when the plane hit."

"My God," she breathed. "That poor man." Oddly, she seemed more upset by this stranger's death than by her husband's. I remembered Prescott's questions about Richard's life insurance policy, and for the first time I found myself wondering if she might have had something to do with her husband's death. *Was she unhappy in the marriage? Could she—a Mexican, after all—be the real link to the drug lord Guzmán?* I felt her eyes on me, and I realized that I was staring at her intently. I flushed, hoping she wasn't able to read my suspicious thoughts. After a moment, she turned back to Prescott. "Are you sure that this other man's death was just a coincidence?"

"Not a hundred percent," Prescott conceded. "But it's the best explanation for what we found. I'll let Dr. Brockton explain it in more detail."

She looked at me again, her face neutral and mask-like now. Opening a second manila folder, I pulled out four photos and slid them across the table to her. "The picture on top shows the wreckage of the aircraft's nose. The nose hit first, obviously, so it was the last layer we got to as we excavated down through the debris." Her eyes flicked rapidly across the image, scanning and then lingering, scanning and then lingering, and I wondered if she was searching the image for traces of her husband's remains. When she looked up, I continued. "The next picture shows what we found underneath the nose—crushed between the nose and the rock face of the mountainside." She flipped to the second photo. As she studied the image, her eyes narrowed, and I could tell that in spite of herself, she, too, was fascinated by the grim tableau. "As you can see, the man wasn't alone on the mountainside when the plane hit. There was a mountain lion just above him—in the act of pouncing on him, as best we can tell—at the moment of impact. It's like a freeze-frame image of the moment they died." She shook her head slightly—not in doubt, I sensed, but in wonder. "The last two pictures are close-ups. As you can see from those, the man and the mountain lion were crushed directly against the mountainside—frankly, if you'll forgive my bluntness once more, we had to scrape them off the rocks. That tells us they were definitely *outside* the plane, not *inside*."

I was about to launch into more detail when I felt Prescott's foot nudging me under the table, and he smoothly took the reins from me. "Obviously this was not the focus of our work up there, Mrs. Janus—far from it, but it's the sort of thing the media is likely to play up, so we wanted to make sure you knew about it."

Instead of acknowledging this, she turned to the NTSB investigator. "Mr. Maddox, I have two questions for you. First, was my husband's crash an accident, suicide, or murder?"

Maddox blinked. "Well . . . I'm not sure we can answer that question. I can't, at any rate." He shot a quick look at Prescott, but Prescott ignored him, so he went on. "What I *can* do is tell you that I've seen no evidence of mechanical or structural failure, sabotage, explosives, or anything remotely suggesting an attack on the aircraft. I've also seen no signs that your husband ever lost control." He seemed to shift gears—to take a step back into "briefing" mode—and continued, sounding more at ease. "He took off normally, made a climbing turn, changed course, and then leveled off. All those maneuvers were smoothly executed." Maddox, too, had brought a folder of visuals to the meeting, but unlike me, he doled out the images one by one instead of giving her the whole set at once. "These are diagrams showing the aircraft's radar track and altitude, from just after takeoff until the moment of impact." He slid the first image across the table to her. "This one shows the radar track, superimposed on a map of Brown Field and the surrounding area. The red arrows indicate significant events in the flight, as well as the time they occurred. As you can see, the radar picks up the aircraft almost immediately after takeoff. It flies northeast for three miles—about sixty seconds. Then, over Otay Lake, it turns south, toward Mexico, shortly before leveling off. It continues south for another thirty seconds, the remainder of the flight." She looked up, her face grim but expectant, and he slid the next page across the table. "This second diagram plots the aircraft's altitude against the profile of the terrain. As you can see, a mile from the summit, the plane levels off at thirty-three hundred feet"—he reached across the table and, with the tip of a pen, indicated a spot on the line—"but the terrain continues rising steeply. So on that particular course, at that altitude, the collision was inevitable." He waved the pen over the pair of diagrams, as if it were a wand, conjuring up the plane's final moments. "Taken together, these indicate that the aircraft was in controlled flight the entire time. Again, nothing wrong with the plane, as far as we can tell at this point. Nothing obviously wrong with the pilot, either, judging from the flight path—no indications that he suffered a heart attack or seizure or stroke." He paused briefly, then asked, "Are you aware of any medical problems that might have incapacitated him?"

"No. Richard was a strong and healthy man."

Maddox nodded. "Let me go back to the question I said I couldn't answer. Without any radio communications or other information that would shed light, I can't say whether he hit the mountain accidentally or intentionally. On the one hand—the 'accident' hand—there's no lights on that mountain, so even though it's big, it's almost invisible on a moonless night, especially if there's any haze—and there *was* some haze that night. If he didn't have a terrain warning alert on his GPS system, or if he hadn't studied the aviation sectional chart closely—and frankly, the peak altitude of that mountain is printed in *very* small type—he might not have realized he was headed straight for it." He paused, gave a pained frown. "On the other hand—the 'intentional' hand; the 'suicide' hand—if he *did* intend to take his life, he flew that plane in a way that would guarantee the outcome. And would minimize the risk of killing or injuring anyone else."

"But he did," she said. "He did kill someone else."

"One-in-a-million odds," Maddox replied. "One in a billion."

To my surprise, she gave a small, ironic smile. "Not much comfort to that unlucky one."

"No, ma'am, I suppose not." A long silence ensued. Finally he prompted, "Did you have another question for me, Mrs. Janus?" She looked puzzled. "You said you had two questions for me. The first was whether it was murder, an accident, or suicide. Is there something else you'd like to ask me?"

"Ah. Yes. Was my husband's death painful?"

Maddox shook his head emphatically. "No, ma'am. As I say, that mountain's essentially invisible. He might not have seen it till the last second; maybe not at all. And at that speed—four hundred miles an hour—he would have died instantly. A millisecond. Less than the blink of an eye."

She shifted her attention to me. "Dr. Brockton? Do you agree?"

"Absolutely," I assured her. "He didn't feel a thing." I believed—and I prayed—that it was the truth.

Prescott had scheduled the press conference for the building's largest courtroom. Even so, it was jammed. A forest of camera tripods had sprung up around the perimeter and in the aisles, and nearly every seat was taken. On the cameras, as Prescott led Maddox and me to a podium in front of the judge's bench, I saw logos for CNN, NBC, ABC, CBS, Fox, E!, and a dozen other cable networks and local stations.

"Good afternoon," Prescott began briskly. "I'm Special Agent Miles Prescott of the FBI's San Diego field office. With me are Mr. Patrick Maddox, a crash investigator from the National Transportation Safety Board, and Dr. William Brockton, a forensic anthropologist from the University of Tennessee. Mr. Maddox and Dr. Brockton will brief you on their findings, but before I turn the podium over to them, I'll start by confirming that we have positively identified the remains of Richard Janus. Mr. Janus was the pilot of the jet that crashed the morning of June 19. He did indeed die in the crash, and he was the only person aboard the aircraft."

The reporters shouted questions, but Prescott motioned for silence. "Please hold your questions until the end." He then summoned Maddox to the podium to reprise what he'd told Mrs. Janus, and once Maddox was done, he brought me up to do the same. After I'd finished, Prescott opened the floor for questions. Maddox swiftly dispensed with the idea that the plane had been shot down or sabotaged or bombed, as well as the suggestion that Janus had lost control of the aircraft, and then I answered a few basic questions: yes, I was confident that teeth were as reliable as DNA for purposes of identification; no, I didn't think DNA testing would be possible, though we would certainly give it a try; yes, it was true that I ran a facility called the Body Farm, where corpses were allowed to rot in the name of research.

Then Prescott himself asked a question—one that he'd told me to expect, asking me to save my final images until he gave me the go-ahead. "Dr. Brockton," he said, "did you find anything noteworthy at the crash site besides the remains of Richard Janus?" I raised my eyebrows inquiringly, to make sure I understood his cue correctly, and he gave a slight nod.

"Noteworthy? Yes," I said. "In fact, I'd say it was quite remarkable. Under the wreckage, crushed by the nose of the plane, we found the body of another man—a Mexican immigrant, as best we can tell. We also found the body of a mountain lion, which appeared to be pouncing on the man at the moment of the crash." The end of my sentence was nearly drowned out by a chorus of gasps, exclamations, and questions as I flashed the image of the two carcasses flattened against the rocks. If Prescott had intended to create a stir, his strategy had succeeded in spades. Catching my eye, he pointed to the screen and spun an index finger in a go-ahead signal. I clicked forward to the close-ups, and the room buzzed again. When the buzz subsided, I described in more detail how we'd found them—man and beast—plastered to the bluff's bare rock, and how the insect activity confirmed the freshness of their deaths.

After a barrage of questions, Prescott returned to the podium, checked his watch conspicuously, and began winding things down. I was admiring his media-management savvy—if he'd scripted the entire event, it couldn't have gone more smoothly—when a voice from the back of the room interrupted brashly. "What about the FBI's arrest warrant for Richard Janus?" Everyone, including Prescott, suddenly sought the speaker. The crowd parted slightly as a young reporter—the reporter the FBI agents had frog-marched to the TV news helicopter a few days before—stepped into the center aisle. "Mike Malloy, Fox Five News," he announced. Prescott raised both hands, pointed to the rear corners of the room—corners where two FBI agents were standing—and then aimed both fingers at Malloy. "My sources tell me the FBI was planning to arrest Richard Janus the night he died," Malloy shouted over the din. "What role did the FBI play in Richard Janus's flight, and his crash? Did the FBI drive him to suicide?" By now the two agents had muscled through the crowd and taken hold of Malloy's elbows. But the damage was done: half a dozen television cameras had swiveled toward the reporter and recorded the dramatic turn of events, and Prescott—his jaw clenched, a large vein at his forehead standing out like a purple tree root—gestured to the agents to release the reporter.

Prescott gave the microphone three quick, attention-getting taps—taps so hard, they popped like gunshots. "As most of you know," he said, "we have a policy of not commenting on open criminal investigations. But in view of the inflammatory, irresponsible nature of the question, I will respond briefly." The crowd fell silent. "We have no indication that Richard Janus meant to commit suicide. In fact, we believe he was attempting to flee to Mexico. As you've heard, he had filed a flight plan to Las Vegas, Nevada. Almost immediately after takeoff, though, he changed course, turning directly toward Mexico. He was less than two miles from the border when the aircraft struck the peak of Otay Mountain. A hundred feet higher and twenty seconds more, and he'd have made it." Again the room buzzed; again Prescott signaled for quiet, waiting for quite a while before he got it. "The night of his death, we were indeed preparing to take him into custody, on charges of drug trafficking and money laundering, among others. Behind the façade of a humanitarian organization, Richard Janus was a drug trafficker. He faced multiple felony charges; he faced millions of dollars in fines—and life behind bars." Over the din of shouted questions and whirring cameras, Prescott raised his voice one more time. "That concludes this briefing. No more questions." He stepped away from the podium, beckoned curtly to Maddox and me, and led us toward the side door.

We were followed by a hail of questions about the criminal allegations—amid the din, I heard the words "cocaine" and "DEA" and "cartel" and "Guzmán"— but Prescott paid no attention. As he opened the door, I glanced back at the clamoring throng, and suddenly I caught sight of a familiar face at the edge of the crowd—a face that looked oddly out of place in the scrum of scrubbed young journalists. The face belonged to a man who was fat and aging; even from a distance, his reddish-gray hair and sallow skin looked unkempt, unclean, and greasy. And somehow, over the noise of the crowd, I heard—or imagined I heard—a moist, whispering sound: the sound of labored breath, wheezing in and out of a mountain of flesh.

It made the hair on the back of my neck stand up, and I froze. A moment later, I felt Prescott's hand on my elbow, leading me out of the room. Ten minutes later, still shaky, I was in a black Suburban, with one of the younger agents driving me to the airport. This time the airport was San Diego International, not Brown Field; this time my ride wouldn't be the FBI director's sleek

Gulfstream, but a cattle-car commercial airliner—one where I'd been assigned a middle seat in the last row.

But it didn't matter. I'd done my job, as Kathleen had urged me to do, and I was finished.

I was headed home.

Home to Kathleen.

Part Two

The Cudgel

No mortal could cross the threshold of birth or
death until Janus had wielded both the objects
he held in his hands: both the key and the
cudgel. Passages and transformations are never
easy or cheap, and the price is often reckoned
in pounds of flesh and buckets of tears.

—Sofia Paxton, *Ancient Teachings,*
Modern Wisdom

And the LORD said to Satan, "Have you
considered my servant Job, that there is none
like him on the earth, a blameless and upright
man, who fears God and turns away from

evil?" Then Satan answered the LORD, "Does Job fear God for no reason? Hast thou not put a hedge about him and his house and all that he has, on every side? Thou hast blessed the work of his hands, and his possessions have increased in the land. But put forth thy hand now, and touch all that he has, and he will curse thee to thy face."

—Job 1:8–11

You can plan all you want to. You can lie in your morning bed and fill whole notebooks with schemes and intentions. But within a single afternoon, within hours or minutes, everything you plan and everything you have fought to make yourself can be undone as a slug is undone when salt is poured on him. And right up to the moment when you find yourself dissolving into foam you can still believe you are doing fine.

—Wallace Stegner, *Crossing to Safety*

Chapter 17

The black FBI SUV—the one that had whisked me from the press conference to the airport—screeched to the curb of San Diego International at 1:09. I was cutting it close; my flight was at 1:44, but I could see the Delta ticket counter just inside the glass doors, and the line was short. "Want me to wait?" asked the driver, another of Prescott's seemingly infinite supply of young, well-groomed agents.

"Nah, I'll be fine. Thanks for the lift." I hopped out, scurried inside, and got in line with my bag and the plastic bin of teeth and bone shards. Only two people were ahead of me, and three ticket agents were working the counter. *Piece of cake,* I thought, hoping that the security screeners wouldn't freak out and waylay me over the remains. One of the agents finished checking in a passenger, but then, instead of calling "next," he turned and walked through a door, disappearing from view. I glanced at my watch; it was now 1:12. Suddenly nervous, I divided my attention between the two remaining ticket agents on duty, willing them to hurry. One of the agents was a sour-faced older woman who wasted no time on pleasantries; the other, a pretty twentysomething, chatted and laughed with her customer, a lanky young man whose British accent she seemed to find charming. Sour Face quickly dispensed with one of the two people ahead of me; incredibly, Pretty Girl continued chatting with the Brit as if she had the entire afternoon to devote to the conversation. "Oh, I *love* London," she gushed. "It's so much more *continental* than our American cities." *Oh, please,* I thought, and then—checking my watch again—*Oh, please hurry!* Her colleague, Sour Face, sent another traveler on his way and took the next in line. There was no longer anyone ahead of me, but I was running out of time. I waved my arms to catch the girl's attention; it took a while, but finally she looked at me, and I tapped my watch. "Sir, I'll be with you in a moment," she said, her voice less animated than when she was chatting with the Brit. The man looked around and seemed to have a clearer sense of my problem, or more compassion, for he took his boarding pass, thanked her, and then gestured me toward the counter.

"Sorry to rush you," I said, handing her my itinerary, "but I'm cutting it pretty close here."

She studied it, frowning. "Sir, that flight leaves at 1:44," she said. "That's less than thirty minutes from now. I'm sorry, but I can't check you in."

"My watch says 1:14," I said. I was fibbing, but only by two minutes. "And I'm not checking baggage. All I have is this carry-on."

"I'm sorry, sir. It's 1:15. And the thirty-minute cutoff is a TSA rule. Homeland Security."

"Come on. Sixty seconds. Besides, I was in line with time to spare. If you hadn't been flirting with that guy ahead of me, I'd have been standing here two minutes ago."

She flushed, but she didn't budge; in fact, her expression hardened. "Look at me," I pleaded. "Do I look like a terrorist? I'm a college professor." Fumbling at my waist, I unclipped my TBI shield and laid it on the counter. "Look. I'm a consultant to the Tennessee Bureau of Investigation. I just came from helping the FBI. I'm one of the good guys."

But she had stopped making eye contact. "Sir, I'm sorry. I don't make the rules. The best I can do is book you on the next available flight."

I sighed. "When is that?"

"Tomorrow morning at six-thirty."

I stared, dumbfounded. "You're kidding me, right?" The look she gave me indicated that she wasn't. "It's still *lunchtime*. You mean to tell me there's no way to get to Knoxville—no way even to *start* toward Knoxville—until tomorrow?"

"That's correct, sir. Do you want me to book you on that six-thirty A.M. flight?" Her fingers clattered rapidly over the keyboard. "That would get you into Knoxville at . . . 3:53 P.M."

Unbelievable, I thought. The idea of hanging around, killing time, for the next sixteen hours seemed unbearable. There had to be a way to get home sooner. "What about Los Angeles?"

"What about it? What is it you're asking, sir?"

"How far away is L.A.?"

She shrugged, looking as if she might be getting irritated. "Two, two and a half hours by car. Fifty minutes by air."

"Surely LAX has more flights today. When's the next plane to LAX? If I caught that, could I get home tonight?"

Her fingers clacked and clattered, with more force this time. "The next flight to Los Angeles is at 1:46."

"I'll take it. Get me on it."

"Sir, it's now 1:17. That flight leaves in twenty-nine minutes. I can't put you on it."

"But I was standing right here at 1:15. Thirty-one minutes before the flight."

"But you weren't *booked* on that flight, sir. You still aren't. And you *can't* be—it's not possible. Those are the *rules,* sir."

I wanted to scream. Instead, through clenched teeth, I said, "And when is the next flight to L.A. that I *can* be on?"

More furious keyboarding. "Four P.M. Arriving 4:48."

"And when could I get the hell out of Los Angeles for Knoxville?"

By now she, too, had given up all pretense of cheery politeness. "There's an eleven P.M. to Detroit, with connections to Atlanta."

"Come on, there has to be something earlier than that."

"Yes, sir. There's a 1:45 flight from LAX to Atlanta. But obviously you can't take that. Then there's nothing eastbound until eleven o'clock tonight."

"Christ," I muttered. "And what time would I get to Knoxville? If nothing went wrong in Detroit?"

"At 10:31 tomorrow morning."

I no longer wanted to scream. Now I wanted to weep. Feeling more defeated than I had in ages, I fished out my wallet and sighed, "I'll take it."

Exiting the terminal at McGhee Tyson Airport the next morning—after spending what felt like an eternity shoehorned in the last row of seats to Detroit and then again to Knoxville, directly in front of lavatories that seemed not to have been cleaned in weeks—I was stunned when I stepped into the swelter of Tennessee's summer. On the sauna-dry slopes of Otay Mountain, my sweat had evaporated almost instantly; here, it was as if I had swum into a steam bath. Or a sweat bath. *How soon we forget,* I thought, hunching a shoulder to mop my brow. *But how fast we're reminded.*

Heading toward the parking deck, I suddenly stopped, muttering, "Well, crap." My truck wasn't in the parking deck, I'd just remembered; it was parked a half mile away, at Cherokee Aviation, the charter air terminal where the FBI's Gulfstream had swooped down to fetch me. Looking to my left, across a long ribbon of hot asphalt, I could just make out the truck, shimmering in the distance like a mirage. Slinging the strap of my boxy bag over my sleep-deprived shoulder, I began the trudge.

Ten sweaty minutes later, my sodden shirt plastered to my skin, I unlocked and opened my truck—the rubber weather stripping made a ripping sound as it pulled away from the hot metal of the door frame—and tucked the bag behind the front seat, then cranked the engine and put the air-conditioning on high. Leaving the truck idling, I stepped inside Cherokee to mop off and use the courtesy phone to call Kathleen, as my cell phone's battery had died somewhere between California and Tennessee. But the courtesy phone appeared to be surgically grafted to the ear of a commercial pilot, a glossy-haired, pretty-boy Casanova type in a pseudo-military uniform. I tried hovering, hoping he'd take the hint and finish his conversation; instead, he turned his back and cupped a hand around the mouthpiece. Judging by his quiet murmuring and occasional chuckles, the pilot wasn't filing a flight plan; he appeared to be cooing to a woman he had just bedded or, more likely, hoped to bed, as soon as his next flight was over. Too weary to wait, I returned to my truck and headed toward campus. I would check in at my office, then go surprise Kathleen at hers.

I passed the medical center and crossed the Tennessee River, flowing green and welcoming beneath the high span of the Buck Karnes Bridge. Looking to my right—upstream, between the hospital and a condominium complex—I saw the three-acre patch of woods housing the Body Farm. Across the river, a bit farther upstream, loomed the towering oval of Neyland Stadium, which housed the dingy offices and classrooms and labs of the Anthropology Department.

The river separating these two odd offices of mine was, for reasons I didn't entirely fathom, a powerful touchstone for me. As I crossed the channel on the high span of concrete, I filled my lungs and exhaled loudly—the sound somewhere between a sigh and a hum—feeling myself only now to have truly landed. *Home*, I thought. Smiling, I turned onto Neyland Drive and headed upriver, as reflexively and instinctively as some four-wheeled salmon. Making my way to the stadium, I threaded along the one-lane service road at the base of the grandstands and stopped beside the service tunnel that led to the field's north end zone.

Reaching behind the seat, I unzipped my bag and removed the bin of teeth and bones, then entered the dim, echoing concrete stairwell and headed up one flight of steps: up to my private office, my sanctuary, my hideaway; the place where I holed up when I needed to focus on science and forensics, not bureaucracy. I set the bin on the hallway floor and turned the key in the lock of my door, tugging gently as I twisted, to loosen the deadbolt from the grip of the warped door frame. When the bolt rasped and thunked free, I turned the knob and hipped the door open, then bent down, picked up the bin, and set it on my desk. Then I dialed Peggy, my secretary, who kept watch over the Anthropology Department's main office, a hundred yards away—all the way at the opposite end of the stadium, beneath the south end zone's grandstands. Peggy answered halfway through the first ring. "Anthropology," she said, her voice sounding strange and strained.

"Hi, honey, I'm home," I joked, hoping to ease the tension I heard in her voice.

"Good *God*, where have you been?" Over the past dozen years, I'd heard Peggy sound testy many times. But this was beyond testy—miles beyond it; light-years beyond it.

"San Diego, remember?" I was starting to feel some anxiety myself. "You don't sound too happy to hear from me."

"Three hours ago I would have been happy to hear from you," she snapped. "Yesterday you told me you'd be in first thing this morning. I've been trying to call you for hours."

"Oh, sorry," I said. "There was a problem with my flight. And my phone died. I just got in. What's wrong? Should I come up?"

"You mean to tell me you're on *campus*?" It sounded more like an accusation than a question.

"Well, I am now," I hedged. "My flight landed twenty minutes ago. I drove straight here. Came in the back door. Just now. Literally this minute. I'm down in my other office."

"Would you please come to *this* office instead? Quickly?" The sarcasm would have dripped from her voice if the iciness of her tone hadn't flash-frozen it first.

"You've got me feeling kinda gun-shy," I said. "Want to tell me what this is about?"

"There is a television news crew here from Channel Four in Nashville. They have been camped in my office for the past *three hours*. Please come immediately. If not sooner."

Chapter 18

As I walked in the door of the departmental office, Peggy glowered at me from behind her desk as an attractive young woman—*of Italian ancestry? no, Greek,* I guessed—stood up and turned toward me. I put on what I hoped would pass for a courteous smile. "Hello, I'm Dr. Bill Brockton," I said. "What can I do for you?"

She held out her hand. "Dr. Brockton, I'm Athena Demopoulos, Eyewitness Four News." Her handshake was firm—aggressively firm, as if she were trying to prove something. She nodded slightly toward a pale young man behind her; his frumpy clothes were a stark contrast to her chic, tailored suit. "This is Rick Walters, my cameraman." His handshake, like his clothes, was much more relaxed than hers.

"Ms. Demopoulos, I'm sorry I've kept you waiting," I said. "My flight was delayed, and my phone was dead." Pulling out my pocket calendar, I flipped it open and scanned the current day's empty page. "Did we have an appointment that I failed to write down?"

"No, we didn't. We're investigating a news story that's breaking now. It has come to our attention that you're conducting experiments with human bodies."

"We are indeed," I said cheerily. "I'm not sure I'd call that 'breaking news'—we've been doing it for more than a decade. I guess news travels slowly from here in the hinterlands." I smiled again. "You might have gotten wind of my research a little sooner if the prevailing winds blew from east to west instead of west to east." I winked to make sure she got the joke.

She frowned; I couldn't tell whether she was confused or upset. "I don't think you understand the gravity of the story," she said. "If you'll let me finish, I can make it clear to you. It has come to our attention that you're conducting experiments on the bodies of military veterans. Men who put their lives on the line to defend our American way of life. Do you deny that?"

Her question took me totally off guard. "No, I don't deny it, but I can't confirm it, either," I said.

"Don't be coy, Dr. Brockton."

"I'm *not* being coy," I said. "I'm being blindsided. I have zero information on this. If you've got any information at all, you've got more than I do. How about you start by telling me what you've heard, and where you heard it? How did the story come to you, and why?"

"I can't reveal my sources," she said, her voice a mixture of self-importance and smugness. "But they're quite credible, I assure you. I have the names of at least four veterans whose bodies were sent to you." She rattled off the names. "Are they here? Yes or no? If they are, please tell our viewers—and the families of these four men—what kind of experiments you're doing on them, and why?"

Somehow a microphone had materialized in Athena Demopoulos's hand and had positioned itself directly in front of my face. Meanwhile, the cameraman had hoisted a video camera to his shoulder, and the blinking red light above the lens led me to believe that he was filming. Filming me. I shrugged, shaking my head. "I don't know if they're here."

She gave me a look of disgusted disbelief. "You're saying you don't even keep track of whose bodies you're experimenting on?"

I winced at the phrase *experimenting on*—it made me sound like Josef Mengele, the Nazi death-camp doctor. "No, I'm not saying that at all. What I *am* saying is that we don't refer to our research subjects by name. When bodies come in, we give them case numbers—to protect their privacy—and we always refer to them by those numbers." She looked puzzled, so I explained. "For example, suppose a funeral home brings over a donated body this afternoon—a TV reporter, let's say, whose story on the joys of skydiving didn't turn out quite the way she'd planned." She looked startled by the scenario, which was okay by me. "She'd be the thirty-eighth body donated to us in 2004. That means we—my graduate students and I—would refer to her, and would think of her, as '38-04,' not as Melissa or Carissa or Athena or whatever her name was." She no longer looked startled; now she looked angry. "My point," I said, "is that we *do* keep track of the bodies we have—very careful track—but we also keep their names confidential. So if you'll write down the names, I'll go check our master file." She eyed me suspiciously, as if I were trying to pull a fast one on her, but then pulled out a small notepad and began scrawling names. "By the way," I added, "did your secret source give you the dates these bodies supposedly arrived?" She looked up from the notepad, scowling. "Because if you can narrow down the time, it won't take me as long to check the files. Which means I can answer your question sooner." She added a year beside each name, then ripped the page from the pad.

Before handing me the paper, she held the microphone in my face again. "You haven't answered my other question yet," she said. "Why are you experimenting on these bodies? Have you no respect for the dead?"

"Ms. Stephanopolus—"

"Demopoulos," she corrected sharply.

"Ms. Demopoulos," I resumed, "I assure you, I have enormous respect for the dead."

"You toss them on the ground and let them rot," she shot back. "You call that respect?"

"I call it *research*. We don't 'toss' them; we lay them. Carefully. Respectfully. We conduct scientific research on human decomposition during the extended postmortem interval. It's never been done before."

"Maybe there's a good reason for that," she countered.

"Nobody ever *flew* before," I shot back, "until the Wright brothers did. Were they wrong to study flight?"

She opened her mouth to speak, then closed it. Instead, she looked down, her gaze traveling down to my left hand. Then she locked eyes with me again, her expression now smug. "I see you're wearing a wedding ring, Dr. Brockton," she said. "If your wife died, would you take her to your Body Farm? Would you throw her in the woods, for the bugs and the buzzards to eat?"

If she'd been a man, I might have clenched my fist and hit her. Instead I clenched my jaw and silently counted to ten. Then I asked, in as neutral a tone as I could muster, "Are *you* married, Ms. Demopoulos?"

Her eyes hardened. "That's a personal question. I don't discuss my personal life on camera."

"Neither do I," I said coolly. I reached out and took the names from her. "Now, if you'll have a seat, I'll go check the files."

I hurried down the long, curving corridor beneath the stadium to my other office, at the far end. The walk did me good—partly because it got me away from the reporter, and partly because it allowed me to let off a bit of steam in a way that was more constructive than taking a swing at a TV reporter. I thought back to the way the Fox 5 reporter in San Diego had ambushed Prescott, and I envied the FBI agent his coolness under fire.

Ten minutes after leaving the news crew cooling their heels in Peggy's office, I returned and handed the list back to Athena Demopoulos. I had put a check mark beside each of the names, confirming that all four bodies had indeed been sent to us. "Your sources did get the names right," I told her, "but not the context." I motioned toward the open door of my office. "Please. Come in, and let me explain a little more about what we do." She and the cameraman followed me in. He set up a tripod, latched the camera onto it, and gave her a "ready" nod.

She laid a microphone on the desk. "You admit that you're experimenting on the bodies of military veterans," she began. "How do you justify that?"

"Let me back up and give you a little background first," I began. "So you'll have some context. We get bodies in two ways. From two different sources. About half are donated—in a person's will, or by their next of kin—in exactly the same way bodies are donated to Vanderbilt Medical School, there in Nashville." She seemed on the verge of interrupting, but I held up a finger and kept talking. "Others—and this is the category that includes the four veterans you've asked me about—are bodies that are unclaimed after death. These come to us from medical examiners all over the state." As she processed this piece of information, I hurried on. "If a body goes unclaimed—maybe the person is an unidentified John or Jane Doe; maybe they've got no relatives; maybe their relatives are estranged—whatever the reason, if a body's unclaimed, the cost of burying that body falls on the county where the death occurred. Now, bear with me just a minute more. It costs about a thousand dollars to bury a body, and a lot of Tennessee counties don't have that kind of money to spare. If they send the body to me, it's a win-win: They save money, and our research program grows. And the more research we do—the better we understand how bodies decay after death—the more help we can give police in solving murder cases."

"How? How does letting veterans' bodies rot in the woods help solve murders?"

She wasn't making this easy. I took a breath to collect myself before going on. "By giving us more data on which to base our estimates of time since death. Our research lets us tell the police, with a high degree of scientific certainty, how long ago someone was killed. By comparing the decomposition of the victim's body with what we've observed in our research—and by taking variables like temperature, humidity, and so forth into account—we can help the police narrow down the time of the murder, to within a matter of days or even hours. Earlier, you sounded distressed when you mentioned bugs. Even the bugs are an important part of our research. By knowing what bugs come to feed on a body—and when, and how fast they grow—we can be even more precise."

Her cameraman, I noticed, looked interested in this, but her face registered nothing but disgust. "You still haven't explained why you're conducting these experiments on the bodies of U.S. military veterans."

"It's not like I'm *seeking* the bodies of veterans. Look, when a funeral home or a medical examiner sends me a body, I don't do a background check. I don't investigate whether the deceased was a veteran, just like I don't investigate whether he was a priest, or a prisoner, or a teacher, or a TV reporter. I say, 'Thank you very much,' and I assign a case number and a research question, and I try to learn something from that body."

"But why don't you think veterans deserve a dignified burial?"

"I *do*." I turned my palms up. "I think *everybody* deserves a dignified burial. The last thing I'm trying to do is keep a veteran—or anyone else, for that matter—from getting a decent, dignified burial. The thing is, Ms. Demopoulos, when these four men died, no one claimed them. No one *tried* to arrange a dignified burial for them. If you've come across relatives who *want* these bodies, I'm happy to *give* them the bodies. They'll be a little the worse for wear now, but unfortunately, I can't help that." I shrugged, trying to read her expression. "Does that answer your questions?"

"It's a step in the right direction," she said. "But we also need to see your facility. The Body Farm, that's what you call it, right?"

I felt myself getting testy again. "That's what a lot of people call it."

"And you think that name shows respect for the dead?"

This woman had a knack for nettling me. "I'm not the one who came up with it," I snapped. "An FBI agent coined the name, and it stuck. So that's what it's usually called—by police, by medical examiners, and by reporters. Reporters who—up until now—have been able to understand that our research helps the good guys catch the bad guys." I shouldn't have needled her that way, but she'd gotten under my skin, and I was mad. What was it Mark Twain said about journalists— "never argue with people who buy ink by the barrel"? I was battling a person who bought videotape by the truckload, but it was too late to back out now. "As for taking you out there and showing you around—letting you shoot footage—I can't do that."

"Why not?"

"It's a research facility, not a tourist attraction. The work we do there is sensitive. And it's certainly not fodder for tabloid television."

She flushed, and I could tell that she, too, felt nettled now. "This is not tabloid television," she practically hissed. "This is journalism in the public interest. We are investigating a major news story here—the disrespect being shown here to the bodies of American servicemen. I will go to the university's president or board of trustees if that's what it takes to get your cooperation."

"I *am* cooperating," I insisted. "I've checked our files, I've confirmed what you asked me to confirm, and I've explained—or *tried* to explain—what we do, and why. But I can't let you go roaming around in there with your camera, looking for lurid footage. Because turning you loose in there with a camera and a big chip on your shoulder? *That* would be treating the dead with disrespect."

She stood up so suddenly her chair scraped the floor and nearly toppled backward. If looks could kill, the glare Athena Demopoulos shot in my direction would have laid me out like a lightning bolt, and I'd have joined the ranks of the dead—veterans and civilians alike, indistinguishable in death—who were mustered out, and falling apart, behind the fence of the Body Farm. "Cut," she snapped at the cameraman. "We're out of here." Then, to me: "But we *will* be back."

Of that I felt sure. Awfully and dreadfully sure.

Pressing the heels of my hands into my temples, I worked my scalp in slow circles, first in one direction, then in the other, trying—but failing—to release the tension. Next I closed my aching eyes and rubbed them with the thumb and fingers of my right hand.

The Nashville reporter had the basic facts correct: We did have the remains of four veterans at the Body

Farm. All four had come from Nashville. All four had died, during the prior eighteen months, at the VA Hospital there, and when no next of kin had claimed their remains, Nashville's M.E. had sent the bodies to me for research. Nothing underhanded or sinister had been done; the men had simply died alone and unloved. In that regard, those four—the Nashville Four—were like too many other veterans, especially Vietnam War veterans.

Vietnam: I myself had been lucky enough—young enough—to stay out of the war. I turned eighteen during the war's final year; the draft hadn't yet ended, but I had a high lottery number—high enough that I didn't get drafted. By that time most Americans seemed to agree that Vietnam had been a foreign-policy failure: an unwinnable fight, and a terrible waste of lives. As a result, our conflicted feelings—our national shame, it might even be called—had created an unwritten but undeniably tragic domestic policy: a policy of pretending that Vietnam had never happened, and of turning a blind, indifferent eye to Vietnam vets and their postwar troubles.

The College of Social Work at UT was large and well regarded. One of the faculty there—a friend of mine—had made a long-term study of Vietnam vets. What he'd found had shocked me. Twenty or more years after returning from Southeast Asia, four out of five Vietnam vets still suffered from chronic symptoms of PTSD, posttraumatic stress disorder. Compared to nonveterans, they also had higher rates of alcoholism, drug abuse, depression, and suicide. And unlike veterans of World War II, who were widely celebrated as national heroes, Vietnam vets tended to be unappreciated, unacknowledged, sometimes even scorned. It was almost as if we were all avoiding eye contact with a homeless beggar—a beggar who might, come to think of it, be a Vietnam veteran.

I didn't know the specific stories or circumstances of the four veterans who had ended up at the Body Farm. All I knew was that in the end, no one had cared enough to claim them, to arrange for the honor guard and the folded flag and the well-kept grave their service should have earned them.

Who had contacted Channel 4 about the story, and why—and why *now*, at this particular time? Initially, I'd assumed that the reporter was pursuing the Janus story, and when she'd started talking about veterans, I'd wondered if she was working some sort of angle related to Janus's Air America stint in Southeast Asia. But her barrage of questions and accusations had quickly made it clear that this was a Tennessee story—a Body Farm story—and a veteran story. For all I knew, we might've had dozens of veterans' corpses at the Body Farm over the past dozen years. Was it really high-minded concern about the treatment of dead soldiers that was behind this, or was there some unspoken subtext—some power play or hidden agenda? The reporter had dodged my question about who her source was. If I pressed the point, I felt sure that she'd bristle and bluster and begin waving the freedom-of-the-press flag as if she were its lone standard-bearer and staunchest defender.

Still rubbing my temples and eyes with one hand, I used the other hand to call Kathleen. "I'm back," I told her glumly. "I need you to feel sorry for me for just a minute."

"I didn't realize it was such a hardship to come home," she said, her tone hovering somewhere between teasing and defensive.

"I didn't either," I said. "I was really looking forward to it. But then I had the trip from hell. And then things got even worse."

"Poor baby. What's wrong? Tell me about it."

So I did, skipping the trip and going straight to the ambush interview by the TV reporter.

"Sweeps week," she said scornfully.

"What?"

"Sweeps week. It's when the networks pull out all the stops. They measure their ratings—their

viewers—during sweeps week. The higher their ratings, the more they can charge for ads. So they show
blockbuster movies, sensational stories, anything they
think'll get viewers. Don't take it personally, hon. It's
all about money, not about you."

"It sure *feels* like it's about me," I squawked. "It's
my work—my facility; my reputation—in the cross-
hairs of that . . . that . . ."

"Language, Bill. *Language.*"

"That *reporter.* That mudslinging, muckraking,
holier-than-thou reporter. Am I allowed to call her
that?"

"Of course, sweetheart—to me. I wouldn't say it
to her, though. Not unless you want every television
viewer in Nashville to think you're a grumpy old man."

"Grumpy? *Me?* Hmmph," I said. "I'll be nice as pie.
She'll be eating out of my hand."

"If I catch her lips anywhere near any part of you,
her next story can be about her colonoscopy. The one I
administer with her own video camera."

I laughed, in spite of myself. "I should've come to
your office instead of my office," I said. "I'm thinking
I might have gotten a warmer welcome."

"I'd've been nice as pie," she cooed. "You'd've been
eating out of my hand."

"Hold that thought for a few hours," I told her.
My spousal flirting was cut short by the buzz of my

intercom. "Rats," I said. "Peggy's buzzing me. Probably more bad news. See you at home." I pressed the intercom button. "Tell me you've good news, Peggy."

"Can't," she answered. "You've told me never to lie to you. Do you want door number one, or door number two?"

"Excuse me?"

"You have two callers on hold. The dean's on line one, and the general counsel's on line two."

"The general counsel? As in Amanda Whiting, UT's top legal eagle?"

"Bingo."

"Jeez," I said. "If line three rings, don't answer—it'll be the Angel of Death calling."

"No, he's coming to see you in person," she cracked. "He'll be here in ten minutes."

"Swell," I said. "I'll tell the dean to talk slow—that way maybe I can skip the lawyer altogether." The truth was, I rather liked the general counsel, but given that the Channel 4 reporter was probably already badgering her, I doubted that she was calling with good news. The dean, on the other hand, had long been a reliable, agreeable ally, from the moment I'd first pitched my unorthodox research program to him, years ago. *How many years? Ten? No, twelve,* I realized as I pressed the blinking button. *That was 1992. Where does the time go?*

"Hello," I said to the dean. "Are you calling to fire me?"

"I can't," he said. "You've got tenure. Good thing, too, because you've stirred up a hell of a hornet's nest."

"I didn't stir it up," I protested. "I just happened to be standing near the tree. Somebody else took a whack at the hornet's nest. I don't know who, and I don't know why."

"Actually, I'm calling to make sure you know I'm in your corner," he said. "You do good work. You're a credit to the university. Let me know if I can help."

"You good with a pair of tweezers?"

"How's that?"

"It might take you and me both to pull all the stingers out of my hide."

He chuckled. "You'll be all right. Good luck, Bill."

"I need it. Amanda Whiting's on the other line."

"Ah. You *do* need it," he agreed, and for once I wished he weren't quite so agreeable.

General Counsel Amanda Whiting was less agreeable than the dean had been. "We've got one hell of a mess on our hands," she said. Her words were muddled, and for a bizarre moment I wondered if she was drinking. Then I heard the clatter of a knife on a plate, and I realized she was eating. "How do we clean this up and make sure it never happens again?"

"I've offered to give the bodies back," I told her. "If anybody takes me up on it, I'll gladly deliver the bodies myself. As to how to make sure it doesn't happen again, I suppose we can check with the Veterans Administration every time we get a body. But what a pain. We screen bodies for AIDS and hepatitis; I didn't realize we needed to screen them for prior occupation."

"We live in litigious times, Bill. We can't afford to risk lawsuits—million-dollar claims for pain and suffering—filed by relatives of those science-project guinea pigs you've got rotting on the ground."

"What an eloquent description," I snapped. "Mind if I borrow that? It would give that Nashville reporter a much better grasp of the merit and dignity of our research. 'Science-project guinea pigs, rotting on the ground': Have I got that right?"

"Sorry," she said. "That was out of line. You know that's not what I really think. I'm looking at it as a lawyer; putting it in the worst possible way—the way a plaintiff's attorney would, if somebody slapped us with a lawsuit. It could happen."

"Someone could claim my research caused pain and suffering? Seriously?"

"Seriously."

"What about the pain and suffering of dying alone? Where were these sensitive, caring relatives when these poor guys were staring death in the face, with no one to hold their hand or say how much they'd meant?"

"It stinks," she agreed. "No pun intended. But we need to tread carefully here. *I* know you have respect for the dead. We just need to make sure that others know that, too." She paused, then cleared her throat. "The reporter's pushing hard to get in."

"No surprise there." I sighed. "Look, I think it's a bad, bad idea. We turn her loose in there with a camera, she'll crucify us. You've never been out to the research facility. It's not pretty, Amanda, what the body goes through after death. That's why the funeral industry is so huge—that's why we spend billions of dollars a year to make the dead look like the living. Because we don't want to confront the ugly reality of our mortality. The buggy, bloated, putrefying reality."

"Bill, I'm eating *lunch* here. Or was."

"If there's rice on your plate, make sure it's not wiggling," I said. She groaned, and I laughed. "But seriously, we don't want her in there with a camera. She's got an ax to grind. And she wants to put our necks—*my* neck—on the chopping block. Tell her no."

There was silence on the other end of the line. "We're in a bit of a bind here, Bill," she said finally. "We're a publicly funded institution. We're responsible—we're *accountable*—to the taxpayers of Tennessee. We don't have the option of concealing what we're doing with their money."

"I'm not trying to conceal it," I said. "I'm just trying not to rub their noses in it. Because frankly, even though this work is important, it's not real pleasant. You remember that old TV commercial—for shampoo or hair color?—that showed a gorgeous woman running toward a guy? Slow motion, her long blond hair bounding up and down, up and down, with every stride?"

"Yeah, that rings a bell. Vaguely. Your point being . . . ?"

"Remember the tag line? 'The closer he gets, the better you look'? The Body Farm's not like that, Amanda. We're the opposite. The closer you get, the *worse* we look. And the worse we smell."

"I get it, I get it," she said. "But we have to find some way to accommodate this journalist. It's a legitimate news story. It might be slanted, it might be unfair, it might be unfavorable—"

"No 'might be' about it," I snapped. "It's a total hatchet job. I wish I knew who put her onto this, and why."

"I've done some asking around," she said. "Sounds like it was a disgruntled employee at the VA Hospital.

They weren't even going after you—they wanted the hospital to do better by dead and dying vets. It was the reporter who made the story about us."

"So why do we even have to cooperate?"

"Because now it *is* about us, Bill. And even if it's bad news, it's news, and we've got to make a good-faith effort to cooperate. Otherwise, the story snowballs— it's no longer just about these four dead veterans, it's about *us*, about our secrecy and skullduggery. What other dark deeds might be going on behind that fence? We need a solution. How can we meet her halfway— give her something, but not give away the store?"

I sighed, although I'd guessed she might say something of the sort. "Okay," I said. "There's a guy in the public relations office. Name's Buck. He's done a few press releases about us. About our research, about forensic cases we've helped the police solve. Buck used to work for WBIR, and he's asked me a couple times about shooting footage at the Body Farm. Wants to make a science documentary, for the Learning Channel or National Geographic or some such. How 'bout I take Buck over, let him get some shots, and give the footage to the Channel Four folks?"

"Good idea. Nothing too graphic, though."

"Lord no," I assured her. "Very . . . tasteful."

"Eating," she reminded me.

"Sorry. Very discreet. I'm thinking a fresh body—freshest we've got, anyhow—and some bare bones. A nice white skeleton."

"I don't think we should muddy the water with race," she said.

"Huh? With what?"

"Race. You said 'a nice white skeleton.' I wouldn't bring up race."

I laughed. "The bones," I said, "not the donor. White bones. Bare bones. Sun-bleached bones."

"Oh," she said. "Right. I knew that."

Chapter 19

An hour after my phone calls with the dean and the legal eagle, I crossed the river, looped past the medical center, and threaded through the hospital employees' parking lot. The lot was nearly full; the only unclaimed spaces were in the farthest corner, beside the high wooden fence surrounding the Body Farm. Those spots were almost never taken; they were the last resorts of hospital workers too late to be choosy—especially on hot summer days like this one, when the research facility gave new meaning—literal, eye-watering meaning—to the phrase "body odor."

A single vehicle was parked in the normally vacant spots. But it was not parked between the lines, nose to the fence. Instead, it was parked parallel to the fence, straddling three parking places. It was a white Chevy

Blazer labeled EYEWITNESS 4 NEWS, and on top of the Blazer was a tripod, and on top of the tripod was a video camera, and peering through the viewfinder was the cameraman from Channel 4. Perched beside him, looking almost comically incongruous in her tailored suit and power pumps, was my nemesis, Athena Demopoulos.

I stopped fifty yards away. Taking out my phone, I scrolled through my contacts to the number of the medical center police and pressed "call." "*Dis*-patch," answered a woman with an East Tennessee twang.

"This is Dr. Brockton," I said. "There's a television news crew parked outside the Body Farm. They're up on top of their car with a video camera."

"Yes, sir," said the dispatcher, and to my surprise, she chuckled. "Emmett said he'd be sleeping on the sofa for a week if his wife saw him helping that gal get up there."

"Emmett? Who's Emmett? What are you talking about?"

"Emmett. Officer Edmonds. He had to boost that lady reporter up. It took a push to the tush, if you know what I mean."

"Wait," I said. "You're telling me that one of your officers has already seen them? And *helped* them?"

"Well, yes, sir," she said, suddenly sounding nervous. "She—the lady—she said you were on your way.

Told them to meet you here. She told him you'd got snagged on a phone call with the chancellor or some other muckety-muck, but you said to go ahead and get started, and you'd be right there." She paused. "Are you . . . *not* there?"

"I *am* here," I said. "Would you please radio Officer Friendly and ask him to come right back?"

"Sir?"

"I need Emmett to escort his new girlfriend off the premises."

"But she said—"

"I don't give a damn what she said," I snapped. "It's not true. I didn't tell them to meet me here, and I certainly don't want them looking over my fence with a TV camera."

"Yes, sir. I'm sorry, sir. I'll send him right away."

"*Thank* you."

I hung up and pulled forward, tucking in behind the Blazer. Athena Demopoulos glanced my way, then muttered to her cameraman, who kept his eye glued to the viewfinder. As I was getting out, I heard the wail of a siren, and a police cruiser lurched to a screeching stop beside the Blazer. The door opened and a stocky young officer got out, his face flaming, his brow beaded with sweat. "Dr. Brockton, I'm so sorry," he said. "She told me—"

"I know what she told you. She told you a lie."

He walked to the Blazer. "Ma'am? Sir?" He rapped the rear windshield with his knuckles. "I need you to get down off your vehicle and leave the premises."

Athena Demopoulos looked down, feigning innocence and surprise. "Is there a problem, Officer?" She was clearly stalling for time, and the cameraman kept shooting.

"Yes, ma'am. The problem is, you don't have permission to be here filming. I need you to turn off the camera and get down off of there. Right now, please."

"We don't need permission," she said. "This is public property." Her colleague swiveled the camera slightly and adjusted his focus.

"No, ma'am," the officer replied. "Technically—legally—UT Medical Center is private property. I've asked you, as nice as I know how, to shut off that camera and get down from there. I'm going to ask you one last time, and if you don't do it by the time I count to three, I'll arrest you for trespassing. One . . ." She laid her hand lightly on the cameraman's shoulder; he held up a just-a-second finger. "Two . . ." She gave the shoulder a squeeze. "*Three.*" The officer touched the radio transmitter on his shoulder. "This is Officer Edmonds," he said, his head angled toward the mike. "We have a trespassing incident at the Body Farm. I need backup."

The cameraman straightened up and raised his hands. "Hey, everything's cool," he said. "No worries. Just takes a minute to power this thing down. We're leaving right now, aren't we, Athena?"

"Absolutely," she said. She looked at Edmonds coyly. "Help me down?" Edmonds folded his arms across his chest and glared. She turned to me, raising her eyebrows. I shook my head slightly. "I guess it's true." She sighed. "Chivalry really is dead."

"That's right," I said. "It died right after journalistic integrity gave up the ghost."

Chapter 20

Waiting for the Channel 4 story to air was like waiting for a firing squad to raise their rifles and pull the trigger. Time seemed to move at a fraction of its normal speed, and I oscillated wildly between wishing the event simply wasn't happening, and wishing it would just hurry the hell up and be done. I twisted in the wind like that for two days; on the afternoon of the third day, I got a phone call. "Bill, it's Amanda Whiting," I heard the general counsel say.

"You're calling to tell me you've gotten an injunction to block the story?"

"Sorry; not possible," she said. "I'm calling to tell you the story airs tonight. I just got a courtesy call from Channel Four's attorney to let me know."

"Courtesy call," I scoffed. "Well, that call is about the only courtesy they've shown. How bad's the story?"

"I don't know. He didn't say, and I didn't ask."

"Guess we'll hear all about it tomorrow from friends in Nashville," I said. "I'm glad it's airing there instead of here." She didn't reply—she conspicuously didn't reply—so after the silence dragged on a while longer, I said, "Amanda? What?"

"It is airing here, Bill. Channel Four is NBC. The NBC affiliate here, WBIR, is picking it up, too."

"Channel Ten?" My heart sank; WBIR was Knoxville's leading news station, and I'd always enjoyed a good relationship with reporters there. "I thought they liked me."

"I'm sure they *do* like you, Bill. But if their sister station in Nashville runs a big news story about you, WBIR can't ignore it."

Why not? I heard a voice in my head shrieking. *Why the hell not?*

As the newscast loomed, Kathleen tried her best to cheer me up, but I wasn't having any of it. She made one final attempt. "Should I pop some popcorn?"

"Sure," I grumbled. "But instead of butter and salt, give it some strychnine and arsenic."

"Oh, good grief," she said. "Get down off that cross and come sit by me on the sofa. It can't be as bad as you think."

During the Knoxville anchor's lead-in, Kathleen appeared to be right. "The University of Tennessee's 'Body Farm' is making headlines tonight in Nashville," he began. "The research facility, created by UT anthropologist Bill Brockton, uses donated cadavers to study postmortem human decomposition. The Body Farm's research helps homicide detectives make accurate time-since-death estimates."

Kathleen nudged me. "See? Nothing to worry about."

But the newscaster's face turned serious as he continued. "But some critics are charging that the Body Farm's research isn't just macabre, it's disrespectful—and possibly even unpatriotic. From Nashville, Athena Demopoulos reports."

The image switched to a row of neat white headstones in a military cemetery. Then the shot tilted up and widened to show many more tombstones, all identical, and a woman—my new nemesis—walking between them, speaking directly to the camera. "Most veterans rest in peace after death," she began, "buried with honors in military cemeteries like this one in north Nashville." The screen showed close-ups of several tombstones, then switched to four photographs of soldiers in uniform. "But for these four Nashville-area veterans—men who were prepared to make the ultimate sacrifice for their country—there is no peaceful burial. By rights, they should be here. Instead, after death, their bodies ended up at a gruesome Knoxville facility known as the Body Farm." The peaceful cemetery images were replaced by sinister-looking shots of the Body Farm's main gate and fence—wide shots, then close-ups zooming in on the gate's rusting padlock, the heavy steel chain, and the barbed wire and concertina topping the fence. Then—in a sequence that Buck, the PR staffer had shot—I appeared on-screen. Walking up to the gate, I unlocked it and stepped inside, then closed the gate, vanishing from view. "The Body Farm is the creation of this man, Dr. Bill Brockton," the reporter continued, "a University of Tennessee anthropologist whose obsession with death and decay drives him to perform macabre experiments on human bodies—including these four Nashville-area veterans. Dr. Brockton refused to allow us inside the grounds of the ghoulish facility." Once more—this time in slow motion—I stepped through the gate and closed it, as if I were closing it in Athena's face—"but reliable sources gave Channel Four disturbing details of the indignities inflicted upon the dead. Human bodies are tossed on the ground to rot. The remains are infested with insects, preyed upon by scavenging animals."

Suddenly the screen filled with the face—the tear-streaked face—of a thirtysomething-year-old man. The shot widened to show him walking across lush, carefully clipped grass, between tidy rows of tombstones at the Nashville military cemetery. "But one man is vowing to set things right, for his grandfather and other veterans as well. Adam Anderson—grandson of Lucius Anderson, one of the four Nashville veterans at the Body Farm—says he'll do whatever it takes to get his grandfather back and give him the dignified burial he deserved."

"It ain't right," the young man said, shaking his head and wiping his eyes. "He served his country. He deserved better than this. We got to put a stop to this."

"Anderson isn't the only one ready to do battle over the treatment of veterans' bodies," Demopoulos said. Now the camera showed a portly, glossy-haired man striding into an office lined with law books. "He's found a powerful ally in Wayne Wilson, a state senator from Jackson, Tennessee.

"I was shocked," Wilson pronounced, "to hear what's being done to these veterans—and to other deceased individuals—in the name of science." He added, "Don't get me wrong, I'm not antiscience. There's a place for it. But this isn't science; this is just morbid obsession. And I believe the people of the great state of Tennessee would want their elected representatives in Nashville to right this grievous wrong."

I practically leapt up from the sofa. "*Grievous wrong!*" I sputtered. "What a load of crap! I'll give you some grievous wrong, all right!"

"Shhh," said Kathleen. Latching onto my arm, she pulled me back to my seat beside her and patted my leg.

The footage cut to a close-up of Athena Demopoulos's face, filled with compassion. "Adam Anderson says he's grateful for Senator Wilson's vow to help. He just wishes it had come sooner—in time to help give his grandfather dignity in death."

The shot widened to show Anderson standing beside her in the cemetery. "It just breaks my heart," Anderson told her, "that they're allowed to treat him that way . . ." He wiped his eyes again, and Athena leaned closer, handing him a tissue and giving his shoulder a comforting squeeze. "It breaks my heart they're allowed to treat *anybody* this way," he said, his voice breaking. She nodded earnestly, then—when he put his face in his hands and wept—she enfolded him in a hug. Then she stretched out one hand, fingers raised and spread wide, to block the camera's view—a gesture the lens captured in loving, lingering detail throughout her final, somber line of voice-over: "Athena Demopoulos, Eyewitness Four News."

Kathleen had been right: The story wasn't been as bad as I'd thought it would be. It was worse. Much, much worse.

Unable to sleep, I reached for her in the night. "Tell me you love me," I said. "Tell me everything will be all right."

"I do love you, darling," she said. "I'm so glad you're home." But a moment later, as my hand slid up her hip and toward her breast, she laid her own hand over mine, immobilizing it. "I'm still out of commission, honey. I'm sorry."

I pulled back to look at her in the dim light of the bedroom. "You still have your period? How can that be? It's been almost two weeks. You need to go to the doctor."

"I called. Nothing to worry about. But if it keeps on much longer, I'll go in." She gave a short, ironic laugh. "Funny way for menopause to start, huh—the nonstop period? Like having a month of monsoons just before a forty-year drought sets in."

She was trying to be game about it, but her words gave me a sharp pang. Was it hearing her use the word "drought" to describe the change her womanly body was about to undergo? Or was it the combination of images—drought and flood, a pair of biblical-sounding plagues—that suddenly made me feel the grip of cold, bony fingers closing around my heart like some scaly and pitiless claw?

Chapter 21

Is it possible, as priests and mystics believe, to conjure
up evil beings simply by speaking their names—
out loud, or even silently, in the fearful shadows of
the heart and mind? Earlier in my life, I would have
scoffed at the suggestion. Yet now, in my hand—my
trembling hand—I held powerful evidence to the contrary. Unscientific evidence, yet no less convincing and
frightening for all that.

Satterfield read the return address on the padded
envelope I had just taken from the mailbox. Nothing
more, just the name. But the name was enough. More
than enough.

Standing there at the end of the driveway—one hand
clutching the envelope, the other still holding the tab
on the mailbox door, which I'd noticed was ajar when

I'd walked out to retrieve the newspaper—I wheeled and scanned in all directions, as if Satterfield might somehow have slipped through the bars of his cell and returned to haunt us.

Apart from the alarms shrieking in my head, it was an idyllic Sunday morning in a pretty, woodsy neighborhood. A few doors down the street, a dad in shorts and T-shirt jogged alongside a small bicycle, which a girl who looked about Tyler's age was pedaling proudly. "Good *job*," the dad praised. "Pretty soon you'll be too fast—I won't be able to keep up!" Behind me, in the small park across the street from our house, a young mother—the bicyclist's mom?—was pushing a swing, evoking burbles of delight from the toddler cradled in the seat. My quiet street, shaded by maples and hemlocks, was the very picture of suburban safety and tranquility. It had been, that is, until I'd seen—until I'd silently said—the name on the envelope in my hand.

Tucking the package back in the mailbox, I fished my cell phone from my jeans. Scrolling through my contacts, I found Brian Decker's name and pressed "call." After four rings he still hadn't picked up, and I began mentally composing a voice mail—one I hoped would sound more rational than I felt—but on the fifth ring he answered. "This is Captain Decker," he said.

"Deck, it's Bill Brockton," I said.

"Hey, Doc. How the hell are you? Haven't talked to you in way too long." He sounded pleased to hear from me, but there was an understandable undertone of sadness in his voice, too.

Decker headed the Knoxville Police Department's SWAT team. We'd met twelve years before, at the end of Nick Satterfield's string of sadistic serial killings, when Decker arrived at my house just in time to help keep Satterfield from murdering my family and me.

"Deck, can you check on a prisoner for me?" The words rushed out without preamble. "Make sure he's still in custody?"

"Sure, Doc. City, county, state, or federal?"

"State. South Central Correctional Facility. In Clifton."

"Ah," he said. "Prisoner's name wouldn't happen to be Satterfield, would it?"

"Yeah. How'd you know?"

He knew because no one understood Satterfield's menace better than Decker, whose own brother had died while searching Satterfield's house for booby traps. I heard a deep breath on the other end of the line. "You sound spooked, Doc. What's going on?"

"I'm standing at my mailbox, Deck. There's an envelope here—a padded envelope—with a return address that just says 'Satterfield.' Nothing but the name."

"Shit—don't open it!" I'd never heard alarm in Decker's voice before, but I was hearing it now, loud and clear.

"Okay, I won't open it."

"Put it down—*very gently*—and get away from it."

"You think it's a bomb?"

"The guy has a thing for explosives."

"He has a thing for snakes, too," I reminded him, "but I don't think this envelope has room for either a bomb or a boa constrictor. Anthrax or ricin, maybe. But it's probably just a hateful letter. What I want to know—besides is the guy still behind bars—is how the hell he got this to me?"

Decker didn't speak for a moment; in the background, I heard computer keys clattering. "Hang on. I'm checking on him." More clattering. "Well, according to this—the state's Felony Offender Information database—he's still there. And I sure haven't heard anything about an escape. Which I would have. And so would you. 'Serial killer breaks free'? You *know* the media would go nuts over that."

He had a point there, I had to admit. "So how was he able to send this to me? Can convicted killers just mail stuff to anybody they please?"

"Unfortunately, yeah," he said. "There are a few rules, but they're pretty minimal. Basically, inmates aren't supposed to send threats to victims or victims' families."

"Wait. Did you say 'rules'? And '*supposed* to'? The system assumes a serial killer's gonna play by the rules for good *mail* manners?"

"Sounds lame," he conceded. "But there's a safety net, sort of. If the warden thinks a piece of mail poses a threat, he can have it opened. But that requires a bunch of paperwork, and prison wardens probably have enough paperwork already, without creating more for themselves. Still, Satterfield's no ordinary prisoner, and the warden would know that the two of you aren't exactly pen pals." There was a pause, then: "It's Sunday. Did you not check your mail yesterday?"

"I did," I said, the realization—*no mail on Sundays*—hitting me for the first time as I checked for a postmark. "Shit. This wasn't mailed. This was hand delivered."

"Listen, Doc, the safest thing would be to get the bomb squad over there."

"That would freak Kathleen out," I said. "I don't even want her to know about this, much less think it's about to blow our house to smithereens."

"So take her out for brunch. Stay gone for a couple hours, let the guys check it out, then we give you a call once we're gone."

"And the neighbors wouldn't notice a thing, right?" I pictured the series of scared and angry phone calls we'd get. "She'd be twice as mad at me—first for tricking her, then for upsetting everybody in Sequoyah Hills."

"Well, we gotta do something with it, Doc. And you damn sure shouldn't just tear into it. What do *you* suggest?"

Out of the corner of my eye, I saw the dad and the girl on the bike looping back toward me, thirty yards away and closing fast. "Hang on just a sec," I said to him, then took a casual step sideways, putting my body between the envelope and the child. Decker was right; we had to do something, and fast—get the package out of the neighborhood, away from innocent bystanders. "I'll take it to the forensic center," I told him after they had passed. "We've got a portable x-ray machine; I can wheel it outside, onto the loading dock, and shoot an x-ray. If it shows any wires, I'll call the bomb guys. If it doesn't, I can take it inside and open it under an exhaust hood, in case it's some sort of nasty powder."

"I don't like this," Decker grumbled.

"I don't like it either," I said. "But the less fuss the better. Like I said, it's probably just a hateful letter."

"Then how come it's not in a regular envelope?" I didn't have a good answer for that. "Let me come get you, Doc."

"Just meet me at the forensic center, Deck."

"I'm on my way," he said. "How soon can you be there?"

"I'll leave right now. I'll be there in fifteen minutes." I thought about how to explain my abrupt departure. "I'll tell Kathleen the M.E. needs me to come look at a skull fracture."

"Hurry up, but be careful, Doc. Don't handle it any more than you have to. I don't suppose you're wearing gloves?"

"Come on, Deck. Do *you* put on gloves when *you* go to the mailbox? Does the mailman wear gloves? The mail sorters?"

"Yeah, yeah," he groused.

"Besides," I went on, "y'all can get prints off whatever's inside, right? And it's not like Satterfield's trying to hide—hell, he's put his name right here on the envelope. He may have licked the flap, too, which gives you DNA. What more do you want—a video of him sealing and mailing the package?"

"That'd be helpful."

"Yeah, well, good luck with that. Okay, I'm signing off. Gotta go in and make my excuses to Kathleen. See you in twenty?"

"Put it in the back of your truck. Hurry up—but drive slow."

"Deck, you're talking to a man who's never gotten a speeding ticket in his whole life."

"I'm not worried about you getting a ticket. I'm worried about you going kablooey."

"You're talking to a man who's never gone kablooey, either."

Fifteen minutes later, I eased down a one-lane drive-way and parked beside UT Medical Center's loading dock, which adjoined the morgue and the East Tennessee Regional Forensic Center. Decker was already there, pacing the loading dock. The KPD cruiser he'd arrived in was parked fifty yards away.

"I see you're not taking any chances with city property," I teased as I got out of the truck. When I closed the door, he flinched.

"Gently, Doc, *gently!*"

I gave him a look. "You think I carried it here on a cushion? Hell, I hit a dozen potholes between the house and here. It's not gonna blow up if we breathe." Heading to the back of the truck, I opened the cargo hatch and lifted out a small, heavy box—a fireproof document safe where Kathleen and I stored our passports and wills.

Decker gave the safe an approving nod. "Good thinking."

"Even a blind squirrel finds a nut once in a while," I said. I set the safe—gently—on the edge of the concrete loading dock. "The machine's inside. I'll be right back."

The portable x-ray camera was tucked in a corner near the roll-up garage door. It had been bestowed on me by the head of the hospital's Radiology Department several years before, shortly after I had wheeled a particularly ripe corpse—a floater found in the Tennessee River—into Radiology and had asked a tech to check for bullets. To hear the Radiology folks tell the story— and over the years, I had heard most of them tell it, repeatedly—the entire floor had cleared out the instant the floater and I arrived. "Damnedest thing I ever saw," the department head liked to say. "Everybody— staff, patients, visitors—flat-out hauling *ass* out of there. It was like a miracle on steroids. The lame didn't just walk out of there, they *sprinted* out."

Leaving Decker to keep nervous watch on the document safe, I unlocked a steel door, stepped into a dark basement hallway, and pressed a button on the wall to raise the roll-up door. The door rattled and clattered open, like some immense, industrial scale-up of a rolltop desk. My mind flashed to the rolltop desk that had once occupied pride of place in my father's law office: the lustrous quarter-sawn oak; the small, dark pigeonholes stuffed with fountain pens, inkwells, staplers, magnifying glasses, stamps, sealing wax, whatever. There were no fountain pens or inkwells pigeonholed here, of course, only corpses—as many as half a dozen at any one time—cached in the cooler down the hall, each silently awaiting its turn in the autopsy suite.

Wheeling the x-ray machine out the door and onto the dock, I set a film cassette on the concrete, then opened the safe, removed the envelope, and laid it gingerly atop the film. "You might want to step inside," I told Decker as I lowered the camera into place. "Unless you want to nuke your boy bits." He scurried inside, and I set the exposure and the shutter, which had a ten-second delay to allow me to scuttle to safety with *my* boy bits. Through the doorway, I heard *whir-clunk*, the distinctive sound of the shutter on the radiation source.

The morgue was in the basement—morgues always are, in accordance with some unwritten law of the universe—so we had nowhere to go but up. After two flights, I could hear Decker laboring to breathe. "Doesn't this place have elevators?" he panted.

"Man up," I said. "It's only four floors. Besides, don't you have to take a fitness test every year?"

"Every five," he gasped. "I've got three more years to enjoy being fat and out of shape. Then I diet and exercise like crazy for three months, so I can pass the physical. Then I get to eat and lay around for another four years."

"Knoxville's Finest," I teased. Glancing back as we emerged on the fourth floor, I saw him mopping sweat from his brow. "Deck, my friend, you put the *hot* in *hot pursuit.*"

Radiology was just around the corner. The receptionist—Jeanette? no: Lynnette—gave me a sunny smile. "Dr. Brockton! Nice to see you again. How's business at the Body Farm?"

"Pretty lively," I said. "People are dying to get in. Lynnette, this is Captain Brian Decker, one of Knoxville's finest."

"Hi," she said. "Actually, it's Shawnette. Nice to meet you."

Decker gave her a sweaty wave across the counter.

"Sorry, Shawnette," I said, my face now as red as Decker's was. "You got a tech back there who might be able to develop a picture for us?"

"Sure," she said. "Stacy. Go on back. I'll tell her you're coming."

Stacy—a pale, chubby young woman with a strong East Tennessee accent—met us outside the first radiology suite and held out her hand for the cassette.

"Lemme guess," she said. "You're lookin' for another bullet in somebody that's burned up or fallin' apart?"

"I don't know *what* I'm looking for," I said. "Just trying to see what's inside an envelope."

"And you cain't just open it?"

"Not sure what would happen if I did. That's why we're hoping you can give me a sneak peek, if you wouldn't mind."

"You know I don't care to," she said, which was an East Tennessee way of telling me she didn't mind at all. She disappeared into the lab, situated between two of the imaging suites.

Decker and I waited in the hallway for a couple of minutes. Then we heard a signal indicating that she had finished developing the image. The signal was Stacy's voice, emitting a high, loud shriek.

Decker slit the envelope carefully, then tipped the opening down toward the blue surgical pad we'd laid across the tailgate of my truck. A lumpy packet— blue-lined notebook paper, folded several times— slid out. With purple-gloved fingers, Decker eased open the folds one by one until the object inside was revealed.

"Yeah," he said slowly, "I'd say that's a human finger, all right." He picked it up gently and inspected it, then handed it to me.

The finger was small—a child's finger—severed as neatly at the base as Kathleen's had been. I stared at it, trying to make sense of it. It had come from Satterfield; I felt no doubt about that. But whose finger was it? How had he come by it? How had he sent it—and why?

The notebook paper wasn't just a wrapping; it was also a message, in a handwriting that I recognized from prosecution exhibits at Satterfield's trial. "As token and pledge," the note read, "I send you this: a finger from my firstborn son. When the time is right, I will bring him to retrieve it, and the two of us will rain down vengeance upon you and your family."

I handed the note to Decker, the paper rattling from the tremor in my hand. He read it, then looked at me, his face grave. "You ever hear anything about Satterfield having a kid?"

I shook my head, but suddenly I had a sick feeling. "There was a woman," I said, "at Satterfield's trial. A weird woman. Most people were looking at him like he was a monster, you know? This woman was different. She was looking at him like he was . . . her hero or *beloved* or something."

He nodded. "I've heard about women like that. Like rock-star groupies, but instead of singers or drummers, these gals get obsessed with serial killers. It's a power thing—they're attracted to all that dark energy or something. Remember Charles Manson? That whole harem he had? All those creepy women in what he called 'the family'?"

"I remember," I said. "And 'creepy' is putting it mildly. They all shaved their heads during his trial, right? Carved pentagrams in their foreheads?" I thought for a moment. "Didn't Ted Bundy have groupies, too?"

Decker nodded again. "Lots. He even managed to marry one of 'em, right in the middle of his murder trial. Pulled some kinda jailhouse-lawyer stunt in the courtroom; conned the judge into pronouncing them man and wife—monster and wife—right there on the spot." A strange look passed across his face; I could see that he was on the verge of adding something, but then he bit it back.

"What?" I asked. He frowned, looking pained. "*What?* Spit it out, Deck."

"He got her pregnant, too. Bundy."

"What? *How?* I mean, besides the basic egg-meets-sperm part. Do death row inmates get conjugal visits?"

"Not supposed to," he said. "But then again, it was in Florida. Crazy shit happens in Florida." He shook his head—whether about Florida or about the idea of Bundy as a dad, I couldn't be sure. "One thing you can be sure of, though," he added. "That snake Satterfield would've read about Bundy making a baby. And you know what they say about imitation. Highest form of flattery."

"Sickest sort of perversion," I responded. "But Satterfield didn't manage to get married during *his* trial. So for *sure* he wasn't eligible for conjugal visits."

"Maybe there was a turkey baster involved," he mused. "Or a spunk-filled condom. Or a rubber glove." We looked at each other and grimaced in unison, repelled by the images his words had conjured up.

"He's a convicted serial killer," I protested. "He shouldn't be able to pass a spunk-filled *anything* to a visitor."

"You're right. He shouldn't." Decker shrugged. "But prisons are bureaucracies. Systems. And any system can be gotten around or abused, if the price is right. Grease enough guards, do enough favors, gather enough dirt to get somebody under your thumb? You can break any rule—or bend it into any shape you want."

Glumly I turned my attention back to the finger. The digit was in good condition—slightly shriveled, but not decomposed. "The forensic guys can get prints off that, right?"

Decker plucked the finger from my palm and peered closely at the tip, inspecting the delicate ridges and whorls. He nodded, then shrugged. "Not sure there's much point, though. I doubt the kid's gonna show up in AFIS"—I knew he was referring to the FBI's Automated Fingerprint Identification System. "Not unless he's some kind of child-prodigy criminal." Seeing my disappointment, he hurried to add, "I'll check, though. Like my mama always said, nothing ventured, nothing gained." He rewrapped the finger and slid it back into the envelope, then said, "So . . ."

"What?"

He held the envelope toward me. "The fact that this was hand delivered. So to speak. I'm not liking that." He looked at the KPD cruiser parked fifty yards away, as if it contained the answer to some question he was pondering. "Wait here," he said. "I've got something for you." He walked back to the cruiser, opened the driver's door, and laid the envelope on the passenger seat. Then he reached under the driver's seat and took out a small bundle of black fabric. He brought it to me, offering it up on both palms.

I took the bundle, surprised by its heft. "What is it?"

"Insurance," he said.

"Feels like a lot of it." I unwrapped the cloth— velvet, with a thick, soft nap—which was rolled around the object several times; unspooling it made me think of unwinding a burial shroud. And in a way, it turned out, I was unwrapping death, for swaddled within the soft black fabric was a handgun, its precisely machined surfaces lustrous with a thin coating of oil. I stared at it, then at Decker. "Jesus, Deck. What are you doing? I don't want this. I've never had a gun in my life. I *hate* guns; they scare me." I handed it back to him.

"I know," he said, although I doubted that he knew how deep-rooted my aversion to guns was, how painfully personal: my father had shot himself in the head when I was young, and my mother and I had found him. "But Satterfield scares you, too," he went on. "And he *should*. You ask me, that guy's ten times scarier than this thing. Look how close he came to taking out your whole family—and in a really bad way." I didn't need Decker to remind me of that terrible night. "The good news is, he's behind bars. Solid, well-guarded bars. But if he did manage to get out—or to send somebody else gunning for you, some dark night—wouldn't the odds be better if you had this beside the bed? Tucked in the drawer of the nightstand?"

"I don't know, Deck." It was hard to think rationally; the message from Satterfield—the finger from Satterfield—felt like talons tearing into my belly.

"Look, Doc, I don't know what he's up to. And I don't think he can get out of there. And I'll go pay him a visit, if you want—discourage him, shall we say, from messing with you. But take this, for now, just in case. If not for your own sake, take it for Kathleen's." He hesitated, then plowed ahead, into territory I wished he'd stay the hell out of. "He thinks he's got unfinished business with you. He started with Kathleen last time, and he'd start with her again if he got a chance. And he'd make you watch it all."

At that moment—the moment I reached out and took possession of the gun—I wasn't sure who I hated most: Satterfield, Decker, or myself.

Chapter 22

I checked the time as the garage door clattered down behind my truck in the basement of my house. I hadn't quite made it home within the sixty-minute deadline I'd set for myself, but I'd missed it by only seven minutes. As I climbed the steps to the kitchen, I rehearsed what I would tell Kathleen about the skull fracture that had supposedly required my sudden trip to the morgue.

She met me at the top of the stairs, her face strained. "The phone has been ringing like crazy the whole time you've been gone. The house phone. Your cell, too—you left it here. You have a bunch of voice mails." She handed it to me.

"Oh, hell, I'm sorry, honey," I began. "I didn't—"

She cut me off with a shake of the head. "I'm not fussing at you. Sounds like you've got plenty of other folks ready to do that."

"What now? Who called?"

"Amanda Whiting, the UT lawyer. And a TV reporter. And the FBI."

"*Damn* that Athena Demon-whatever," I snapped. "Now she's dragged the FBI into this veterans thing?"

"No, not the Channel Four woman from Nashville," she said. "This is some smug, self-important guy from San Diego."

"San Diego?" As I skipped over the general counsel's message, my mind flashed back to the intrusive San Diego reporter who had arrived at the crash site by helicopter—and later created a stir at the FBI's press conference. His cocky, challenging words seemed to echo in my mind, and a fraction of a second later—like the delay in a public-address announcement—I heard the same words, in the same voice, coming from the cell phone at my ear: "Mike Malloy, Fox Five News." As the message continued to play, I felt the blood rising to my face . . . and then I felt it draining.

"Jesus Christ," I whispered.

Kathleen looked worried. "What's wrong? Honey? What's happened?"

I held up a hand to quiet her as Malloy's message began to play. I closed my eyes and felt my head sag toward my chest. "No," I whispered. "No, no, no. *Please,* no." I felt Kathleen's hand on my arm, squeezing and then shaking it to get my attention, but I just shook my head, my eyes still tightly closed. I felt behind me with my free hand and found one of the chairs tucked beneath the kitchen table. Tugging it out, I sat down— or, rather, collapsed into it.

When the third message began—the FBI message— my eyes flew open, and I stared at Kathleen as if I'd seen a ghost. She no longer looked worried; now she looked downright alarmed, and she backed away slightly, as if I myself might be cause for alarm. When the third message ended, the phone fell silent for a moment. Then a robotic voice intoned, "To replay your messages, press one. To save your messages, press two. To delete your messages, press three."

I cued up the reporter's message again, put the phone on "speaker," and turned it toward Kathleen, motioning for her to sit. Her eyes still riveted on me, she sat down across the table, poised on the edge of the seat as if ready to spring up and flee at the slightest provocation.

"Mike Malloy, Fox Five News," I heard the brash voice again. "Dr. Brockton, I need to ask you some questions about the remains you identified as those of Richard Janus. I have information from a reliable source confirming that Janus is actually still alive. My source tells me that Janus had his teeth pulled and put a decoy body in the aircraft. I'd like to ask you to explain more about how you reached the conclusion you did, and how Janus was able to fool you, since you're supposed to be one of the world's leading experts on human identification."

I felt Kathleen's hand on my wrist. "Oh, darling," she said. "Bless your heart."

"Wait," I said over the dial tone at the end of the reporter's message. "It gets better."

"Dr. Brockton," the third message began in a tight, clipped tone, as if each word were being bitten instead of spoken. "SSA Prescott, San Diego." As if I needed to be reminded where Prescott worked. "We have one hell of a shitstorm here, the epicenter of which is your botched identification of Richard Janus. I have two questions for you, which might, at this point, be moot, but I'll ask them anyway. First, did you check the teeth for tool marks, or other evidence of extraction? Second, why the hell didn't you ask more questions about that spinal cord stimulator?" There was a pause in the message, and Kathleen opened her mouth to speak, but again I held up a hand to tell her to wait. "We need you to return the teeth and skeletal material immediately," Prescott went on, "so we can send the teeth to a qualified forensic odontologist." The phrase—*qualified forensic odontologist*—practically dripped venom. "Please deliver them to the FBI's Knoxville field office as soon as you get this message. They'll be expecting you. Needless to say, you're not to make any further comments to the media about this case." And with no further sign-off, he hung up.

"Oh, Bill," said Kathleen. "I am so, so sorry."

The fourth and final voice mail was from a blocked number. The message began with what might have been the heavy breathing of an obscene call, but then the breathing became torn and ragged, as if the caller were struggling to regain control. "Please," said a woman's voice, hoarse and anguished and barely recognizable. "Do not play games with me. I must know. Is my husband dead, or is he alive? Tell me the truth, please. I beg you. Please." The breathing grew even more ragged as she gasped out a San Diego telephone number, and then the call ended.

Kathleen stared at me from across the table. One hand remained on my wrist; the other was over her mouth. "My God," she breathed. "Was that . . . ?"

"Yes." I nodded. "Carmelita Janus."

"How awful." Kathleen's eyes were wide. "What on earth do you do now?"

I considered my options, not liking any of them. "I give the teeth and bones back to the FBI. But first I spend some time with them." I heard another voice, and I realized that my cell phone was nagging me to replay, save, or delete my messages. Instead, I simply disconnected the call, and left the phone on the table. "I *think* the voice-mail system keeps those marked as new messages until I tell it to do something with them," I told Kathleen. "I'm leaving now, but I'm not taking that with me."

"Where are you going?"

I was about to tell her—it was my nature to tell Kathleen everything, although I'd made an exception when the finger from Satterfield had arrived—but I just shook my head instead. "If anybody calls looking for me, you don't know where I am. All you know is, I'm out, and you don't know where I am, and I forgot to take my phone with me." A sudden thought struck me—a terrible thought: the thought that Satterfield might send someone to the house while I was gone. "Kath, why don't you go spend the night at Jeff and Jenny's?"

"What?"

"Sure! Do it, Kath. I'm likely to get a zillion calls— hell, maybe even people coming to the house looking for me—and that'll drive you crazy. You could babysit, and let Jeff and Jenny have a dinner date. The boys would love it. *You'd* love it."

Her eyes searched my face, and I suspected she could tell I was holding something back besides my whereabouts. If she had to find me in an emergency, she could probably guess where I'd gone, but if I didn't tell her, she wouldn't have to lie to anyone.

"How long will you be gone?"

"I'm not sure. Tonight. Probably all day tomorrow. I hope I'll be back tomorrow night."

Her eyes flickered with an expression I couldn't quite read, and I wondered if she was upset about my disappearing act. "What?"

"Nothing," she said. "I'll be off the grid tomorrow, too."

"What's up?"

"Nothing," she repeated. "A journal article I'm writing. Tomorrow's the deadline. I've never had such a hard time finishing something. It's been like pulling—" She interrupted herself.

"Don't you dare finish that sentence," I growled, smiling in spite of myself. Then I raised her hand and kissed it, pushed away from the table, and hurried back to UT—not to the hospital's loading dock this time, but to the small, grimy office tucked beneath girders and grandstands, a bone's throw from Neyland Stadium's north end zone.

Hurrying up the stairs, I turned the balky lock of my office door and dashed to my desk to retrieve a small plastic bin: the bin that contained the mortal remains of Richard Janus—or those of a convincing decoy. Grabbing the bin, I raced back down the stairs, hopped into my truck, and hurried away.

Chapter 23

I didn't have far to drive. A hundred yards from Neyland Stadium—hunkered in a low spot of the asphalt that surrounded the stadium like an alluvial floodplain—was a dilapidated blue building of corrugated metal, the paint cloudy with age and streaked with rust. The building still bore a sign that read ANTHROPOLOGY ANNEX, but the sign, like the building, was faded and rusting. Years before, until we'd built the Regional Forensic Center, with its high-tech processing rooms, the annex had been the place where our donated bodies had finished shuffling off their mortal coil—or, rather, simmering off their mortal coil—in large, steam-jacketed kettles, to which we added a bit of Biz and a dash of Downy to sweeten the pot.

I parked the truck behind the building, then flipped through my many keys, searching for the one that fit the annex's garage door. My secretary, Peggy, occasionally scolded me about the jangly mess that was my key ring, but now—as I found the snaggletoothed key that unlocked the garage—I felt vindicated for all the years I'd hauled around this spiky excess baggage of brass and steel. "See," I said smugly to an imaginary Peggy, twisting the door's latch. As if by way of an indignant retort, the latch let out a screech that made my fillings shudder in my teeth, and as the door clattered and groaned upward, it unleashed a shower of dust, rust, and crumbled bird droppings.

I didn't care. I retrieved the truck from behind the building and eased it into the dusty garage bay, then lowered the door and went missing. AWOL. The Invisible Man.

It took five minutes just to remove the many layers of wrapping from the plastic bin of remains. As I snipped and tugged, I felt almost as if I were unwinding a modern-day mummy, this one wrapped not in linen but in Saran Wrap and packing tape—our makeshift maneuver to avoid stinking up not only my carry-on bag—my "carrion bag," I had jokingly dubbed it—but the entire plane. As I unwound the

final layer of plastic, I caught a faint whiff of odor—
not the familiar, overpowering smell of decomposing
flesh, but the charred aroma of burned meat.

Opening a dusty supply cabinet, I found a disposable
surgical sheet—made of absorbent blue paper—and
unfolded it on the counter that ran the length of one
wall. Then I laid out the teeth and bone fragments in
anatomical order, or in as close an approximation of anatomical order as I could achieve, given the high degree
of fragmentation. The teeth, being the most intact, were
the easiest; they were also of greatest interest and greatest consternation to me. What was it Prescott had asked
about? *Tool marks or other evidence of extraction?* His
question had sounded angry, but not merely angry; it
had sounded surprisingly specific, too, and I wondered
what had prompted such specificity. As far as I knew,
none of the FBI agents had reexamined the teeth after
we had recovered them and sent them to the medical
examiner's office, along with the bits of burned bone.
The morning of the press conference, Prescott had sent
one of his subordinates to the M.E.'s office to retrieve
the material, which the M.E. was glad to release, the
identification having been made—positively and correctly, to the best of everyone's knowledge at the time.
So what had changed since then? What new information, or allegations, or accusations, had come to light

to undermine the identification—*my* identification; my work; my reputation?

An old magnifying lamp, its lens gray beneath a blanket of dust, still hovered over the counter, its articulating arm creaky and arthritic with age. I flipped its switch, not expecting anything, but after a moment, the fluorescent bulb that encircled the lens flickered to life. "Hmm," I said, then quoted a line from a Monty Python comedy, a scene in which a plague victim is being carried prematurely to a cart of corpses: "I'm not *quite* dead," I cracked in my best—or my worst—Cockney accent. Then, after I'd said the words, they took on a new and unexpected meaning, and I imagined them being spoken by Richard Janus. Was Janus quite dead, or was he—like me—merely missing, AWOL, the Invisible Man?

Even after cleaning the magnifying lens and examining the teeth through it, I still couldn't answer the question. *Someone* was dead, all right; that much was absolutely clear from the bones: vertebrae; shards of shattered limbs; charred chunks of pelvis; curved cranial fragments. But were those bits and pieces from Richard Janus?

The teeth were his; that, too, was beyond doubt. But other things were now entirely in doubt. Could it be true—as both Prescott and the television reporter indicated—that the teeth had been extracted, then placed in the plane with a decoy body? If so, that meant the decoy's teeth had been pulled, too, because if they hadn't, we'd have found two sets of teeth.

The teeth were damaged—their roots almost entirely broken and burned away. At the scene, I'd been surprised at the lack of jawbone surrounding them, but then again, the jaws themselves—both the mandible and the maxilla—had been reduced to fragments. I'd asked Maddox if such extreme fragmentation was normal; he'd shrugged and nodded. "I'm surprised there's this much left," he'd said. "A high-impact crash like this? Usually all we find is a smoking hole." I must have looked surprised, because he'd added, "If it were a helo crash, or a military aircraft, I'd expect more. Those guys wear helmets, so it gives a little protection. Poor bastards don't have a snowball's chance of surviving, mind you. The helmets just mean we get to pick up bigger pieces."

The day before the press conference, I'd told Prescott I wanted to take a second look at the teeth, but he'd resisted the idea. The high profile of the Janus case had put too much pressure on him—pressure from the Bureau's uppermost level. Now—now that it was too late; now that things were a royal mess—I was finally getting that second look.

I still didn't see "tool marks"—which I took to mean marks from dental extraction forceps, or perhaps from ordinary pliers—but I wouldn't really know until I'd cleaned the teeth thoroughly. So what had prompted the question, or the accusation, from Prescott? I could think of only one explanation that fit the facts: Someone had told Prescott—or the Fox reporter, or both—that the teeth had been extracted, and that Janus's death had been faked. But who? And why?

Hours later—hours of cleaning and scrutinizing later—I still had no idea where the revelation had come from, or what had motivated it. But I *had* found signs of abrasions and fractures in the enamel of many of the teeth: abrasions and fractures that were more consistent with compressive and torsional forces— gripping and twisting—than with impact. With a heavy heart and sinking spirit, I concluded that the teeth had indeed been extracted before the crash. But I still didn't see the big picture. In fact, if anything, I was more baffled than ever. Had Richard Janus indeed faked his death? If so, how the hell had he done it?

Chapter 24

I was surprised to find a phone still hanging on the annex wall, draped in Halloween-worthy cobwebs, and I was downright astonished to hear a dial tone when I lifted the dusty receiver to my ear. Digging deep into my wallet, I found the business card—formerly crisp and imposing, now dirty and crumpled—that I'd gotten from Pat Maddox, the NTSB crash investigator, and dialed the number. The phone rang half a dozen times before a deep, gravelly voice rumbled, "Uh . . . yeah . . . Maddox."

"Oh hell, I woke you up," I said. "Sorry, Pat. I didn't think about the time change. It's only, what . . ." I glanced at my watch.

"Six fifteen here."

"I apologize."

"I might possibly forgive you," he growled—still sounding like a balky diesel engine on a cold morning—"if you'll tell me who the hell this is, and what's so damn important."

"Oh, sorry, Pat. It's Bill Brockton. The anthropologist. From Tennessee. I'm calling about the Janus crash."

"Oh, Doc," he said, his voice warming up. "What can I do for you?"

"I'm not sure," I said. "In fact, I don't have a clue. Which is the problem, I guess. I got a call—a voice mail—yesterday from Miles Prescott, the FBI case agent."

"Ah, yes," he said. "I saw him on the news last night. Special Agent Prescott, not looking 'specially happy. Was he calling to say 'thanks again for the great work'?"

"Not exactly," I said. "How much news coverage have you seen?"

"Not much. Just the one story last night. Talking about the teeth. By that jerk from Fox News."

"You mean 'Mike Mal-*loy* . . . *Fox* Five News!'?"

Maddox gave a dry laugh. "Yeah. That guy. You've got him nailed. He called me yesterday—no, day before—fishing around. Sounded like he had some kinda scoop, but he wouldn't say what. All I gave him was a suggestion about what he should go do to himself. Not politically correct—not anatomically possible, either—but it made me feel better to say it."

"You think it was Malloy who told Prescott the teeth had been extracted?"

"Dunno," said Maddox. "Maybe. Probably. He seems to have a real hard-on for this story."

"But where'd *Malloy* get the information? I've spent all night looking at those teeth, Pat, and he's right— they *were* extracted. Pulled. Thing is, I had to clean 'em off and look at 'em under a magnifying glass before I could tell. It's not like some reporter could take a quick glance and spot the marks. Besides, how could he have even seen them—the teeth, I mean?"

"Well, I'm guessing *you* didn't give him a look," he said.

"Hell, no."

"Okay, so who *could've*?"

"Nobody," I said. "The only people who had access to those teeth were us." Suddenly something occurred to me. "Wait. *Not* just us. The medical examiner did, too."

"Just the medical examiner himself? Nobody on his staff?"

"I don't know," I admitted. "All the material went to the morgue—just overnight—so the M.E. could write up the death certificate. Maybe somebody on his staff snuck the reporter into the morgue."

"But why?"

"Hell, I don't know," I said. "Maybe Malloy's girlfriend—or boyfriend, or cousin, or somebody—works for the M.E."

"Maybe," he said, but he didn't sound convinced. "Any chance somebody wanted to make you look bad, Doc? You done anything to piss off the San Diego medical examiner?"

"Of course not. Not that I know of, anyhow." I thought for a moment. "Unless he felt like I was stepping on his toes just by being there."

"You mean, like maybe it was an insult—a slap in his face? Like he wasn't good enough—smart enough—to make the I.D. himself?"

"Could be, I reckon," I conceded. "I've worked with a lot of medical examiners over the years, and most of them are great. But some of 'em are pretty weird."

"Hell, Doc, what do you expect from guys who spend all their time with dead bodies?" I felt my hackles begin to rise—being a guy who happened to spend a lot of time with dead bodies myself—but then Maddox added, "Only folks weirder than *that* would be sickos who get their kicks poking around in plane crashes, right?" He chuckled.

"Right," I said, almost smiling in spite of myself. Maddox's wit was one of the things I'd liked about him while we were working the crash.

"So what does Prescott want you to do now?"

"Get lost, basically," I said. "Stay away from the media. Stay away from the case. I've got to take the teeth and bones over to the FBI's Knoxville field office. Should've already done it, but I wanted to take a closer look first—see if it's true about the teeth."

"And?"

"It is. The damn Fox guy got it right."

Maddox didn't speak for a moment. "So . . . I'm guessing this puts you in a kinda awkward spot, huh?"

"Kinda awkward. Like the pope is kinda Catholic."

He grunted a sort of laugh, then said, "Sorry to hear that, Doc."

"Makes two of us." I blew out a long breath. "If the FBI was about to come down hard on Janus, I get *why* he might fake his death. But I don't get *how*. How'd he get that plane to crash into that mountainside, carrying a decoy body and his bloody teeth?" Maddox didn't answer, so I ventured a guess. "The autopilot?"

"The autopilot? How do you mean, Doc?"

"Could Janus program the autopilot to make the plane take off on its own, then turn south and level off?"

"Sure, Doc," Maddox said, "if this was a Hollywood movie. Or if that Citation was a CIA drone. Otherwise, no way. He had to've been at the controls."

"But *how?*"

Maddox sighed. "I'm probably not supposed to tell you."

"Tell me what?"

"Turns out there might've been a way—there *was* a way—for Janus to jump from the plane in flight."

I pulled the handset away from my ear and stared at it, as if the phone were Maddox himself. "But you said there *wasn't.* You said he'd've smashed into the engine right after going out the door."

"He would've—if he'd gone out the cabin door. Which, you may recall, couldn't be opened in flight. So that's all true."

"Then *how?*" I was starting to sound like a broken record.

"Like I say, I shouldn't be telling you things. But I can't keep you from guessing, can I? So think about it, Doc. If he couldn't go out *that* door . . ."

He'd made it easy for me to finish that sentence. "He went out another door—a different door." I searched my mental data banks and called up an image of the aircraft. "But *what* different door? You showed us the cutaway. There *is* no other door on a Citation."

"Well . . . not when it rolls out of the Cessna factory, there's not." He waited, as if he had given a big enough hint to allow me to solve the riddle.

"Ah," I said, the light dawning. "Janus had the Citation modified, didn't he? Bigger engines. Bigger fuel tanks. 'So he could crash harder and burn hotter'— wasn't that how you put it?"

"Good memory. Those were *among* the mods . . ."

"So he had other changes made, too," I said. "Like adding another door somewhere."

"Bingo. And what kind of door might a guy like Janus—a guy delivering stuff to remote villages—want to add?"

"A cargo door. But could that be opened in flight?"

"Depends on the kind of cargo door," he said. "You know what a clamshell belly door is?"

"Is that like a bomb-bay door on a B-17?"

"Bingo," Maddox said. "Main difference between a bomb and a cargo pallet is what happens when it hits the ground."

"And the belly door on the Citation could be opened in flight?"

"That's the whole point of a belly door," he said. "Pretty crazy—the Citation can't carry a lot of cargo, and it must've cost a damn fortune to install that door. But I guess it paid for itself the first time he dropped a pallet-load of cocaine." He paused briefly, as if considering whether or not to tell me something. "You know he had a little private airstrip a few miles from Brown Field, right? Perfect place to do drug drops on his way back from Mexico."

I was still playing catch-up, but it was all starting to make sense. "So you're thinking Janus took off, opened the belly door, and bailed out just before the plane hit?"

"Sure looks like it."

"But he wouldn't have time to open a parachute, would he? That mountain was coming up fast to meet him."

"At the end, yeah, but not at first, Doc. I've looked again at the terrain profile and the aircraft's altitude. The airport, Brown Field, is about five hundred feet above sea level, and so is Lower Otay Lake, where he changed course and headed south. We all thought he was turning toward Mexico, you know? But I think he was aiming straight for Otay Mountain all along. If he jumped when he was over his airstrip, he'd've been a good fifteen hundred feet AGL."

"AGL?" The term wasn't familiar to me.

"Above ground level."

"Fifteen hundred feet? That's high enough to jump?"

"If you know what you're doing," he said. "And if you're lucky. Skydivers are required to pull the cord by two thousand feet AGL. Gives 'em time to pop their reserve chute, if the main doesn't open. Combat jumps can be as low as five hundred feet. But those lunatics that jump off buildings and bridges—BASE jumpers, I think they're called? Some of them jump from two, three hundred feet. Dumb-asses with a death wish."

"So he could've done it."

"Hell, yeah, he could've done it. Would've been pretty fascinating, though."

"Fascinating?" It seemed an odd word to use.

He chuckled. "Sorry. Slang. Means 'scary as hell.' Dark night, rough terrain, fast as he was going? *Extremely* fascinating. Remember D. B. Cooper—Dan Cooper? Hijacked a commercial airliner about thirty years ago?"

"Vaguely," I said. "He got money and a parachute, right, and made the plane take off again?"

"Right," said Maddox. "The plane he picked to hijack was a Boeing 727; damn things had stairs back near the tail that could be lowered in flight. Cooper bailed out around midnight, somewhere over the Columbia River Gorge. To this day, nobody knows whether he survived or not. Maybe that's where Janus got the idea. *In*-ter-esting. Fascinating. Risky as hell, though." He gave a small grunt. "If the Feebies were about to lock him up forever, though, I guess *not* jumping looked risky as hell, too."

Two things still bothered me. I asked Maddox about the first. "So how come we didn't figure this out while we were out there working the scene?" I hoped that the word "we" wouldn't sound accusatory, but he saw right through my politeness.

"You mean, how come the hotshot crash expert missed something as big as a pair of belly doors in the wreckage?" He sounded surprisingly unruffled by the implied criticism.

"Well, okay. Yeah. How come you missed that?"

He chuckled again. "I dunno. Same reason you missed the tool marks on the teeth, maybe?" He didn't sound spiteful; he sounded matter-of-fact, or even slightly amused. "For one thing, the fuselage was pretty thoroughly fragmented."

"True," I conceded. "Looked like it'd been through a shredder."

"A shredder plus an incinerator," he said. "For another thing, the evidence techs—not the ones working with you, but the other four, the ones gathering up the scattered chunks?—they were sending up stuff faster than I could sort through it. I didn't get a chance to start combing through everything till after the press conference. Two days ago, I saw some parts I didn't recognize—a couple hinges and latches—so I dug deeper, started asking around. That's when I found out about the belly door. So I got on the horn to Prescott."

"What'd he say when you told him?"

"Not much. That's the weird thing. It was almost like he'd been expecting it; like somebody'd already told him something. He sounded mad when he picked up the phone. First thing he said was, 'And what's *your* good news?' Like he'd just gotten some other bad news, you know?" He paused. "Maybe he'd just gotten a call about the teeth from Mike Mal-*loy*, *Fox* Five News." He did a pretty good imitation of *my* imitation of the pushy, self-important reporter.

My second question was one Maddox wouldn't be able to answer—it was one maybe nobody could answer—so I thanked Maddox and hung up, leaving the question unasked, except in my own frustrated mind: If it wasn't Janus strapped into the Citation when it hit Otay Mountain, who the hell was it?

Suddenly a third thought struck me. This one wasn't a question, but an inescapable conclusion, and it was the most disturbing of the three. If he really had faked his death and sent a decoy corpse hurtling into the mountainside, that could mean only one thing: that Richard Janus—a man I had admired deeply—was not just a hypocrite and a drug trafficker, but a diabolical killer, too.

Chapter 25

S he answered on the first ring, her voice as flat and expressionless as a computer's. "Yes?"

"Mrs. Janus?" She didn't respond, so I went on. "Mrs. Janus, it's Bill Brockton—Dr. Brockton, the forensic anthropologist—returning your call."

"Oh, thank you, Doctor," she said, and it was as if a switch had flipped: Her voice was no longer mechanical and flat; now it was warm, expressive, and deeply sad. "Thank you. I am very grateful. No one else will return my calls—no one except reporters, and I don't want to talk to them. It is extremely painful, this sudden . . . *not knowing.*"

The phrase, *not knowing*—or, rather, the deep chord it struck in me—took me by surprise. I'd heard the same phrase many times over the years, most often from the parents of abducted kids, runaway girls, or missing young women; I'd also heard it from the families of Vietnam War soldiers who were still, after decades, missing in action. I had pegged Mrs. Janus as different from such simple, open grievers. I had sized her up as cool, calm, and collected—or maybe I had judged her to be complicit and guilty. Now, in response to her comment, I felt my shields lowering and my sympathy rising.

Still, I knew that if not knowing was her problem, I was in no position to solve it. "Unfortunately, Mrs. Janus," I said, "I probably can't tell you anything that will help you. The truth is, I don't know what's going on. I no longer have any idea whether your husband is dead or alive. I wish I did. And I've got your number. If I find out anything, I promise to call you."

"Wait," she said, her voice urgent. "Don't hang up. *Please.* You are my only hope."

"Me? But I just told you—I don't know anything. Really, I don't. I've never been so confused and frustrated by a case." As I said the words "a case," I realized they might sound cold and callous to her. "I'm sorry; I don't mean to sound insensitive or unkind."

"I understand," she said. "And you don't. But tell me, please—at the meeting, you sounded convinced that it was Richard in the plane."

"At the meeting, I was," I said. "But now? Now I don't know."

"The media and the FBI are saying that it *wasn't* Richard," she said. "That it was someone else. That Richard had his teeth pulled, and he killed someone else, and pulled that man's teeth, too. But how can this be, Doctor? It cannot be."

"It *might* be," I said, thinking—just as Maddox had, one phone call and five minutes earlier—that I shouldn't say anything more. But then, just like Maddox, I kept talking. "The only new information I have is this. I just now reexamined the teeth—your husband's teeth—and it's true that they had been pulled. Extracted." I heard what sounded like a soft gasp on the other end of the line. I went on: "I couldn't see that when I found them in the wreckage, because the teeth were covered with soot and grease. But I just now finished cleaning them. And when I looked at them under a magnifying glass, I could see marks—little scratches and cracks—made by forceps or pliers or some other tool."

"*Dios mío*," she whispered. *My God.* "But who could have done this? Could . . . Richard do that himself? Pull all his own teeth, so he could fake his death?"

I hadn't even considered this grisly possibility. "I don't know," I confessed. "I've never heard of anybody pulling out all their own teeth. One or two, sure, but a whole mouthful? There would be a lot of pain. And a lot of blood. I suspect the body would go into shock long before all the teeth were out."

"So if Richard did this—if he faked his death—he would have needed help. An accomplice."

"I think so," I said, wondering if *she* might be the accomplice. I tried to imagine Carmelita Janus—the elegant woman I'd sat across the table from only a few days before—yanking tooth after bloody tooth from her husband's mangled mouth. I couldn't picture it. Suddenly I recalled the FBI's struggle to obtain Janus's dental records. "He might have had a dentist do it. To minimize the pain and the damage. Even so, it would have been a drastic step." I recalled stories I'd heard about coyotes and wolves, caught in traps, gnawing off their own legs to free themselves, but I stopped myself from mentioning those to her. Instead, I simply said, "He would have to be very desperate to do that. But it sounds like maybe he was."

"No. He *wasn't*," she said. Her voice broke, and her breath turned quick and ragged and jerky, like that of a hurt child or an injured animal. "He . . . was worried, yes. Afraid, even. He had agreed to do something dangerous . . . to . . . help someone. But it was almost over, he said, and everything was going to be all right. That was the last thing he said to me. 'I'll be back soon, and everything will be all right.' And then he said, 'I love you so much.' And then . . . he was gone."

I didn't know what to say, so I kept quiet, and she kept sobbing. Finally she spoke again, her voice now thick and gluey. "To think that he was dead—it broke my heart. To think he might be alive—it would make me . . . *happy* . . ." Something about the way she said it—the pause before she said the word; the upward inflection that left the end of the sentence hanging in midair—seemed to contradict her words. "But it also makes me very confused. I thought I knew my husband, Doctor—I thought I knew, absolutely, who he was. Now, I cannot say that, not with conviction. But not to know the truth? That is the worst of all. It will drive me insane. And that is why I beg you to help me."

Perhaps she was just a practiced liar and a good actress, or perhaps I was reacting out of my own wounded pride, but I found myself believing her—and wanting to ease her pain. "Mrs. Janus, I would help you if I could," I said. "But frankly, I don't see how I can. I've been taken off the case. The FBI thinks I botched it. And maybe they're right."

"The FBI." Her voice had turned steely. "The FBI wanted Richard dead. Maybe enough to kill him."

"*Wait* a minute," I said. "They're a law enforcement agency. They're the good guys. They would never do that."

I heard a sharp exhalation. "I see that you're an idealist, Dr. Brockton." There was a note of sadness, or even bitterness, in her words. "Just like Richard. You believe in the goodness of people. And sometimes, yes, that is a gift. A prophecy and a catalyst."

"Excuse me?"

"Sometimes believing that people are good *inspires* them to be good. Inspires them to try harder. Maybe they begin to see themselves the way that you see them; maybe they like what they see, and so they try to *become* it—try to become honest, or kind, or generous; more noble than they have been before. Sometimes." She paused, then added, "But other times, believing good things about people allows them to take advantage of you. Or deceive you. Or even destroy you." She drew another breath, this one long and steady. "Be careful, so this doesn't happen to you also."

This conversation was not going the way I'd expected it to. "As I said, Mrs. Janus, I'm not at all sure I can help you. But maybe you can help me. I'm very confused, too. I still feel sure that those were your husband's teeth in the wreckage."

"Yes, without a doubt," she agreed. "Even if the rest of the remains were someone else's, the teeth were Richard's."

"But the spinal cord stimulator," I pointed out. "That's evidence that the remains—"

"*That,*" she interrupted, "is evidence that the FBI cannot be trusted."

"Why do you say that? The FBI now seems to think that it wasn't Richard in the plane. But the spinal cord stimulator suggests that it *was* him."

Again she surprised me, this time with a brief, bitter laugh. "Not at all," she said. "Richard did not have a spinal cord stimulator."

"I don't understand," I said, more confused than ever. "I saw his medical records. I saw the x-ray. *You* saw the x-ray."

"He *used* to have a spinal cord stimulator," she said. "But it wasn't working, so he had it removed. More than a year ago."

"Then why didn't his medical records say that he'd had it taken out?"

"Because Richard decided that the doctor who put it in was a quack. He stopped going to that doctor. He had it taken out in Mexico City, when we were visiting my family."

My mind was racing. "But why didn't you tell us? Why didn't you say something, when I talked about finding the stimulator in the wreckage? When I showed you the x-ray?"

"You were with the FBI," she said simply. "I did not trust them, so why would I trust you? Why would I tell you anything? If I thought Richard was still alive—hiding somewhere—why would I tell that to the FBI? They would just keep looking for him."

My next question seemed the obvious one. "Then why are you telling me now, Mrs. Janus?"

"Because I have changed my mind about you, Dr. Brockton."

"Why?"

"Two reasons. First, you told me something about yourself that day—a small but important fact, something easy for me to check, to find out if it was the truth or a lie."

"What fact?"

"You told me that you give money to support Richard's work. I checked, and it's true. That tells me that you're an honest man, and also a good man. That is one reason I changed my mind."

"What's the other reason?"

"Because now the FBI has betrayed you, too," she said, her voice cold with contempt. "There is an old saying, Doctor, 'The enemy of my enemy is my friend.' You know this saying?"

"I know the saying, Mrs. Janus," I said, suddenly uncomfortable, "but it doesn't apply here. I don't think I've been betrayed. And the FBI is certainly not my enemy."

"Are you sure, Doctor? The FBI seems to consider *you* an enemy."

I was just about to answer her—disagree with her again—when the building's corrugated metal siding boomed and rattled so loudly I nearly dropped the phone.

"Dr. Brockton," I heard a deep voice calling. "Are you in there?"

What the hell? I thought. *And* who *the hell?*

As if in answer to my question, a voice called out, "Dr. Brockton, if you're in there, I need you to open the door. It's Special Agent Billings. FBI."

Chapter 26

Special Agent Cole Billings—a tall, muscled young man in a suit and a hurry—fixed me with a piercing stare when I tugged open the annex's rusty door. "I'm glad to see you, Dr. Brockton," he said, but his tight jaw and hawkish eyes looked the opposite of glad. "We were getting worried. Nobody seemed to know where you were."

"Oh, sorry to cause a fuss." I gave him my most conciliatory expression. "I've been right here since . . ."—I looked at my watch and gave a vague shrug—"sometime yesterday."

"You don't seem to've told anybody where you'd be," he said. "Your wife said she didn't know. Your secretary, either."

I shook my head, rolling my eyes in what I hoped would pass for embarrassment at my own incompetence.

"You know what they say about absentminded profes-
sors," I told him. "And I've got plenty to make my
mind especially absent lately. A Nashville TV station
has opened a real can of worms. Raising a big stink—
pardon the pun—about veterans' bodies at the Body
Farm. You seen any of that coverage?"

"A little." He said it dismissively, so I'd be sure not
to make the mistake of thinking it mattered to him in
the least.

"What a mess," I went on. "I've been getting phone
calls all hours of the day and night. Reporters circling
my office, even coming to my house. Driving me nuts."
His eyes flickered impatiently. "Anyhow. I'm glad
it's you that found me, not that damn woman from
Nashville. Channel Four." I motioned him inside. "I've
actually been working on something for you guys—
your San Diego colleagues. Cleaning the teeth and
bone fragments."

If possible, he looked even less glad than before,
possibly even alarmed. Apparently this was something
he *did* care about. "From the Janus plane crash?"

I nodded. "I didn't get a chance to clean them out
there. We were scrambling pretty fast. Now that I've
got the soot off, I can see things I couldn't see before.
Tool marks on the teeth. They'd all been pulled!
Damnedest thing I ever saw." I pointed toward the

counter where the material was spread on blue surgical drapes. "Here, let me show you."

His expression turned stone-cold, and I knew he wasn't buying my show of uninformed friendliness. "I'm sure that'd be very interesting, Dr. Brockton, but I don't have time for that. I'm here to pick up that material from you. I'd better just get it and go."

"Oh," I said. "Okay. Of course. It'll take me a few minutes to pack it up. You can help, if you want to, or just look over my shoulder. Make sure I don't miss anything."

His eyes searched my face for signs of sarcasm, and it was quite possible that he found them. As I packed and padded the teeth and bits of bone, giving a verbal accounting of the items, he stood at my side, watching closely, and he reread the evidence receipt three times before signing it, bearing down so hard that the point of the pen almost tore through the paper.

By the time I finished cleaning the annex—not only the slight mess I had made, but also the accumulated dust, dead bugs, and cobwebs of two prior years of neglect—it was six P.M.; I had been holed up for well over twenty-four hours, scrubbing and studying the teeth, my only sustenance the two apples and the three packs of peanut butter crackers I'd brought from home. Even though I was tired, hungry, and dirty, I hated to leave, because leaving meant plunging into the turbulence of the two storm systems swirling around me: the Janus case, where I was being made to look incompetent, and the Channel 4 ruckus—"Vet-Gate," one newspaper reporter had dubbed it—where I was being portrayed as uncaring and unpatriotic. Not to mention the other problem, which wasn't just painful but potentially deadly: Satterfield.

Raising the metal garage door, amid another chorus of metallic banshee shrieks, I stepped outside, blinking and stretching in the golden, slanting light. Drawing a deep breath, I smelled something unpleasant—something that I quickly realized must be me. I took a deep, analytical sniff and came to the conclusion that if I had been the subject of a multiple-choice exam question— "Which of the following does Bill Brockton stink of?"—the correct answer would be "(d) all the above." Suddenly, to my surprise, I detected a delightful aroma amid the malodorous miasma, and my mouth began to water, as reflexively and reliably as those of Pavlov's dogs. *Ribs*, I realized, my nostrils dilating, my head swiveling into the breeze like some ravenous, carnivorous weathervane. A quarter mile away, a thin plume of smoke spooled upward from the kitchen of Calhoun's on the River and wafted my way. *Do I dare,*

I wondered, *dirty as I am?* I took another deep drag of the divine scent. *I do, I do,* I decided; I could ask for an outside table, on the patio overlooking the water, and I could duck into the bathroom on my way into the restaurant and do a bit of damage control at the sink. Life was looking up.

Reflexively I reached for my cell phone to call Kathleen. She probably wouldn't want ribs again so soon (had our anniversary dinner really been less than two weeks ago? It seemed like months). But my hand came up empty, and I remembered that I'd left my phone on the counter at home, so that Kathleen and I could both truthfully say that I didn't have it with me. What was the phrase the CIA had coined back in the 1960s—when they were hatching political-assassination plots they didn't tell the president about? *Plausible deniability*: the I-didn't-know legal loophole. I'd left my cell phone at home so I could say I didn't know that the FBI was looking for me, but now plausible deniability was circling back to bite me in the butt—or at least to make it hard to score a dinner date with my wife. "Crap," I muttered, ducking back inside to call her from the annex phone.

Kathleen didn't answer her cell or the house line. Finally I remembered that she'd mentioned being off the grid today, too—something about a journal article she desperately needed to finish writing. I dialed her office on campus, on the off chance that she was holed up there, now that everyone else had likely left for the day. No luck. "Crap," I repeated, not wanting to eat alone. Deflated again, I backed my truck out of the corrugated cave, wrestled down the screeching door and locked it, heading for home and for leftovers in lieu of ribs by the riverside.

On an impulse, instead of heading directly home, I detoured to Kathleen's building, hoping for a chance to tell her about my conversations with Maddox, Mrs. Janus, and Special Agent Billings. I didn't see her car in the parking lot, though, and her office window looked dark. Only then did I remember that she had planned to hole up in the library.

I parked in a fire lane outside the library's main entrance on Melrose Avenue, switching on the truck's flashers in hopes that they might ward off a ticket or a tow truck. I took a quick spin through the coffee shop and the study areas on the main floor without spotting her, then peered through the doors of several study rooms, before it occurred to me that she might be downstairs in Reference. I didn't see her there, either, but I did see a librarian I knew slightly, peering at a computer screen. *Thelma? Velma?* Neither of those names seemed quite right. "Hello there," I said to her. "How long before actual books are a thing of the past?"

She looked up, reflexively smiling when she recognized me. Then something flickered in her eyes, and she looked slightly embarrassed, as if she'd remembered something unseemly about me. "Oh. Dr. Brockton. Hello."

"I don't suppose you've seen my wife in here this evening," I said.

"No, but I've been staring at this screen pretty hard. Feel free to take a look around."

"I already did. Didn't see her. She's working on an article, so I thought she might've needed help finding something."

"Well, not that I know of, but if I see her, I'll tell her you were looking for her."

"Thanks." I nodded and started away, but then stopped and turned back. "Oh, long as I'm here . . . is, uh, Red working tonight?"

"Who?"

"Red. That's her nickname. I don't know her actual name. Young woman. Smart. Sarcastic, but in a fun way." Thelma/Velma/what's-her-name was giving me a blank stare. "You know, *Red,*" I repeated. "I think that's the color of her hair."

"I can't think of anybody who fits that description. Not in Reference, anyway. Maybe she's in Periodicals?"

"No," I said, feeling embarrassed and awkward—stupid, even—but also stubborn, not quite ready to give up. "Reference. I've talked to her two or three times. She was working the late shift one night a couple weeks ago when I called. June . . . twentieth, I think. Just before midnight. You could check the staff schedule."

"I don't need to," she said.

"Excuse me?"

"I don't need to check the staff schedule to tell you that there was nobody named Red working late that night. Nobody named *anything*."

"I don't understand."

"The library's open till midnight during summer session," she said, "but the Reference Desk is only staffed until ten."

I stripped in the garage, tossed my clothes into the washing machine, and stepped into the shower in the basement bathroom. I stayed there, slumped under the spray, until the water turned cold. I was physically exhausted—I hadn't slept in almost forty hours—but I was unmoored and off kilter, too, from the roller-coaster ride of all the recent revelations, confrontations, implications, and miscommunications: Prescott's angry message, Maddox's new information, Mrs. Janus's mistrust of the FBI. The last two back-breaking straws had been my unsuccessful search for Kathleen, followed by the disquieting discovery that

"Red"—to whom I had confided about the Janus case—was a stranger and an imposter of some sort, someone whose motives and machinations were utter mysteries to me.

Shivering as I stepped out from under the chilly water, I dried off, wrapped the towel around me, and trundled upstairs, where I found Tupperware containers of baked beans and potato salad deep in the fridge: the remains, I realized, of our anniversary dinner. The beans looked and smelled fine; the potato salad was slightly suspect, with a gauzy layer of mold floating above the chunky surface. It seemed more like a layer of ground fog than a deeply established colony of fungus, so I commenced a culinary version of an archaeological dig, removing the top stratum and setting it aside before excavating in earnest, shoveling it into my mouth.

By the time I'd finished the potato salad and baked beans, my whole body was buzzing with fatigue. Shuffling back to the bedroom, I pulled on a soft, ragged pair of sweatpants and a paint-spattered T-shirt, then returned to the living room and settled onto the sofa to watch a bit of the History Channel until Kathleen came home. Outside, the summer light began to fade. Inside, the sights and sounds of World War II filled the room. Within minutes, the menacing growls of warplanes and the lethal clatter of machine-gun fire lulled me into a deep, dreamless sleep.

I awoke to daylight—bright morning daylight—streaming through the living room windows. Surfacing from fathomless depths, I felt disoriented, staring around the room as if it were unfamiliar territory. The television screen was dark and silent, so evidently Kathleen had come in at some point during the war and switched it to peacetime mode. But why hadn't she waked me, even if only to lead me to bed?

"Kathleen? Kathleen! Are you here?"

"I'm in the kitchen, honey. About to leave."

Swinging my feet onto the floor, I levered myself into a sitting position and pushed myself off the couch. Rounding the corner into the kitchen, I saw Kathleen rinsing her coffee cup, her briefcase already slung over one shoulder. Still groggy, I moved toward her, hoping for a kiss. "Why didn't you wake me up? What time did you get in?"

"Really late," she said. "Midnight, maybe? You were really out of it—I could hear you snoring from down in the garage, as soon as I got out of my car—so I figured I should just let sleeping dogs lie."

"I wish you'd woken me up. I really wanted to see you."

"Sorry, hon. I was afraid you wouldn't be able to get back to sleep if I woke you up. And I was desperate to get to sleep by the time I got home last night. After you left yesterday—no, day before yesterday; God, I'm so tired—the phone started ringing off the hook. Reporters and FBI agents calling all afternoon and half the night. So I didn't get much sleep Sunday night. And yesterday was . . . well, intense." She picked up her keys from the counter.

I glanced at the microwave clock. It read 8:15—later than my usual departure time, but earlier than hers. "Do you have to go right now?" I heard a note of petulance in my voice, and I realized that my feelings were hurt.

"I have a meeting at eight-thirty, darling." She came and gave me a peck on the cheek, then slid off and headed downstairs for the garage. "I'll talk to you this evening," she called up the stairs. "Love you."

"Love you, too," I murmured to the empty doorway, my unheard voice a mix of wistfulness and resentment.

Chapter 27

Peggy glowered when I entered the Anthropology Department office at nine on Tuesday—not because I was an hour later than usual, but because I'd been AWOL for all of Monday, hunkered down in the abandoned annex. I knew she was about to light into me, but I held up a preemptive hand and shook my head. "Not now, Peggy. Messages on my desk?"

"A few *dozen*." Her tone was as biting as a pair of fingernail clippers.

"Thank you." I headed through the doorway into my administrative office—the one where I met with struggling students, frustrated faculty, and bean-counting bureaucrats—and gathered up the mound of pink messages. If anything, Peggy had understated the number. Curling them into a haphazard scroll, I cinched them with a fat rubber band and headed back out through Peggy's office.

"You're already *leaving?*"

"No. Just heading down to my other office to sort through all this. Buzz me if Kathleen calls. Or the dean. Or the FBI." I sighed as a bleak thought occurred to me. "Or the general counsel, I guess. But reporters? I'm in an all-day meeting."

"What meeting? You don't have a meeting on your schedule." It wasn't like Peggy to be dense, so I suspected that she was subtly gigging me, slightly punishing me.

"The meeting between my butt and the chair at the far end of the stadium. The quiet end of the stadium."

She opened her mouth, but—perhaps seeing the warning in my eyes—shut it and simply nodded.

I made it to the north end of the stadium without encountering another soul in the long corridor that curved beneath the grandstands. Breathing a sigh of relief, I unlocked the door of my private sanctuary, hung out the DO NOT DISTURB sign, and locked myself inside.

Ten minutes later, there was a knock at the door. I knew it wasn't Peggy; in twelve years as my secretary, she had made the long, dark trek to this end of the stadium only twice—both times in her first week on the job. I considered who it might be. The last thing I wanted to do right now was talk to a graduate student. Or a colleague. Or anyone else, I realized, with the exception—the *possible* exception—of Kathleen. I ignored it. After a pause, the knocking resumed, louder this time. Again I ignored it. "Hello? Dr. Brockton? You in there?" I recognized the voice of Brian Decker, and I considered him friend, not foe.

"Oh, just a second, Deck," I called, hurrying to open the door. "Hey. Sorry to keep you waiting. I was preoccupied"—I pointed an accusatory finger at the heap of phone messages—"trying to figure out which of these alligators is gonna take the biggest bite out of my ass. What's up?"

"The plot thickens," he said. "You were right."

"Well, *that's* not something I've heard much lately," I said. "About what?"

"About running the print from that finger. That kid's pinkie. I got a hit."

"No kidding? The kid's already got a record? He *is* a prodigy."

"Not a criminal record," he said. "An I.D. record."

"I'm not following you," I said.

"There's been a big push, the last few years, to put kids' prints on file," he said. "So if a kid goes missing, we've got something besides photos to work with."

"You mean if a body turns up?"

He frowned; nodded. "Yeah, but not just that," he said. "Also, if the missing kid—or someone who *might* be the kid—turns up years later."

"Makes sense," I said. "Like putting a computer chip in your dog's neck, right?"

He nodded. "Like that. The new version of that is DNA—parents can buy DNA kits now—collect a cheek swab and send it off to a company that'll run the profile and store it."

"For a fee," I said.

"For a fee. But fingerprints are free."

"But we're talking about Satterfield's kid here," I said. "So putting the kid's fingerprints in a database seems like the last thing Mom and Dad would want to do."

Decker raised his eyebrows. "Like I said, the plot thickens," he repeated. "This isn't Satterfield's kid."

"How do you know? And if it's not his, whose is it?"

"It's Tim and Tammy Martin's kid," he said. "And I know because I talked to them."

I stared at him, dumbfounded. "And their kid's missing a finger?"

"Unfortunately, their kid's missing a lot more than that," he said. "Their kid's dead."

"Jesus," I said. "Murdered?"

He shook his head. "Accidental death. Two weeks ago. Riding his bike. A seventeen-year-old girl ran over him. She was dialing her cell phone." I frowned, partly because I was appalled by the senseless death, partly because I couldn't imagine how these puzzle pieces fit together. Decker reached into his shirt pocket and pulled out an index card, which he handed to me.

Except it wasn't an index card, it was a photo: a headshot of a woman looking—scowling—directly at the camera. The woman was five feet seven inches tall; I could tell this from the inch-by-inch measurements stenciled on the wall behind her. I looked from the photo to Decker, puzzled. "This looks like a mug shot," I said. "But if she's seventeen, I'm not a day over twenty."

"She's not. Take another look." I studied it again. She looked familiar, but I was having trouble placing her. Decker raised his eyebrows, watching me closely. "Recognize her? From Satterfield's trial?"

I felt a mixture of excitement and dread rising in me. "My God, it's her! The weird groupie woman?"

"Give that man a cigar," he said. "Or a finger."

I stared at him, baffled. "I still don't get it, Deck. Connect the dots for me."

"Think about it," he said. "I'll give you a hint. The kid still had the finger when he was hit by the car."

I was about to snap at him—about to tell him I didn't have the time or energy for guessing games—when I realized that playing twenty questions with Decker was probably the most fun I would have all day. *All day? Hell, maybe even all week,* I thought, glancing again at the pile of angry, insistent messages.

"So the parents," I mused. "I'm guessing they're not connected to Satterfield, or the package—that they had nothing to do with cutting off their son's finger."

He shook his head. "They were horrified when I told them about it. And furious."

My mind sorted through various possibilities. "So the girl runs over the boy. Somebody calls 911. The EMTs and the police—city, or county?"

"County. Sheriff's deputies."

"The EMTs and the deputies arrive. Is the kid alive or dead when he goes into the ambulance?"

"Alive. Dies on the way to the hospital. Head trauma—no helmet—and internal injuries."

"Poor kid. But his finger's still attached, you say."

"Right."

"And then he's taken to the morgue. Is that where the parents first see him?"

"Yes. Took a while to track them down."

I could feel the picture coming into focus. "So they I.D.'d the body at the morgue. And the finger must've still been on his hand then. Because if it wasn't, they'd have noticed and started asking questions. And anyhow, Garland"—Dr. Garland Hamilton, the Knox County medical examiner—"would've pounced on that. An amputation that clean? He'd have been on that like a duck on a June bug." Decker nodded, smiling slightly, and I continued, on a roll now. "So the boy still had the finger when he was in the morgue. But unless somebody dug up his body"—I felt almost as energized now as when I was working a death scene—"the finger must've been amputated between the time he left the morgue and the time he was buried." Decker was beaming now. "My God," I said, "so Satterfield's groupie-woman works at the funeral home? She cut off the finger while she was embalming the boy's body?"

"See," he said, "I knew you could figure it out."

"He must've told her to be on the lookout for a finger to send me. A woman's or a kid's. They're pen pals, right?"

"Pen pals, and more," he said. "The mailroom says they swap letters two, three times a month. And she visits once or twice a year."

I looked again at the mug shot. In addition to her name, the placard in the image bore a calendar date.

I looked up. "She was arrested *yesterday*?" He nodded, looking pleased, and I pressed on. "For this?"

"Yup. Desecrating a corpse."

"Any evidence? Besides circumstantial?"

"We got *so lucky* on this one," he said. "There was a big scandal, couple months back, about a Memphis mortician who was having sex with female corpses."

"I remember that. Really disgusting."

"No kidding, Doc. Anyhow, the guy that owns the funeral home handling this boy's burial? He got spooked by that Memphis stuff. Had hidden cameras installed in all the embalming rooms. So when I showed up yesterday, asking who had access to the kid's body, he puffs up, all proud, and says, 'Here, let's take a look.' He calls up the footage on his computer with me sitting right there. Doc, you should've seen that man's face when it showed this gal—his employee, mind you—slicing off the kid's finger. That man was shitting bricks. Probably still is. I'm guessing the kid's parents are gonna sue the pants off him."

"I wouldn't worry too much about his pants," I said. "Most funeral homes have huge insurance policies. That's one reason funerals cost so damn much." I looked again at the mug shot. "So she's in custody. She talking? About Satterfield?"

He made a face. "Nah, she's all lawyered up. My guess is, she'll end up trying to cut a deal. And maybe the D.A. will require cooperation as part of that." I frowned, and he went on. "Meanwhile, I'm thinking I might take a little road trip over to Clifton. South Central Correctional Facility."

"To see Satterfield?"

"See him. Talk to him. Rattle his cage a little. Have a frank, man-to-man chat in a private interview room." He began to nod slowly, a dark glint in his eyes, his fingers clenching and unclenching rhythmically. "Suggest that it's not a good idea to bother you and your family."

For a moment, I allowed myself to imagine what I suspected Decker himself was imagining: Decker, built like a linebacker, beating the crap out of Satterfield. I imagined it, and I liked it. I liked it a lot. I felt myself yielding to the idea, being taken over by it. It was as if I were spellbound, enchanted by the siren song of violent vengeance. It almost seemed as if I myself were the one slamming Satterfield's face against a cinder-block wall, kicking Satterfield's splintering ribs. Suddenly my fantasy took an unexpected and horrifying turn. During a split-second pause in the carnage, Satterfield managed to turn his face toward me, and through the bloody lips and the broken teeth, he grinned at me: a mocking, malicious, complicit grin. "Gotcha," the grin seemed to say. "How do you like it, becoming me?"

"*No!*" My voice—my shout—startled me from my waking dream. Was I shouting at Satterfield, at myself, or at Decker? I had no idea.

Decker stared at me. "Doc? What's wrong?"

I felt a shudder run through me. "Nothing. Sorry. Just . . . probably not a good idea to go see Satterfield. But, Christ, that guy is still under my skin. Like some dormant virus, or a cancer cell—lurking, biding its time, you know?" He nodded. A thought struck me. "Know much about shingles?"

"Roofing shingles?"

"Medical shingles. The disease."

"Not much," he said. "Old people get it, right? Very painful, I've heard."

"Ever have chicken pox, as a kid?"

"Sure. Itched like crazy."

"The virus that caused it? You've still got it," I said. "When your immune system kicked in, it killed most of the virus, but not all. Some of it survived; it's hiding at the base of one of your spinal nerves, coiled up like a snake. One day when you're fifty or sixty or seventy, something reactivates it—nobody really knows how or why—and it comes slithering out."

Suddenly Decker grabbed the edge of my desk with both hands. He went pale and began to breathe in quick, sharp pants; sweat beaded on his forehead and began to run down his face. His eyes were wide and wild, staring with an expression of utter horror at something that was either miles away from my office, or deep within himself.

"Deck? What's the matter?"

"Kev," he whispered, then—louder: "Kevin! No!"

I leaned across the desk and squeezed one of Decker's forearms. The muscles were clenched so tightly, his arm felt like a bar of cast iron. Then I realized what must have happened. Decker's younger brother, Kevin—a bomb-squad technician—had died while searching Satterfield's house for explosives: killed not by a booby trap, but by a deadly snake, a fer-de-lance, that had been set loose in the house. Comparing Satterfield to a lurking virus—and then comparing the virus to a snake—must have taken Decker back to the scene of his brother's death. It was as if I had poured gasoline on Decker's memory, then held a lighted match to it, and I cursed myself for my stupidity. "Hey, Deck," I said, squeezing his arm tighter. "Deck, can you hear me? It's Bill Brockton, Deck. We're here in my office at Neyland Stadium." I waved my other hand in front of his staring eyes, but it had no effect. Trying to get his attention, I began snapping my fingers near his face, moving the hand slightly from side to side, all the while calling his name. His body was now trembling, as if shivering hard, and I had visions of his heart giving out or an aneurysm in his brain bursting. *I've got to get him out of this,* I thought, and in desperation, I began tapping his cheekbone with my fingertips. He seemed not to notice, so I tapped harder, still to no effect, and then I began to slap him gently—*the sound of one hand clapping,* I thought absurdly—still calling his name and telling him mine. I was beginning to despair— wondering whether to call 911 or someone in the Psychiatric Department at UT Medical Center—when he reached up and seized my wrist, with a grip that felt like a vise, and brought my hand down to the desk. "Deck," I said, struggling not to cry out. "Deck, it's Bill Brockton. Can you hear me, Deck? I need you to hear me. I need you to stay with me, Deck. Come back from wherever you've gone. Come back to Neyland Stadium, to my office by the north end zone."

At that moment my phone rang. With my free hand I reached to answer it, but just before I did, I noticed that Decker's eyes had flickered at the sound, so I decided to let it keep ringing, in hopes that somehow the phone would manage to reel him back from wher- ever he'd gone. *Keep ringing,* I prayed, and it did: two times; three; four. By the fourth ring, his eyes seemed to be coming into focus, searching for the source of the sound. "That's the phone on my desk ringing," I said. "It might be Kathleen, my wife, calling me. You remember Kathleen, don't you, Deck? Remember that lunch we had at Calhoun's?" I caught myself just in the nick of time—just before saying "right after Satterfield's trial?"—and changed course to say, "You remember that huge pile of rib bones we left on the table?" The phone was still ringing. "You wouldn't believe how much my phone's been ringing lately, Deck. The FBI thinks I screwed up a case in San Diego, and I have about fifty reporters wanting to interview me about what a dumb-ass I am."

He blinked and seemed to be trying to get his bearings. I kept talking. "I have another fifty wanting to tar and feather me for disrespecting veterans—using them in our research at the Body Farm." He blinked again, then turned to look at me, his expression suggesting that he vaguely remembered me but couldn't quite place me. I plowed ahead, encouraged that he seemed to be heading in the right direction, namely, the direction of sanity. "I'm afraid they might try to shut down the Body Farm, Deck. I know the police understand how important our research is. So do prosecutors. But bureaucrats and politicians? I'm not sure they know or care. What should I do, Deck? How do I protect the work I care about?"

"I don't know," he said, then: "Sorry, what? I think I spaced out for a second there. What were we talking about?"

"Beats me, Deck," I said. I nodded at the phone—still ringing, now for at least the twentieth time—and added, "That damned thing just won't quit ringing. Made me forget whatever it was I was saying." He nodded, looking almost normal now, so I ventured, "Hey, Deck?"

"Yeah, Doc?"

"You reckon maybe you could turn loose of my wrist? I'm starting to lose the feeling in my fingers."

An hour after Decker left—finally sounding sane but still looking haunted and harrowed—my fingers were still tingling from his viselike grip on my wrist. Before he departed, I had nervously circled back to the subject of Satterfield, urging Deck not to go to the prison and "rattle his cage," as he'd put it. "If you do," I said, "he'll know he's getting to me." Deck had grunted, then nodded—conceding, apparently, that cage rattling might not be a brilliant idea. I appreciated the concession. I just wished it had seemed more convincing.

After Decker's departure, I had begun scaling the mountain of messages—the Everest of Insistence—that Peggy had left for me. I started by sorting them into three categories: Not Important, Urgent, and 911. After leafing through the first ten messages, I saw that the Not-Important stack contained no messages; all ten had ended up in the 911 stack. I redefined the categories—Bad, Worse, and Worst—but the outcome was similar, with all the messages landing in Worst. Next I briefly considered (and swiftly rejected) Worst, More Worst, and Most Worst, then settled on Oh Shit, Holy Shit, and Somebody Shoot Me. Still no change.

Clearly a paradigm shift was required. Instead of sorting by urgency, I decided to categorize by caller: Media Meddlers, UT Honchos, and Other. This time, the results were different, and though I certainly didn't think I had conquered, I had, at least, divided: The callers were split almost evenly between two categories, Media Meddlers and UT Honchos, with only a few outliers in Other. Many of the messages were duplicates, I noticed: UT's general counsel, Amanda Whiting, had called four times; the dean had dialed me twice; my newswoman nemesis, Athena Demopoulos, had tried me three times; and one persistent caller—the record holder—had left me seven messages, each of which bore the same San Diego number, followed by the words "Mike Malloy, Fox Five News!!!" I tossed the duplicate messages—and all of Malloy's—and found to my relief that I actually had only a dozen callers chasing me, rather than two or three dozen. Better yet, I decided I could safely ignore most of the reporters, though not, alas, my Nashville nemesis.

The one caller whose name stood out as a pleasant surprise was Wellington Meffert, a Tennessee Bureau of

Investigation agent who was better known, to lawmen and lawbreakers in the mountainous East Tennessee counties he covered, as "Bubba Hardknot." Meffert had left me only two messages, but because I actually looked forward to talking with him, I moved Bubba to the head of the line. I was reaching for the phone to call him when the intercom buzzed. "Well, crap," I muttered to myself, then—picking up the handset—answered with, "Yes, Peggy. Which particular pain in my ass is about to flare up?"

"Two of them, actually," answered an echoey female voice that sounded familiar but didn't sound like Peggy. My heart sank and my face flushed as the voice continued, "It's Amanda Whiting, Dr. Brockton. The dean and I decided to drop by for a visit. Peggy was kind enough to put us on speaker when she paged you."

"That *was* kind," I said drily.

Sitting in the leather swivel chair behind the oak desk in my administrative office, I occupied the seat of power, at least furniture-wise. But looking across at the grim faces of the dean and the general counsel, perched on the ladder-back chairs normally occupied by failing students, I knew that my position was tenuous, at best. Amanda Whiting, UT's top legal eagle, seemed ready to tear me to shreds with her Harvard-honed talons, and the dean—long one of my staunchest supporters—was relegated to the role of onlooker and sympathetic spectator as the shredding commenced and the blood began to flow. "Dr. Brockton, I appreciate the contribution that your research facility has made to forensic science," Whiting was saying for at least the third time.

Methinks thou dost protest too much, I thought, but what I interrupted her to say was, "Not just 'has made,' Amanda."

"Excuse me?"

"You said 'has made.' We're still making contributions. Present tense, and future tense. We've got a dozen studies under way right now, and more coming down the pike, some of them really exciting."

Whiting responded with a nod that acknowledged what I'd said and yet somehow, at the same time, dismissed it as utterly irrelevant. "I understand," she said, and then proceeded to demonstrate that she didn't, in fact, understand and also didn't care. "But surely *you* can understand that the university needs to prioritize risk management and damage control."

"Can I?" I could feel my blood pressure ratcheting up. "My understanding has always been that the university's priorities are the pursuit of knowledge and the education of students. When did those get replaced by playing it safe and covering our asses?"

She flushed, not from embarrassment but from anger. "Don't play the simpleton," she snapped, and I felt my own color rising. Before I could retort, she barreled on. "How much of our funding comes from the state?"

"A lot."

"You're damn right, a lot. A hundred fifty million dollars this year, give or take a few million. And if the state decided to take a few million—or more than a few—how do you propose that we fund the pursuit of knowledge and the education of students? You ready to teach for free?"

"What's your point, Amanda? You want to cut off my salary?"

"No, dammit, but the legislature might."

"Oh, please," I said. "Now who's playing the simpleton?"

The dean shifted in his chair, scraping the legs across the floor, as if the chair were clearing its throat for attention. "Hang on, both of you. Can we maybe dial this back a notch or two?" Whiting and I continued to glare at each other, and he tried again. "We're all on the same side, remember? And you've both got a point. Amanda, Bill's research has made the Anthropology Department one of the best in the country." I felt better, but only until he added, "But, Bill, the hornets that the Channel Four story stirred up might be about to sting us bad."

I turned my full attention on him. "Sting us how? What do you mean?"

He frowned. "You remember that state senator in the story?"

"That grandstanding dummy from Jackson? What about him?"

"Apparently he wasn't just grandstanding. He's drafted a bill for the next legislative session. If you don't shut down your research program, it would cut the university's state funding."

"You've got to be kidding," I said, but I could tell by his expression that this was no joke. "Cut our funding? By how much?"

Amanda Whiting answered for him. "By one hundred percent," she said. She no longer sounded angry; now she sounded demoralized and defeated. "Every damn cent."

Chapter 28

The next morning I got up at five, an hour before my alarm was set to go off, and slipped from bed. Kathleen lay motionless, her breathing steady, and I decided not to wake her—if, indeed, she was sleeping, though I half suspected she was not.

We had been off kilter and cross all through the prior evening, to a degree that was rare and perhaps even unprecedented for us. I still hadn't told her about Satterfield's threat, and withholding that information meant that I couldn't tell her about Decker's meltdown in my office, either. My secrecy almost certainly contributed to my testiness—partly because withholding anything from Kathleen ran deeply counter to my nature. I had tried several times, on the other hand, to talk about both the Janus case and the political assault on the Body Farm. But Kathleen, usually so solicitous and sympathetic, had seemed distant and preoccupied. By bedtime, our conversation had cooled to curt mono-syllables, and we had slept, to the degree that either of us succeeded in sleeping, with our backs to each other.

Threading my way through our neighborhood in the predawn darkness, I turned onto Cherokee Boulevard, which was flanked on one side by mansions and on the other by a long ribbon of riverfront parkland. A low layer of fog, only a few feet thick, blanketed the fields and river; as I drove, my headlights created a luminous oval pool within the fog, but the air above the lights— the air up where I sat—was clear, so I had the odd sensation that my truck had been transformed into a boat, and that I was not so much driving as navigating, finding my way through a channel whose margins were outlined by the familiar hedges and streetlamps rising from the depths and piercing the surface. At the bou-levard's roundabout, the big, illuminated fountain— normally spouting from a waist-high round basin—had been transformed into a marine geyser, jetting up through the fog as if from some undersea vent or fault line. As I curved past it, I slammed on the brakes. A solitary runner, visible only from the chest up, was rounding the fountain. The bizarre image—a human-headed sea monster swimming past a waterspout in the ocean—haunted me for the remainder of the drive to campus. *Signs and omens,* I thought, *but of what?*

I parked my truck in the cool dark beneath the stadium's south end, down beside the basement door leading to the bone lab. In the quiet of dawn, I could hear the truck's engine ticking with heat, and the sound seemed to echo some ominous interior ticking I sensed but couldn't pinpoint: the ticking of something about to explode. *Satterfield? The Janus debacle? The backlash over the veterans? None of the above? All of the above?* I couldn't shake the feeling that in some soft blind spot, a creature with claws was clutching at me. Another unsettling image flashed into my mind, displacing that of the sea-monster man swimming through the fog: a naked man chained to a rock, a ragged wound in his side, a sharp-beaked eagle tearing at his liver. *Prometheus,* I remembered. But Prometheus—an immortal—had stolen fire from the gods. Had I committed some great transgression? Was I guilty of hubris, the arrogant pride that went before a fall, in both Greek mythology and Christian teaching? In seeking to unlock the secrets of death, was I guilty of overweening ambition—of trespassing in divine realms where mere mortals were not allowed?

The ticking—of the truck's engine or of the more ominous cosmic machinery—seemed to grow louder, and just as I recognized the sound of footsteps, a face loomed in front of me. I jumped, and then realized, with a mixture of fear, relief, and embarrassment that the last, loudest ticking I'd heard—a split-second afer the footsteps—had been the sound of someone tapping on my window to get my attention. "Dr. Brockton?" I blinked, disoriented, then recognized the face of Steve Morgan, a former student who now worked for the Tennessee Bureau of Investigation.

"Steve?" I rolled down the window. "You scared the crap out of me. Am I under arrest?" I said it as a joke—or *thought* I did—but in my skittish, spooked state of mind, it came out sounding more paranoid than humorous. I tried to smooth over the awkwardness with another joke. "Looks like I could learn a trick or two from the TBI. I never could motivate you to get to class by eight."

This one didn't fall quite so flat. He smiled, though in the watery light now coming from the eastern sky, the smile looked faint. "Doc, could I talk to you about something? A personal matter?"

I felt a rush of sympathy and relief. "Sure, Steve. I'm always happy to help a former student, if I can." Rolling up the window and opening the door, I got out and shook his hand. For the first time I noticed the black Crown Victoria parked fifty yards away. "You been staking me out? Or did you just know I'd be up with the chickens?"

"I remembered you were an early bird," he said. "But also, I couldn't sleep. Figured I might as well come on down and wait for you."

"You *are* in a state. Come inside."

He frowned. "Mind if we stay outside? Walk and talk? I don't want to bring this into your office."

"Sounds serious. Sure, let's go." I clicked my key fob to lock the truck, then we started out along the narrow service road that circled the base of the stadium, weaving in and out of concrete footings and angled steel girders. We walked in silence a while; I didn't want to press him, and he was in no hurry to begin.

When we reached the other end of the stadium—where an access tunnel led through the base of the grandstands to the playing field—I noticed that the chain-link gate was unlocked and standing open. Pointing to it, I walked through. We emerged at one corner of the north end zone. The transition—from the dark, narrow passageway to the vast bowl of the stadium opening before us—seemed to free up something in Steve.

"I don't know much about marriage," he began, stopping and leaning against the padding around the base of the goalpost. "Sherry and I have only been married three years. I'm still trying to figure out how it works."

"Me, too," I said, giving his shoulder a sympathetic squeeze. Sherry, his wife, had been my student, too; in fact, my osteology class was where they had met, and where Steve had first asked her out. "I've been married thirty years now, and sometimes I still find myself scratching my head, wondering what the hell just happened." His only response was a ruminative grunt, so I went on. "What's got you worried, Steve? Your marriage in a rough patch?"

"No, sir," he said. "I think maybe yours is."

I took a step back. "Excuse me?"

He turned to face me. "Do you know where your wife was day before yesterday, Dr. Brockton? What she was doing?"

I stared at him, baffled and filled with a sense of dread. "She was in the library at UT. Writing a journal article."

"No, sir," he said again, shaking his head with what appeared to be deep sadness. "She was in Nashville. At the Vanderbilt Plaza Hotel."

"What the hell are you talking about?"

"I saw your wife in Nashville that day, Dr. Brockton. At the Vanderbilt Plaza Hotel. With a man. They were having lunch. He was holding her hand."

I felt confused. I felt sick. And I felt mad as hell at Steve. "You're mistaken," I said angrily. "Kathleen was here—on this campus, in the library—all day and most of the evening." He shook his head, and I wanted to hit him. "You barely know her, Steve—you've seen her, what, two or three times in your life? I can't believe you'd accuse her of something like this." I spun and walked away, across the goal line, toward midfield.

"BDK 643," he called after me.

I stopped in my tracks, then turned to look at him. "What did you say?" It was a reflexive question, one I needn't have asked.

"BDK 643," he repeated. "That's the tag of the car she drove away in. Toyota Camry with a Knox County plate. I ran it. It's registered to you."

"I know," I said. My knees had gone weak. I motioned to a bench by the sideline and sat down heavily. I felt as if someone—someone big, like a UT defensive lineman or cornerback—had just knocked me flat. "Tell me what you saw. Start at the beginning. Don't leave anything out."

Thirty minutes later, Kathleen opened her office door. When she saw me sitting behind her desk, she dropped her keys. They clattered to the floor with unnatural loudness. "*Bill.* You scared me to death. What are you doing here?"

"Who is it, Kathleen?"

"What?"

"Who is it? Who is he? You're having an affair. I want to know who the sonofabitch is."

She gave me an odd look. There was no shame in it, as I'd expected there would be; instead, I saw . . . what? Grimness? Sorrow? Disappointment? "No," she said after a moment. "I'm not having an affair."

"Dammit, Kathleen, stop lying to me. You said you were in the library all day Monday. Writing. Trying to meet a submission deadline. That's a lie. You were in Nashville." Her eyes narrowed and her chin lifted slightly—a warning sign, one that might have given me pause under any other circumstances. "You were with a man at the Vanderbilt Plaza Hotel. Don't even think about telling me you weren't, because I *know.*"

"You've been *spying* on me?"

"No, I have *not* been spying on you," I said. "Steve Morgan saw you there. Saw you holding hands with some man. He thought I deserved to know." I shook my head. "I told Steve he was wrong—told him it couldn't've been you, because you were here at UT, working in the library. But then he showed me a picture of your car, and your license plate. And then he showed me a picture of you and your boyfriend." I had expected to stay furious—*intended* to stay furious—but I felt my anger crumbling, and I felt tears rolling down my face. "*Why*, Kathleen? You're always talking about what a good life we have. What a good marriage we have. Why would you risk throwing all that away?"

"And *you*," she said. "Why would you be so quick to doubt me?" Her briefcase fell to the floor and she slumped backward against the door, then hung her head, putting her face in her hands. I heard her breath grow ragged, and by the time she dropped her hands and looked up—only a few seconds later—she had aged a decade, her face slack and bleak. "Oh, honey," she whispered. "I've been needing to talk to you. But I've been afraid to tell you . . . because it's really hard . . . and I knew . . . it would make you . . . *so* sad." She fought for breath, shaking her head slowly. "It's not . . . what you think."

I slapped the top of the desk, so hard it sounded like a rifle shot, and she flinched so hard the door rattled in its frame. "Jesus, Kathleen, don't give me that crap," I began, but she held up a hand, and the haunted expression in her face stopped me.

"It's not . . . an affair," she said. "It's worse. Much worse." She stared straight at me now. "All that cramping and bleeding I've been having? The nonstop period? I thought it was just menopause and fibroids, or maybe endometriosis. But it's not. It's cancer, Bill. A fast, mean kind of uterine cancer." She drew a shuddering breath and held it for a moment, but when she breathed out, the exhalation sounded oddly steady; calm, even, as if saying the dreaded word had freed her from something. Meanwhile, as she regained her equilibrium, I began to lose mine. The room seemed to spin, the floor—the abyss—to open beneath me. "It's called leiomyosarcoma," she went on. "Smooth-muscle tumor. I'd never heard of it. Have you?" I just stared, and she suddenly smiled an ironic, heartbreaking smile. "That man in Nashville—my 'boyfriend'? That was Dr. Andrew Spitzer, from Vanderbilt. He's a gynecologic oncologist—a specialist in cancer of the lady parts. That hand-holding over lunch? That was when he gave me my test results. Gave me my death sentence."

"What are you talking about? *Stop*," I said, struggling to catch up, struggling to keep it together. "Tests can be wrong. We need to get a second opinion."

She shook her head. "Spitzer was my second opinion. I saw my regular ob-gyn while you were out in San Diego. She referred me to Spitzer; got him to work me in on an urgent basis. I didn't tell you. I didn't want to worry you with it."

"I'm your *husband*, Kathleen. I *want* to be worried, if you're worried. But this can't be right."

"It might not be right," she said, "but it's real. Remember last year, when I had that fibroid cut out?"

"Sure," I said. "Power . . . power something-or-other?"

"Power morcellation," she said. "Remember the tool the surgeon used? Looked like my handheld blender, the one I call the 'Wand of Power'?" I stared, not quite following the thread. I was miles behind, but she didn't wait for me to catch up. "Turns out power morcellation wasn't such a great technique. The blade chopped up the fibroid, like they said it would. But it wasn't just an ordinary fibroid. And they didn't get out all the pieces—all the morcels—when they flushed me out afterward."

"But the pathology report came back clean," I reminded her. "Not cancer."

"Not in what they looked at," she said. "But there must have been tumor cells hiding in there somewhere. That's what Spitzer thinks, anyhow. And the tool they used to cut up the fibroid—the power morcellator? It scattered those cells like seeds." She shrugged. "And now, those seeds have taken root, all over the place, and I've grown a bumper crop of tumors." She gave a short, bitter laugh. "Funny thing," she said. "That surgery was supposed to help me, but instead, it killed me."

"Kathleen, stop talking like that," I said. "We'll fight this. We'll beat this."

"We can't, Bill. It's not beatable. It's too far along. The CT scan at Vanderbilt showed cancer all over my abdominal cavity. It's already in my lungs, too. Spitzer said radiation and chemo might—*might*—give me an extra few months—"

"Can we do it here, or do we need to go to Vanderbilt?"

"No," she said.

"No, what? No, we don't need to go to Vanderbilt?"

"No, we're not doing it. Either place. *Any* place."

"What are you talking about? Of course we are. How soon can we start?"

"*No.*" Her face was no longer slack; it was now set, as hard as I'd ever seen it. "You don't get to decide this, Bill. This isn't *we*, this is *me*, and I say no." She shook her head, her expression resolute. "Listen to me. Spitzer said the treatment would be brutal, and any extra time it gave me would be pure hell." I started to argue, but she cut me off again. "Pure hell. Those were his words. I won't put myself through that, Bill. And if you love me, you won't try to make me." She gave a wry half smile. "Funny, I was always so sure you'd be the one to die first. I figured some ex-convict would come gunning for revenge, or maybe you'd have a heart attack from working so hard. I never once thought I'd go first. And I sure never thought it'd be so soon."

"Tell me this isn't happening, Kathleen," I pleaded. "Tell me this is a bad dream."

"I can't, honey. I wish I could, but I can't."

"Don't leave me, Kathleen. Please. I can't bear it."

"Yes, you can." She gave me an appraising glance. "It won't be easy for you, though. You're going to miss me when I'm gone."

I knew she was right, because I could already feel a deep, black fissure cracking open within me—a fault line zigzagging down to depths I could not even begin to fathom.

Chapter 29

Kathleen had finally persuaded me to leave her office—"I have a lot of things to take care of," she'd said as she propelled me gently into the hallway—and I'd made my way in a daze back to the dark quietude of my private office, where I sat staring out the window at the stadium's crisscrossed scaffolding of gritty, rusting girders. My own scaffolding—the underpinning of my life—suddenly felt old and rusty, too, though in hindsight the rust had been eating away at it for quite some time.

Through the grimy window, a faint flicker of movement caught my eye: a small, oblong shape twitching slightly atop a grayish-white lump. I stood up and walked to the window for a closer look. On the other side of the glass, six inches from my face, a paper wasp was scrabbling around, atop a small nest suspended beneath an I-beam. The wasp's antennae and mandibles and forelegs twitched as it bustled across the shallow structure. The nest, about the same size as the face of my wristwatch, contained several dozen open hexagonal cells. Inside the nearest cells, I saw small, glistening larvae, and as the wasp moved from cell to cell, it darted its head briefly inside cell after cell, dispensing tiny taste treats: a dollop of chewed-up caterpillar, perhaps, or a masticated maggot—maybe even a maggot plucked from a corpse across the river, at the Body Farm. To one side of the nest, a dozen other wasps sat motionless, like airplanes parked on the deck of an aircraft carrier. Just beyond the small nest—no more than six inches from it—hung the prior year's nest, empty and abandoned, like some entomological version of a blighted suburban strip mall. As I watched, I heard a sharp hissing sound, and suddenly a powerful jet of water shot up from somewhere below, swooshing and fanning across my window. Every few years, the university's maintenance crews pressure-washed the windows of Stadium Hall, and today, it seemed, was the appointed day. The stream made several passes back and forth, sending sheets of muddy water cascading down the glass and off the sills. As the view cleared, to the extent that the view from these windows ever cleared, I looked out at the girder I'd been study-ing minutes before. The wasps—along with their new nest—were gone: swept away in the blink of an eye. Six inches from the obliterated construction site, the old nest hung, dripping but undamaged. In my mind, I seemed to hear the words of some Old Testament prophet, his voice as harsh as wormwood and gall and my own bitter heart: *Vanity, vanity—all is vanity—and we are as dust in the wind.*

My cell phone rang for the umpteenth time of the agonizing afternoon, and for the umpteenth time I reached for the "ignore" button. A moment earlier, I had ignored a call from Carmelita Janus—I felt bad about that, since I had promised to try to help her, but I also felt as if I were drowning in a sea of my own troubles, unable to haul her to safety. I glanced at the display, to see if Mrs. Janus had hit "redial," but the display showed me a different name: "KPD Decker." I had already ignored two calls from Decker shortly before lunchtime; I didn't think I should ignore a third, given how precarious his mental state had seemed the last time I'd seen him. Feeling edgy, I an-swered the call. "Hey, Deck. How you doing?"

There was a brief silence on the other end, then a male voice I didn't recognize said, in an oddly busi-nesslike tone, "Hello? Who is this, please?"

"This is Dr. Bill Brockton," I answered. "At the University of Tennessee. Who are *you*, and why are you calling me on Captain Decker's cell phone?"

"Dr. Brockton, did you speak with Captain Decker this morning?"

The question seemed to come out of nowhere. "Excuse me?"

"I asked if you spoke with Captain Decker this morning."

"No, I didn't. Why?" I felt confused, and in the back of my head, an alarm was beginning to sound.

"His cell phone shows that he called you twice. First at 10:23 Central Time, for twenty seconds, and again at 10:54, for five minutes."

"I don't understand," I said, feeling testy now. "*Who* are you? Why are you calling me? And what business is it of yours who calls me, and when?"

There was another silence, then: "Dr. Brockton, this is Special Agent Henry Fielding with the TBI. I need to know whether you spoke with Captain Decker this morning."

"No," I said. "I think he tried to call me, but we didn't talk. I have a backlog of voice mails I haven't listened to yet. There might be one from him. I can check, and call you back, if you want."

"Not right now," he said. "Right now I need to ask you a few questions."

The alarm bell in my head was almost deafening now. "Tell me what's happened," I demanded. "Is Deck hurt? Has he been in an accident?" The word "suicide" flashed into my mind, but I didn't want to say it, because the act of saying it might somehow make it real. Suddenly a phrase the TBI agent had used connected with a circuit in my brain, and I felt a jolt that was almost electric. "You said 'Central Time.' Decker was calling me from Middle Tennessee this morning?" I prayed that it wasn't so, but deep down, I knew that it was.

"Yes, he was."

"Jesus. Please tell me he wasn't calling me from Clifton," I said. "Please tell me he didn't go to the prison."

"What do you mean, Dr. Brockton?" The agent's question—and his tone of voice—couldn't have been more casual if he'd been asking about the weather. And that told me, beyond a doubt, that something was badly wrong.

"Is Deck hurt? Is he in some sort of trouble?" The agent didn't answer, and I snapped. "Goddamnit, Fielding, what the *hell* is going on? Quit playing games with me. If something's happened to Captain Decker, tell me what it is, and tell me how I can help."

I heard the agent take a long, deep breath, and then I heard him exhale it. "Captain Decker's in the ICU at

Vanderbilt Hospital," he finally said. "He's lost a lot of blood. They're not sure if he's going to make it."

"Oh dear God," I said. "He did go to the prison, didn't he? This happened to him there."

"What makes you say that, Dr. Brockton?"

"Because he mentioned it a couple days ago, when I saw him. He's working a case involving an inmate there. Nick Satterfield. The serial killer. Satterfield's . . . girlfriend, his groupie—I don't know what to call her—she helped Satterfield send a threat to me. A threat and an amputated finger. Decker came to see me a few days ago, to tell me they'd arrested her. While he was here, he said something about paying a visit to Satterfield."

"What, exactly, did he say?"

I hesitated; I didn't want to create more problems for Decker, but I didn't see any clear alternative to the truth. "He said he might go see Satterfield, might rattle his cage a bit."

"Did he use those words? 'Rattle his cage'?"

"I think so. Would you please just tell me what's happened?"

"Bear with me, Dr. Brockton. Was it Captain Decker who suggested rattling Satterfield's cage? Or was it you?"

"*What?*" He didn't respond. "No, it wasn't me," I said. "It was Decker who mentioned it, but he wasn't serious. He was just talking, you know?"

"No, sir, I don't know," he said. "What I do know is that Captain Decker went to see Mr. Satterfield. And there was a violent confrontation in the interview room. And Captain Decker nearly bled out on the floor."

I had a terrible sense of déjà vu—of Satterfield uncoiling and striking down a good man, out of pure malevolence and unadulterated evil.

"I don't understand how that could happen," I said. "Aren't the prisoners behind glass, or bars, or a wire screen, or something? Aren't they shackled, or cuffed? Or at least *guarded*?"

"Captain Decker requested a private interview," the agent said. "In a room. And he asked the guard to remove the prisoner's restraints."

"Jesus," I said. "*Jesus.* Why would he do that?"

"I don't know, sir. I thought maybe you could tell me."

"But what *happened*? You said Decker lost a lot of blood. Did Satterfield have a knife? A shiv—is that what it's called?"

"He had a razor blade," said Fielding. "Hidden in his mouth. He must've been expecting trouble."

"He was *causing* the trouble," I snapped. "He sent that finger, and he waited. It was a trap. Bait. And how the hell did he get hold of a razor blade?"

"You'd be amazed what inmates can get hold of. Drugs. Phones. Weapons. Women. Anyhow, by the time the guards got in and broke up the fight, Decker was cut pretty bad. Satterfield went for the neck—he cut the jugular vein, and he was still cutting when they pulled him off. Almost got the carotid artery, the ER docs said."

"That sick sonofabitch," I said. I didn't know whether to weep or scream. "I guess he just wants to take as many people down with him as he can."

"That's not the way he tells it, Dr. Brockton," said the agent.

"What do you mean?" I was echoing the question Fielding had asked two minutes earlier, but my tone—unlike his—was anything but casual.

"Satterfield says it was self-defense. Says Decker was trying to kill *him*. Says Decker came there to kill him."

"That's not true," I said. "That can't be true."

"No? That's not all he says, Dr. Brockton. He says Decker was doing it for you."

"Oh, bullshit," I snapped.

"For you and your wife," the agent went on. "Decker told Satterfield you and your wife promised him ten thousand dollars."

"How *dare* you?" My voice sounded both loud and muffled—as if I were shouting, but shouting from somewhere far away. "Do you even know who Satterfield is, and what he's done?"

"Yes, sir, actually, I am familiar with Satterfield's record."

The words "Satterfield's record" seemed a mockery to me.

"Do you know what he did, *actually*, to the four women he killed?"

"I've seen the autopsy reports, if that's what you mean."

"That's only a small part of what I mean," I snapped. "Can you imagine the pain and the terror he put those women through, on their way to those autopsy reports?"

"No, sir, I guess I can't."

"I guess not. And do you know that he cut off my wife's finger—in front of me, and our son, and his girlfriend—just for kicks? Just to give us a little taste of what he had in store for us?"

"I am aware of that," he said. "And I certainly don't condone it."

"Don't *condone* it?" I was practically roaring now. "Well, that's mighty big of you, Agent Fielding, not to *condone* it."

"Dr. Brockton? Sir? I need you to take a step back and calm down. I'm sorry if my choice of words offended you. No doubt about it, Satterfield's done terrible things. But those things aren't the issue right now. The issue right now is, he's alleging crimes have been committed, by Captain Deck—"

"Give me a break," I interrupted. "You're going to take a convicted serial killer's word over a police officer's?"

"Let me finish," he said. "He's alleging crimes were committed by Captain Decker, and by you and your wife. Attempted murder by Captain Decker, and conspiracy to commit murder, by you and your wife."

"My wife," I spat, "is dying. And frankly, Agent Fielding, in light of that, I don't give a good goddamn what Satterfield says. If you've got an ounce of decency in you, neither will you."

Whatever response he had to that, I didn't hear it. I had already hit "end."

Chapter 30

After the call about Decker, I left campus—as if by leaving my office, I could leave my worries—and headed toward home. But as I turned west onto Kingston Pike—toward the mansions that signaled the boundary of Sequoyah Hills—I felt myself slowing, and then turning into the parking lot of Second Presbyterian Church. *Our* church: the church where Kathleen and I had worshipped for years, first as young marrieds, then as young parents, then as youth-group leaders for Jeff and his friends.

The church, a soaring neo-Gothic structure of tan sandstone, sat high on a green rise, looking timeless and serene. Blessedly, the sanctuary was both unlocked and empty, its stained-glass windows ablaze with afternoon light. Slipping into a pew near the back, I bowed my head and prayed—or *tried* to pray. But the words felt lost in space; they echoed in my heart as loudly as they might have echoed in the vault of the nave, had I shouted them at the top of my lungs.

Tucked into racks on the backs of the pews, alongside well-worn copies of the *Presbyterian Hymnal,* were copies of the Bible, not so worn. Slipping a Bible from the nearest rack, I flipped through it until I came to the Book of Job. I'd never actually read it, but I'd heard the story countless times over the years: Job was a good and pious man, brought to the breaking point by an onslaught of misfortunes. Through it all—tragedy upon tragedy, all of them undeserved—Job's faith held firm, and in the end, God rewarded him. Maybe I could learn something from Job, I thought, as I began to read. Maybe Job could help me make sense of what was happening, or at least help me face it with faith and peace. Maybe Job could even teach me how to do the real trick: to snatch True Happiness from the bloody jaws of tragedy.

The story's opening was much as I had expected: God praises Job's piety to Satan, and Satan responds by taunting God—challenging God. "He's rich and happy," Satan sneers. "Of *course* he's pious." And so begins a contest, a wager, between God and Satan; a tug-of-war, with Job as the rope, tested by a torrent of tragedies. In the space of a single chapter, a series of messengers arrives, one on the heels of another, reciting loss upon loss—all Job's possessions—7,000 sheep, 3,000 camels, 500 teams of oxen, 500 female donkeys—as well as the demise of all of his farmhands, shepherds, and servants.

But worse—far, far worse—is yet to come. Another messenger arrives immediately, informing Job that his seven sons and three daughters, feasting together in a son's house, have all perished in a fierce, house-leveling windstorm. Like each of the prior bearers of bad tidings, this one concludes by saying, "And I only am escaped alone to tell thee."

The litany of his losses complete, Job stands up, rips his clothes, and shaves his head. Then, a sentence later—to my astonishment—Job gets over it. In what struck me as the world's swiftest resolution of grief, he simply shrugs it off. "Naked came I out of my mother's womb," he says, "and naked thither I shall return: The Lord gave, and the Lord hath taken away; blessed be the name of the Lord."

Baffled, I reread that passage—reread it several times, in fact; it didn't take long. I stared and squinted at the page. "Them's the breaks," Job seemed to be saying. "Easy come, easy go." By the time I'd read his words enough times to memorize them, I was no longer just puzzled; I was also, I realized, angry. I could understand, and I could admire, Job's tranquility in the face of material losses. Stuff, after all, is only *stuff*, if you ignore the countless corpses of servants and livestock littering Job's property. But to suffer such slight, offhand pain—a torn robe, a shaved head, and an "oh well"—at the death of his children? His *ten* children? I didn't get it. I didn't believe it. Was Job a man—an actual flesh-and-blood father? Or was he something else, some colder-blooded creature masquerading as a man?

I decided to give Job the benefit of the doubt, or at least to try. After all, I'd read only the first chapter. Maybe Job would get more real; more believable; more human.

Instead, Job got clobbered again.

In round two, God gives Satan permission to ruin Job's health. Before you can say "Jack Robinson," Job breaks out in boils from head to toe. Sitting in a pile of ashes, he's reduced to scraping his scabrous, oozing skin with a shard of pottery.

It was there, midway through Chapter Two, that I came to an electrifying expression of humanity—but not from Job himself. From his wife. "Curse God and die," she tells him, practically spitting the words through her tears. As I read those bitter words again and again—"Curse God and die"—it dawned on me that the bitterness must have poured directly from the fissure in her heart: a heart broken not just by her children's deaths, but also by their father's offhandedness and aloofness. In just four words, Job's wife expressed deep, primal pain. Facing the loss of Kathleen, the person I loved best in all the world, I understood and liked and *believed* Job's wife, in a way that I didn't understand or like or believe Job.

And what is Job's response to his anguished wife? He tells her to shut up. And then he begins to talk. And talk. And talk. For *forty chapters*, Job and four other guys talk. They argue about God, about suffering, and about Job himself. Why do the righteous suffer? Why do the wicked get off scot-free? How come God's being such a jerk when I, Job, have played by all the rules?

As I read the debate—as Job kvetched ad nauseum about his undeserved suffering and his spotless conscience ("I'm pure gold," he says at one point)—I found myself getting madder than ever.

Eventually even the Almighty has had enough of Job's self-righteous whining. Speaking from a whirlwind in a mighty voice, God puts Job in his puny place, pointing out in no uncertain terms what a tiny, trivial, know-nothing Job is compared to God, the creator of the universe. Job apologizes, and at that point God rewards him: God cures Job's pox, makes him richer than ever, and gives him a passel more kids. All's well that ends well.

I closed the Bible, still confused, and still mad—furious, in fact, for reasons I couldn't quite put my finger on. Tucking the book back into the rack alongside the hymnals, I stood up, stretched my back, and looked around at the magnificent architecture: the high, vaulted nave; the mighty stone columns; the graceful arches; the stained glass, its blues deepening to indigo in the waning light, its reds darkening into wine and blood.

I stepped outside and let the sanctuary door sigh shut. As it closed, I heard a latch snapping into place with a metallic click. Reaching back, I gave the handle a tug. The door, which had been open when I'd arrived, was now locked tight. Was it an omen? A punishment—banishment—for my cynical response to Job? Or was it simply a spring-loaded piece of steel popping into place, as it was designed to do?

It was after six when I pulled into the garage at home, but Kathleen's space was still empty. I called her cell, but the call went straight to voice mail, which meant either that she was on a call or that her phone was switched off. She hadn't left a note on the kitchen table, the usual place for notes; when I checked for messages on the home phone, I found voice mails from half a dozen reporters—including Athena Demopoulos of Nashville's Channel 4 and Mike Malloy, Fox 5 News!—and, at the end, a message from Kathleen: "Hi, honey. I've gone to a meeting at the Wellness Community. A support group for people with cancer. I'll call you when I get done."

I listened to the message three times. Its matter-of-factness baffled me; from the brevity and the tone, she might just as easily have been telling me that she was at the grocery store, or swinging by the public library to return a book. I hung up the phone and wandered back to the bedroom, thinking, *How did this happen? How did we become the cancer family?* I half expected the doorbell to ring, and to find myself face-to-face with a neighbor delivering a casserole and pity.

Sitting on the bed to take off my shoes, I noticed the nightstand drawer slightly ajar. I reached out to close it, but then—instead—I slid it open. Nestled deep in the drawer, hidden beneath a wavy, outdated telephone directory, I found it: the nine-millimeter pistol loaned to me by Decker—Decker, who had foolishly, and perhaps fatally, put himself within striking distance of Satterfield's fangs.

Contrary to her message, Kathleen did not call; she simply came home, unannounced, sometime after nine. "Tell me about the support group," I said, anxious—desperate, perhaps—to reconnect with her; to feel that I was somehow a part of the experience, a part of *her* experience, a partner.

"I'm not ready to talk about it yet," she said, and I felt hurt and excluded. "I'm exhausted. What I'd really like is to take a shower and go to bed. Can we do that? Could we just curl up and go to sleep?"

"Of course," I said. "Whatever you want."

But I'd promised more than I could deliver. I lay awake for hours, trying to sort out the tailspin that was now our life. When at last I fell asleep, I dreamed of Job—a pair of cynical, sacrilegious dreams, both of them set at the end of Job's tribulations.

In the first dream, God bent down and ruffled Job's hair, scratching him behind the ears as if he were a dog, cooing, "*Who's* a good boy? *Job's* a good boy! *What* a good boy!" Then God lobbed a treat into the air, whereupon Job leapt into the air and caught the morsel in his mouth.

The second dream was even stranger than the first. In this one, God looked like a TV game-show host—specifically, like the host of *Let's Make a Deal*—and Job was a contestant who had just won. To celebrate Job's victory, the angel Gabriel gave a loud blast on his trumpet, and the Almighty beamed beneficently as the heavenly hosts clapped and cheered. When the applause subsided, God commanded, "Gabriel, tell Job what he's just won!" The angel lowered his horn and said, in a silky announcer's voice, "God, Job's Grand Prize package starts with *one thousand* fertile female donkeys. But that's only the beginning. To work the fields, Job gets a thousand teams of oxen—a total of *two* thousand oxen!" A woman in a skimpy robe led a donkey and an ox out to stand on the cloud beside Job. "To travel the deserts in style," Gabriel went on, "Job receives *six thousand* new top-of-the-line dromedary camels! And to round out his livestock portfolio: how about *fourteen thousand* fluffy sheep!" As another woman led out a camel and a sheep, Job raised his arms exultantly, and the angels cheered again. "But that's not all, God," continued Gabriel. "To make sure he has plenty of time to enjoy his new prosperity, Job gets another *one hundred forty years of life!*" More ecstatic applause ensued, along with a chorus of strumming harps; Job gasped and wiped away tears of gratitude with the sleeves of his robe. "Last but not least, Lord, Job gets a *fabulous new family*—ten new kids, *twice* as smart and good-looking as the old ones!" As the children appeared, all ten of them, Job whooped and hollered, pumping his fists in the air triumphantly.

I woke up at that, shocked from sleep by the irreverent image. As I got my bearings—lying beside

Kathleen, outwardly in the same way I had for the past three decades, but with everything between us now changed—I found myself thinking about the one key character who had not appeared in my sacrilegious dreams: the same character who hadn't, I suddenly realized, appeared in the Bible story's happy ending. *Job's wife*, I thought. *Where's the woman with the broken, bitter heart?* I also thought of the ten new children. Were the new children conceived and carried by the same old wife? Did they fill the void left by the ten dead ones? Or are some losses beyond recompense or redemption?

I lay still, listening—listening for a whirlwind, and a Voice within it offering eloquent answers—but all I heard were crickets and cicadas, and the waning wail of a freight train keening somewhere in the distant dark.

Chapter 31

I didn't pressure Kathleen to drop her opposition to treatment—not overtly, at least—but I did persuade her, through a combination of cajoling and browbeating, to let me speak with Dr. Spitzer, the Vanderbilt specialist who had diagnosed her cancer. At the appointed time, we called him from our living room, sitting together but listening and talking separately, each on our own cordless phone. Kathleen spoke first, sounding oddly formal and slightly embarrassed to be imposing—or to have *me* imposing—on Spitzer's time. Brushing aside her apology, he asked how she was feeling. "Pretty good, I guess, for a dying woman," she said, and her matter-of-fact fatalism made me wince. "I get short of breath when I go up stairs. Also, I feel really bloated now, as you predicted, and I can't eat more than a few bites before I feel stuffed."

"I'm not at all surprised by any of those things," he said.

"Why not?" I asked him. "What do they mean?"

"The bloating is ascites," he said. The word—it rhymed, in some slantwise, cruelly ironic way with the festive-sounding "invitees"—was familiar to me. A few years before, I'd witnessed a murder victim's autopsy—an alcoholic who would have soon died of liver disease, if his son hadn't crushed his skull with a cinder block first. That man's belly had been grotesquely distended, as if he were eight months pregnant. "The peritoneal cavity—that's the abdominal cavity, but you probably know that . . . ?"

"I do," I said.

"In advanced leiomyosarcoma," he resumed, "the peritoneal cavity fills with cancerous fluid." I looked at Kathleen in alarm, but she was looking out the window, carefully avoiding eye contact with me. "Kathleen, you might want to consider having that drained," Spitzer added. "It won't change the course of your disease, but it might make you more comfortable."

"Would I have to be at Vanderbilt for that?"

"Oh, certainly not," he said. "It's an outpatient procedure. You could have it done in Knoxville. Think about it, and let me know if you want a referral."

"I will," she said. "Thank you."

"What about the shortness of breath, Dr. Spitzer?" I asked. "Is that also caused by the fluid? Pressure on the diaphragm or lungs?"

"No, I'm afraid not," he answered. "What it means is that the tumors in the lungs are blocking or crushing the bronchii. Closing off the airway. Kathleen, are you coughing up any blood?" I stared at her, horrified.

"A little," she said. "Is that going to get worse?"

"It's possible. You could start to hemorrhage," he said. "Or you could throw a clot."

"Jesus," I said. "What do we do, if one of those things happens?"

"Frankly? Unfortunately, Dr. Brockton, there's not much that can be done, if that happens. As I'm sure Kathleen has told you, her disease is quite advanced, and it's not amenable to treatment."

I stared across the room at her, her face in profile and silhouetted against the window, and said, "How the hell did this get so far before we found it?" I wasn't sure which of them I was asking—both, perhaps—and the question sounded almost like an accusation. But if either of them took offense, they did a good job of masking it.

"Thing about the uterus," said Spitzer, "is that you don't need it to live." I was puzzled by the statement. "It's not essential to staying alive," he explained. "Not like the heart or the brain or the lungs. The only time it's essential is during pregnancy, right?"

"Right," I said, suddenly struck by how ironic it was that Kathleen's uterus—the organ whose sole purpose was to nurture life—had become the agent and angel of her death. "But I'm not sure I'm following you."

"Well, because it's not essential," he went on, "it's not immediately apparent when something's going wrong. Women tend to overlook things like bloating or unusual bleeding. Some of that just goes with the territory." After thirty years of Kathleen's monthly cycles, I recognized the truth of that. "Even if the bloating is fairly severe," he said, "they might think they're just gaining weight. Also, uterine leiomyosarcoma is pretty rare. Some ob-gyns never see a single case. I've seen a lot, but that's because patients get referred to me from all over the country."

"Dr. Spitzer," I asked, "are you married?" For the first time, Kathleen turned toward me, looking startled and possibly angered by the question.

"I am," he said. "I've been married to a lovely woman for thirty-two years."

"If *your* wife got this diagnosis, what would you do? What kind of treatment would you want her to get?"

He thought for a moment. "The best treatment I could give her," he said. "I'd make sure she knew how much I loved her. I'd make the most of whatever time we had together. And I'd get ready to grieve like hell."

"You can't just sit around and wait for me to die," Kathleen said finally. We were still sitting in the living room long after the call had ended. She had been looking out the window, into the fading light; I had been looking at her, watching as her features softened and grew less distinct in the gloom. "I need you not to hover," she went on. "Hovering over me—tiptoeing around, watching me like a hawk for any little signs and symptoms? That would drive me crazy. It'd be the worst thing you could do for me."

The comment stung, and I started to object, but Kathleen knew me too well—it *would* be my way to hover. "Okay," I said, "I'll try not to."

"Thank you."

"It won't be easy for me, Kath."

"It won't be easy," she agreed. "But it'll be important." After a moment, she added, "Don't shut down after I'm gone. You'll probably want to, but you can't. Or shouldn't, anyhow. And don't pull away from Jeff and Jenny and the boys. You'll need them."

"I need *you*," I told her. "You're the one I need."

"Well, we can't help that," she said. "You'll need to keep busy, too." I started to protest, but she held up a hand to keep me from interrupting. "Don't get discouraged about these setbacks you've had lately. The politics. The grandstanding and game-playing. Stand up for yourself. Stand up for your work. Stand up for the Body Farm."

"They can have the damn Body Farm if they want it, Kathleen."

She shook her head. "You don't mean that. You'd better *not* mean it. You've put too much into that place. And so have I."

I didn't quite follow that last bit. "I'm not . . . How do you mean?"

She turned, and even in the dim light, I could see the impatience in her eyes. "All those nights and weekends you spent working—at the Body Farm and in the morgue—instead of home with me? You think those didn't cost me anything?" The words felt like a knife in my chest, but she waved her hand to shoo away my guilt. "I'm not trying to make you feel bad, honey. I know I wasn't always gracious and generous about it, but I tried, because I knew it mattered so much to you. It must've mattered to me, too, or I wouldn't have put up with it. So don't you dare give up on it. If you do, I swear I'll come back and haunt you."

She forced a smile, and I tried to laugh at the brave joke, but the laugh got tangled up somewhere between my heart and my throat.

"One more thing, while we're on the subject," she said. "I see how miserable this Richard Janus thing has made you. You've had this cringing, hangdog look ever since the FBI and Fox News made it sound like you'd screwed up. Get over it, Bill. That, or get back into it."

"I can't get back into it," I said. "They've shut me out." I held out my hands, palms up, and gave a shrug.

"See?" The sharpness of her tone startled me. "That's exactly what I'm talking about. What on earth has happened to your backbone?"

In spite of myself—in spite of wanting to be so kind and loving that I could somehow magically keep Kathleen alive and well—I felt a flash of anger. "Gee, I don't know," I said. "Maybe I lost my backbone out there on that mountainside. Or maybe it's tied to the whipping post."

"Well, untie it, then," she snapped. "Or go find it. Or grow another one, if you have to. 'Cause being without it sure doesn't become you. I'm the one who's dying, Bill. Quit acting like it's *you* that's nailed to the cross." I drew back, stunned, but then she reached over and squeezed my hand. "You've always made me so proud, Bill. Don't stop now. Don't stop when I'm gone. That would just make it sadder, don't you see?"

We sat a while longer; by now the room was growing dark around us, but something had shifted—eased, at least for a moment—and we sat in a sort of companionable isolation, each absorbed in our own thoughts and feelings.

When the streetlights outside came on, Kathleen leaned over to the end table between us, took a box of matches from the drawer, and lit the thick white candle—her wine-drinking candle, she sometimes called it. "One more thing," she said. I braced myself for more scolding, but she smiled, her face glowing in the warm light of the flame. "I wouldn't consider it hovering if you brought me a glass of wine."

Chapter 32

It wasn't easy, taking my mind off Kathleen and refocusing it on my work. But she was right, and I owed it to her—and to my own sanity—to try.

I'd been taken off the Janus case by Prescott, cut off from everyone in the FBI's San Diego field office. It was possible, though, that Mac McCready would still talk to me. I dialed his Quantico number, and he answered on the third ring. "McCready here."

"Mac, it's Bill Brockton, in Knoxville. Are you still speaking to me, or is the entire Bureau shunning me?"

"Still speaking, but I'm not sure I'm much of an asset to you. I'm not exactly the golden boy around here, either. Prescott's pretty pissed at me, too. Hard to blame him—he's been getting chewed up pretty bad himself, by big dogs with sharp teeth."

I hadn't taken time to consider the awkwardness of Prescott's position—he was, after all, the public face of the troubled case—but whatever compassion I felt for him was offset by my slight resentment of the time pressure he'd applied . . . and by the powerful sting of feeling like the scapegoat. "Not fun for any of us," was the best I could muster. "Listen, Mac, I'm still trying to figure out who told Prescott about the teeth. Do you know?"

"It was that reporter. Malloy. Guy's a prick, but you gotta hand it to him—he was a giant step ahead of us."

"But how'd he get there, Mac? Who told Malloy the teeth had been pulled? Who *knew*? I sure didn't. Not till I cleaned 'em off the other day—*after* Prescott called to fire me."

"Had to've been somebody who was in on it," McCready mused. "Maybe it was the guy with the pliers. Hell, maybe it was Janus himself."

"Why? Why would whoever faked the death—Janus or his DIY dentist—put a bug in a reporter's ear?"

"Good question, Doc. Figure that one out, and you're nearly there."

"You think Janus wanted to embarrass the Bureau?" As soon as I said it, I decided it was highly unlikely, given that the Bureau wouldn't just be embarrassed;

the Bureau would be gunning for vengeance. "Nah, not that," I said. "Janus would know that the FBI would move heaven and earth to catch him if he's humiliated y'all. Maybe he promised the dental assistant a big payoff, but stiffed the guy instead."

"That could work," he agreed. "Listen, I gotta go—I'm teaching a fresh batch of recruits at the Academy about one of your favorite topics today: bugs. 'Trust the bugs,' right? Keep the faith, Doc. It'll get better."

As I hung up, I couldn't help wondering, *Will it? How? And when?*

Among the many mean surprises that accompanied the Ultimate Mean Surprise—Kathleen's death-sentence surprise—was the secretarial surprise: the mountain of insurance forms, financial forms, legal forms, and other forms of forms to be scaled. In a perverse corner of my mind, I imagined the grim reaper, twenty-first-century style, no longer mowing down mortals with a scythe, but simply burying them alive beneath truckloads of paper.

In the seven days since our telephone conference with Dr. Spitzer, Kathleen and I had come to an unspoken agreement, an uneasy détente. We distracted ourselves from the bigger issues of mortality and grief by focusing on what we began calling "the business of death and dying." We dealt with the business—the bureaucracy—at the kitchen table, sorting papers into stacks and categories that sometimes covered every square inch, despite the fact that we'd added a leaf to the table. There was a certain amount of apt irony, Kathleen noted early on, in dealing with death at the kitchen table, where she had almost perished at the hands of Nick Satterfield years before. "Not with a bang, and not with a whimper," she'd joked, "but with a notarized signature in triplicate." At moments like that—moments of understated heroism—I admired the hell out of her and wondered how on earth I'd be able to bear losing her.

I was doing a surprisingly good job of not falling apart—even Kathleen commented on it—until she slid me an official-looking form headed with the logo of the Tennessee Department of Health and Environment. "What's this?" I asked.

"An advance directive. It's the state's new version of a living will." I felt a jolt of fear shoot through me as I scanned down the page. Near the top, directly beneath her own name, Kathleen had designated me as her "Agent"—the person authorized to make health-care decisions for her—but in a series of boxes beneath my name, she had systematically tied my hands, checking the "No" box beside every possible treatment option: No cardiopulmonary resuscitation. No defibrillation. No life support. No surgery, antibiotics, or transfusions. No tube feeding or IV fluids.

I stared at the form—its grim specifics, the litany of life-extending options she was refusing—and then looked up. She was watching me closely; it was all I could do to meet her gaze. "Looks like you've got your mind made up," I said, trying to keep the pain—sadness and also self-pity—out of my voice. "Nothing here for me to do."

"Yes, there is," she said. "You make damn sure they abide by this. I've heard of too many cases where hospitals ignored these things—jump-starting people's hearts, putting people on respirators or feeding tubes—even when the patients had living wills on file. If anything like that starts to happen, you fight tooth and nail to stop it, you hear me?" I nodded. "I need you to say it. Out loud. Promise me you won't let them keep me alive."

I felt tears running down my cheeks. "God, Kathleen."

"*Promise* me." Her voice was like steel.

"All *right,* dammit. I promise." It was all I could do to choke out the words.

"Thank you." She pulled a handful of paper napkins from the holder and passed them across to me.

I wiped my eyes and blew my nose, with a wet, honking blast.

"Nice," she said. "It's your table manners I'll miss most in the afterlife."

"Something to look forward to, while you're waiting for me." I gave another Gabriel-worthy trumpet blast, then flipped to the form's second page. "So I just sign down here, as a witness?"

She shook her head. "You can't." She reached across and pointed at a block of fine print that excluded relatives, by blood or marriage, as witnesses. "I guess the powers that be want to make sure you're not trying to get rid of me."

"Good for them," I said. I glanced up at the organ-donation section of the form and saw that she had specified only her corneas. I glanced up at her.

"My organs can't be used," she said. "They might give cancer to somebody else. The corneas are safe, though."

I nodded. "Well, I know that's important. Be a shame if you couldn't donate those, after all your work to help people's vision."

"I'm glad you brought that up," she said. "I want to do more, if you're willing."

"Like what?"

"Well, it looks like we're in pretty good financial shape, right?"

"I wouldn't exactly call us rich, but yeah, looks like we're not in any danger of going belly-up. Especially since you're refusing expensive treatments like Band-Aids and aspirin."

"Don't be a smart-ass," she said, but I caught a twinkle in her eye, and I managed a half smile. "That life-insurance policy we took out on me years ago, when Jeff was a baby?"

"Yeah?"

"Well, he's still listed as the beneficiary," she went on. "Seems like he doesn't need it now. His accounting practice is growing like crazy."

"You want to change it so the boys are the beneficiaries? Set up college funds for them?"

"I want them to get half of it," she said. "Twenty-five thousand apiece. Enough to help, but not enough to make them lazy."

"Seems Solomonic of you," I said. "What about the rest?"

"I want to give it away, Bill. To charity. Do a little good on my way out." She reached across and took my hand. "I want to give twenty-five thousand to my foundation, to hire a part-time director and fundraiser. So Food for Sight can keep going—and start growing—instead of just limping along, or dying with me."

Her generosity touched me; her foresight astonished me. I rubbed my thumb across the back of her hand. "Do you have any idea how much I admire you?"

"You've mentioned it once or twice." She gave my hand another squeeze.

"That leaves another twenty-five thousand," I said. "Who's that for? UT?" She shook her head, so I guessed again, mentally reviewing her list of favorite causes. "League of Women Voters?" Another head shake. "Doctors Without Borders?"

"No. Airlift Relief International."

I blinked. "Airlift Relief? Janus's thing?"

"Yes."

"But . . ."

"But what, Bill?"

"Well, for starters, he's dead."

"So? I hope people keep giving to my 'thing' after I'm dead."

"But you're not a drug trafficker, Kathleen."

"Neither was he. I don't believe it, Bill. I think he was set up."

"You think he was framed? By the FBI? Come on, Kathleen."

"Maybe not the FBI. Maybe somebody else—some other agency, or the real drug traffickers. I don't know who. But I do know that a lot of poor people in Central and South America will die in disasters if people don't step up and keep that outfit going."

"I think we need to think about this some more," I said.

"I don't. It's done. I mailed the beneficiary-change form today."

I stared across the table at her, my thoughts and emotions swirling. As they swirled, three questions kept rearing their unsettling heads: What would the FBI think, if they learned of my wife's big gift in memory of an accused drug smuggler? What if the money ended up, directly or indirectly, in the pockets of narco traffickers and killers? Last but not least—in fact, worst of all—was it possible that I was resisting the idea because I was actually jealous of a dead man?

Suddenly Kathleen clutched my hand, and for a moment I wondered if she had somehow read my ungenerous thoughts. Then I heard her gasp—a ragged, wrenching effort to draw a breath—and saw the expression of terror on her face.

"Kathleen? Honey, what's wrong?" She jerked her hand from mine and gripped the table, pushing upward with both arms, as if to keep herself from being pulled underwater. "Oh God," I said. "No. Please, no."

Her eyes opened wide, and then wider and wider still—impossibly wide—and she reached across the table, her hands scrabbling, searching for mine. Her gaze remained locked on me, and as I stared, frozen with horror, the fear in her eyes gave way to something else—dawning awareness, perhaps, followed swiftly by sorrow and then—at the last moment—by something I would have sworn was gratitude.

Chapter 33

Knoxville News Sentinel
July 13, 2004

Kathleen Walker Brockton, Ph.D.
Scientist, teacher, humanitarian, wife, and mother

Kathleen Walker Brockton died Tuesday after a brief bout with cancer. She was 50. A native of Huntsville, Alabama, Dr. Brockton earned her B.S. degree from the University of Alabama and her M.S. and Ph.D. degrees from the University of Kentucky.

Dr. Brockton was a professor in the University of Tennessee's Nutrition Science Department, where she taught for fourteen years. Before moving to Knoxville in 1980, she taught at the University of Kansas in Lawrence. A respected scholar as well as a popular teacher, Dr. Brockton's research interests focused on the health effects of nutritional deficiencies in children. Her 1997 journal article "Vitamin A Supplements: Saving Sight, Saving Lives" brought widespread attention within her field to the problem of vitamin A deficiency, a problem that causes blindness in an estimated 500,000 Third World children every year and kills approximately half of those children within a year after losing their sight. Chosen as "Author of the Year" by the journal's editorial board, Dr. Brockton used the award's monetary prize to establish a nonprofit foundation, Food for Sight, to provide vitamin A supplements to Third World children. During its first three years, Food for Sight provided vitamin A supplements to more than 100,000 children in Asia and Africa. "It costs fifty cents to keep a child from going blind," Dr. Brockton was often heard to tell prospective donors. "Fifty cents. Who couldn't—who wouldn't—give the gift of sight to a child?"

A woman of exceptional intelligence, vision, and compassion, Dr. Kathleen Brockton is survived, mourned, and missed by her husband, Dr. William Brockton; their son, Jeff; their daughter-in-law, Jenny; and two grandsons, Tyler and Walker.

Arrangements are still pending, and a memorial service will be held at a later date. In lieu of flowers, the family requests that donations be made to the Food for Sight Foundation.

Chapter 34

A dozen years had passed since I'd last sat in this particular chair, in this particular role: in the role of troubled parishioner, seeking counsel from the senior minister at Second Presbyterian. At the time of that visit, I'd been working a series of sadistic sexual murders—murders committed by my nemesis Satterfield. What had brought me here, back in 1992, was a question that had been raised, crudely but powerfully, by a young woman infuriated by the cruelty Satterfield had inflicted on his victims. "Why," she had raged, "are men such shits to women?"

The minister on that prior occasion was the same as the minister on this occasion: the Right Reverend Michael Michaelson, D.Div., more often (and more simply) referred to by most of his flock as Rev. Mike.

I still remembered Rev. Mike's answer to the memorably crude question about men, women, and the problem of evil. On that occasion, he had responded with a disquisition that was long, learned, and fascinating, one that viewed the issues through a half-dozen different lenses: theology, of course, but also evolutionary biology, sociology, and abnormal psychology. In the end, though, Rev. Mike's learned comments had proven to be far less illuminating than Kathleen's brutally efficient explanation: "Why? Because they *can* be."

In the years since that counseling visit, I'd worked a hundred homicides, give or take a dozen—none as brutal as Satterfield's misogynistic butcherings—and that particular "why?" had drifted into one of the distant, dusty corners of my mind, displaced by other questions that were less rhetorical and more immediate, as well as more *answerable*: "Doc, what made that checkerboard crosshatching on that punched-in circle of skull?" (Answer: The milled head of a framing hammer.) "Doc, how come them maggots to look burnt?" (Answer: Because the killer left the body in the woods for a week, then came back and torched it.) "Doc, did that dude get blowed up by a bellyful of dynamite?" (Answer: No, the abdomen burst from the buildup of decomposition gases in the gut.)

This time, sitting in the pastor's study, I asked a question not on behalf of countless suffering women, but on behalf of just one woman. How could an omniscient, omnipotent, and benevolent God, I asked—the kind of God we heard about again and again in the stained-glass sanctuary of this majestic church—allow health-conscious, humanity-helping Kathleen Brockton to be stricken down, in the prime of life, with an aggressive, untreatable cancer?

The right reverend sat silent, his eyes on me—not looking *at* me so much as looking *toward* me, somehow, his gaze seeming to send compassion in my direction. Kathleen and I had known him, and had liked him, ever since he'd arrived at Second Presbyterian fresh from seminary, as an energetic young assistant pastor. After a long while, he gave a sorrowful shake of his head. "I won't pretend I have a good answer for you," he said. "This is one of the toughest questions of all. Why do bad things happen to good people? Why does God allow suffering—undeserved suffering, in particular? Why do some people—even terrible people—lead charmed lives, while others—including wonderful people like Kathleen—get dealt brutally bad cards? That's the central question, as you probably know, of the Book of Job."

I made a face. "I don't buy it. Job."

"How do you mean?"

I told him how I'd sought solace in the story of Job, and how unsatisfying and infuriating I had found it. I also confessed my two sacrilegious dreams about Job: Good-Boy Job and Game-Show-Winner Job.

Instead of looking shocked, he actually smiled slightly. "That's an interesting spin on it," he said. "I don't believe I've come across that in any of my Old Testament textbooks. I might just use that in a sermon someday, if I really want to rile people up."

"Be my guest," I said. "While you're at it, tell folks how offensive it is to say things like 'Everything happens for a reason' or 'His will be done.' Kathleen's secretary actually said that to me when I went in to clean out her office. I had to walk away to keep from hitting her."

He winced. "My secret name for that is the 'God's Perverse Plan' doctrine. If you take it to its logical extreme, you end up arguing that God planned the pain of every battered woman, every molested child, every black man strung up by a lynch mob, every Jew sent to the gas chambers of Auschwitz." He clasped his hands, his fingers interlaced and his index fingers extended, and I couldn't help thinking of the nursery rhyme *Here is the church, and here is the steeple* . . . "A poet I like a lot once put it this way: 'If God is God, he is not good;

if God is good, he is not God.' Strong words, but they do get at the heart of the problem."

"I'm not sure I follow. I never was good with poetry."

"He's saying that if God's omnipotent, he must be a jerk, to allow so much innocent suffering. And if God's *not* a jerk, then he must not be all-powerful, because if he were, he'd protect people."

Amen, brother, I caught myself thinking.

Chapter 35

*D*oes *suicide run in families?* That was the question I found myself pondering after I had left Rev. Mike's study and returned to my empty, echoing house.

The answer, I well knew, was *of course it does.* Over the years, I'd read scores of books and articles about suicide; its dark causes, and the long shadow it could cast on the lives of the loved ones left to clean up the mess, literally and figuratively. I also, though, knew the answer in a deeper, darker way: I had felt its tug on occasion, during my adolescence; had heard its sinister siren song, calling me toward the rocks of doom. But adulthood—the twin rudders of a career and a family— had steered me into safer waters.

Until now.

In the blink of an eye—the catch in a throat—my mind traveled back almost half a century. I was four years old. I was trundling up the stairs to my father's law office, a few steps ahead of my mother, who climbed slowly so that I could be the one to burst through the door crowing, "Daddy, Daddy, we came to s'prise you!" Only we were the ones, she and I, who were surprised: surprised by the figure slumped sideways in his swivel chair, the eyes vacant and clouding; surprised by the dark splotches and smears fanning across the wall behind him; surprised by the odors of brimstone and blood and bleakness in the air.

We never spoke of it, my mother and I—not once in the next forty years; not once before her own death. And so, because it was never spoken of, it was never really laid to rest.

And now, here it was again—suicide, my unseen, lifelong shadow—sitting beside me on my bed. On *our* bed: the bed I'd shared for thirty years with Kathleen. Young, willowy Kathleen. Pregnant, rotund Kathleen. Dough-bellied, big-breasted, nursing-mom Kathleen. Weary working-mother Kathleen. Midlife, tennis-toned Kathleen. Swiftly cancer-stricken Kathleen.

I reached for the drawer of the nightstand and slid it open, then wormed my hand once more beneath the phone directory. Closing my fingers around the pebble-textured grip, I pulled upward and outward, removing the pistol Decker had loaned me a lifetime ago, back when I had mistakenly believed that what I needed to fear was a malevolent man, not a microscopic murderer called cancer.

I turned the weapon over slowly in my hands, inspecting its angles and contours, its meticulously milled surfaces. Pulling back the slide, I noticed the smoothness of the action, the precision and solidity of the metallic click as the weapon cocked. I turned the barrel toward me and studied the small round opening, a darkness as black and deep as my despair.

The siren song grew louder, accompanied by the sound of blood roaring in my head, roaring like the sea. Then I heard something else: I heard voices. *Children's* voices. "Grandpa Bill! Grandpa Bill! Where *are* you, Grandpa Bill?" I heard two pairs of small feet running down the hall, running toward my bedroom. I hid the gun, tucking it behind my back, sliding it surreptitiously beneath my pillow.

Tyler was the first to reach the bed. Without breaking stride, he launched himself like a missile, soaring upward in a graceful, gleeful arc, then belly-flopping onto the mattress with enough force to rattle the headboard against the wall. Walker, smaller and slower, tried to emulate him, but barely cleared the edge of the mattress, landing like a spent fish—but giggling as exuberantly as his aerobatic brother. When I reached out and gathered them in my arms, holding them hard, Tyler squirmed halfway free and looked up at me. "Are you crying, Grandpa Bill?"

"No, honey," I lied. "I just have something in my eyes."

Walker snuggled against me. "I didn't see Grand-mommy in the kitchen," he said. "Where is she?"

"Grandmommy's gone, buddy," I said hoarsely.

"Where did she go?"

"To heaven, *stupid*," said Tyler.

"But when will she come *back*?" There was a new note of urgency in his voice.

"She's not coming back, buddy," I whispered. "She can't."

I could not have said who felt the worst: the yearning three-year-old, the heartsick fifty-year-old, or the tough-guy five-year-old, who was perhaps just big enough to reach the bitter fruit of the Tree of Knowledge, and to grasp that something precious to him was lost beyond all finding, broken beyond all mending.

We ate the take-out pizza Jeff and Jenny had brought as a surprise, or a gesture of kindness, or an act of pity. Sitting around the kitchen table, we made awkward small talk, all the adults careful not to look at Kathleen's chair, which loomed monumental in its emptiness. I took a bite, but the crust felt and tasted like cardboard in my mouth, and I laid the wedge on my plate. The boys, on the other hand—their tears dried, their upset trumped by their hunger and the pizza's aroma—wolfed down two slices apiece, then bolted from the table and ran squealing down the hall.

Jeff nodded at my virtually untouched food. "No dessert unless you clean your plate," he said with a wink, echoing a line he'd heard from me a thousand times growing up.

I shook my head. "It's good—and y'all were sweet to bring it. But I've got no appetite tonight."

Jenny reached across the table and laid a hand on my arm. "I'm worried about you," she said. "You're skin and bones—like one of your skeletons." She looked me up and down. "I've seen coat hangers fill out a shirt better than you do these days." It was a good line, and I did my best to give her a smile, but it felt more like a grimace.

Down the hall, the rhythmic creak of bedsprings ceased, and the boys' chatter changed tone, shifting from giggling to squabbling. Jenny noticed it first, of course. "I founded it," protested Walker. "Give it back. Give it *back!*"

"You're too little," scoffed Tyler. "You're just a baby."

"Boys," Jenny called toward them. "Cut it out!"

"Give it back!" wailed Walker. "Give it *back!*"

Suddenly a terrible realization hit me. "Oh dear God," I gasped, leaping up so suddenly my chair toppled backward. "Please no." I ran from the kitchen, my feet scrabbling on the tile as I made the turn into the dining room and dashed down the hall.

"Let go. Let *go!*" yelled Walker. I heard a growl like that of some wild, angry animal, and then a howl of pain.

My feet seemed mired in mud or concrete, moving in excruciating, exhausting slow motion. "*Boys,*" I called out desperately. "Stop! Don't move!"

"Dad? What's going on? *Dad?*" Behind me, as I ran toward the bedroom, I could hear panic in Jeff's voice.

"Jeff, *go,*" I heard Jenny saying, her voice panicky. "Hurry! Something's wrong!"

"Boys, don't move!" I shouted again. I reached the bedroom doorway and froze in horror. My grandsons, on my bed, were wrestling over a nine-millimeter handgun, the weapon seesawing back and forth in their hands as they fought for possession. "Boys! *Stop* it! Put it down!"

But they were too caught up in the struggle to hear or to heed. I hesitated, afraid to grab for the gun but terrified *not* to. Jeff and Jenny lurched against my back, then craned to see what was happening in the bedroom. Then came a jolt and a scream as Jenny hurtled past me. An instant later a gunshot cracked, and voices around me and within me began to shriek.

Chapter 36

The Emergency Department at UT Medical Center was surprisingly quiet, the waiting room empty except for the three of us. Jeff, Tyler, and I sat without speaking. I sat hunched over, my elbows on my knees, my chin in my hands. Jeff cast occasional glances at me, his expression a mixture of confusion, anger, and sorrow.

Jenny emerged from the treatment area, shaking her head, and sat down beside Jeff and Tyler, ignoring me. Tyler crawled into her lap, and she wrapped her arms around him, enfolding him to her breast, one hand over the ear that wasn't pressed against her. She drew a deep breath and blew it out slowly. "Well," she said to Jeff. "They just finished splinting the fingers. Luckily, the breaks weren't bad. And kids heal fast." She gave a quick, almost imperceptible smile. "Walker's in love with the nurse. He's listening to her heart through a stethoscope. She said she'd bring him out in a minute."

Jenny looked at me for the first time, and I braced myself against the anger I saw in her eyes. "The doctor asked me how it happened," she went on. "I told him the boys were fighting over a gun, and Walker's fingers got twisted in the trigger guard." I nodded grimly; the police were probably on their way to arrest me, and I deserved it. Leaving a loaded handgun lying around where kids could find it—what would the charge be, criminal neglect? Reckless endangerment? She held my eyes, then, after an uncomfortable pause, added, "I told him it was a cap gun." I stared at her, dumbfounded. She shrugged, though her eyes still glittered with anger. "Now, why the *hell* was that thing laying right there where the boys could get ahold of it?"

How could I explain? "Decker—Captain Decker, from KPD—loaned it to me," I said lamely, "when Satterfield sent me . . ." I trailed off, not wanting to say too much in front of Tyler. "When Satterfield sent me that package. Decker thought I might need it."

Jeff frowned. "But what was it doing on the bed?" he demanded. "You said Satterfield's in solitary, and his girlfriend's in jail." I nodded but didn't offer any other explanation; I was too ashamed to tell them the truth, and I didn't have it in me to conjure up a plausible lie. Jeff's eyes bored into me. "Tyler told me you were crying when we showed up."

"Well, I'm pretty sad these days, son, you know?"

"Well, yeah, Dad, I *do* know," he snapped. "I am, too. Mom's gone, and it hurts like hell. Hurts you most, maybe, but hurts me, too. *And* Jenny. *And* the boys, even though they don't really understand it. But here's the thing you don't seem to get. If something happened to you—if we lost you, too?" He was speaking low now, in an angry whisper, so Tyler couldn't hear. "Do you have any idea how damaging that would be for these boys?" I blinked, blindsided by the turn the conversation had taken. "You lost your dad when you were a kid," he went on, "and that *sucks*, and I'm *sorry*," he said, though he sounded more fierce than sympathetic. "But you had your grandparents—all four of 'em, all good as gold, the way you tell it. Tyler and Walker just lost one. Don't you dare take another one from them." With that, he stood up and strode to the far side of the waiting room, staring out the window at the ambulance parked outside.

Jenny lifted Tyler from her lap and stood him up. "Why don't you and Daddy go look at the ambulance," she said. "There's a helicopter out there, too. I bet he'd take you to see that, too." He scurried off, and she shifted into the chair beside me. She gave me a long, long look, shaking her head slowly. Her cheeks were splotchy and her eyes brimming. "I am so mad," she said quietly, "that I want to slap the bejesus out of you. You put my kids in terrible danger. It's a miracle one of them's not dead." I nodded miserably. "But god-damnit, I *love* you, and we *need* you. So how 'bout you cut the crap, quit feeling sorry for yourself, and rejoin the land of the living?" While I was still taking in this wide-ranging message, she leaned over and kissed my cheek. At the same time, she reached across and gave my other cheek a quick slap—a slap that was half play-ful, half serious. Before I had time to respond, I saw a door opening, and a pretty young nurse led Walker into the lobby, two of his fingers taped into a splint, an x-ray clutched in his other hand.

He came running over. "Grandpa *Bill*," he said, holding up the injured hand, "Tyler broke *this* finger and *this* finger. Look—they took a picture of the bones!" He handed me the x-ray proudly.

"Yup, those are broken, all right," I said. "But you know what? Soon they'll be good as new. Even better—stronger than before."

"I know," he said. He beamed up at the nurse. "She told me. It's a miracle!"

"I guess it is, buddy," I said. "I guess it is."

It was dark by the time I left the hospital and headed for home. Crossing the Tennessee River, I stopped on the bridge at the center of the span. The shoulder was wide—they'd built the bridge optimistically broad, big enough to accommodate two or three additional lanes at some point in a prosperous future—so by parking close to the concrete guardrail, I had a good ten feet of clearance between my door and the nearest lane of traffic. Standing by the front bumper, I put my hands on the rail and leaned over, peering at the water. The great river, black and silent, spooled past far below, unaware and indifferent to me and my recent troubles; indifferent to my past joys, too, for that matter. It flowed onward, ceaselessly southward, called by the sea—or blindly bound by the laws of gravity and fluid dynamics. In the swirling water, I had no reflection and no significance. The realization was humbling, but it was liberating, too. What did it matter, really, if I lived or died—or, more accurately, what did it matter *when* I died?

The nine-millimeter pistol—which I had taken from the house and locked in my glove box when we'd hurried to the hospital—hung at my side, dark and heavy, as if a piece of the night itself had condensed and crystallized in my hand. If I leaned over the concrete railing of the bridge, I reflected, I could blow my head off without leaving a mess for anyone to clean up. If I sat on the railing and leaned backward as I pulled the trigger, I could topple into the water and sink beneath the surface. *Or do a backflip off the railing first,* I thought, *and pull the trigger on the way down.* That way, even if my nerve failed me, I was still committed. *If the bullet don't get ya, the water will,* I told myself, in a hillbilly twang. It sounded like a parody of a country music tearjerker, and it brought an ironic smile to my lips.

I remembered Jenny's parting words to me in the ER's waiting room. "You *owe* these boys now," she'd said to me. "If you do something stupid and self-destructive, they'll think it was their fault somehow. Just like *you* thought that *your* dad's death was *your* fault." Had I told her that in an unguarded moment, or had she intuited it? Either way, she was right. "Don't you do that to these boys," she'd added, punctuating her final four words by jabbing a fierce finger at me. "Don't you fucking dare."

Shifting my grip to the gun's barrel, I cocked my arm and flung the weapon into the darkness—a sidearm throw that sent it spinning out across the black water like some small, lopsided boomerang. *Don't come back,* I silently ordered it. A moment later I heard it hit: *plunk;* the sound seemed faint and far away, as fleeting and insignificant—as unexpectedly miraculous, too—as if a fish had just leapt from the water to launch itself, for one brief and exuberant moment, headlong into the air.

Standing at the rail in the darkness, I fished out my cell phone and dialed a number I knew by heart. "Book a flight," I told the computer that answered Delta's phone. "A new reservation . . . San Diego, California."

Part Three

The Key

And the end of all our exploring
Will be to arrive where we started
And know the place for the first time.

—T.S. Eliot, "Little Gidding"

Chapter 37

San Diego, California
August 2004

M y return to San Diego, six weeks after my first
visit, felt like a low-rent case of déjà vu: Instead
of landing in a posh Gulfstream V, I thumped down in
a weather-beaten 737, my knees bruised by the seat-
back ahead of me, my elbows chafed by the men seated
on either side of me, their rolls of fat spilling over the
armrests and into my personal space.

Thirty minutes after landing, I was in a helicopter
once more, headed back to Otay Mountain. This time,
though, instead of the combat-grade Bell 205 from the
San Diego County Sheriff's Department, I strapped
myself into a civilian chopper whose cockpit appeared

to have both the shape and the structural strength of an eggshell. The craft offered seating for four people, but horsepower for only two. With three adults and one suitcase aboard, the thing hesitated, as if considering whether to lift off or simply sit and tremble on the tarmac. Finally, with funereal slowness, we slipped the surly bonds of earth and crept off the ground, though the word "skyward" would have been a wild exaggeration. "Not quite as sporty as the one I rode in last time I was here," I told the pilot. "But maybe that's a good thing. That last ride scared the crap out of me."

It was only when the pilot laughed and apologized that I recognized him as the very same pilot who had scared the crap out of me. He wasn't wearing a deputy's uniform this time, but he was definitely the one whose hovering above the burning Citation had damn near killed three FBI agents and me. "Only scary thing about this machine is how underpowered she is," he said. "The good news is, she gets pretty zippy once we burn off about forty gallons."

I knew I shouldn't take the bait, but I couldn't help myself. "And what's the bad news?"

"The bad news is, when she gets zippy, you know she's running on empty."

"Don't scare him," said a woman's voice—Carmelita Janus's voice—from the cramped rear of the cabin, which she shared with my baggage. "Dr. Brockton needs to concentrate, not worry."

When I had finally returned her calls, after weeks of ignoring her during Kathleen's brief, brutal death spiral, Mrs. Janus had sounded shocked and saddened to hear my news. She had also withdrawn her plea for help—"I know you have many other things on your mind," she'd said—but I had insisted on coming, assuring her that immersing myself in work would take my mind off my troubles. And so at my request, she had chartered a helicopter—piloted, to my surprise, by the off-duty deputy. The deputy's name was Charles Throckmorton; his nickname, though, was Tailskid—Skidder, for short—a handle whose origins I was afraid to ask about. Skidder had been a friend of Richard's, I learned—something he hadn't mentioned to the FBI agents or to me that first day, although he had told us they had flown together a few times. Probably just as well that he hadn't said they were friends, I realized. As before, Skidder's mission on this trip would be to fly me back to the crash site. This time, though, we would follow, as precisely as possible, the dogleg route the Citation had flown the night of the crash.

To get to our starting point at Brown Field, we skirted the edge of San Diego Bay, the skyline of downtown out the left side of the canopy's bubble, the low, narrow strand of Coronado Beach across the bay on our right. When we reached the end of the bay, the pilot banked to the left, and the San Ysidro Mountains—including Otay Mountain—reared up in the distance, high and dry in the August heat. "Brown Field's straight ahead," said the deputy. "Six miles." He pressed a radio-transmitter button on the control stick and notified other aircraft in the vicinity that we'd be making a low pass over the runway from the west and then departing to the northeast. "If we land," he explained to me, "we'd have to get this thing off the ground all over again. Better to keep flying, so we can pretend we're rolling down the runway like a jet." I could see his point.

We skimmed the runway a hundred feet above the asphalt, then began to climb. A half mile beyond the airport, we banked to left, turning northeast, which put Otay Mountain off to our right. "Think of this as a slow-motion replay," said Skidder. "The Citation was climbing two thousand feet a minute that night, accelerating to three hundred miles an hour. Our rate of climb and our airspeed are about one-fourth of the jet's. So you'll have plenty of time to look around." After a moment, he added, "If you don't mind my asking, what is it you're looking *for*, Dr. Brockton?"

"I don't know."

"But you'll know it when you see it?"

I held out my hands, palms up, and shrugged. "Hope so. All I know is, I *won't* see it if I don't look."

Mrs. Janus's voice came through the headset. "That reminds me of Richard. 'Better to die trying than to live without trying,' he used to say."

"Christ, Carmelita," squawked the pilot, "and you told *me* not to scare him."

Ahead of us, I saw what at first glance might have been a pair of immense shopping malls. As we got closer, I noticed tall watchtowers and coils of razor wire, and I remembered passing the entrance road to a prison on my prior trip. "That's quite a prison," I said. "State penitentiary—am I remembering that right?"

"The one on the left is," the pilot answered. "Donovan. The one on the right's county, mostly, with a little federal thrown in for good measure." Beyond the prisons lay a blue-green lake, one I'd seen before, but from a different angle, looking down from the crash site.

I pointed. "Otay Lake?"

"Lower Otay Lake, technically. You see the arm stretching to the east? We'll turn south when we get to the far end of that." He pointed to a dial on the instrument panel. "Miracle of miracles, we're almost at thirty-nine hundred feet."

Mrs. Janus spoke again. "You see the little airstrip just beyond the tip of the lake? And the two hangars? Richard's maintenance shop is there. 'Janus Junkyard,' he called it. You can see a DC-3 carcass he cannibalized for parts, to keep ours flying."

"Why didn't he just do everything at Brown Field?"

"Too expensive," she said. "He bought this whole place from a skydiving school, for about what it cost to park the Citation at Brown Field for a year. He would've kept the jet here, too, but the runway's too short."

"Damn rough, too," added the pilot.

"Not as rough as those jungle clearings," she pointed out.

"Well, no," he agreed. He glanced down at a chart spread across his lap. "Okay, I'm turning south, descending to thirty-three hundred feet."

I turned toward him, though his attention was focused on the gauges and the horizon, not on my puzzled face. "Descending? Why?"

"Because that's what the Citation did that night."

"But I thought the plane was flying straight and level when it hit."

"It was," he said. "For the last two miles. But before that—right after the last turn—it came down five hundred feet, pretty quick."

"Came down? Why the hell would it do that?" I asked, but immediately, I answered my own question.

"To make sure it hit the mountain." Then, after a moment, another question occurred to me—one I was not able to answer for myself. "Could the plane's autopilot have made it descend and level off?"

"No," said the pilot and Mrs. Janus in unison.

"An autopilot's more like cruise control," added the pilot. "It can keep the wings level, and keep the plane on course, but it's not designed to maneuver the plane."

"Then that tells us something useful," I said. "Tells us that if somebody bailed out, they didn't jump until after that maneuver, right?"

"Guess so," said Skidder.

"Assuming that's true," said Mrs. Janus, "what do you make of it? What's the significance?"

"Don't know," I said. "All I know is that I'm looking for *something* . . ."

"Though you don't know what it is," the pilot reminded me.

"I don't know what it is," I echoed, "but if you'll tell me when we level off . . ."

"Right . . . about . . . *now*."

" . . . then I'll know where to start looking." He gave a nod, and I looked down. Below us, the flat terrain surrounding the lake and the airstrip began giving way to hills and valleys. Somewhere down there must be the spot where a parachute jumper had landed in the darkness. Even in daylight, the terrain looked forbidding.

If I searched the terrain below, might I come across a parachute—attached to a man who had broken both legs upon landing, slowly dying on a rocky mountainside? I scanned the ground for signs of a 'chute, but unless it was the color of desert camo, there wasn't one.

Two miles ahead of us, up the longest and straightest of the valleys, loomed Otay Mountain. As I stared out at it—its ridgeline stretching from one side of the canopy to the other, its peak aligned directly with the bubble's vertical center support—I had the uneasy feeling that the helicopter was a rifle scope centered on a target . . . and that I was a human projectile streaking straight for the bull's-eye. I thought about the Citation streaking toward it—far faster than this—and I thought about the other jet that had crashed into Otay Mountain earlier, back in 1991. Maybe that crash—clearly an accident—had inspired Janus, or whoever was at the controls that night, to aim the Citation at the same dark peak.

Soon the peak was rearing directly before us, and as Skidder continued hurtling toward it, I felt my fingers digging into my thighs. I'd thought that the deputy had pushed his luck—as well as the envelope of flight and the boundaries of sanity—when he'd hovered the sheriff's helicopter a stone's throw from the burning aircraft wreckage. Today, in the helpful light of hindsight, that maneuver seemed comparatively tame:

Skidder was now aiming our flying egg toward a small rock shelf jutting from the mountainside, just below the crash site. As the spinning rotor edged closer and closer to the trees and boulders, I found myself clenching the sides of my seat. Afraid of looking, but terrified of closing my eyes, I focused my gaze out the left side of the canopy, where the hazards lay slightly farther away. "Looks like a mighty tight fit here," I said, trying to sound braver than I felt.

"Skidder could do a backflip and set us down on that spot," said Mrs. Janus. "Those helicopter chase scenes you see in Hollywood movies? Skidder does the flying for some of those."

I spoke before I thought. "You mean the ones where the chopper collides with a train—or a tumbling car or a motorcycle—and then explodes?"

"Don't forget the one where the chopper gets taken down by a bow and arrow," Skidder said. "*Rambo Three.* Or by a squadron of fierce flamingos—*Sheena, Queen of the Jungle.*" I felt the skids settle onto the rock, and he shut down the engine.

"Nice," I said, my admiration exceeded only by my relief.

The last time I'd seen the crash site—the day we'd hoisted the Citation's flattened nose off the rock face, revealing the crushed corpses of the Mexican and the mountain lion—the place had been bustling, still swarming with people and vehicles from the FBI, the sheriff's office, the fire department, the U.S. Forest Service, and the National Transportation Safety Board. Now, as I stepped out onto silent scorched earth, the place seemed out of kilter and surreal, as if its transformation back to wilderness were not just implausible, but somehow unnatural.

Carmelita Janus called to me from the helicopter's cabin. "How can we help, Dr. Brockton?"

"Let me take a look around first," I said. "I need to get my bearings again. Get my head back in the game."

"We'll sit tight," said Skidder. "Just holler when you need us."

As I surveyed the vertical bluff, some thirty yards upslope from where we had landed, I conjured up a mental image of the debris field as it had been the first day after the crash, with pieces of engine cowling and wingtips strewn across the narrowing valley, the shredded rubble of the fuselage still smoldering. As I picked my way up the rocky slope, I replayed the excavation, fast-forwarding through three days of digging in just three minutes.

Nearing the base of the bluff, I began to glimpse remnants of wreckage amid the rocks: shards that would have required weeks of tedious tweezering to pluck from their nooks and crannies and crevices. I found the presence of these fragments strangely comforting—confirmation, perhaps, that I was indeed in the right place; reassurance that I hadn't just imagined the entire episode.

For some reason—perhaps a continuation of my earlier sensation of being a human projectile aimed at the mountainside—I felt drawn to the impact's epicenter, the broad, shallow crater created by the jet's missile-like strike. During the excavation, we'd spent three days crouching and stooping beneath that crater, picking our way steadily down, down, down, until we'd cleared the rubble and reached bare rock at the base of the bluff. Now, as I approached, I found myself looking up, not down: up at the wide, shallow crater; up at the still-fresh fractures radiating outward, like some gigantic spider's web etched into the stone above my head. And in one of those fractures, I caught a glimpse of something—of several small somethings, in fact—that called out for a closer look, and a climb.

Years before—for my forty-fifth birthday, when Kathleen had decided that I was sliding into some sort of midlife rut—she'd given me a weekend of instruction at a rock-climbing school in the mountains of North Carolina. The lessons hadn't transformed me into Spider-Man by any stretch of the imagination, but they had shown me how to find toeholds on surprisingly small ledges, and how to jam a few fingers or cram a whole fist into a crack, twisting it to lock it into place and to create a powerful handhold—one that was "bombproof," as my instructor liked to say. Now, standing at the base of the cliff, I studied it from a fresh perspective: sizing it up not as a forensic scientist, but as a climber. I noticed a half-dozen or so small, blocky bumps zigzagging upward—a simple ascent for a serious climber, though not for a rank, rusty amateur like me. But the crash itself had worked in my favor, I realized: Besides creating new cracks and sharp edges in the rock, the impact had subtly altered the angle of the rock face. The lower half of the crater was no longer *absolutely* vertical, but—because of its concavity—only *relatively* vertical now. If I was lucky, that subtle difference in geometry might just be enough. *Might.*

Reaching overhead, I hooked my fingertips over two bumps in the rock. Then I took a small step up with my right foot, and a bigger step with my left, stretching wide and splaying myself against the rock. I clawed higher with my left hand, then raised my right foot, feeling for a foothold that had looked within reach but that suddenly seemed to elude me. Again and again I scrabbled—with my toes, with the side of my foot, with my toes again—seeking but not finding purchase. The muscles in my hands and forearms began to tremble and shriek, and just as I finally found the foothold I needed, my grip failed, my fingers loosened, and I felt myself toppling backward. In that instant—the instant when I realized I was falling—I had just enough time to recall the last person who had fallen to the base of this cliff: a supremely jinxed man who had jumped from the frying pan of Mexico's hardships and fallen straight into the combined fires of perilous terrain, a powerful predator, and a hurtling jet.

My descent ended not in a bone-breaking thud onto rocks, but in an unexpected embrace, of sorts: Skidder, to my surprise, was there to catch me, sort of, or at least slow my fall. "Damn, Doc," he grunted as I half slid, half staggered to my feet in front of him. "What the hell you doing? I thought *I* was the only crazy stunt-man around here."

Carmelita Janus was hurrying toward us. "My God, Dr. Brockton, are you hurt?"

"Just my pride," I said. "I was trying to get a closer look at something up there. Probably nothing, but seemed worth checking out."

"I don't think you should try it alone," she said. "Let us help you. Please."

Reluctantly—ashamed of my clumsiness and weakness—I assented. Skidder interlaced his fingers to create a stirrup for my right foot, hoisting it as high as his waist. As I raised my left foot, feeling for a toe-hold, Carmelita Janus grabbed my shoe and guided it to a ledge I had not noticed. Then Skidder did the same with my right foot—angling it into a niche that was as high as his head—and after one more step with my left foot, this time unaided, I reached a stable, sustainable position, my feet secure, my fists wedged into cracks that would hold me with virtually no effort required. "That's about as high as we can get you, Doc," Skidder said.

"It's as high as I need to be." I felt a second wave of adrenaline kicking in, and this one was not from my fall or my fear.

"You've found something," said Carmelita. "What is it?"

"Look at this," I said, freeing my left hand and plucking a small, cigar-shaped object—twice the size of a grain of brown rice, but hollow and almost weightless—from a nook in the rock. "I'm going to drop it now. Watch close." I released it and watched it float down, as light as a tiny feather.

Carmelita caught it in midair, the way a child might catch a snowflake. She peered at it, then looked up at me. "What is it?"

"It's a puparium," I told her, wedging my fist back into the crack. "An empty pupa case. From a maggot that turned—that metamorphosed—into an adult fly. If y'all look close, you can see more of these down lower, in crevices here and there."

"Yes," she said after a moment, pointing. "Here's one. And here's another."

"I wanted to climb to see how high they went. I followed them all the way up here."

"Huh," Skidder grunted. "You're sounding kinda excited about this, Doc."

"I am. It means there were maggots up here."

"You sound surprised," said Carmelita. "But didn't you tell us, that day in the meeting at the FBI office, that you had found maggots? I thought that was one way you knew the Mexican man died the night of the crash."

"You have a good memory," I said. "That's true. But those maggots were down near the ground. These are too high to be from that guy, or from the mountain lion. Maggots can fall, but they can't climb. I'll tell you like I tell my students: Trust the bugs. The bugs never lie."

Skidder furrowed his brows. "And the truth that these new bugs are telling you . . . ?"

"I *think* they're telling me that some pieces from our guy—the guy in the cockpit—came through the windshield and landed in some of these crevices. If those pieces were shielded from the fire, maybe they didn't get cooked."

"And if you can find uncooked pieces, maybe you can get DNA after all," he finished.

"Exactly." I peered into every crack I could see from where I stood, clinging to the rock. As I bobbed my head and craned my neck, I caught a sudden glimmer of reflected light to my right. "Hang on," I called, freeing my right hand this time and reaching into the recess where I'd glimpsed the reflection. "I think I might see a piece of windshield."

"Be careful," he said. "That could be jagged. You don't want to get cut."

"I'm not worried about cuts," I said. "I'm worried about snakes." I reached in gingerly. My hand now blocked my view, so I was working blindly, strictly by touch, praying not to encounter the open mouth of a rattlesnake. Beneath my fingertips, I felt the feather-light shells of more puparia—dozens of them!—and I groped on, eagerly. Suddenly I felt something shift against my fingers, and I heard a dry, hollow rustling—*a rattlesnake's tail buzzing?*—and with a yelp, I yanked my hand from the opening. I lost my balance again and felt myself toppling backward once more—this time from much higher—but luckily, my left fist was wedged tightly enough into its crack to hold. *Bombproof,* I thought gratefully.

"Jesus, Mary, and Joseph," said Carmelita. "What happened?"

"Sorry," I said. "And *ouch.*" My left hand felt as if it had argued with a belt sander and a claw hammer—and lost both arguments—but at least my brains weren't spattered on the rocks. "I heard something that I thought might be a rattlesnake," I explained sheepishly, "so I jerked my hand back." She gasped, so I hurried on. "But it wasn't. It was just my hand knocking a bunch of dry puparia out of the way, rustling them. Dumb. Okay, let's try this again." I reached into the recess once more, willing myself to ignore the rustle of the insect shells.

"You look like you're putting your hand in the Mouth of Truth," said Carmelita—a reference to an ancient Roman carving of a face—a man or a god—with a gaping mouth. "Tell a lie with your hand in the mouth, legend says, and the mouth bites it off."

"The truth is, this makes me very nervous," I said. It must not have been a lie, because my hand remained attached and unhurt. My fingers eased through the cluster of pupa cases and then came to a larger, heavier object—the thing that had shifted when my fingers grazed it. I had thought it might be a piece of windshield, but as I closed my fingers carefully around it, it felt different from a piece of shattered acrylic. It felt greasy, and it felt familiar.

"Are you *sure*?" asked Carmelita, staring at the small, curved fragment I had pulled from my pocket once I'd made it safely down.

"Absolutely," I told her. "Look at the edge here. See the cross section? There's a hard layer of bone on the outside and the inside, separated by a spongy layer in between. It's definitely a piece of cranium. A skull fragment."

"What are *those*?" asked Skidder, pointing at the inner surface, which was etched with branchy indentations. "They look like riverbeds. Dry gullies."

"Close," I said. "Those are meningeal grooves—grooves where blood vessels ran. More proof that it's a skull fragment."

"It might be from an animal," Carmelita said.

"Might be, but it's not," I said. Turning the piece over, I showed them the outer surface. It still had a bit of dried scalp and a tuft of short, gray hair attached. "That's human hair."

"My God," Carmelita whispered. "That's Richard's hair." She clutched Skidder's arm for support. "My husband really is dead."

After giving Mrs. Janus a few minutes alone, I circled back to her. "Do you still have something of Richard's, like a toothbrush or a baseball cap? Something that could be used for DNA comparison?" She might be right—it might be a tuft of Richard's hair, and a bit of Richard's skull, in her hand. But *might be* wasn't good enough, wasn't certain enough. I couldn't afford to be accused of botching the identification a second time.

"I have his favorite cap," she said. "Also a hairbrush. You need hairs that still have the follicles attached, yes?"

"Yes," I said, surprised and impressed. "How did you know that?"

"I've been through this already with the FBI. I gave them a comb and a hat."

"Oh, great—never mind, then," I said. "They've already got something to compare to this."

She glanced at Skidder, then at me again, suddenly looking wary. "What do you mean?"

"I mean, since they've already got the hat and the comb, all we need to take them is the skull fragment."

She stared at me. "We can't take this to the FBI," she said.

"But . . . we *have* to. It's their case."

"But the FBI has told everyone Richard faked his death," she protested. "They've told everyone he's still alive, somewhere in hiding. This piece of skull would prove them wrong. I don't think they will admit their mistake."

"Come on," I said. "They won't ignore clear proof that he's dead. Teeth are one thing; teeth can be pulled—Richard's teeth were pulled. But you can't just pull out a piece of skull and walk away. If the DNA matches, they'll believe it."

"I don't trust them," she said. "I think they're more interested in protecting their image than in finding the truth."

Suddenly I had an idea—an idea that I was shocked to hear myself suggesting. "What about that obnoxious Fox News reporter, Mike Malloy?" Carmelita and Skidder shot glances at each other. "What?" I said. "Look, I don't like him either—he's pushy as hell—but he's actually done the best job of covering this. Seems like he'd love another big scoop. The latest twist in the world's most twisted case."

Carmelita shook her head. "Mike Malloy is dead," she said.

I stared at her, then at Skidder. He nodded. "Found dead in his bed yesterday," he said. "A leather strap around his neck and the bedpost."

"He hanged himself?"

The deputy grimaced. "Not on purpose. There was a bunch of porn in the bed. Looks like an accidental autoerotic asphyxiation." As I struggled to take this in, he went on, "Supposedly it increases the intensity of orgasm if there's less oxygen in the brain. So some people—kinky people . . ." He trailed off awkwardly.

"I get it, I get it," I said. Suddenly a thought struck me. "What if it was staged? What if he'd kept poking around, looking for the story behind the story? What if he'd managed to track down his source—whoever it was that knew about the teeth? What if he'd found out that it really was Richard in the wreckage—that the whole thing was an elaborate double fake? Malloy might have looked like a threat."

Carmelita was nodding excitedly. "I think you're right," she said. "Maybe he figured out who the killer was."

Skidder cleared his throat. "That could be true," he said. "But meanwhile, we've got to do something with this piece of skull. I have an idea. Carmelita, I understand your concerns about the FBI. But what we've just found is a game changer. I propose a compromise. I'm not in uniform today, but I *am* a law enforcement officer. How 'bout if I take custody of this piece of evidence? I can transfer it—or a piece of it—to a forensic lab that's not part of the FBI. And I can transfer custody of the rest of it to Prescott, if the outside lab confirms that it's Richard."

"*When* the outside lab confirms that it's Richard," said Carmelita grimly.

One of the consolation prizes of being an aging professor is that you teach a lot of students over the years—students who go on to become doctors and lawyers and research geneticists. One of my former students had ended up running a genetics lab at UCLA Medical Center, in Los Angeles. It took just five minutes on my cell phone—high on Otay Mountain, I got a great signal—to ask if he could do a DNA analysis, comparing a bit of scalp tissue with a sample from a comb or a cap. "Piece of cake," he said. "Can you overnight it?"

"I might be able to do better than that," I said. I turned to Skidder. "Any chance you could fly this up to UCLA Medical Center?"

"Sure thing," he said. "I know that helipad like the back of my hand." I relayed this information to my student, who was suitably impressed with the speed, and assured me he'd be waiting, and could be at the helipad within five minutes' notice.

After thanking him and hanging up, I asked Skidder how soon he might be able to make the handoff.

"Three, four hours," he said. Seeing my disappointment, he explained, "I gotta turn in this bird and get one from the sheriff's fleet. Plus I'll need to brief the sheriff." Now my disappointed expression turned to a look of alarm, but Skidder gave a don't-worry wave of his hand. "The sheriff had a lot of respect for Richard. Plus he's a master of the interagency-cooperation game. Trust me—he'll find a way to spin this thing so Prescott can't possibly bitch. Hell, Prescott'll probably end up having to give the sheriff a public pat on the back, for being such a great team player and all."

A moment later we climbed back into the helicopter for the quick flight down to Brown Field. I had reserved a rental car there, and—despite their protests that I should stay someplace nicer—I'd booked a room in the Otay Mesa Quality Inn: a cruddy but convenient base from which to do the exploring I'd planned for the following day. Besides, in a twisted sort of way, it felt like my home away from home.

As the engine throttled up and Skidder raised the stick, the helicopter practically leapt upward. I was pleasantly surprised by its newfound nimbleness— until I remembered what Skidder had said earlier about the aircraft getting "zippy" just before the tank ran dry. I shot a quick, panicky look at the instrument panel, trying to spot the fuel gauge. Skidder must have noticed. "No worries," he said. "It's all downhill from here. We can coast in, if we have to."

"Skidder," I said, "how come every time you try to reassure me, it scares the crap out of me?"

Chapter 38

The Otay Mesa Quality Inn was shabbier than I remembered—and I had remembered it as damn shabby. "Memory is a trickster," as one of my UT colleagues, a pompous English professor, was fond of saying.

I asked the desk clerk for a room on the hotel's quiet side. "Define 'quiet,'" said the clerk, a sallow young man with greasy black hair and cynical eyes. "No traffic, or no gunshots?"

He didn't appear to be kidding. "Tough choice," I said, "but I'm gonna go for no gunshots."

He handed me a key. "All the way at the end," he said, nodding toward the freeway. I thanked him, moved the car, and carried my bag to the room.

As I turned the key in the lock, a truck roared past on the freeway, rattling my door and window. *Home sweet home,* I thought, echoing Prescott's description of the hotel when he'd brought us here our first night. But the truth was, I didn't much mind the shabbiness. I'd be sleeping in an empty bed; that was the worst part—far worse than the torn carpet and stained bedspread. *Just don't let me get bedbugs,* I prayed. Like the desk clerk, I was dead serious.

Maybe Kathleen really *was* haunting me—not about the Janus case, as she'd threatened, but about the backlog of old voice mails on my phone. Throughout our teaching careers, our offices had been a study in contrast: hers always neat and tidy, mine always . . . less so. As with our desktops, so with our voice mails. I tended to procrastinate, avoiding messages I knew would be unpleasant (a category that nowadays seemed to encompass virtually all of them). "Okay, Kath," I announced over the rumble of traffic, "I'm clearing my decks. You'd be proud."

Mercifully, most of the messages were so old that they had become utterly irrelevant, and I found myself hitting the "delete" key many times in swift succession. Muckraking talk-radio host badgering me about disrespecting veterans? Delete. Obituary-stalking strangers who'd read about my wife's passing in the newspaper? Delete. Neighborhood widows offering a soft shoulder and a warm casserole? Delete delete delete.

The message I most dreaded hearing—the one I saved for last—was the voice mail I'd received from Captain Brian Decker shortly before his throat had been cut in a prison interview room by Nick Satterfield. Decker was still at Vanderbilt Hospital, still barely alive—still in a coma, in fact—and merely seeing his number on my phone's display was enough to make me feel bad all over again: guilty, somehow, even though I'd urged him not to go rattle Satterfield's cage. The TBI agent investigating the incident—if *investigating* was the right word for an inquiry that gave any weight at all to Satterfield's version of events—had said that the call had lasted five minutes. As I punched the series of keys that would play the message, I braced myself for bad tidings: a grim reminder of Satterfield's virally infectious venom, at the very least, and possibly even a self-incriminating revelation from Deck about what he'd intended to do to Satterfield. I considered erasing it without listening—what was the point, besides pain?— but decided I owed it to Decker to hear him out.

As the message began to play, all I heard was random background noise—doors opening and closing; metal chairs scraping on a concrete floor; a staticky, scratchy sound that I finally recognized as the rustle of fabric against a microphone. Decker must have pocket-dialed me, I realized, accidentally hitting "redial" as he'd slid his phone into his shirt. Through the rustle and static, I suddenly heard Decker speaking, and then—to my horror—I heard Satterfield answering. His voice came across the miles and the weeks in a soft, sinister hiss, taunting Decker about his brother's death. Weeks after their bloody fight, I found myself eavesdropping on their confrontation, as mesmerized and terrified as if I were actually in the room with them.

I expected to hear Decker respond with threats and violence, but he didn't. Satterfield kept it up—kept goading Decker with cruel details about the agonies his brother had suffered—but Decker wasn't taking the bait. Suddenly I felt a jolt like an electric shock, as Satterfield said my name. "I've got unfinished business with Brockton. I'll be back to deal with him. All of them. And I'll take up right where I left off."

"Don't even think about it," said Decker. "I should've shot you last time, but I let Brockton talk me out of it. I won't make that mistake next time."

"Here's the thing, asshole," said Satterfield. "You won't be around next time. You're about to bleed out on this floor." All at once the message erupted into noisy chaos: crashing furniture, thudding bodies, and a strangled shriek of pain. Then, in midshriek, the phone went silent. Two seconds later, a computerized voice prompted me: "To replay this message, press

one. To delete it, press three. To save it, press two." My
fingers shaking, I carefully pressed two. Then I dialed
Steve Morgan, the former student now working for
the TBI. Not surprisingly, I got *his* voice mail. "Steve,
it's Bill Brockton," I said. "I'm about to forward you
a message—a recording of what went down between
Captain Decker and Nick Satterfield. I'd appreciate it if
you'd share it with Agent Fielding. And I'd appreciate
it if Fielding would get off my ass. If he really wants to
do the right thing, he might also drop by Vanderbilt
Hospital and apologize to Decker. Who knows, Decker
might actually hear it. Might fight a little harder to pull
through."

I ended the call, then returned to my voice mail and
forwarded the recording to Steve. That done, and my
decks clear, I got back to the business at hand. The
business that had brought me back to California, back
to Otay Mountain, and back to this seedy motel and
this rough-edged border crossing.

Somewhere nearby, I heard a loud bang: gunshot, or
backfiring engine? Out here, I was having trouble telling the difference.

The Otay Mesa branch of the public library was just
ten minutes west but a world away from the seamy-
underbelly freight district where I was staying. Instead

of the dilapidated warehouses and rusting shipping containers of my neighborhood, the library nestled amid neat houses, tree-lined streets, baseball fields, and basketball courts. The library's reference desk occupied a back corner of the main reading room, flanked by low shelves of encyclopedias on one side and bound volumes of old *Life* magazines, decades' worth, on the other. "Excuse me," I said to a reference librarian whose steel-framed spectacles matched the silvery curls of her hair. "Do you keep files of news clippings about local stories?"

"Vertical files? Oh, yes," she said, smiling sweetly. "Some of them are a bit out of date, though. The Internet, you know—it's making newspaper clippings obsolete." She pointed to a set of chest-high filing cabinets, which appeared to be approximately the same age as my own venerable self. "The files are there. Can I help you find something specific?"

"I'm interested in several topics," I said. "A San Diego man named Richard Janus, who founded a charity called Airlift Relief International. He's been in the news lately."

"Indeed," she said, her radiant smile giving way to a pursed, prunish expression. "Most unfortunate." I didn't know if she was referring to the plane crash or the drug-running allegations. Perhaps both.

"I'm also interested in a man who runs a Mexican drug cartel," I went on. "His name is Guzmán." I spelled it for her. "El Chapo Guzmán. I seem to remember hearing about some sort of connection between his drug trafficking and Otay Mesa."

Her mouth had gone from slightly pursed to tightly puckered, and not in a kissing kind of way. From the look of prim disapproval, I might have been asking her to help me find pornography. "The files are arranged alphabetically," she snipped. "You can try looking up the last names of the two . . . *people*. I believe there might also be a file called DRUGS." I got the distinct impression that not only did she disapprove of drugs themselves, she also disapproved of news coverage that mentioned them—and of anyone who might have the brass to read such coverage.

"Thank you," I said pleasantly. "You've been most helpful." *She's no Red,* I thought as I walked toward the files. *But then again, Red's no Red either—not the reference librarian she pretended to be, anyhow.*

The Richard Janus file contained a thick sheaf of clippings—yellowing with age, untarnished by the recent scandal—praising him for his humanitarian service. During his flying for Air America back during the Vietnam War, several clippings reported, Janus had delivered rice to starving peasants in Laos—experiences that he consistently described as "deeply rewarding" and "the inspiration for Airlift Relief International." None of the clippings mentioned Air America's drops of "hard rice"—guns and ammunition—or of home-made napalm, cooked up in oil drums by the CIA and dispersed over villages thought to harbor Communist guerrillas. Had Janus napalmed villages? Had he fer-ried opium to fund U.S.-friendly warlords in the poppy-growing region known as the "Golden Triangle"? The press clippings shed no light on those questions.

One interesting side note I found in Janus's file was a brief bio of his wife. As a young woman from an aristo-cratic family in Mexico City, Carmelita Janus had been a beauty queen, model, and honors law student, well on her way to a promising legal career. She had left Mexico in her early twenties—with Richard Janus—shortly after the murder of her father, a high-ranking judge. In light of the widespread, well-documented corruption of Mexico's police, army, and prosecutors by narco traffickers, I couldn't help wondering: Had her father been killed because he'd opposed drug lords like Guzmán? Or had he sold out to one drug lord, then gotten gunned down by a rival?

El Chapo's file was far slimmer than Janus's. It con-tained just three clippings, which had merited clipping and filing, as best I could tell, because each of the three quoted "knowledgeable DEA sources in San Diego." The first story reported Guzmán's 1994 arrest and imprisonment; the second recounted his 2001 escape; and the third—the one I recalled Red mentioning—described how DEA agents discovered an elaborate underground railroad, used to haul drugs through a tunnel beneath the U.S.-Mexico border. The drugs—tons of them, according to the "knowledgeable DEA sources"—were loaded into carts beneath a house in Tijuana, wheeled the length of the tunnel, and then unloaded. The rail line's northern terminus, said the story, was a warehouse fifty yards north of the border, in the industrial sector of Otay Mesa. *In the Quality Inn sector of Otay Mesa,* I realized with a shock. It was likely that I had wandered past that very warehouse my first evening in town—*The fenced building with the guard-dog sign?* I wondered—before I'd ended up at the IHOP, overhearing the argument between Miles Prescott and the fat, wheezing warrior from the DEA or the CIA or whatever federal agency it was that waged war on badasses.

The pursed-lipped librarian's clippings did not, however, shed light on the things that had been gnawing at me all afternoon and evening, ever since I'd found the bit of bone that seemed to have come from the shattered skull of Richard Janus: If Janus had in fact been murdered—if a killer had strapped Janus's body into the cockpit, aimed the plane at the mountainside, and then parachuted to safety—a whole series of baffling questions reared their heads, clamoring for answers. Why had the killer pulled Janus's teeth? Why had he tucked a spinal cord stimulator behind the body? Why had he told the Fox reporter and the FBI agent that tool marks could be found on the teeth? In short, why had the killer gone to such elaborate lengths to do a *double* fake: to start out by creating the illusion that Janus had died in the fiery crash, but then to shatter that illusion, replacing it with a second illusion—the illusion that Janus was alive and on the lam somewhere?

For years, I had preached the gospel of Occam's razor, a rule of logic stating that the simplest explanation that fits the facts is almost certainly the *correct* explanation. This case, though, seemed to be turning Occam's razor on its head: the more complex and bizarre the explanation, the closer it seemed to stumble toward some grotesque, distorted, funhouse-mirrored travesty of truth.

That night, in my lumpy bed in my shabby motel, I dreamed of Janus—not the American pilot Janus, but the Roman deity, the one with two faces. That Janus, the one who gazed unblinkingly at both the past and the future, had been the guardian of doorways and transitions and transformations; he'd been both the keeper of the key and the wielder of the cudgel. In my dreams, the key to the mystery remained just out of reach, my fingertips not quite touching it as first my hand, then my entire arm, plunged into the Mouth of Truth.

I knew that the key must be close at hand, though, because as I groped blindly, my motions accompanied by the soft rattlings of dry pupa cases or snake tails, I felt myself being cudgeled. Rhythmically, ceaselessly cudgeled.

Chapter 39

After an early breakfast of petrified bagel, I stocked up on water and snacks at a nearby convenience store—a place sporting so many signs in Spanish, I half wondered if I had somehow strayed through a gap in the border fence—and aimed the rental car toward Otay Mountain, guided by the detailed topographic map I'd gotten from Carmelita Janus.

The topo map confirmed what I had already noticed: The area around the airfield and my motel was pancake flat, the streets following straight gridlines. To the north and east of town, though, the terrain began to rise and the roads began to undulate, following the contours.

My first stop was the grass airstrip at the eastern end of Lower Otay Lake—the home of "Janus Junkyard," where Airlift Relief had kept spare parts, picked-over airplane skeletons, and a maintenance shop. Pat Maddox, the NTSB expert, had sounded certain that the airstrip was where the Citation's pilot—the actual, living pilot—would have steered his parachute. It made sense, I'd agreed, as I'd studied the topo map: the airstrip and the area around it were flat and free of hazards, except for a couple of hangars, a windsock tower, and a handful of airplane carcasses. Would I be able to find evidence of a parachute landing somewhere out there, in forty acres of grass and weeds? Or was I wasting time and energy on a fool's errand? "Only one way to know," I muttered, turning down the dusty dirt lane that led to the airstrip.

I'd gone only a hundred yards when I came to a farm gate that blocked the road, a thick chain and padlock cinching the gate to a stout fencepost. The gate itself wasn't much of an obstacle; its construction—horizontal tubes of galvanized steel, spaced eight or ten inches apart—made it a makeshift ladder. No, the real obstacle was the yellow-and-black crime scene tape stretched across the gateway, along with a laminated notice bearing the FBI logo and a stern NO TRESPASSING warning. I cast a furtive look around, found the coast was clear, and stepped onto the gate's second rung, my hands gripping the top crossbar.

One step up, I paused, partly because of the NO TRESPASSING notice—specifically, its mention of video surveillance—but also partly because of something I remembered from the prior day's flight retracing the jet's route. According to Skidder, an expert pilot, the Citation was still maneuvering when it crossed the airstrip. In fact, the jet's five-hundred-foot descent and leveling off had occurred only after it had made its turn toward the mountain. The jumper must not have landed here.

Returning to the car, I pulled out the topo map and spread it on the hood, studying the lay of the land and the way the roads wrapped around its contours. Shortly before I'd reached the turnoff to the airstrip, I had passed another dirt road—this one heading south, into the broad valley that funneled up to the peak. The day before, retracing the Citation's route in the air to the crash site, I'd hit pay dirt. Maybe I'd get lucky again this time, following the ground track.

As I doubled back and entered the mouth of the valley—*the Mouth of Truth?* I heard myself wondering—I quickly realized my rental car was a poor steed for this ride. I had asked for an SUV, but the Hertz counter at Brown Field didn't have any; instead of a Jeep Cherokee or Ford Expedition, I was bucking up a washboard road in a low-slung Chevy Impala, dodging football-sized rocks and wincing with every scrape of the oil pan against jutting ledges. The road ended a half mile up the valley, in a wide hollow with a flat, sandy turnaround area. Stopping thirty yards short of the turnaround, I got out and walked, my eyes scanning the ground. I could see tire tracks, but unlike the crisp tread marks I'd left in my FBI training exercise at the Body Farm, these furrows—plowed in dry, soft sand—revealed nothing about the tires or vehicles that had made the marks.

As I neared the turnaround, where the tracks looped back, I saw other signs of disturbance: sandy heaps and hollows, which I suspected had been sculpted by the scuffing of feet. Then I spotted something that made my heart race: a midden of cigarette butts strewn beside the tire tracks, as if someone had emptied an ashtray there . . . or had parked and waited for an hour or two, chain-smoking an entire pack, using each cigarette's final embers to light the next, then dropping the dying butt to the ground beneath the car's open window.

Suddenly I stopped, my eye caught by what appeared to be another artifact—an odd, enigmatic, and therefore electrifying creation. At the center of the wide turnaround, five fat cigar butts, each as thick as my thumb, jutted upward from the sand a couple of inches apiece. With one at the center and the other four radiating outward from it—each five feet or so from the center—they formed a large, precise geometric shape: like the five dots on dominos or dice . . . or like a giant + sign, measuring ten or twelve feet from tip to tip. A small circle of sand at the base of each stub was black with soot, and as I edged closer, I saw that the cigar butts weren't cigar butts at all, but the remnants of signal flares stuck into the ground. Set alight in the blackness of this wilderness, they would have created a blazing bull's-eye here: here in the softest, safest spot for a parachutist leaping into the blackness from a streaking jet.

Hands shaking, I dialed Skidder's number. *Deputy* Skidder's number. Given that he was briefing the sheriff—had probably briefed the sheriff the day before—about the piece of skull, he'd need to relay this information, too. But my call didn't go through, and when I looked at my phone I saw why. Down in this hollow, miles from town, I had no signal. Zero bars. "Crap," I muttered; I'd need to return to civilization to make the call. As I turned back toward my car, I spotted signs of civilization—a grim sort of civilization—on the skyline only a few miles away: the guard towers of the state prison. My first thought was a bad pun: *plenty of bars at a prison.* My second thought was less silly, and maybe even useful: *Maybe one of the guards saw something that night.*

It took every particle of patience I had to thread the car slowly back down the rocky road and out of the hollow. Once I reached the main road, I floored the gas pedal, gunning the small-caliber engine. I made a skidding turn at the sign pointing toward the prison, then—glancing at my phone and seeing that I had four signal bars—I pulled to the side and phoned the deputy to tell him what I'd found. "This is Skidder," said the voice-mail greeting. "Leave me a message and I'll call you back."

"Deputy, this is Bill Brockton," I said. "I think I found where Richard's killer came down when he bailed out that night. Call me back soon as you can."

Next I scrolled down my list of contacts until I found Special Agent Miles Prescott. I debated the pros and cons of calling him. On the one hand—the call-now hand—an FBI Evidence Response Team would have the best shot at finding any significant evidence, if indeed I was right about what I'd seen; with luck, there might even be recoverable DNA on the cigarette butts, and possibly fingerprints on the unburned bases of the flares. On the other hand—the slow-down hand—the San Diego County sheriff was supposedly engaged in some delicate interagency diplomacy with the FBI, possibly even at this very moment; if I called Prescott directly, rather than letting the sheriff finesse things, I might accidentally sabotage his efforts to refocus the investigation.

I decided to seek a second opinion. This time the call was answered by a human, not a recording. "Safety Board. Maddox."

"Pat," I said. "Bill Brockton here."

"Doc," he said heartily. "How the hell are you?"

"Well, I'm okay," I said. "It's been rocky lately. My wife passed away recently. Unexpectedly."

"*What?* Did you just say your wife died?"

"Yes. But—"

"My God, Doc, I'm so sorry to hear that."

"Thanks, Pat. I appreciate that. But that's not what I'm calling about."

"Well, no," he said, "I realize I might not be your main go-to guy for emotional support. What's up?"

"You'll be very interested in this," I told him. "And I'd appreciate your advice."

"Advice? Hell, Doc, I stopped giving advice a long damn time ago. I noticed I was nearly always wrong, but even when I was right—*especially* when I was right—people ended up getting pissed off at me."

I laughed. "I promise not to get pissed off."

"I'll hold you to it, Doc. So to paraphrase the 911 dispatchers, what's the nature of your advice emergency?"

"So, remember when we talked a few weeks ago? When you said there was a way to bail out of a Citation—out of *that* Citation—in flight?"

"Sure," he said. "I don't surprise that easy anymore, old as I am, but I gotta admit, you coulda knocked me over with a feather when I found out about those belly doors."

"Well, get ready for another surprise. I found where the guy landed."

"Come again?"

"I found where he landed. The guy that bailed out."

"Yeah, sure," he said. "Seriously, Doc, what's on your mind?"

"No kidding. Hand-on-the-Bible serious. I came back to San Diego, and I found the place, Pat. Not where you thought, though—it's about a mile south of that airstrip." I described the scene—the dead-end road, the pile of cigarette butts, the giant + sign formed by flares. "In the middle of the night, right under the flight path, no other lights around? That signal would've stood out like a *searchlight*."

"Maybe," he said. "If that's what it was. And if that's *when* it was."

"How do you mean?"

"Coulda just been kids, out there some other night. Drinking, smoking dope, playing with fire. You know—kids."

"I've got a good feeling about this, Pat. Those flares, arranged in that pattern? That wasn't made by stoned kids messing around. I'm telling you, Pat, that was a signal. I think maybe I should call Prescott, let his evidence guys see what they can find."

"Special Agent Prescott? I thought you were number one on his shit list."

"Well, yeah," I conceded. "That's why I called you. To see what you think. You're a fed, Pat. Would Prescott actually listen to what I have to say? Or would he just dismiss it, since he thinks I'm full of crap?"

"Hmm. Interesting question, Doc. Tricky." He paused to think. "Here's an idea. I'm just thinking out loud here. I'm *not* on Prescott's shit list. What if I came down and took a quick look? If it's all you say it is, maybe I could make the call to Prescott—soften him up a bit—and then hand the phone over to you. Might help him listen with an open mind if I ran a little interference for you."

"I see your point," I said, "and I appreciate it. But I'm nervous about just leaving it for a day or two, or whenever you can get away and get down here."

"And you think Prescott and Company are gonna rush right over there? Not bloody likely." Maddox chuckled. "You've never ridden with me, have you, Doc?"

"Well, no. Why?"

"Because if you had, you'd know it's like ridin' in a low-flying plane. I can be there in two hours. That soon enough for you?"

I checked my watch. "Really? Three o'clock? *Today?*"

"Three-thirty, tops, if there's not a wreck on the 405. Can you wait that long? You could run back to town and grab lunch, if you haven't already eaten."

"Nah, I've got snacks in the car. Besides, I've got something else I want to do out this way. I'll plan on meeting you at three, or as soon after that as you can get here."

"Where? Can you tell me how to find this place?" I gave him directions, and as I finished, he said, "I see it on the map, and I'm printing it out right now. I'll see you in a couple hours."

"Drive safe, Pat."

He chuckled again. "*Clearly* you've never ridden with me, Doc."

Donovan State Prison occupied the entire top of a low, oblong mesa. The terrain was dry and dun colored, and the few bits of scrubby vegetation that hadn't been bulldozed looked as brown and desiccated as the rocks and dirt. A road encircled the complex, skirting the base of three parallel chain-link fences, fifteen feet high and ten feet apart. Out of curiosity, I circumnavigated the complex on the perimeter road, keeping count of the cellblocks and guard towers. If my count was correct, there were twenty cellblocks and a dozen guard towers, each tower thirty or forty feet high.

I'd seen forbidding penitentiaries before. Tennessee's Brushy Mountain State Prison—whose hard-core convicts had once included James Earl Ray, the assassin of Dr. Martin Luther King Jr.—was a forbidding stone fortress, complete with crenellations that looked transplanted from a medieval castle. Donovan State Prison, by contrast, had nothing even grimly ornamental about it. It was almost as if Donovan's designers and builders had carefully, purposefully excluded any scraps of ornament or history or humanity. Donovan had the bare-bones, bleached-bones look of a bottom-rung industrial complex: a slaughterhouse of the human spirit, as efficient and utilitarian as any meatpacking plant where cows were conveyor-belted to their deaths.

The one exception to the grimness was the administration building, set outside the triple fencing amid grass, shrubbery, and even a few palm trees. After my brief sightseeing circuit, I parked in front and entered the glass doors. A receptionist behind glass asked if she could help me. "I hope so," I said, introducing myself and flashing my TBI consultant's badge—an official-looking brass shield, especially impressive if the word "CONSULTANT" was masked by a strategically placed knuckle.

"Tennessee," she said. "You're a long way from home."

"I sure am," I said, smiling. "The FBI asked me to help with a case out here. I'm hoping I could talk to the watch commander—if that's the right term—who was supervising the guard-tower staff during the graveyard shift on a night back in June."

"Well, the night-shift watch commander wouldn't be on duty now," she said. "But he reports to the assistant warden for security, who *is* here. Could he help you with this?"

"Well, it's worth a try," I said.

"Walter Jessup," said the assistant warden ten minutes later, extending his hand across a desk. "I understand you're interested in events the night of June eighteenth, early morning of June nineteenth?"

"Yes, sir. I'm wondering if any of the watchtower guards saw something unusual, around one in the morning."

"*Any* of them? *All* of them. Have to be blind to miss that fire on the mountain."

I smiled. "Yeah, and I reckon you don't put a lot of blind men up in those guard towers. Actually, though, I'm hoping somebody saw something before the fire. Before the plane hit."

"You mean the parachute?"

I blinked. I stared. I blinked again. "Are you serious? Somebody really saw a 'chute?"

"Yep. Tompkins. Minute or so after the plane flew over. Minute or so before it hit. A little south of the usual spot, though."

"Excuse me?"

"Not quite the same place the 'chutes usually come down."

"Let me make sure I'm following you," I said slowly. "Are you telling me this happens regularly? Nighttime parachute jumps over wilderness?"

"Not regularly. More like irregularly. Occasionally. Three, four times a year, maybe. But usually, like I say, usually they're a little farther north—right over that little airstrip by the lake. And usually they're before the plane lands, not after it takes off. Propeller plane, in the past. Not a jet. So this time was same thing, only different."

I didn't like the sound of this. "How long has this been going on?"

He shrugged. "Five years, plus or minus a year. If it's important, we could ask some of the guards if they can pin it down closer than that."

"Ever reported it to anybody?"

"You bet. Plane comes in at night from south of the border, drops something at a private airstrip a few miles from town before landing at a port of entry? Doesn't take a rocket scientist to figure out they're running contraband."

I felt my heart sinking and my anger rising. "Who'd you report it to?"

"DEA. I talked to the guy myself, face-to-face. Big fat redheaded fella, sitting right there where you're sitting now, wheezing like he had asthma or emphysema or something. He said he'd look into it, but I never heard back from him. And those parachutes kept on coming down."

Sitting in the car in the prison parking lot, I dialed—jabbed—Carmelita Janus's number on my cell phone. "You lied to me," I said, my voice shaking with rage. "Right to my face, looking me straight in the eye. 'Oh, Richard *hated* drugs,' you said. 'Richard would *never* smuggle drugs.' I can't believe I fell for that load of crap. And I can't believe I crawled out on a limb to help you. Don't ever call me again."

"Wait," she said. "I didn't lie to you. Where are you? What's happened? Why are you saying this?"

"I'm at Donovan State Prison," I said coldly. "The guard towers there have a good view toward Richard's airstrip. They've known about the drug drops for years. So has the DEA. Richard's fat, crooked pal."

"Richard wasn't smuggling drugs," she said. "I swear it. You have to believe me."

"No, I don't, Mrs. Janus. I already made that mistake. I won't make it again. I hope they catch whoever killed your husband. But I can't help you anymore."

"Wait," she said again.

I didn't wait. I clicked off the phone, started the car, and left the prison, circling the complex one last time. This time I seemed to feel myself being watched, and I found myself looking upward: up at the looming towers. In the glare of sunlight glinting off their windows, I seemed to see only blank, blind stares, unblinking and utterly indifferent to whatever crimes and misdeeds were occurring—on either side of the triple fencing and coiled razor wire.

Chapter 40

As I neared the turnaround of the dead-end road—the spot I had come to think of as the drop zone—my small, citified, sissified car bottomed out for what felt like the dozenth time, the oil pan banging and rasping as the metal scraped across stone. When I'd rented the vehicle back at Brown Field, the Hertz agent had done a walk-around inspection with me, marking scrapes and dings on a diagram of the car. *Hope he doesn't check for dents underneath*, I thought, parking in the same place where I'd parked two hours before.

The engine was ticking with heat, but something about the sound struck me as odd—as different—from the usual dry, metallic click . . . and it seemed to be coming not just from the engine but from the ground as well. Kneeling in the sand, I leaned on my elbows and peered beneath the car. *Tick-splat, tick-splat, tick-splat.* "Well, damn," I muttered. "Damn damn damn." Each *damn* was echoed by a fat drop of oil falling from the ripped oil pan and splatting into a fast-growing puddle beneath the engine. Still on all fours, I turned and looked behind the car. A thread of oil trailed down the rocky road, like greasy blood, from the wounded Impala.

Then, as if snuffling along the trail, another vehicle nosed up the road, a black Suburban with big tires and plenty of ground clearance. Clambering to my feet, I walked back toward the SUV. "I'm sure glad to see you," I said to Maddox as the door opened.

But it was not Maddox who got out of the Suburban. It was a fat man with greasy red hair, a sweaty white shirt, a leather shoulder holster, and a stubby revolver. The revolver was still holstered, but the safety strap was unsnapped, and I suddenly wished I still had the pistol I'd thrown into the river a few days before. "*You,*" I said, my blood pressure spiking. Even though the air was bone dry, sweat began rolling from my scalp and seeping from my armpits. "What are *you* doing here?"

"Following you," he wheezed. "I don't believe we've formally met, Dr. Brockton. I'm Special Agent William Hickock. I'm with the DEA. The Drug Enforcement Administration."

"I know what the DEA is," I said. "And I know who you are. You're the guy waging war on the worst badasses on the planet, right? Or are you?"

"What the hell are you talking about?"

"I'm talking about your pissing contest with Miles Prescott and the FBI. I heard you and Prescott arguing in the IHOP that night. The night after somebody aimed Richard Janus's jet—his jet and his corpse and his yanked-out teeth—at that mountainside and bailed out. Were you still in cahoots with Janus at that point, or had you two had a falling-out? Had Janus gotten greedy? Or was it *you* that got greedy?"

"I still don't know what the hell you're talking about," he wheezed.

"Bullshit," I snapped. "If you've been following me, you know I just came from Donovan State Prison. The assistant warden there told you *years* ago about Janus's drug drops. Did you offer to look the other way, for a piece of the profits? Or were you two partners, fifty-fifty? You lined up the product, he flew the planes?"

He stared at me, then gave a guffaw. "Drug drops? Those weren't drug drops."

"Jesus, Hickock, give me a break. You're gonna shoot me anyhow, so there's no point in lying."

"Shoot you?" He looked at me as if I were insane. "I'm trying to *protect* you, Dr. Dumb-Ass."

Now I was the one gaping. "*Protect* me?"

"Hell, yeah. And you're not making it easy." He shook his head. "Janus wasn't dropping drugs from that DC-3. He was dropping people."

"People? *What* people? What the hell are *you* talking about?"

"I'm talking about people who needed to get the hell out of Mexico, under the radar. People who had price tags on their heads. People who were trying to help us bring down the country's biggest drug cartel."

"You mean the Sinaloa cartel? You mean Guzmán?"

"I mean Guzmán." He gave a slight, ironic smile. "And yeah, in my world, at least, he is the baddest badass on the planet."

"You brought Richard Janus in on this? How? Why?"

"Richard and I go way back," he said. "*Went* way back. Forty years. I flew with him in Southeast Asia—Laos—back in the sixties."

"Air America? You were an Air America pilot too?"

"Nah, I wasn't a pilot. I was his kicker."

"Kicker?"

"Cargo kicker. Richard would take us in through the treetops, weaving and juking, dodging branches and bullets. That man had balls of solid brass. Then he'd pop up and level off for about two seconds—just long enough for me to kick the rice out the door—and dive back down to the deck." He shook his head again. "This DEA gig? The pucker factor escalates every now and then, but kicking cargo for Richard? Fascinating, every damn day."

I blinked. "Excuse me. Did you just call it 'fascinating'?"

He gave a wheezy laugh. "Yeah. That's Air America slang—coined by Richard, in fact. It's a whistling-past-the-graveyard kinda term. It means—"

"I know what it means," I said, as alarms started sounding somewhere in the back of my mind. "It means 'scary as hell,' right?"

"Right." He grinned, then—studying my expression—he frowned. "Something wrong? You look like you just saw a ghost."

"I just heard an echo," I said. "Somebody else used that word recently, exactly the same way—said jumping out of the Citation that night would've been pretty fascinating. I don't suppose you know the NTSB crash investigator, Maddox? Any chance he was an Air America kicker too?"

"Pat Maddox? 'Mad Dog' Maddox?" Hickock's expression darkened. "Hell, yeah, I know him. And hell no, he wasn't a kicker. He was a Marine Corps pilot from 'Nam. He got scrubbed—given a fake discharge, civilian papers, a bogus contract—and sent to Laos as a so-called civilian. Mad Dog loved the black-ops stuff, the CIA dirty work. He used to call Richard 'Boy Scout' because he was such a straight arrow. Me, he called 'Mild Bill.' Maddox was a hard-ass. An asshole. But hey, it was war, and war is hell."

"He came from the marines? You know what he flew in Vietnam?"

"Sure. He talked about it all the damn time. He flew F-4s."

"Jets?"

"Hell, yeah. The F-4 Phantom was a supersonic attack fighter. Mad Dog loved to wave his top-gun dick in everybody's face."

I hated the image, but I liked the information. "So if he was flying dogfights at Mach 2 or whatever," I said, "he'd have no trouble at the controls of a mild-mannered civilian jet, right?"

"Well, every aircraft's different, but if he studied up on the pilot's handbook and the panel . . ." He trailed off, and I could see him working to connect the dots that I had just begun to connect myself. "Let me get this straight," he wheezed. "Are you thinking—"

I interrupted. "Maddox told me the Citation was like a Dodge Caravan," I said excitedly. "Almost as if he'd flown one and found it kinda boring."

Hickock held up a hand. "Slow down, slow down. Do you really, seriously—"

I cut him off again. "Fighter pilots get parachute training, too, right?"

Hickock furrowed his brow, then gave a grunt—"Huh"—and began to nod, slowly and tentatively at first, then more decisively. "Mad Dog loved the edgy stuff. Survival skills, commando training, inserting assassin teams. All that macho Rambo shit."

"He was limping," I went on. "The day after the crash. He was wearing a knee brace. He said he'd had surgery, but I bet he hadn't—that'd be easy to find out. I bet he twisted his knee when he jumped out of the Citation—came down hard, or crooked, or something. Came down right over there!" I pointed toward the five burned tubes jutting from the sand. "Those are signal flares. A landing zone. A target. Somebody was waiting here. Maddox phoned just before takeoff, or maybe the guy here just listened for the sound of the jet. He lit the flares, the jet turned, and Maddox made the jump. Then—being the crash investigator assigned to this region—he was in a perfect position to cover his tracks." Hickock rubbed his jaw, considering the scenario.

At that moment my watch began to beep, and when I looked at it and saw the time—two forty-five—I felt a wave of panic. "Oh *shit*," I said.

"What's wrong?"

"Maddox. He's on his way."

"On his way where?"

"His way here."

"*Here* here?" I nodded. "Christ. When?"

"Now," I said. "Actually, twenty or thirty minutes from now. That beep from my watch was reminding me to finish up at the prison and head back here to meet him."

"But why, Doc? Why the hell'd you call him, if you think he killed Richard?"

"I didn't think that when I called him," I pointed out. "I called him two hours ago. Before you told me all this stuff about him and Richard. Before I put the pieces together." He still looked confused and mad. "Look, I called to tell him I'd found the spot where Richard's killer came down when he bailed out that night. Maddox offered to dash down from L.A. to take a look." But as I said it, I realized that taking a look was the last thing Maddox needed, because Maddox had seen this spot already, at least three times: first, when he'd scouted it out; later, when he'd placed the flares in the sand, probably the afternoon before the crash; finally, when he'd floated down through the night sky toward the fiery marker, lit by an accomplice with a lighter, a bad nicotine addiction, and a getaway car. No, Maddox wasn't coming to see what I'd found. Maddox was coming to kill me and scrub the site.

"We gotta get out of here," I told Hickock. "Before he gets here."

"Too late for that, I'm afraid," said a voice, and Pat Maddox—Mad Dog Maddox—stepped from behind a bushy mesquite tree, a short-barreled shotgun pointed at Hickock. "Mild Bill," he said pleasantly. "Long time, no see. How you been?" Out of the corner of my eye, I saw Hickock's eyes flicker toward his revolver. Maddox must have seen it, too. "Go for it," he said, nodding at the agent's gun. "But I'd bet my life that your head'll be gone before you can clear leather."

I said the only thing I could think of. "How'd you get here from L.A. so quick?"

"I have a confession," he said. "I lied, Doc. Sorry about that. I was already down here when you called."

Something in my head clicked. "You came down and killed Malloy, the Fox News reporter."

"He was damned annoying," said Maddox. "You said so yourself."

"You're the one who tipped him off about the teeth." He gave a slight, smug smile, which I took as acknowledgment, and I rattled on, my mind racing. "Anonymously—but then he tracked you down somehow. He was onto you. So you went and strangled him and staged the porn." I was partly stalling for time, but mainly I was still working the case, finally figuring things out, and I was absurdly excited, for a man about to be shot.

It was Hickock, not Maddox, who interrupted me. "I should've figured you for this, Mad Dog. Somebody told me you were mixed up in that Iran-Contra mess—running drugs and guns for the CIA in Nicaragua—but I thought he was just blowing smoke up my ass. When I heard you were working for the NTSB, I thought you'd settled down. Stepped up onto the straight and narrow."

"I had," said Maddox. "I got scared straight for a long time. Remember that C-123 got shot down in Nicaragua in 1986? The one that could've brought down Ronald Reagan and George Bush, if Ollie North hadn't taken the fall? I was supposed to be flying that plane, but I was sick. Appendicitis. I didn't fly, so I didn't die. I pulled some good-old-boy strings and got a job investigating crashes. Not too boring, as jobs go."

"And you played by the rules?" asked Hickock.

"I was a good boy for fifteen years."

"Then what happened?" I asked.

"Then I worked a crash about a hundred miles from here. A seaplane, bringing in a load of cocaine to the Salton Sea, up in the Imperial Valley. Bad weather, lousy pilot; the plane flipped and sank. I got a call from one of my old buddies, offering me a nice little nest egg if I could retrieve the cargo and hand it over. The rest, as they say, is history. I started doing a little moonlighting for Chapo Guzmán—two, three flights a month. Good money, and a lot more fascinating than civil service. But then somebody started sneaking snitches out of the country. Didn't take a genius to figure out it was Saint Richard. Ever the Boy Scout."

"So you took him out," I said. "Damage control."

He nodded. "Should've done it sooner. I let nostalgia get in the way."

There was one more thing I still didn't get. "Tell me," I pressed, "why the double fake? First you staged it to look like Janus accidentally crashed, or killed himself. But then you told the reporter and the FBI he'd faked his death. How come?"

"Diversionary tactics," he said. "Divide and conquer. I could tell the DEA was closing in. If I could make the FBI look like screwups—like they'd scared Guzmán into hiding—the DEA would be royally pissed at the Bureau. And less likely to follow the trail to *me*. Right, Chubby?" Hickock didn't respond. "But if I could also make it look like Janus was actually still alive—that he'd faked the whole thing—the FBI would get pissed, too . . . and they'd be hell-bent on finding him instead of helping Fatso here."

"But Prescott said that Janus had gotten an FBI agent killed," I persisted. "What'd he mean by that?"

Maddox made a face. "Janus snuck another snitch out of Mexico back in the spring," he said. "Swooped down and scooped up the guy right out from under the nose of one of Guzmán's enforcers. Turns out an FBI agent was tailing the snitch, and the assassin killed the FBI agent instead of the snitch. Wasn't Janus's fault, but the Bureau was too dumb to know that. That, or they chose to spin it that way so they could make Janus the scapegoat." He drew a breath, as if to clear his head, and when he exhaled, loudly and slowly through his nostrils, the rush of air had the sound of finality. "So. Boys, this has been fun, but I've got other fish to fry, and one of *mis amigos* will be here to pick me up in a few minutes. So if you two would be so kind as to get down on your knees, we can get this show on the road."

"You're kidding," said Hickock. "Or you're stupid. You're gonna blow away a DEA agent and an FBI consultant, and you think you can just walk away scot-free?"

"I'm not stupid," said Maddox. "And I'm not going to blow you away." I felt a glimmer of hope, but then he added, "An assassin from the Tijuana drug cartel is." Shifting the shotgun into his left hand, he reached behind his back and pulled a nine-millimeter pistol from his belt. "Shocking, that a veteran DEA agent walked into a trap with no backup. And tragic that his bad judgment cost the life of a respected forensic scientist, too." He shook his head and gave an ironic *tsk-tsk*. "Quite a lucky break for Guzmán and the Sinaloa cartel, though." He gave a sigh of mock sadness, then said, "On your knees. *Now*."

"Fuck you," said Hickock. "You might kill me, but I sure as hell won't die kneeling."

Maddox rolled his eyes. "Christ, Hickock, you're still the same self-righteous prick you were back in Laos. Okay, have it your way." He aimed the pistol at the agent's chest, and I saw his finger tighten on the trigger.

In desperation—having no better ideas, and having nothing to lose—I raised my arms over my head and waved them frantically, looking up at the low ridge across the hollow. "Take the shot!" I shouted. "Take the shot! *Now!*"

All hell suddenly broke loose beside me. Maddox's attention wavered from Hickock for an instant, and in that instant, Hickock yanked the revolver from its shoulder holster and swung it upward. I heard the crack of a shot—or was it two?—and then a sort of ripping sound in the air beside my right ear, and then another crack rolling in from somewhere in the distance. Maddox jerked forward, his arms flailing, and the short shotgun in his left hand thrashed and boomed. Something whacked me in the head, and I felt myself falling to the sand.

"Doc? Hey, Doc—can you hear me?" I felt my eyelids being tugged open, and as my eyeballs leveled and came into focus, I recognized the face of Special Agent Miles Prescott. "Doc? You back with me now?"

"Yeah," I said, sitting up abruptly and staring wildly at the scene. Sprawled on the ground ten feet away lay Maddox—or most of Maddox, from the chest down. His head—or most of his head—lay off to one side a ways, and I'd worked enough shotgun deaths to know how it had gotten there. I also noticed a large bloody wound in his chest. From the size of it, it looked like an exit wound, which would mean he'd been shot from behind, but I didn't see how that could have happened, since he and Hickock had been face-to-face when the shooting started. *Hickock,* I thought in sudden panic. *Where's Hickock?* I looked beside me, where he'd been standing, but he wasn't there. I whirled, scanning in all directions, and finally saw him twenty feet behind me, sitting on the ground, leaning against the left front wheel of my car. "Hey, Hickock," I said. "From now on, you're *Wild* Bill. Nothing mild about you at *all.* Fastest gun in the West, man."

I waited for his wheezy answer, but he was silent—utterly, unnaturally silent—and when I looked closer, I saw that his eyes were glassy and the sand beneath him was red, his blood mingling with the puddle of oil the Impala had hemorrhaged a quarter hour before. A lifetime before.

I turned and stared the question at Prescott, and he shook his head. "Right in the heart," he said. "Amazing he managed to walk that far."

"Well, damn," I said softly. To my surprise, I felt tears come to my eyes and roll down my cheeks. "He was a good man. I misjudged him at first, but he was a damn good man."

"You're right," said Prescott, his voice suddenly a little thick. "I did, too. And yeah—as good as they get."

I got to my feet, but the movement caused a searing pain in my head, and when I rubbed it, my hand came away sticky with blood.

"We need to get that looked at," said Prescott. "I think Maddox's pistol flew out of his hand and whacked you in the head, but we oughta get that wound cleaned up. Maybe get an x-ray, too. Before we do anything else, though, I gotta ask one thing."

"What's that?"

"You yelled 'Take the shot.' How the hell did you know we had a sharpshooter up there?"

"I didn't," I said. "You *did*?" He looked as confused as I was, then he nodded. "I was totally bluffing," I told him. "He was about to shoot Hickock. I was hoping to distract him long enough to let Hickock get off a shot. Guess it didn't work."

"Actually, it did," Prescott said. "You can't see it now, because of the exit wound from the rifle round, but Hickock nailed him. Maddox was walking dead when the rifle bullet hit him."

I turned and looked again at the body of the DEA agent. "Hickock said he was trying to protect me. And by God he did, didn't he? He died waging war." Prescott nodded. "So now *I* gotta ask one thing," I said. "How the hell did you know to put a sharpshooter out here?"

"We had a GPS tracker on your car. And a tap on your cell phone. We even managed to get a shotgun mike up on that ridge in time to record that last part of Maddox's little speech."

I was impressed, but I was also confused. "You did all that? Why?"

"One of our partner agencies—the San Diego County Sheriff's Department—shared a key piece of new evidence with us yesterday. A skull fragment, which confirmed that Richard Janus was murdered. That took the investigation in a new direction. It also suggested that the killer might attempt to . . . uh . . . *contact* you."

I pondered the implications of all this. "Are you saying you used me as bait for a killer, Agent Prescott?"

I remembered a brief bit of banter from our first ride down Otay Mountain weeks before and gave him a grin. "Did you just throw me under the bus?"

"Of *course* not, Dr. Brockton," he said, grinning back. "We never throw anyone under the bus. And if a forensic consultant just happens to *fall* under the bus? While we're standing nearby with our hand on his back? We do our very best to pick him up and dust him off and remind everyone how glad we are that he's okay." He paused to let that sink in, then added, "I'll be recommending to SAC that we hold a joint press conference tomorrow, together with the DEA and the sheriff, to update the media and set the record straight on Richard Janus's case. I'd like to get Mrs. Janus there, too, if she's willing to accept an olive branch and bury the hatchet. If you could find it in your heart to join us, there might even be a letter of commendation in it for you. A *very* lavish letter."

"When you say lavish," I said, "do you mean embossed with the FBI seal? In color?"

"You know the Bureau doesn't make promises," he said. "But I'll recommend color and embossing. In the strongest possible terms."

Chapter 41

Knoxville, Tennessee

We held Kathleen's memorial service at Second Presbyterian Church in late August, a week after the university's fall semester began—a long time after her death, but the only way to include the university community that had meant so much to her. Jeff, Jenny, and the boys sat with me in the front row. So did Carmelita Janus and helicopter-jockey Skidder, who had given up his law enforcement job to become chief pilot for Airlift Relief International. Carmelita was getting the organization back on its feet again, thanks to Kathleen's bequest and a flood of other donations in Richard's honor, which began pouring in once the media began portraying him as a misunderstood and martyred saint, of sorts. Last but not least, in a wheelchair parked at the end of our pew, was KPD Captain Brian Decker, still weak but out of the woods and expected to recover from his close brush with death.

Behind us, in the second pew, sat Kathleen's colleagues from Nutrition Sciences. At my request, they all wore their academic robes as a way of honoring Kathleen as a teacher and scholar. The sight of them reminded me yet again that Kathleen's death was a loss to many people, in many walks of life—some of them children in faraway places. They would never lay eyes on her, but they would see the world itself, as a result of her foundation's eyesight-saving work.

My own colleagues and students turned out in droves, too. So did the dean, UT's provost and president, and even the sharp-taloned legal eagle Amanda Whiting, who had actually worked behind the scenes to rally legislative support for the Body Farm: Amanda had enlisted police chiefs, county sheriffs, and district attorneys from throughout the state in a campaign to remind their senators and representatives that the Body Farm's research helped solve murders throughout the great state of Tennessee, and that voting against the Body Farm might be perceived as getting soft on crime. The strategy worked brilliantly, and the legislative assault on the facility ended not with a bang, or even a whimper, but with utter silence.

The service itself was fairly brief. I wasn't able to say much—I choked up pretty quickly, so about all I was able to get out was something about what a privilege it had been to share thirty years of my life with such a wonderful woman. Jeff did better than I did, but the real prizewinner was Jenny, who talked about becoming family with Kathleen: about finding a haven, and a friend, and a role model, and a hero all rolled into one in this remarkable woman. *Amen,* I thought.

The receiving line, after the service, lasted for nearly two hours. By the end I was exhausted, having trouble recognizing faces and remembering names. The last person in line was a young woman, and when I looked at her, I drew an utter blank. She looked to be around twenty or so, an attractive redhead with lively eyes. She had probably taken one of my intro classes; by now, thousands of UT students had.

"Hello," I said, extending my hand, as I had hundreds of times in the past two hours. "Thank you for coming."

"We haven't met, Dr. Brockton, but we've talked on the phone," she said, and I knew her voice instantly. She must have seen the shock of recognition on my face, because the next thing she said was, "Yes. I'm Red. I'm not really a reference librarian, and I apologize for misleading you. The phone was ringing, you seemed to need some help, and . . . I . . . I just got carried away. It was just so . . . *fascinating*."

"Fascinating," I said, smiling. "I've been hearing that word a lot lately. It's my new favorite word."

She looked confused, which was understandable. "Anyhow, I'm very sorry you lost your wife."

"Thank you. Me, too."

"And I'm sorry I tricked you."

"It's okay," I said. "You helped me a lot, too. A lot more than the actual reference librarian I talked to, out in Otay Mesa."

"Otay Mesa? That's the place where El Chapo—you know, 'Goose Man'—ran that underground railroad under the border from Tijuana!"

"See," I said. "You're good, Red. The offer's still open. If you want to switch fields—turn anthropologist—let me know."

She blushed, and she smiled shyly. "Actually," she said, "I've sent in my application."

"That's great," I said. "I'll look for it. Will I find it filed under *R*, for *Red*?"

"No," she said. "You'll find it in the *L*s. Under Lovelady. Miranda Lovelady. Does this mean I'm in?"

"I'm like the FBI, Miranda," I said, grinning. "I don't make promises. But I'll recommend you to myself. In the strongest possible terms."

Writer's Note: On Fact and Fiction

During ten years of writing Body Farm novels, I've often noted the blurred boundary—the semi-permeable membrane; the oft-crosssed border—between fact and fiction in the books. Given that the stories are informed by years of Dr. Bill Bass's forensic casework, how could it be otherwise?

This book is no exception. One factual underpinning is the death of Ann Bass, Bill's first wife, who died in 1993. Our fictional character Kathleen Brockton is not interchangeable with the late Mrs. Bass, but she obviously shares traits with her, just as Dr. Brockton—who is not exactly interchangeable with Bill Bass—shares many traits in common with him. The specifics of Kathleen's illness and of Dr. Brockton's grief are products of my own writerly imagination.

Tragically, the 1991 crash on Otay Mountain that's mentioned in the book was not a product of my imagination. Country music singer Reba McEntire lost seven musicians and her band's road manager in the early morning hours of March 16, 1991, when a twin-engine jet—piloted by a crew unfamiliar with the mountainous terrain to the east of San Diego—took off from Brown Field Municipal Airport and slammed into the dark peak of Otay Mountain. Astonishingly, in October 2004, another twin-engine jet—this one an air ambulance—hit the mountainside in the dark, killing the pilots and three medical crew members. After the 2004 crash, the Federal Aviation Administration revised its procedures and charts to reduce the chances of additional collisions with the dark, dangerous terrain lurking to the east of Brown Field.

Four decades ago, Dr. Bass investigated the high-velocity crash of an Air Force plane high in the Great Smoky Mountains, and that case clearly took root somewhere in the nooks and crannies of my mind. But I have a deeper, more personal interest in aviation crashes, too: As an amateur pilot myself, I've read numerous NTSB crash-investigation reports, partly in hopes of learning lessons, and partly because of morbid fascination with the fate that has come close—terrifyingly close—to claiming my own life on several occasions.

A bit farther afield and less personal but also based in fact—contentious, murky fact—is the role the CIA played in drug trafficking in Southeast Asia during the Vietnam War, and in Central America during the Iran-Contra affair. British journalist Christopher Robbin's 1979 book *Air America: The Story of the CIA's Secret Airlines* sheds light on the agency's dealings in Southeast Asia's "Golden Triangle," as well as illuminating the remarkable derring-do of the Air America pilots who flew perilous missions to deliver rice, weapons, commando teams, and more questionable cargo. Numerous reports have chronicled the links between CIA-backed Nicaraguan "Contra" rebels and known drug traffickers. Among those reports is an official government document informally called "The Kerry Report," which was published in 1989 after a three-year investigation headed by then-Senator John Kerry. At the time, Kerry chaired the Senate Subcommittee on Terrorism, Narcotics, and International Operations; he is now U.S. Secretary of State. Do the ends justify the means? It's a question American foreign policy gives us the chance to ponder on a regular basis.

Joaquin Guzmán Loera—"El Chapo"—is a real-life, larger-than-life drug lord who did indeed escape in 2001 from what was supposedly Mexico's top-security prison. Guzmán's remarkable drug distribution network—which included a fleet of planes, a flotilla of boats (and even submarines), and the ingenious tunnels beneath the border fence in San Diego's industrial suburb, Otay Mesa—made him the world's wealthiest and most powerful narco trafficker for years. El Chapo remained at large for thirteen years after that escape, heading the Sinaloa cartel, until February 2014, when he was recaptured in a beachfront condominium with his young wife (a former beauty queen) and their twin two-year-old daughters (born, ironically, in America). El Chapo's recapture marked another victory in the War on Drugs . . . and created another opening at the top for the next ambitious, ruthless entrepreneur, someone able and willing to meet the seemingly insatiable demand for drugs in *El Norte.*

—*Jon Jefferson*
Tallahassee, FL

Acknowledgments

A s always, we have the privilege of thanking many people for helping with this book. We'll start with the FBI—always good friends for crime novelists to have. Angela Bell and Ann Todd, both of the FBI's Office of Public Affairs, were gracious and swift to line up interviews with technical experts. And those experts were terrific: Special Supervisory Agent Richard Marx, of the Evidence Response Team Unit, answered many, many questions about evidence recovery procedures, and Special Agent Freddie Vela shared valuable insights into drug trafficking, Mexican cartels, and undercover drug investigations.

Aviation expert Bob Macintosh—a longtime investigator for the National Transportation Safety Board until his retirement—was extremely generous with his time and expertise. We've repaid Bob's kindness by giving our fictional NTSB investigator a pivotal role in the action. (This might be an appropriate time to remind Bob and other readers of the standard fiction disclaimer: "Any resemblance between actual persons, living or dead, is purely coincidental . . .")

Ace pilots (and good friends) Don Shreve, Rob Cherney, and Ed Dumas helped with details about airplanes, jets, and autopilots, and Jim Gerrish of Sierra Industries, Ltd.—the go-to company for performance-enhancing modifications for Cessna Citation jets—was patient, enlightening, and good-natured in response to countless questions about customizing our ill-fated fictional aircraft. On a grimmer but equally helpful front, search-and-rescue expert Kimberly Kelly offered helpful perspective on searching for fragmented remains of crash victims.

Many forensic-anthropologist friends and colleagues pitched in to share their expertise. Anthony Falsetti, Angi Christensen, and Elias Kontanis offered useful insights into the effects of high-speed crashes and fire on the human body. Robert Mann—who spent years identifying the remains of U.S. military personnel recovered from Southeast Asia—provided helpful perspective on the Vietnam War period of U.S. history. Samm Hurst gave useful entomological and meteorological information about San Diego and the nearby mountains.

Dr. Stephanie Blank, a gynecological oncologist and professor at New York University School of Medicine, provided helpful (and heartrending) details on the aggressive uterine cancer known as leiomyosarcoma; our thanks to her for helping us, and for helping women fight this and other merciless forms of cancer. Thanks also to Ellen Sullivan, communications director at the Society of Gynecologic Oncology, for the referral to Dr. Blank.

Our team at William Morrow Publishers—publishers Liate Stehlik and Lynn Grady, editor Lyssa Keusch, editorial assistant Rebecca Lucash, production editor Stephanie Vallejo, copyeditor Laurie McGee, cover designer Richard Aquan, publicist Danielle Bartlett, and marketing guru Kaitlin Harri—transformed ideas and words into a finished book: a book that people will actually hear about, read about, and even buy! We couldn't be more grateful. Sincere thanks in that vein also to our agent, Giles Anderson, who has kept roofs over our heads and food on our tables for 13 years now.

On the personal front, Cindy and Joe Johnson rode to the writer's rescue yet again by providing a quiet, lovely writing retreat at their off-the-grid cabin on the Ochlockonee River, where the only distractions were the sightings of manatees, dolphins, kingfishers, and alligators. Jim Bass provided wise counsel, legal and otherwise. And last but not least, our wives, Jane McPherson and Carol Bass, kept us—constantly keep us—flying straight and level.

—*Jon Jefferson & Dr. Bill Bass*

THE SKULL

BONES OF

PARTS OF

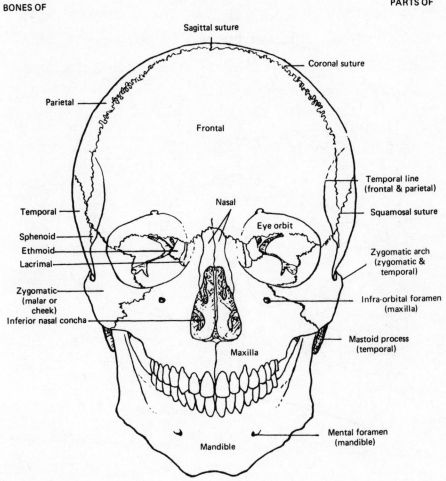

Sagittal suture

Coronal suture

Parietal

Frontal

Temporal line
(frontal & parietal)

Squamosal suture

Nasal

Eye orbit

Temporal

Sphenoid

Ethmoid

Lacrimal

Zygomatic arch
(zygomatic &
temporal)

Zygomatic
(malar or
cheek)

Infra-orbital foramen
(maxilla)

Inferior nasal concha

Mastoid process
(temporal)

Maxilla

Mental foramen
(mandible)

Mandible

BONES OF

PARTS OF

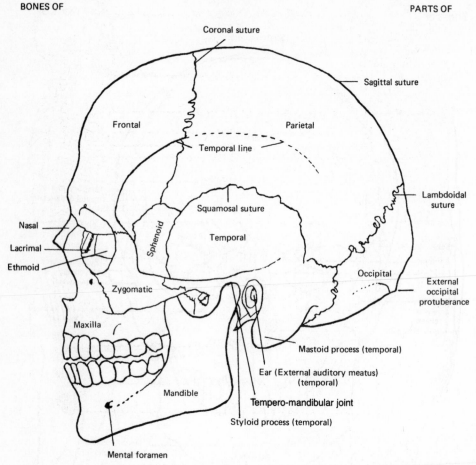

Coronal suture

Sagittal suture

Frontal

Parietal

Temporal line

Lambdoidal suture

Nasal

Squamosal suture

Lacrimal

Sphenoid

Temporal

Ethmoid

Zygomatic

Occipital

External occipital protuberance

Maxilla

Mastoid process (temporal)

Ear (External auditory meatus) (temporal)

Mandible

Tempero-mandibular joint

Styloid process (temporal)

Mental foramen

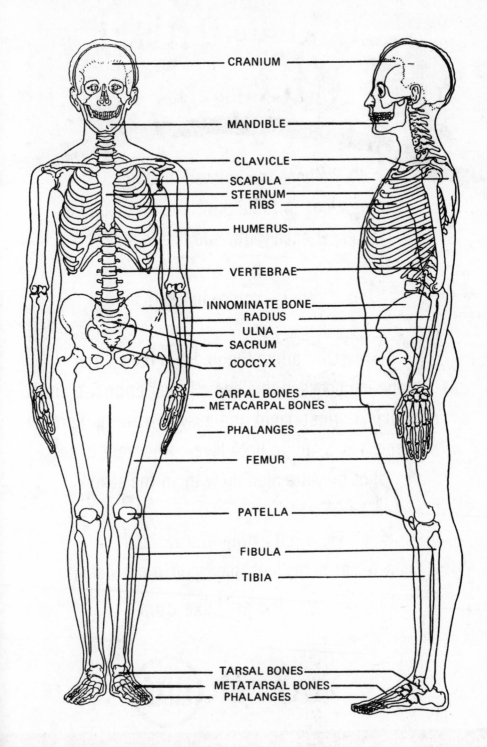

CRANIUM

MANDIBLE

CLAVICLE
SCAPULA
STERNUM
RIBS
HUMERUS

VERTEBRAE

INNOMINATE BONE
RADIUS
ULNA
SACRUM
COCCYX

CARPAL BONES
METACARPAL BONES

PHALANGES

FEMUR

PATELLA

FIBULA

TIBIA

TARSAL BONES
METATARSAL BONES
PHALANGES

THE NEW LUXURY IN READING

We hope you enjoyed reading
our new, comfortable print size and found it
an experience you would like to repeat.

Well – you're in luck!

HarperLuxe offers the finest in fiction and
nonfiction books in this same larger print size and
paperback format. Light and easy to read, HarperLuxe
paperbacks are for book lovers who want to see
what they are reading without the strain.

For a full listing of titles and
new releases to come, please visit our website:
www.HarperLuxe.com